Named one of the Top 10 Books of 2000
by *US Weekly, Newsday,* and *The Dallas Morning News*

A BookSense "76" pick

PRAISE FOR

THE LAST SAMURAI

"Exuberant . . . it is easy to be carried along by the tempo of [DeWitt's] prose, which alternates between short, sharp sentences and sprawling passages that leave you gasping for breath. The writing is playful and engaging, a mix of David Foster Wallace's intellectual colloquialism and the modern fabulism of Aimee Bender. Helen DeWitt shows she is a writer willing to take chances . . . her intelligence provides sparkle as well as promise."

—*The New York Times Book Review*

"One of the outstanding first novels of 2000, Helen DeWitt introduces readers to two of the most interesting characters in modern fiction . . . a wonderfully drawn portrait of a complicated relationship between a mother and her brilliant young son."

—*The Seattle Times*

". . . a witty, wacky and endlessly erudite debut."

—*Kirkus Reviews*

". . . an ambitious, colossal debut novel . . . energetic . . . unpredictable."

—*Publishers Weekly*

"There are stories within stories, layers upon layers in this fresh, fast-paced, wonderfully imaginative book. Delightfully original."

—Booklist

"Helen DeWitt's extraordinary debut, The Last Samurai, is remarkable, profound, and often very funny."

—amazon.com

"Remarkable. More than one reading may be necessary to appreciate fully The Last Samurai's many dimensions."

—The Wall Street Journal

"Fresh, sharp and slyly frisky, it's a daring first effort—a bright and inventive paradigm shift."

—The Dallas Morning News

"The Last Samurai is . . . a triumph—a genuinely new story, a genuinely new form, which has more to offer on every reading but is gripping from the beginning of the first . . . The ambition of this novel is large, and every reading reveals more subtleties . . . [It] is funny and tragic and intriguing and over the top and perfectly controlled. But it is also—in an ordinary and undeniable way—very moving . . . It is exciting for the future of the novel that a writer can do all the basic things readers need . . . and do something new with the form of the tale itself."

—A.S. Byatt, The New Yorker

THE
LAST
SAMURAI

THE
LAST
SAMURAI

Helen DeWitt

talk miramax books

HYPERION

NEW YORK

ISBN 0-7868-6668-3
Paperback ISBN 0-7868-8700-1

First Paperback Edition
10   9   8   7   6   5   4   3   2   1

To

ANN COTTON

ACKNOWLEDGMENTS

In 1991 Ann Cotton went to a school in Mola, a village in a remote rural district of Zimbabwe, with the idea of doing research on girls' education. She ended up talking to two schoolgirls who had come 100 km alone to attend the school. It did not take boarders, so they were living in a hut they had built themselves. They considered themselves lucky because most girls could not go to secondary school, as fees were charged; they dropped out and got married at twelve or thirteen instead. Ann went back to Britain and started raising money for scholarships by selling cakes in Cambridge Market. She founded the Cambridge Female Education Trust in 1993. She persuaded the Body Shop to fund a hostel in Mola. She persuaded other organisations to fund scholarships for more schools, first in Zimbabwe, then in Ghana. She persuaded me to become a Trustee; I could not have finished this book if she had not said 'Of course' each time I said I would do something for CamFed as soon as I had finished my book. Information about CamFed is available from 25 Wordsworth Grove, Newnham, Cambridge CB3 9HH and at http://www.camfed.org.

Professor David Levene has made the book more interesting and less prone to error in too many ways to count; it is impossible to express my debt to his unfailing generosity. I owe more than I can say to my mother, Mary DeWitt Griffin, not only for moral and financial support, but for sharing her remarkable gifts over the course of many years. Tim Schmidt, Maude Chilton and Steve Hutensky have been extraordinary friends; they know how much I owe them.

Alison Samuel of Chatto & Windus brought a fresh eye and keen attention to detail to bear at a stage when both were much needed. I am also grateful to Martin Lam, author of *Kanji from the Start,* for advice on the Nisus program, and to Neil and Fusa McLynn for extensive help with Japanese; also to Leonard Gamberg for casting an eye over the atom, to Chris Done for looking at the astronomy in an early version, to James Kaler for kindly answering a question at the very last minute raised by *Stars and their Spectra,* and to Ian Rutherford for finding a Greek font at the postultimate minute. It should go without saying that they are in no way implicated in any mistakes that remain. I owe a special debt to the many people who helped me appreciate the achievement of Akira Kurosawa; the book would have been very different without their assistance.

Without the enthusiasm of Jonathan Burnham of Talk Miramax Books there would be a manuscript but no book; the extent of that debt speaks for itself.

I am grateful for permission to use copyright material from the following: *The Biographical Dictionary of Film,* by David Thomson; *The Eskimo Book of Knowledge,* by George Binney, by permission of the Hudson's Bay Company; *Theory of Harmony,* by Arnold Schoenberg, translated by Roy E. Carter (English translation ©1983 Faber and Faber Ltd); interview with John Denver, *Melody Maker* 27/3/76, p. 11, © Chris Charlesworth/*Melody Maker*/IPC Syndication; *Foundations of Aerodynamics: Bases of Aerodynamics Design,* by Arnold M. Kuethe and Chuen-Yen Chow, ©1986, reprinted by permission of John W. Wiley & Sons, Inc.; *The Films of Akira Kurosawa,* by Donald Richie (University of California Press), ©1984 The Regents of the University of California; *The Solid State,* by H.M. Rosenberg (©1988 Oxford University Press) by permission of Oxford University Press; *Gesenius' Hebrew Grammar* edited and enlarged by E. Kautzsch, second English edition by A.E. Cowley (1910), by permission of Oxford University Press; *Njal's Saga* (extracts from pages 244-246), translated by Magnus Magnusson and Herman Pálsson (London, 1960) © 1960 Magnus Magnusson and Herman Pálsson, reproduced by permission of Penguin Books Ltd. I would like to thank Kurosawa Production K.K. for permission to reprint material from the screenplay *Seven Samurai (Shichinin no Samurai).*

THE
LAST
SAMURAI

Prologue

My father's father was a Methodist minister. He was a tall, handsome, noble-looking man; he had a deep, beautiful voice. My father was an ardent atheist and admirer of Clarence Darrow. He skipped grades the way other boys skip class, he lectured my grandfather's flock on carbon 14 and the origin of species, and he won a full scholarship to Harvard at the age of 15.

He took the letter from Harvard to his father.

Something looked through my grandfather's beautiful eyes. Something spoke with his beautiful voice, and it said: It's only fair to give the other side a chance.

My father said: What do you mean?

What it meant was that my father should not reject God for secularism just because he won arguments with uneducated people. He should go to a theological college and give the other side a fair chance; if he was still of the same mind at the end he would still be only 19, a perfectly good age to start college.

My father, being an atheist and a Darwinist, had a very delicate sense of honor, and he could not resist this appeal. He applied to various theological seminaries, and all but three rejected him out of hand because he was too young. Three asked him to come for an interview.

The first was a seminary with a fine reputation, and my father because of his youth was interviewed by the head.

The man said: You're very young. Is it possible that you want to be a minister because of your father?

3

My father said he did not want to be a minister, but he wanted to give the other side a fair chance, and he explained about carbon 14.

The man said: The ministry is a vocation and the training we offer is designed for people who feel called to it. I doubt very much that you would benefit from it.

He said: This offer from Harvard is a remarkable opportunity. Couldn't you give the other side a fair chance by taking a course in theology? I believe the college started out, after all, as a College of Divinity, and I imagine they must still teach the subject.

The man smiled at my father kindly and he offered to give him a list of books to read if he would like to do any more in the way of giving the other side a fair chance. My father drove home (they were living in Sioux City at the time) and all the way he thought that this might give the other side a fair chance.

He spoke to his father. The point was made that one course in theology in a strongly secular environment would probably not make a very considerable impact, but all the same my father must decide for himself.

My father went to the second seminary, which had a good reputation. He was interviewed by the Dean.

The Dean asked him why he wanted to become a minister, and my father explained that he did not want to become a minister, and he explained about carbon 14.

The Dean said he respected my father's intentions, but still there was something whimsical about it, and he pointed out that my father was very young. He recommended that my father go to Harvard first and then if he still wanted to give the other side a fair chance he would be delighted to consider his application.

My father returned to his father. The beautiful voice pointed out that a man with a degree from Harvard would find it hard to resist the temptation of going instantly into a career, but it said that of course my father must decide for himself.

My father drove to the third seminary, which was small and obscure. My father was interviewed by a Deputy Dean. It was a hot day, and though a small fan was blowing the Deputy Dean, a red fat man, was sweating hard. The Deputy Dean asked why my father wanted to be a minister and my father explained about the fair chance and about carbon 14.

The Deputy Dean said that the church paid the fees of the seminarians who planned to become ministers. He said that as my father did not plan to become a minister they would have to charge $1,500 a year.

My father returned to his father, who said that he supposed my father could earn $750 over the summer at one of the gas stations, and that he would then give him the rest.

So my father went to a theological college. When I say that he went to a theological college I mean that he enrolled at a theological college & went every Saturday to synagogue out of interest because there was no rule to say you couldn't, and spent most of the rest of the time shooting pool at Helene's, the only bar in town that would serve a 16-year-old.

He waited for my grandfather to ask how he was finding it, but my grandfather never asked.

At the synagogue my father met someone ten years older who ran the services and did most of the readings. He looked a lot like Buddy Holly, and in fact people called him Buddy (he preferred it to Werner). At first my father thought this was the rabbi, but the town was too small to support a rabbi: The services were run by local volunteers. Buddy had wanted to be an opera singer, but his father had insisted he train as an accountant, and he had come from Philadelphia to take up a job as an accountant. He too spent a lot of time shooting pool at Helene's.

By the end of three years my father was very good at shooting pool. He had saved up about $500 from his winnings, and he played carelessly so as not to win too much or too often. He could beat everyone in the bar, but one night a stranger came in.

By some accident the stranger played everyone else first. He played with smooth, economical movements, and it was obvious he was in a different class from anyone my father had played so far. My father wanted to play him; Buddy kept trying to warn him off. He thought there was something not quite right about the stranger; either he would win more than my father could afford to lose, or he would lose and pull a gun. My father thought this was ridiculous, but then the stranger's jacket rode up as he bent over and they saw a gun strapped to his waist.

The game came to an end and my father walked up. He said: My friend here says you're dangerous.

The stranger said: I can be.

My father said grinning broadly: He says you'll kill me if I win.

The stranger said: Are you so sure you'll win?

My father said: There's only one way to find out.

The stranger said: And who might you be?

My father said he was at the seminary.

The stranger expressed surprise at finding a seminarian in the bar.

My father said We are all sinners, brother, in a rather sarcastic tone of voice.

The stranger and my father played a game and five dollars changed hands.

The stranger said: Do you want your revenge?

They played another game which took longer. My father was still playing carelessly; he naturally did not talk while the stranger was playing, but when it was his own turn he answered the stranger's questions with sarcastic stories about the seminary. The stranger was a man of few words, but he seemed amused. My father won in the end with a lucky shot and five dollars changed hands.

The stranger said: Now let's make it interesting.

My father said: How interesting do you want to make it?

The stranger asked how much money my father had in the world and Buddy Holly mouthed the words NO NO Don't tell him you stupid jerk from behind his back and my father said he had $500.

The stranger said he would give any odds against the $500. My father couldn't tell if he was serious.

He said: A hundred bucks. Best of five.

The stranger said in that case he'd like to see the color of his money, because he had to get back on the road and he was not going to hang around for a hundred bucks. He said 5 to 1.

My father had $25 on him. He borrowed $25 from Buddy and the rest in tens and fives from people in the bar who knew he was good for it.

They played two games and the stranger won them both easily. They started the third game and the stranger began to win easily, but then my father's luck turned and he pulled himself together and won. He won the fourth game, though it was a hard fight, and then he won the fifth game and it was silent in the bar. Other people in the bar had seen the gun too.

The stranger reached inside his jacket and everyone froze. Then he took out a wallet. He extracted five $100 bills from a thick stack.

He said: I don't suppose you've had this much money all at one time before.

My father pointed out that he already had $500.

The stranger said: $1,000! That's a lot of money.

He said: I hate to see a man with money who doesn't know what to do with it.

My father said: What do you mean?

The stranger said if you knew something a little ahead of other folks you could sometimes make money if you already had money.

My father said: What do you know?

The stranger said he wouldn't be surprised if the new highway was built that way.

My father said: If you know that for a fact why don't you do something about it? Buy some real estate.

The stranger said: I don't like property. It ties you down. But if I didn't mind owning property, and I had $1,000, I'd know what to do with the money.

The bar closed and the stranger drove off. It happened that Mrs. Randolph, Buddy's landlady, wanted to sell her house and move to Florida, but no one was buying. My father pointed out that if the stranger was right they could buy this house and turn it into a motel and make a lot of money.

If, said Buddy.

The fact was that they were both convinced that the stranger knew what he was talking about; the gun lent a mysterious conviction to the story.

My father said he wasn't going to have time for that though, because once he was through with the seminary he was going to Harvard. He had written to Harvard to take up the earlier offer.

A few weeks went by. A letter came from Harvard explaining that they would like to see what he had been doing for the past few years and asking for his grades and a reference. My father provided these, and a couple of months went by. One day a letter came which must have been hard to write. It said Harvard was prepared to offer him a place based on his earlier record, and it went on to explain that scholarships however were awarded purely on merit, so that it would not be fair to other students to give one to someone with a D average. It said that if he chose to take up the place he would need to pay the normal cost of tuition.

My father went home to Sioux City for Easter. Buddy went home to Philadelphia to celebrate Passover. My father took the letter to his father.

My grandfather looked at the letter from Harvard, and he said that he believed it was God's will that my father should not go to Harvard.

Four years earlier my father had had a brilliant future. Now he faced life with a mediocre degree from an obscure theological college, a qualification absolutely useless to a man incapable of entering the ministry.

My father was struck speechless with disgust. He left the house without a word. He drove a Chevrolet 1,300 miles.

In later years my father sometimes played a game. He'd meet a man on his way to Mexico and he'd say, Here's fifty bucks, do me a favor and buy me some lottery tickets, and he'd give the man his card. Say the odds against winning the jackpot were 20 million to 1 and the odds against the man giving my father the winning ticket another 20 million to 1, you couldn't say my father's life was ruined because there was a 1 in 400 trillion chance that it wasn't.

Or my father might meet a man on his way to Europe and he'd say, Here's fifty bucks, if you happen to go to Monte Carlo do me a favor, go to the roulette table and put this on number 17 and keep it there for 17 spins of the wheel, the man would say he wasn't planning to go to Monte Carlo and my father would say But if you do and he'd give him his card. Because what were the odds that the man would change his plans and go to Monte Carlo, what were the odds that 17 would come up 17 times in a row, what were the odds that if it did the man would send the money on to my father? Whatever they were it was not absolutely impossible but only highly unlikely, and it was not absolutely certain that my grandfather had destroyed him because there was a 1 in 500 trillion trillion trillion chance that he had not.

My father played the game for a long time because he felt he should give my grandfather a sporting chance. I don't know when he played it for the last time, but the first time was when he left the house without a word and drove 1,300 miles to see Buddy in Philadelphia.

My father parked in front of Buddy's house. A piece of piano music was being played loudly and bitterly in the front room. Doors were slammed. There were loud voices. Somebody screamed. The piano was silent. Somebody started playing the piano loudly and bitterly.

My father found Buddy who explained what was going on.

Buddy had wanted to be an opera singer and was an accountant. His brother Danny had wanted to be a clarinettist and worked in his father's jewelry business. His sister Frieda had wanted to be a violinist and worked as a secretary before marrying and having three children. His sister Barbara had wanted to be a violinist and worked as a secretary before marrying and having two children. His youngest sister, Linda, wanted to be a singer and she had now refused point-blank to go to secretarial college; his father had refused point-blank to let her study music. Linda had gone to the piano and begun to play Chopin's Prelude No. 24 in D minor, a bitter piece of music which gains in tragic intensity when played 40 times in a row.

The fact was that their father was Viennese and had very high standards. The children could all play five or six instruments with flair but they hated to practice: They emerged from each piece either bloody but unbowed or miraculously unscathed, and they had all assumed they would be musicians. Buddy was the first to find they would not. Mr. Konigsberg thought that either you had talent or you did not; none of his children played like a Heifetz or a Casals or a Rubinstein, therefore they did not have the talent to be professionals; therefore they would be better off just enjoying their music, and he explained when Buddy finished high school that he thought he should be an accountant.

Buddy said to my father: You know at the time I didn't want to upset my father, I didn't want to make a big thing of it, I thought who am I to say I could be a singer, but then all the others gave in without an argument. I keep thinking, what if it's my fault? If I'd put my foot down maybe my father would have gotten used to the idea whereas instead they all thought they didn't have a choice, I keep thinking what if it's all my fault?

& he waited hopefully—

& my father said: Of course it's your fault. Why didn't you stand up to him? You let the whole side down. The *least* you can do is make sure it doesn't happen again.

My father knew that he would always hate himself for respecting his own father's wishes, and he now thought that at least someone else could avoid this mistake.

Does she have a place? he asked.

No, said Buddy.

Well she should go for an audition, said my father, and he went into the front room followed by Buddy to argue for this point of view.

In the front room was a 17-year-old girl with fierce black hair, fierce black eyes & ferocious red lipstick. She did not look up because she was halfway through her 41st consecutive rendition of Chopin's Prelude No. 24 in D minor.

My father stood by the piano and he suddenly thought What would be the odds against going to a seminary and going to *synagogue* and learning to play *pool*, just suppose he fell in love with a Jewish girl from Philadelphia and made a fortune in motels and lived happily ever after, say the odds were a billion to one that was still not the same as impossible so it was not actually impossible that his father had not, in fact—

Linda plunged down to the bass and hammered out three bitter low notes. Doom. Doom. Doom.

The piece was over. She looked up before starting again.

Who are you? she said.

Buddy introduced my father.

Oh, the atheist, said my mother.

i

— Let's make bamboo spears! Let's kill all the bandits!
—You can't.
—That's impossible.

Three farmers (Seven Samurai)

A small village is yearly invaded by bandits and the farmers lose their crops and sometimes their lives. This year the elders decide to do something about it. They have heard of a village which once hired masterless samurai and was saved. They decide to do the same and send some of their number to search for willing samurai. Since there is no pay, merely food, a place to sleep, and the fun of fighting, the farmers are fortunate that they first meet Kambei (Takashi Shimura), a strong and dedicated man who decides to make their cause his own. A young *ronin*, Katsushiro (Ko Kimura) joins him, then he accidentally meets an old friend, Shichiroji (Daisuke Kato). He himself chooses Gorobei (Yoshio Inaba) who in turn chooses Heihachi (Minoru Chiaki). A master swordsman, Kyuzo (Seiji Miyoguchi) joins, and so, eventually, does Kikuchiyo (Toshiro Mifune), a farmer's son himself, who has been following them around for some time, attracted—as all of them are—by Kambei.

Once in the village they prepare for war. Not waiting for the first attack, they storm the bandits' fort, burn it and kill a number of the bandits—though Heihachi is also killed. The bandits attack the village and they repulse them, though Gorobei is killed. Then they hit upon the plan of allowing a few in and spearing them to death. In the final battle both Kyuzo and Kikuchiyo are killed—but the bandits are all dead.

It is spring, once more the rice-planting season has come. Of the original seven samurai, only three are left and they soon will go their separate ways.

Donald Richie, *The Films of Akira Kurosawa*

1

Do Samurai Speak Penguin Japanese?

There are 60 million people in Britain. There are 200 million in America. (Can that be right?) How many millions of English-speakers other nations might add to the total I cannot even guess. I would be willing to bet, though, that in all those hundreds of millions not more than 50, at the outside, have read A. Roemer, *Aristarchs Athetesen in der Homerkritik* (Leipzig, 1912), a work untranslated from its native German and destined to remain so till the end of time.

I joined the tiny band in 1985. I was 23.

The first sentence of this little-known work runs as follows:

Es ist wirklich Brach- und Neufeld, welches der Verfasser mit der Bearbeitung dieses Themas betreten und durchpflügt hat, so sonderbar auch diese Behauptung im ersten Augenblick klingen mag.

I had taught myself German out of *Teach Yourself German*, and I recognised several words in this sentence at once:

It is truly something and something which the something with the something of this something has something and something, so something also this something might something at first something.

I deciphered the rest of the sentence by looking up the words Brachfeld, Neufeld, Verfasser, Bearbeitung, Themas, betreten, durchpflügt, sonderbar, Behauptung, Augenblick and klingen in Langenscheidt's German-English dictionary.

This would have been embarrassing if I had been reading under the eyes of people I knew, since I should have been on top of German by now; I should not have frittered away my time at Oxford infiltrating classes on Akkadian, Arabic, Aramaic, Hittite, Pali, Sanskrit and Dialects of the Yemen (not to mention advanced papyrology and intermediate hieroglyphics) instead of advancing the frontiers of human knowledge. The problem is that if you have grown up in the type of place that is excited to be getting its first motel, the type of place that is only dimly (if, indeed, at all) aware of the very *existence* of the Yemen, you want to study dialects of the Yemen if you can because you think you may well not get another chance. I had lied about everything but my height and my weight to get into Oxford (my father, after all, had shown what can happen if you let other people supply your references and your grades) and I wanted to make the most of my time.

The fact that I had completed an undergraduate degree and gone on to get a scholarship to do research just showed how much more appropriate the grades and references were which I had provided myself (straight As, natürlich; lines like 'Sibylla has wide-ranging interests and an extraordinarily original mind; she is a joy to teach') than anything anyone I knew would have come up with. The only problem was that now I had to do the research. The only problem was that when a member of the scholarship committee had said, 'You're on top of German of course,' I had said airily, 'Of course.' It *could* have been true.

Roemer, anyway, was too obscure to be on the open shelves of the Lower Reading Room with more frequently consulted classical texts. Year after year the book gathered dust in the dark, far below ground. Since it had to be called up from the stacks it could be sent to any reading room in the Bodleian, and I had had it sent to Reserve in the Upper Reading Room of the Radcliffe Camera, a library in a dome of stone in the centre of a square. I could read unobserved.

I sat in the gallery looking out across a bell of air, or at the curving walls crammed with extraordinarily interesting-looking books on non-classical subjects, or out the window at the pale stone of All Souls, or, of course, at *Aristarchs Athetesen in der Homerkritik* (Leipzig, 1912). There was not a classicist in sight.

I formed the impression that the sentence meant: It is truly a fallow and new field which the author has trod and ploughed through in handling this subject, so especially might this statement sound in the first moment.

This did not really seem worth the trouble it had taken to work it out, but I had to go on so I went on, or rather I was about to go on when I glanced up and I happened to see, on a shelf to my left, a book on the Thirty Years War which looked extraordinarily interesting. I took it down and it really was extraordinarily interesting and I looked up presently and it was time for lunch.

I went to the Covered Market and spent an hour looking at sweaters.

There are people who think contraception is immoral because the object of copulation is procreation. In a similar way there are people who think the only reason to read a book is to write a book; people should call up books from the dust and the dark and write thousands of words to be sent down to the dust and the dark which can be called up so that other people can send further thousands of words to join them in the dust and the dark. Sometimes a book can be called from the dust and the dark to produce a book which can be bought in shops, and perhaps it is interesting, but the people who buy it and read it because it is interesting are not serious people, if they were serious they would not care about the interest they would be writing thousands of words to consign to the dust and the dark.

There are people who think death a fate worse than boredom.

I saw several interesting sweaters in the Market but they seemed to be rather expensive.

I tore myself away at last and returned to the fray.

It is truly a fallow and new field which the author has trod and ploughed through in handling this subject, so especially might this statement sound in the first moment, I reminded myself.

It seemed extraordinarily uninteresting.

I went on to work through the second sentence, ratio of profit to expense as before, and the sentence after that and the one after that. It took five to ten minutes to read a sentence—an hour a page. Slowly the outlines of the argument loomed out of the mist, like Debussy's drowned cathedral sortant peu à peu de la brume.

In La Cathédrale Engloutie chords of melancholy grandeur break out, at last, *ff* !!!! But when, after some 30 hours or so, I began at last to understand—

49 people in the English-speaking world know what lay in wait. No one else knows or cares. And yet how much hangs on this moment of revelation! It is only if we can conceive of the world without Newton, without Einstein, without Mozart, that we can imagine the difference between this world and the world in which I close *Aristarchs Athetesen* after two sentences and take out *Schachnovelle* in cool disregard of the terms of my scholarship. If I had not read Roemer I would not have known I could not be a scholar, I would never have met Liberace (no, not the) and the world would be short a—

I am saying more than I know. One thing at a time. I read Roemer day after day, and after 30 hours or so enlightenment came not in an hour of gold but an hour of lead.

Some 2,300 years ago Alexander the Great set out from Macedonia to conquer everything in his path. He conquered his way down to Egypt and founded the city of Alexandria, then went on to conquer his way east and die, leaving his followers to fight over his conquests. Ptolemy was already governor of Egypt, and kept it. He ruled the country from Alexandria, and it was he who set up one of the many splendours of the city: a Library built up through an acquisitions policy of singleminded ruthlessness.

The invention of the printing press lay as far ahead of them as the wonders of the 3700s from us; all books were copied out by hand. Mistakes crept in, especially if you were copying a copy of a copy of a copy; sometimes the copyist would have a bright idea and add bogus lines or even entire bogus passages, and then everyone after him would innocently copy the bright idea along with the rest. One solution was to get as close to the original as you could. The Library paid the Athenian public record office a massive deposit to borrow the original manuscripts of the whole of Greek tragedy (Aeschylus, Sophocles, Euripides, the lot) and make copies. It then made sure of having the best possible version by the simple expedient of keeping the originals, returning the copies and forfeiting the deposit.

So far, so not wildly exciting, and yet so much could be said, all fascinating, about the Library and Alexandria and the mad people who lived there, for the writers alone must be the most perverse and wilful the world has ever known. There are people who, needing a place to put umbrellas, go to Ikea and purchase an umbrella stand for easy home assembly—and there are people who drive 100 miles to an auction in the heart of Shropshire and spot the potential in an apparently pointless 17th-century farming implement. The Alexandrians would have been bidding against each other at the auction. They loved to rifle the works of the past (conveniently available in a Library built up by a ruthless acquisitions policy), turn up rare words which were no longer understood let alone used, and deploy them as more interesting alternatives to words people might actually understand. They loved myths in which people went berserk or drank magic potions or turned into rocks in moments of stress; they loved scenes in which people who had gone berserk raved in strange, fractured speeches studded with unjustly neglected vocabulary; they loved to focus on some trivial element of a myth and spin it out and skip the myth—they could make a *Rosencrantz and Guildenstern* of any *Hamlet*. As scholars, as scientists, as mathematicians, as poets who led the flower of Roman youth astray, they crowd their way into books not mainly about them; given a book to themselves they burst out at once into a whole separate volume of footnotes—I speak of course of Fraser's *Ptolemaic Alexandria*, a book I would come back from the grave to possess (I asked for it on my deathbed once and didn't get it). But time is short—the Boy Wonder is watching the video, who knows for how long—what was Roemer's contribution to this marvellous subject?

Roemer was interested in the Homeric criticism of Aristarchus, who was head of the Library a little after 180 BC (the unpleasantness about the tragedies was before his time). Aristarchus had wanted a perfect text of Homer; since an original manuscript did not exist, ruthlessness and cash were not enough: he had to compare copies and spot mistakes. He marked for deletion (athetised) lines he thought did not belong in the text, and was the first to write down his reasoning in commentaries. Nothing by Aristarchus survived. There were marginal notes on the *Iliad* that named no names but were probably third-hand extracts from Aristarchus; there were a few other notes that named names.

Some of the third-hand extracts struck Roemer as brilliant: they were clearly by Aristarchus, who was clearly a genius. Other extracts were too stupid for a genius: clearly by someone else. Whenever someone else was said to have said something brilliant he saw instantly that it was really by Aristarchus, and if any brilliant comments happened to be lying around unclaimed he instantly spotted the unnamed mastermind behind them.

Now it is patently, blatantly obvious that this is insane. If you are going to shuffle all the names around so that one person is always the genius, this means that you have decided not to believe your source whenever it says someone else said something good or the genius said something bad—but the source is your only reason for thinking the genius was a genius in the first place. Anyone who had stopped to think for two seconds would have seen the problem, but Roemer had managed to write an entire scholarly treatise without thinking for two seconds. Having settled on stupidity as the criterion of inauthenticity he went on to discard one stupid remark after another as really by Zenodotus or Aristophanes (no, not the) or misquoted by Didymus, with many sarcastic & gleeful asides on the ineptitude of these imbeciles.

When I first worked out that this was what he was saying I couldn't believe he could really say it so I read another 50 pages (at a rate of 20 minutes/page, thus adding another 16.66 hours to the total) and he really was saying it. I stared at the page. I closed my eyes.

Say you grow up in the type of place that is excited to be getting its first motel, moving from town to town as one motel is finished and another begun. You are naturally not enthralled by school and achieve a solid B− average. Presently you take Scholastic Aptitude Tests and astound everyone by a degree of scholastic aptitude which places the B− average in an entirely different light. Your teachers take the result as a personal insult. You apply to various colleges, who ask for references, and teachers who have reduced you to speechless torpor write complaining of apathy. You are interviewed on the basis of dazzling scholastic aptitude and you are asked about your interests and you have no interests. You have no extracurricular activities because the extracurricular activity was the Donny Osmond Fan Club. Everyone turns down your application on grounds of apathy.

One day you are lying on a bed in one of the motel rooms. Your mother is having a bad day: she is playing Chopin's Revolutionary Etude for the 63rd time on the piano in the adjacent room. Your father is having a good day: a member of the Gideon Society has come to suggest placing Bibles in the rooms, and he has been able to state categorically that he is not having that piece of trash in his motel. Each bedside table, he explains, has a copy of Darwin's *Origin of Species* in the top drawer. In fact it's a really good day because that very morning one of the guests stole the *Origin of Species* instead of a towel. You stare apathetically at the TV. They are showing A Yank at Oxford.

Suddenly you have an idea.

Surely *Oxford*, you reason, would not hold non-membership of the Donny Osmond Fan Club against you. Surely *Oxford* would not insist on mindless enthusiasm just to prove you can be enthusiastic about *something*. Surely *Oxford* would not accept hearsay as evidence. Surely *Oxford* wouldn't hold a reference against you without knowing anything about the writer.

Why not apply?

I thought: I could leave Motelland and live among rational beings! I would never be bored again!

I had reckoned without Roemer. I now thought: Maybe it's my German?

But he really was saying it and I really had spent 46.66 hours reading it. I stared at the page. I stared out across the dome. The space was filled with the soft sound of pages turning. I put my head on my hand.

I had spent 46+ hours on this bizarre piece of logic at a time when I had read not a word of Musil, or Rilke, or Zweig. But I did not have a scholarship to read things that were merely good; I had a scholarship to make a contribution to knowledge. I had squandered 47 hours at a time when people were dying of starvation & children sold into slavery; but I did not have a work permit to do things that were merely worth doing. If I had not needed the work permit I could have dispensed with the scholarship, & if I had gone back to the States I could have dispensed with the work permit, but I did not want to go back to the States.

There is a character in *The Count of Monte Cristo* who digs through solid rock for years and finally gets somewhere: he finds himself in another cell. It was that kind of moment.

I wished I had spent the 47 hours on dialects of the Yemen.

I tried to cheer myself up. I thought: I am in Britain! I can go to a film and catch an ad for Carling Black Label! Because the ads in Britain are the best in the world, and the ads for Carling Black Label were British advertising at its best. I couldn't think of a film I actually wanted to see but the ad would be brilliant. But I suddenly thought that this was exactly the problem, this was the diabolical thing about life: one minute of a Carling Black Label ad to two hours of Ghostbusters XXXV that you didn't even want to see in the first place. So I decided not to go to a film, and if only—

I decided against a film. I thought: Let's go in search of fried chicken.

An American in Britain has sources of solace available nowhere else on earth. One of the marvellous things about the country is the multitudes of fried chicken franchises selling fried chicken from states not known for fried chicken on the other side of the Atlantic. If you're feeling a little depressed you can turn to Tennessee Fried Chicken, if you're in black despair an Iowa Fried Chicken will put things in perspective, if life seems worthless and death out of reach you can see if somewhere on the island an Alaska Fried Chicken is frying chicken according to a recipe passed down by the Inuit from time immemorial.

I cycled out the Cowley Road, past a Maryland Fried Chicken, past a Georgia, and all the time I was trying to think of something I could do without a work permit. I came at last to a Kansas Fried Chicken and dismounted.

I was just locking my bike when I thought suddenly: *Rilke was the secretary of Rodin.*

The things I knew about Rilke were these: that he was a poet; that he went to Paris and got a job as secretary to Rodin; and that he saw some paintings by Cézanne in an exhibition at the Grand Palais and went back day after day to stare for hours, because they were like nothing he'd seen.

I knew nothing about how Rilke got this job, so that I was free to imagine that he simply turned up on the doorstep. Why shouldn't I simply turn up on a doorstep? I could go to London or Paris or Rome and turn up on the doorstep of a painter or sculptor, the type of person who would probably not care about a work permit. I could see things that had just come into the world and stare for hours.

I walked up and down and I tried to think of an artist who might need an assistant.

I walked up and down and I thought that perhaps it would be easier to think of an artist if I were already in London or Paris or Rome.

I did not have a lot of money, so I walked up and down trying to think of a way to get to London or Paris or Rome. At last I went into the Kansas Fried Chicken.

I was just about to order a Kansas Chik'n Bucket when I remembered that I had signed up for dinner in college. My college was famous for its chef, and yet I was tempted to stay where I was, and if only—

I won't think that. I don't mean that, but if only—

What difference does it make? What's done is done.

By coincidence I had signed up to eat in college that night; by coincidence I sat by a former member who was visiting; it was no coincidence that I talked of intellectual monogamy & of work permits since I could think of nothing else, but by coincidence this former member said sympathetically that Balthus had been the secretary of Rilke, by coincidence she was the daughter of a civil servant & so not intimidated by British bureaucracy, & she said that if I could bear the shame of being known to

Why are they fighting?
WHY ARE THEY FIGHTING?

WHY ARE THEY FIGHTING?

Can't you read what it says?

Of COURSE I can read it but WHY

Well they're looking for samurai to defend the village from bandits

I know that

but some of them think it's a waste of time

I know THAT

because the samurai they've asked have been insulted by the offer
of three meals a day

I KNOW that

and now they're saying I told you so

I KNOW THAT BUT WHY ARE THEY FIGHTING

I think this may be too hard for you.

NO

Maybe we should wait till you're older

NO

Just till you're 6

NO! NO! NO! NO! NO!

OKOKOKOKOK. OK. OK.

I think he is probably too young but what can I do? Today I read
these terrible words in the paper:

> In the absence of a benevolent male, the single mother faces an
> uphill battle in raising her son. It is essential that she provide the
> boy with male role models—neighbours, or uncles, or friends of
> the family, to share their interests and hobbies.

This is all very well but Ludo is an uncleless boy, and I don't happen
to know any well-meaning stamp collectors (if I did I would do my
best to avoid them). It's worrying. I once read that Argentine soldiers
tied up dissidents and took them up in planes over the sea and threw

them out. I thought: well, if L needs a role model let him watch
Seven Samurai & he will have 8.

*The farmers see a crowd of people. A samurai has gone to the river's edge
to be shaved by a monk.*

*A man with a moustache and a sword pushes his way through the crowd
and squats scratching his chin. (It's Toshiro Mifune.)*

*A handsome, aristocratic young man asks someone what's happening. A
thief is hiding in a barn. He is holding a baby hostage. The samurai has asked
for monk's robes and two rice cakes.*

*The samurai puts on his disguise. He feels Mifune watching and turns.
His eyes are black in a white face on a black screen. Mifune stares blankly
back. The samurai's eyes are black in a white face. Mifune scratches himself.
The samurai turns away. He turns back and looks at Mifune; his eyes are
black his face is white. He turns away and goes to the barn.*

Mifune sits on a stump close behind him to watch.

*The samurai tells the thief he has brought food, tosses the rice cakes
through the door, and follows.*

The thief runs from the barn and falls down dead.

The samurai drops the thief's sword in the dirt.

The parents of the child rush forward to take it.

*Mifune runs forward brandishing his sword. He jumps up and down on
the body.*

The samurai walks off without a backward look.

type (I had admitted to 100wpm) I could have a work permit & a
job.

I was about to say earlier that if I had not read Roemer on the
30th of April 1985 the world would be short a genius; I said that the
world without the Infant Terrible would be like the world without
Newton & Mozart & Einstein! I have no idea if this is true; I have no

way of knowing if this is true. Not every genius is a prodigy & not every prodigy is a genius & at 5 it is too soon to tell. Sidis knew 12 languages at 8, lectured on solid geometry at Harvard at 12, and ended unknown to all but anxious parents of early over-achievers. Cézanne taught himself to paint in his twenties. But Bernini was a prodigy and a genius, and so was Mozart. It's not impossible. It's possible.

It's possible, but is it likely? If L is a Mozart or a Newton people 10 centuries from now will be interested in the fact that he so nearly

Why did he cut off his hair? Why did he change his clothes?
WHY DID HE CUT OFF HIS HAIR? WHY DID HE CHANGE HIS CLOTHES?
WHY DID HE
He had to disguise himself as a priest so the thief wouldn't be suspicious and kill the child.

Well why couldn't the priest go?

I think Buddhist priests don't believe in violence. Besides, the priest might not have been able to disarm the thief. Anyway the thing that matters is that he does it for nothing, and he does it to rescue a child, because we discover later that his greatest regret—

I would like to tell him to let the film speak for itself. I am about to say this in the confidence that he cannot go wrong when I remember Mr. Richie's comments on the final rice-planting scene. Mr. Richie is the author of *The Films of Akira Kurosawa,* and as I rely on this book for everything I know about the many films of Kurosawa which are not available on video I wish he had not said that the end showed the ingratitude of the farmers and a rice-planting scene as an element of hope. If the film does not speak for itself I will have to say something about the film which I would very much rather

I say to L that I read somewhere that in the Tokugawa period it was punishable by death for a non-samurai to carry a sword. I say that Mr. Richie says that shaving the head would normally be a mark of humiliation for a samurai. I say that the name of the actor with the moustache is Mifune Toshiro because I don't want him to pick up my bad habit of putting the names in the Western order out of laziness and I write it down on a piece of paper for him so he will know it next time. I say that the name of the actor who plays the samurai is Shimura Takashi and I write down after a little thought the characters for Shimura and after a lot of thought the character for Takashi. I say that I have seen Kurosawa's name spelled two ways, the characters for Kuro (black) and Akira (don't know) are always the same, but I have seen two different characters used for Sawa. I write down both versions & I say that it seems more polite to use the form preferred by its bearer. He says which one is Kurosawa and I say he does not appear, he is the director and he says what's a director and I say that it will be easier to explain when he has seen the film. It occurs to me that these pieces of information are flimsy defences against whatever it is that makes a man when told to toss a person from a plane do as told, which is too bad as L instantly wants to know more. He asks me to write down the names of all the other actors so he can look at them later. I say I will try to find them in the autobiography.

never existed; Roemer will be as momentous in his way as the plague that sent Newton home from Cambridge. But why shouldn't he end badly? The business of getting a baby from womb to air is pretty well understood. Out it comes, a dribbling squall. Presently its talents come into the open; they are hunted down, and bludgeoned into insensibility. But Mozart was once a prodigious, prestidigious little monkey.

My father used to say with a mocking smile when things went

wrong, which they for the most part did: Of all sad words of tongue or pen, The saddest are these, it might have been. If L comes to good not by some miracle but by doing the right thing rather than the wrong others may profit from his escape; if he comes to bad (as is not unlikely) his example may spare them.

The farmers look at each other. This is the man they need. They follow him out of town.
So does Mifune.
So does the aristocratic young man. He runs up to the samurai in the road and falls to his knees.

L (reading subtitles): My name is Katsushiro Okamoto. Let me follow you
L: I am Kambei Shimada. I am only a ronin. What's a ronin?
I: A masterless samurai.
L: I am not a samurai and I have no followers
L: Please take me
L: Stand up, or else we can't talk properly
L: You are embarrassing me; I am not very skilful
    Listen, I can't teach you anything special
    I've merely had a lot of fighting experience
    Go away and forget about following me
    It's for your own good
L: I'm determined to follow you, whatever you say
L: I forbid you
    I can't afford to have any followers
Mifune runs up and stares at the samurai. Kambei: Onushi —samurai ka? Mifune (drawing himself up) : [incomprehensible shout]
L: Are you a samurai?
L: Of course!

Kambei and Katsushiro walk away. A farmer runs forward and falls to his knees.

I tell L that in the autobiography Kurosawa has nothing but praise for the marvellous Mifune except possibly that he had a rather harsh way of talking which the microphones had trouble picking up. I say that it's very charming the way the translators have translated the Japanese into Penguin.

L: What's Penguin?

I: It's what English translators translate into. Merely had a lot of fighting experience! Determined to follow you! As it happens most English speakers can understand Penguin even if they wouldn't use it in daily life, but still.

L: Isn't that what they say?

I: They *may* be speaking Penguin Japanese, we can only surmise. Kambei says *Tada kassen ni wa zuibun deta ga, tada,* just, *kassen* is battle or combat according to Halpern (but I wonder whether that isn't just Penguin infiltrating the dictionary), *ni* in, *wa* topic particle, *zuibun* a lot, *deta* happened, *ga* another particle which we won't go into now but which seems pretty common, it's hard to believe *it* is giving the flavour of Penguin to the

L: When are you going to teach me Japanese?

I: I don't know enough to teach you.

L: You could teach me what you know.

I: [NO NO NO NO] Well

L: Please

I: Well

L: Please

Voice of Sweet Reason: You've started so many other things I think you should work on them more before you start something new.

L: How much more?

I: Well

L: How much more?

The last thing I want is to be teaching a five-year-old a language I have not yet succeeded in teaching myself.

I: I'll think about it.

I would like to strike a style to amaze. I think I am not likely to discover the brush of Cézanne; if I am to leave no other record I would like it to be a marvel. But I must write to be understood; how can formal perfection be saved? I see in my mind a page, I think of Cicero's *De Natura Deorum*: across the top one Latin line, the rest English (or possibly German), identification of persons obscure after 2,000 years. Just so will this look if I explain every reference for 45th-century readers, readers who may, for all I know, know the name of a single 21st-century genius (the one now five years old). What I mean is that I see in my mind a page, across the top a line with the words Carling Black Label, the rest a solid mass of small type describing Carling Black Label the beer, Carling Black Label ads the glory of British advertising, Levi's the jeans, stonewashed Levi's ad parodied in classic ad for Carling Black Label, lyrics of I Heard It Through the Grapevine classic song sung by Marvin Gaye in classic jeans and classic beer ad, not to mention terrible deprivation of American audiences of the time able to export the jeans and import the beer but not to sample the glories of British advertising to which these gave rise. What I mean is that I have read books written 2,000 or even 2,500 years ago or 20 years ago and in 2,500 years they will need everything even Mozart explained and when once you start explaining there is no end to it.

HOW MUCH MORE?
HOW *MUCH* MORE?
HOW, MUCH, MORE?

I: Well if you read the *Odyssey* and Books 1–8 of the *Metamor-phoses* and the whole *Kalilah wa Dimnah* and 30 of the *Thousand and One Nights* and I Samuel *and* the Book of Jonah *and* learn the cantillation and if you do 10 chapters in *Algebra Made Easy* then I will teach you as much as I can.

L: Then that's what I'll do.

I: All right.

L: I will.

I: Fine.

L: You'll see.

I: I know.

L: Will you teach me the alphabet while I'm working on the rest?

I: It doesn't have an alphabet. It has two sets of syllabaries of 46 symbols apiece, 1,945 characters of Chinese derivation in common use since the Second World War and up to 50,000 characters used before then. I know the syllabaries and 262 characters which I keep forgetting which is precisely why I am not really qualified to teach it to you.

L: Then why don't you get a Japanese to teach me?

This is a wonderful idea. I could get a benevolent Japanese male to act as an uncle substitute for L! A benevolent Mifune lookalike to come and talk about stamp collecting or football or his car in a language which would conceal the diabolical tedium of the subject. But he would probably want some money.

I: I don't think we can afford it.

I once read a book about an Australian girl who was given an English bulldog; a big truck was sent into town to collect the (as they thought) large animal, and brought back a baby bulldog that could be held in the palm of a hand. At the time I thought I would like a tiny bulldog of my own. Little did I know. L has read Ali Baba and Moses in the Bullrushes and Cicero's *De Amicitia* and the *Iliad* which I started him on by accident, & he can play Straight No Chaser which he learned by listening to the tape & trying to copy it about 500 times—it is wonderful that he was able to do it and yet if you are trying to type 62 years of *Crewelwork Digest* onto computer in the same room it can sometimes be hard to feel a proper

For who was Mozart? Wolfgang Amadeus Mozart (1756–1791) was an Austrian composer of genius, taught music by his father Leopold from the age of five, and displayed in the courts of Europe playing the harpsichord blindfold and performing other tricks. He composed string quartets, symphonies, piano sonatas, a concerto for the glass organ and several operas including Don Giovanni and The Magic Flute. His sister Nannerl received identical training and was not a musical genius. I have heard it argued, and by a clever man too, that this proves that women are not capable of musical genius. How is it possible to argue this, you say, AND to know that a brother and sister may have no genes in common, without being committed to the unlikely theory that any man could be a Mozart with similar training? You say it, and I thought it; but the fact is that a clever man so seldom needs to think

What's a syllabary?
A syllabary is a set of phonetic symbols each representing a syllable

he gets out of the habit.

What's a syllable?

You know what a syllable is

No I don't

A syllable is a phonetic element of a word containing a vowel, take the word 'containing' you could break it down to 'con-tain-ing' and have a symbol for each part. In Chinese each word is just one syllable long, a monosyllable. What would polysyllabic be?

With many syllables?

Exactement.

And oligosyllabic would be with few syllables

It would be, but it's not used much, people seem to work in terms of an opposition between the one and the many

Duosyllabic

It would be better to say word of two syllables on grounds of euphony. In general if you are going to make up a word you should use the adverbial form of the number, which would give disyllabic except people often seem to use bi after mono, monogamy bigamy monoplane biplane. Usually Latin numbers go with words of Latin derivation, so unilateral bilateral multilateral bicameral multinational, and Greek numbers with words of Greek derivation, tetrahedron, tetralogy, pentagon

Trisyllabic

Yes

Tetrasyllabic

Yes

Pentasyllabic hexasyllabic heptasyllabic oktasyllabic enasyllabic dekasyllabic hendekasyllabic dodekasyllabic

Exactly

Treiskaidekasyllabic tessareskaidekasyllabic pentekaidekasyllabic hekkaidekasyllabic heptakaidekasyllabic

And who was Bernini? Gianlorenzo Bernini (1598–1680) was 'the greatest genius of the Italian Baroque', who moved to Rome at the age of seven and was taught by his father

EIKOSASYLLABIC

Pietro, a sculptor. Rudolf Wittkower (German art historian, refugee from the Nazis [where to begin?], author of *Art & Architecture in Italy 1600–1750*) compares him to Michelangelo ([1475–1564]),

enneakaieikosasyllabic
TRIAKONTASYLLABIC

painter, poet, sculptor of genius . . .) in his capacity for superhuman

oktokaitriakontasyllabic enneakaitriakontasyllabic
TESSARAKONTASYLLABIC

concentration. 'But unlike the terrible and lonely giant of the six-teenth century, he was a man of infinite charm, a brilliant and witty talker, fond of conviviality, aristocratic in demeanour, a good husband and father, a first-rate

enneakaitessarakontasyllabic PENTEKONTASYLLABIC
heiskaipentekontasyllabic

organiser, endowed with an unparalleled talent for creating rapidly and with ease.'

And Cézanne? Paul Cézanne (1839–1906) was a French painter of genius, associated with the Impressionist

treiskaihexekontasyllabic

school of painting. He was inarticulate: people called him the Bear.
He worked very slowly and with

oktokaihexekontasyllabic enneakaihexekontasyllabic
HEBDOMEKONTASYLLABIC

difficulty. He is most famous for his landscapes and still lifes. His
method was to apply blocks of paint to the canvas, often with a
palette knife rather than a brush. He worked so

heptakaihebdomekontasyllabic

slowly that even fruit could not

OGDOEKONTASYLLABIC

stand still enough: it rotted

What's the longest word in the world?
I don't know. I don't know all the words in the world.
What's the longest word you know?
I don't know.
How can you not know?
I think it's the name of a polymer. I can't remember how it goes.
duokaiogdoekontasyllabic
Wait a minute. Here's a good one. di(2-ethylhexyl)hexahydroph-
thalate.
Is that the polymer?
No.
What does it mean?

I once knew.

My dad would know.

The hell he would (think I)—I would like to say this but I don't KNOW that he doesn't, there is only an (in my opinion) over-whelming likelihood, & I think I should not blacken his name to L without good hard evidence.

He MAY know. It didn't come up in the conversation.

What did you talk about?

I talked about the Rosetta Stone. He talked about his car and about a writer he admired.

What kind of car does he have?

He didn't say. Diethyl-dimethyl methane. Diethyl-diethyl malonate. Diethyl-methyl-ethyl malonate.

treiskaiogdoekontasyllabic   tessareskaiogdoekontasyllabic pentekaiogdoekontasyllabic

before he was done. He used

oktokaiogdoekontasyllabic   enneakaiogdoekontasyllabic ENENEKONTASYLLABIC

wax fruit instead.

And who was Rilke and who was Zweig and who was Musil? Who was Newton and who was Einstein? Rilke

Why don't you teach me the syllabaries?

WHY DON'T YOU TEACH ME THE SYLLABARIES?

WHY DON'T YOU TEACH ME THE SYLLABARIES?

Well

Are they hard?

Not very

Please

Well
Please
I told you the deal
Heiskaienenekontasyllabic duokaienenekontasyllabic

Glenn Gould (eccentric, brilliant mid-20th-century Canadian pianist and specialist in the works of J. S. Bach [18th-century German

HEPTAKAIENENEKONTASYLLABIC

composer of genius]) said of The Well-Tempered Clavier [forget it],
that the preludes

OKTOKAIENENEKONTASYLLABIC

were merely prefatory

ENNEAKAIENENEKONTASYLLABIC

and of no

HEKATONTASYLLABIC

real musical interest. The

You could teach me ONE syllabary
I told you the deal
Is there a language with only one syllabary?
I think Tamil makes do with one
So Tamil would be a monosyllabaric language
Yes

And Japanese is a disyllabaric language but most people would call
it bisyllabaric
    Yes
    trisyllabaric tetrasyllabaric pentasyllabaric hexasyllabaric

reader

heptasyllabaric

may

oktasyllabaric

take comfort

enasyllabaric

in a plain

dekasyllabaric hendekasyllabaric dodekasyllabaric

preface.

hekkaidekasyllabaric

I will hope to do no worse by

heptakaidekasyllabaric
OKTOKAIDEKASYLLABARIC
ENNEAKAIDEKASYLLABARIC
EIKOSASYLLABARIC
heiskai

You're missing a masterpiece of modern cinema. Finish the
Odyssey and I'll teach you the hiragana, yes?
Done.

Emma offered me a work permit & a job.
I said: Done.

❖

Odyssey 1.

❖

Odyssey 2.

❖

Odyssey 3.

❖

Odyssey 4.

❖

I never meant this to happen. (L is reading *Odyssey* 5. He has read four books in four days. I would carry on from where I left off but I have misplaced my notes.) What I meant was to follow the example of Mr. Ma (father of the famous cellist), who I read somewhere started teaching Yo Yo when he was 2.

Coupez la difficulté en quatre was his motto, which meant that he would reduce a piece of music to a number of very small short tasks; the child was to master one task a day. He used the same procedure with Chinese characters, the child learning a character a day—by my reckoning that makes two simple tasks but you get the picture. I thought that this would be an enormous help to L for very little trouble to myself, & when he was 2 I started him on flashcards.

I think that the first simple task was supposed to be cat. No sooner had he mastered this simple task than he wanted to go on, he wanted every single word in his vocabulary on a card, he sobbed PURPLE PURPLE PURPLE when I tried to stop before writing it down. The next day he started his first book, *Hop on Pop* by Dr. Seuss, no sooner had he started than he started to cry because he did not know Hop and Pop. I saw in a flash that the time required to teach a two-year-old workaholic by the look-and-say method would leave perhaps 6 minutes a day for typing, & so (doubting my ability to make ends meet on 55p a day) I hastily went over a few principles of the phonics system. He learned to say huh when he saw an h and puh when he saw a p and by the end of the week he could read as follows: Hop. On. Pop. The. Cat. in. the. Hat.

I thought: It worked! It worked!

He would sit on the floor and when he found something interesting he would bring it over to show me.

Thunder of tiny feet. He had unearthed a treasure. Yes? I would say

And he would produce from the page—O Joy!—a thing of glory

The

Wonderful!
And here was another find! What could it be? Could it—No—
Yes—*Yes*—It was a

Cat

And he would pluck from the page one marvel after another, until at last he could nonchalantly draw now a rabbit, now a dove, now
a string of coloured scarves from an ordinary empty black top hat.
Wonderful marvellous wonderful marvellous cool
I was not getting as much work done as I had hoped.
One day it occurred to him that there were quite a lot of other
books on the shelves.
He selected a book with pictures, and he came to my side, per-
turbed.

The face on the gutta percha inkstand has a tale to tell

I explained gutta percha, inkstand and tale

it is believed to be that of Neptune, moulded to commemorate the successful use of the material to insulate
the world's first submarine telegraph cable from England to France in 1850.

& I said NO.
I said You know a lot of these words don't you, and he said Yes,
and I said Why don't you practise reading the words you know and

you can pick FIVE WORDS that you don't know and I will explain them.

I don't know how much of this deal he understood. He asked for Neptune, moulded, commemorate, successful, material, insulate and submarine. I explained them in a manner which I leave to the imagination. He read a few words that he knew and put the book on the floor. Then he went back for another book. What a delightful surprise! In, And, To and our old friend The in *Truth and Other Enigmas*! Sadly, however, no sign of gutta percha or Neptune.

He put the book on the floor and went back to the shelf.

20 books later I thought: This is not going to work.

I said: Put the book back on the shelf

& he took it down with a cry of glee

so I put it back and I put him in his playpen and he started to sob.

I said: Look, why don't you look at all the nice pictures in *Classic Plastics,* and whenever you know a word you can read the word, look at this lovely yellow radio

and he sobbed NOOOOOOOOOO

I said: Well look, here's *Truth and Other Enigmas*, that's got lots and lots and lots of words, let's see if you know a word on this page

& he sobbed NOOOOOOOOOOOO and tore the page from the book and hurled the book away.

I thought: Let's think of some other simple task. A simple task that can be mastered on a daily basis that will not lead to the transfer of hundreds of books to the floor.

So I took him to Grant & Cutler and I bought a little French picture book and *Yaourtu la Tortue* and *L'Histoire de Babar* (as well as a copy of Rilke's *Letters on Cézanne* which they happened to have in stock). I taught him a few simple words on a daily basis for a few days and he left the English books alone.

I thought: It worked! It worked!

One day he found some French books on a shelf. I explained five words in *Zadig*. Soon 20 French books had followed it to the floor. Then he went back to the English books.

I thought: Let's think of another simple task.

I thought arithmetic could be the simple task. So I taught him to count past 5 and he counted up to 5,557 over a period of three days before collapsing in sobs because he had not reached the end & I said with the genius of desperation that the good thing about infinity is that you know you'll never run out of numbers. I taught him to add 1 to a number which seemed a simple task & he covered 20 sheets of graph paper with calculations: 1+1=2 2+1=3 3+1=4 until he was carried sobbing to bed. I once read a book in which a boy who studied too much at an early age came down with brain fever and was reduced to imbecility; I have never come across a case of brain fever *outside* a book, but still I was concerned & would have liked to stop but he sobbed if I tried to stop. So I taught him to add 2 to a number and he covered 20 sheets with 2+2=4 3+2=5.

How old was he asks a reader. I think he was about 3.

He settled down now and as long as he could cover 20 sheets with a particular calculation he did not need to go on to infinity. He did not need to take the books off their shelves. I taught him to multiply single numbers & now on 20 sheets he put times tables for the numbers 1–20. I have no idea how you would make a 3-year-old do this if he did not want to any more than I know how you could stop one that wants to, but when he had done it for a couple of months it was easy to explain variables & functions & increments. So by the time he was 4 he could read English & some French & cover 20 sheets with graphs for x+1, x+2, x+3, x+4; $x^2 + 1$, x^2+2 & so on.

About a year ago I snatched a moment to read *Iliad* 16. I had been typing in *Melody Maker* 1976 and had reached the point in an interview with John Denver where the singer explained:

You know, Chris . . . I have a definition of success, and what success is to me is when an individual finds that thing which fulfills
himself, when he finds that thing that completes him and when,
in doing it, he finds a way to serve his fellow man. When he finds
that he is a successful person.

It doesn't make any difference whether you are a ditch-digger
or a librarian or someone who works at the filling station or the
President of the United States or whatever, if you're doing what
you want to do and in some way bringing value to the life of others, then you're a successful human being.

It so happens that in my area, which is entertainment, that success brings with it a lot of other things, but all of those other
things, the money, the fame, the conveniences, the ability to travel
and see the rest of the world, all of those are just icing on the cake
and the cake is the same for everybody.

This was the kind of thing a recent President of the United States
(like Denver, a genuinely nice guy) had tended to say, and as there
was no point thinking about his particular way of bringing value to
the life of others I thought it was a good time to take a break and
read *Iliad* 16. I had been typing for five or six hours so it was a good
day so far.

Iliad 16 is the book where Patroclus is killed—he goes into battle
wearing Achilles' armour to encourage the Greeks & unnerve the
Trojans, since Achilles still refuses to fight. He wins for a while but
he goes too far; Apollo makes him dizzy & takes away his armour, &
he is wounded by Euphorbus, & then Hector kills him. I had remembered suddenly that Homer addresses Patroclus in the vocative
& that it is strangely moving. Unfortunately I could not find *Iliad*
13–24, I could only find 1–12, so I decided to read Hector & Andromache in Book 6 instead.

As soon as I sat down L came up to look at the book. He stared
& stared. He said he couldn't read any of it. I said that was because

it was in Greek & had a different alphabet & he said he wanted to learn it.

The last thing I wanted was to be teaching a 4-year-old Greek.

And now the Alien spoke, & its voice was mild as milk. It said: He's just a baby. They spend so much time in school—wouldn't he be better off playing?

I said: Let him wait to be bored in a class like everyone else.

The Alien said: It will only confuse him! It will destroy his confidence! It would be kinder to say no!

The Alien has a long eel-like neck and little reptilian eyes. I put both hands around its throat & I said: Rot in hell.

It coughed & said sweetly: So sorry to intrude. Admirable maternity! All time devoted to infant amelioration. Selflessly devoted!

I said: Shut up.

It said: Sssssssssssssssssssssssssssssss.

I said: Grrrrrrrrrrrrrrrrrrrrrrrrrrrrrr.

—& I wrote out a little table for him:

A	B	Γ	Δ	E	Z	H	Θ	I	K	Λ	M
A	B	G	D	E	Z	Ē	TH	I	K	L	M

α	β	γ	δ	ε	ζ	η	θ	ι	κ	λ	μ
a	b	g	d	e	z	ē	th	i	k	l	m

N	Ξ	O	Π	P	Σ	T	Υ	Φ	X	Ψ	Ω
N	X	O	P	R	S	T	U	PH	KH	PS	Ō

ν	ξ	ο	π	ρ	σ,ς	τ	υ	φ	χ	ψ	ω
n	x	o	p	r	s	t	u	ph	kh	ps	ō

& I said: There's the alphabet.

He looked at the table and he looked at the page.

I said: It's perfectly simple. As you can see a lot of the letters are the same as the ones you already know.

He looked at the table and he looked at the page and he looked at the table.

The Alien said: He is only four

Mr. Ma said: Coupez la difficulté en quatre

I said patiently:

I said patiently a lot of things which it would try my patience even more to repeat. I hope I am as ready as the next person to suffer for the good of others, and if I knew for a fact that even 10 people this year, next year or a thousand years from now would like to know how one teaches a 4-year-old Greek I hope I would have the decency to explain it. As I don't know this I think I will set this aside for the moment. L seems to be transferring *Odyssey* 5 word by word to pink file cards.

❖

Odyssey 6.

❖

Odyssey 7.

Emma was as good as her word and I was as good as my word.

In the summer of 1985 I began working as a secretary in a small publishing house in London which specialised in dictionaries and non-academic works of scholarship. It had an English dictionary that had first come out in 1812 and been through nine or ten editions and sold well, and a range of technical dictionaries for native speakers of various other languages that sold moderately well, and a superb dictionary of literary Bengali which was full of illustrative material and had no rival and hardly sold at all. It had a two-volume history of sugar, and a three-volume survey of London doorknockers (supplement in preparation), and various other books which gradually built up a following by word of mouth. I did not want to be a secretary & I did not particularly want to get into publishing, but I did not want to go back to the States.

Emma was really the next worst thing to the States. She loved America in the way that the Victorians loved Scotland, French Impressionists Japan. She loved an old Esso station on a state highway in a pool of light with a round red Coca-Cola sign swinging in the wind, and a man on a horse thinking vernacular thoughts among scenes of spectacular natural beauty, and a man in a fast car on a freeway in LA. She loved all the books I'd been made to read at school, and she loved the books we didn't read in school because they might be offensive to born-again Baptists. I did not know what to say.

In my mind I saw a timid little mezzotint in which a lot of cross-hatching and a little hand tinting depicted some place where Europeans first going had been drunk on colour & writing a book had insisted on the Grand Canyon or Table Mountain or the South Seas being shown in a colour engraving, so that what was brilliant cobalt was represented by blue so pale it was almost white, vermilion crimson and scarlet by pink so pale almost white and there would be also a green so pale perhaps yellow so pale perhaps pale pale mauve, so that the reader might taste in a glass of water a real drop of whisky. I thought of Emma's favourites with a scornful laugh, and yet this was stupid, you could just as well think of some other image that would not be contemptible—the black-and-white film does not show the world we see around us in its colours but it is not contemptible. The fact is that though things were better than when I had been reading things people had thrown their lives away on seventy years before at any moment a passion would fling itself on the first idea standing by and gallop off ventre à terre—how quietly and calmly some people argue.

It made me nervous to have these rages and sardonic laughs just waiting to gallop off ventre à terre, it was easier not to say anything or to say something quiet and banal. And yet if someone is very clever and charming you would rather not say something banal, you resolve instead to say something while remaining perfectly calm & in control—

I said that it seemed very quaint that in England books were in English & in France they were in French and that in 2,000 years this would seem as quaint as Munchkinland & the Emerald City, in the meantime it was strange that people from all over the world would go to one place to breed a nation of English writers & another to breed writers of Spanish, it was depressing in a literature to see all the languages fading into English which in America was the language of forgetfulness. I argued that this was false to what was there in a way that a European language could not be false to a European country, just as it was one thing to film Kansas in black & white but for the Land of Oz you had to have Technicolor, & what's more (I seemed to be covering ground more impetuously than I had planned but it was too late to stop) it was preposterous that people who were by and large the most interesting the most heroic the most villainous the newest immigrants could appear in the literature of the country only as character actors speaking bad English or italics & by & large both they & their descendants' ignorance of their language & customs could not be represented at all in the new language, which had forgotten that there was anything to forget.

Emma said: You mean you think they should not be just in English.

Exactly, I said. Once you think of it you wonder why you never thought of it before.

Well, said Emma, they do say desktop publishing is the way of the future—

Would you like me to type a 100-word letter in a minute? I said, for there was work to be done. A 50-word letter in 30 seconds? A 5-word letter in 3?

I hope you're not too bored, said Emma.

I said: Bored!

I know it's not very interesting, said Emma.

I would have liked to say But it's absolutely *enthralling*. I said sensibly: The main thing is it's giving me a chance to decide what I want to do.

This was exactly the kind of banal, boring remark I would rather not have made in the presence of someone clever and charming, but it seemed to me that Emma looked rather relieved. I said: It's just what I was looking for. It's absolutely fine.

The job was absolutely fine, Emma was clever and charming and I was in London. I tried to follow the example of Rilke but it was not so easy. It was not just a question of being overwhelmed by a body of work: Rilke was overwhelmed by Cézanne, but Cézanne could not have used a secretary, nor paid one. I did not like the idea of working for Rodin in order to stare overwhelmed at Cézanne; it seems as though if you turn up on someone's doorstep you should at least be overwhelmed by his work.

Sometimes I rode the Circle Line reading a book on organic

chemistry and sometimes I read *Leave It to Psmith* for the 20th or 21st time and sometimes I watched Jeremy Brett's marvellous grotesque Sherlock Holmes or of course Seven Samurai. I sometimes went out for Tennessee Fried Chicken.

Day followed day. A year went by.

❖

Odyssey 8.

❖

Odyssey 9 & just asking every word as he goes along. He hasn't even been writing them on file cards. It is lovely that he is enjoying the story.

❖

I came into the office one day in June 1986 to find everyone in a state of nervous excitement. An acquisitor had snapped up the firm and had assured everyone that it would remain an autonomous imprint. This sinister announcement was taken to mean that everyone would soon be redundant.

The overtaker was a big American company, and it published many writers admired in the office. There was to be a big party to celebrate the merger in a few weeks' time.

Emma had got me my job and my work permit & she now got me an invitation to this party.

Now not only did the new firm publish many American writers admired in the office but it also published Liberace, and one of the reasons getting me invited was a favour, one of the reasons people were excited, one of the reasons I did not want to go, was that there was a rumour that Liberace would be there. By Liberace I don't, of course, mean the popular pianist who coined the phrase 'cried all the way to the bank', loved no woman but his mother and died of AIDS in the mid-80s. I mean the acclaimed British writer and traveller whose technique rivalled that of the much-loved musician.

Liberace the musician had a terrible facility and a terrible sincerity; what he played he played with feeling, whether it was Roll Out the Barrel or I'll Be Seeing You, and in sad pieces a tear would well up over the mascara and drop to the silver diamanté of a velvet coat while the rings on his hands flashed up and down the keyboard, and in a thousand mirrors he would see the tear, the mascara, the rings, he would see himself seeing the mascara, the rings, the tear. All this could be found too in Liberace (the writer): the slick, buttery arpeggios, the self-regarding virtuosity as the clever ring-laden hands sparkled over the keys, the professional sincerity which found expressiveness for the cynical & the sentimental, for the pornographic, even for alienation & affectlessness. And yet he was not really exactly like the pianist, because though he did genuinely have the emotional facility of the musician he had only the air of technical facility, there being to even a buttery arpeggio not only the matter of running hands up and down the keys but

L wants to know what βίηφιν means. I say he knows perfectly well what it means & he says he doesn't.

At first (because I was explaining that βίηφιν was the instrumental form of βίη, meaning by force or violence) I thought that the writer was like a person who typing puts a hand down one key to the right or left of where it should be, so that an intelligible sentence nrvomrd duffrnly uninyrllihlnlr ot nrstly do, snf yhr gsdyrt you yypr yhr eotdr iy hryd (ψηλαφόων means, can I see the line? it means feeling or groping about), and in my mind I saw the hands of Liberace moving rapidly & confidently up and down the keyboard striking keys now black now white. Now I think (as far as a person can be said to think who is taking the place of a talking dictionary) that even this is not quite right, because though Liberace did strew his work with mistakes they were not the kind (πετάσσας means spreading, it is the aorist participle of πετάννυμι) that you could overlook in that way or rather (you know perfectly well what ὕφαινον means No I don't It means weave and what form is it here 1st person singular imperfect OK) it is not that he overlooked them (ἄρσενες means males) but that he looked straight at them with complacency (just a minute) Breathless with adoration would Liberace litter his work with gaping arguments and images knocked awry, stand back, fold arms, Ed Wood abeam at toppling tombstones and rumpled grass (just a *minute*) Did he notice or not care? He liked I expect the idea of effortless excellence, & being unable to combine the two had settled for the one he could be sure of (δασύμαλλοι: thick-fleeced; ἰοδνεφὲς: dark; λίγοισι: withies; withy: a piece of wickerwork; πέλωρ: You *know* what πέλωρ means No I don't Yes you do Don't Do Don't Do Don't Do Don't Don't Don't Don't It means monster That's what I *thought* it meant—No wonder I am sticking pins in the father of this child). Here was a man who'd learned to write before he could think, a man who threw out logical fallacies like tacks behind a getaway car, and he always always always got away.

❖

Od. 10.

❖

Met. 1.

❖

I Sam. I? [Have not read in years.]

❖

I Sam. II–V? [Hell.]

It is strange to think that Schoenberg's *Harmonielehre* was first published in 1911, a year before Roemer brought out *Aristarchs Athetesen in der Homerkritik*. Schoenberg, who had a wife and two children, was scraping a living as a teacher of music & portrait painter. I think Roemer held a position at the University of Leipzig. Roemer's colleagues might have pointed out the fallacy; I might have spoken fluent German & lost half an hour on it; I might have lost 50 hours a week later—and Ludoviticus would not now be setting Mr. Ma at defiance by mastering 500 simple tasks on a daily basis. The atoms which now direct the application of a pink Schwan Stabilo highlighter to *Odyssey* 10 would be going about some other business, as would I, & the world, for all I know, would be short an Einstein. And yet tactful colleagues, bad German and terrible timing might have conspired to catapult me from an academic career without effect upon Schwan Stabilo & *Odyssey* 10: Schoenberg, distracted by financial difficulties, might have written a stupid book. He might have written a clever book; I might have gone to buy a dress on the day of the party.

On the day of the party I walked down to Covent Garden at lunchtime to buy a dress, and on my way to Boules I thought I would just stop off for a moment at Books etc. I happened to go into the music section, and I happened to pick up Schoenberg's *Theory of Harmony*.

My father used to say, when things went wrong, that man is the cat's paw of fate. I think this is the kind of thing he had in mind.

No sooner had I taken the book from the shelf than I had to buy it; no sooner bought than began to read.

Schoenberg was putting forward arguments for the development of music using a much more liberal notion of consonance, and then possibly eventually of a music using a much wider range of notes (so

that you could have, say, an extra four notes between C and C sharp).
He said:

> It is clear that, just as the overtones led to the 12-part division of
> the simplest consonance, the octave, so they will eventually bring
> about the further differentiation of this interval. To future genera-
> tions music like ours will seem incomplete, since it has not yet
> fully exploited everything latent in sound, just as a sort of music
> that did not yet differentiate within the octave would seem in-
> complete to us. Or, to cite an analogy—which one has only to
> think through completely to see how very relevant it is: The sound
> of our music will at that time seem to have no depth, no perspec-
> tive, just as Japanese painting, for example, affects us as primitive
> compared with our own, because without perspective it lacks
> depth. That [change] will come, if not in the manner that some
> believe, and if not as soon. It will not come through reasoning (aus
> Gründen) but from elemental sources (Ursachen); it will not
> come from without, but from within. It will not come through
> imitation of some prototype, and not as technical accomplish-
> ment; for it is far more a matter of mind and spirit (Geist) than of
> material, and the Geist must be ready.

I thought this was one of the most brilliant things I had ever heard
in my life. The comment on Japanese art was obviously wrong—I no
sooner read it than I saw in my mind an image of Lord Leighton's
Greek Girls Playing at Ball, with its irreproachable, its even masterly
use of perspective in the handling of the girls, the antique landscape,
the airborne drapery, no sooner did I see this than I started to laugh,
so shallow and superficial and even artless did it seem in comparison
with (say) a print by Utamaro. But the basic argument was absolutely
brilliant.

Before reading this brilliant book I had thought that books should
be more like the film The Godfather, in which at one stage Al Pacino

goes to Sicily and the Italian is all in Italian. Now I thought that this was a rather simpleminded way of looking at the question.

If you say that in a book the Italians should speak Italian because in the actual world they speak Italian and the Chinese should speak Chinese because Chinese speak Chinese it is a rather naive way of thinking of a work of art, it's as if you thought this was the way to make a painting: The sky is blue. I will paint the sky blue. The sun is yellow. I will paint the sun yellow. A tree is green. I will paint the tree green. And what colour is the trunk? Brown. So what colour do you use? Ridiculous. Even leaving abstract painting out of the question it is closer to the truth that a painter would think of the surface that he wanted in a painting and the kind of light and the lines and the relations of colours and be attracted to painting objects that could be represented in a painting with those properties. In the same way a composer does not for the most part think that he would like to imitate this or that sound—he thinks that he wants the texture of a piano with a violin, or a piano with a cello, or four stringed instruments or six, or a symphony orchestra; he thinks of relations of notes.

This was all commonplace and banal to a painter or musician, and yet the languages of the world seemed like little heaps of blue and red and yellow powder which had never been used—but if a book just used them so that the English spoke English & the Italians Italian that would be as stupid as saying use yellow for the sun because the sun is yellow. It seemed to me reading Schoenberg that what the writers of the future would do was not necessarily say: I am writing about an Armenian grandfather Czech grandmother a young biker from Kansas (of Czech & Armenian descent), Armenian Czech English OK. Gradually they would approach the level of the other branches of the arts which are so much further developed. Perhaps a writer would think of the monosyllables and lack of grammatical inflection in Chinese, and of how this would sound next to lovely long Finnish words all double letters & long vowels in 14 cases or lovely

Hungarian all prefixes suffixes, & having first thought of that would then think of some story about Hungarians or Finns with Chinese.

An idea has only to be something you have not thought of before to take over the mind, and all afternoon I kept hearing in my mind snatches of books which might exist in three or four hundred years. There was one with the characters Hakkinen, Hintikka and Yu, set provisionally in Helsinki—against a background of snow with a mass of black firs, a black sky & brilliant stars a narrative or perhaps dialogue with nominative genitive partitive essive inessive adessive illative ablative allative & translative, people would come on saying Hyvää päivää for good day there might be a traffic accident so that the word tieliikenneonnettomuus could make an appearance, and then in the mind of Yu Chinese characters, as it might be Black Fir White Snow, this was absolutely ravishing.

I had not really wanted to go to the party, and now in this distracted state I wanted to go less than ever—but I thought it would be rude not to go when the invitation was such a favour, so I thought I could just go for 10 minutes and then leave.

I went to the party. As so often it was much easier to come with the plan of leaving after 10 minutes than to leave after 10 minutes, for instead of making a polite excuse to leave after 10 minutes I found myself describing now to this person now that the brilliant *Theory of Harmony*. Who publish it, they would say, Faber, I would say and they would say Oh. Some people did not seem interested and I naturally dropped the subject but others did and I did not and I ended up staying three hours.

Schoenberg would say: This scale is not the last word, the ultimate goal of music, but rather a provisional stopping place. The overtone series, which led the ear to it, still contains many problems that will have to be faced. And if for the time being we still manage to escape those problems, it is due to little else than a compromise between the natural intervals and our inability to use them—that compromise which we call the tempered system, which amounts to an indefinitely extended truce

& in my mind I would hear languages related like a circle of fifths, I would see languages with shades of each other, like the colours of Cézanne which often have a green with some red a red with some green, in my mind I saw a glowing still life as if a picture of English with French words French with English words German with French words & English words Japanese with French English & German words—I was just about to leave when I met a man who seemed to know quite a lot about Schoenberg. He had lost his last job through a merger and now the writing was on the wall so he was rather distracted but still he started telling me about the opera Moses and Aaron.

He said Of course you know what it's about

& I said Well presumably

& he said No musically, musically it's about, & he paused, & he said in this opera Moses spoke directly to God and he did not sing his part was in Sprechgesang it was speech, harsh speech over music and the Children of Israel could not understand; he had to communicate through Aaron, who was an operatic tenor, it was a beautiful lyric role but of course it's Aaron who proposes the Golden Calf, he doesn't himself understand—

I said what a marvellous idea for an opera the plots were usually so farfetched and contrived

& he said he rather liked that but yes it was a marvellous idea, and he began to tell me in a low-key English way a terrible story about the opera which he described as one of the great lost works of the 20th century. Schoenberg had composed most of the first two acts between 1930 and 1932; then the Nazis had come into power and he had had to leave in 1933 and it had been rather disruptive. He went to America and kept applying for grants to work on it but the foundations did not care for the atonal music. So he had to support his family by teaching, and he went back to composing tonal pieces in support of his grant applications so that his time when he was not teaching was taken up with the tonal compositions. Eighteen years later he had still not composed the music for Act Three of Moses and Aaron. As death drew near he said that perhaps the words could be spoken.

He said: Of course he could be quite a difficult character

& he suddenly said—Will you excuse me? I really must catch Peter before he goes.

He walked off and it was only after he had gone that I realised I had not asked the crucial question, which is Do we ever hear God?

I hesitated and then hesitantly followed but he was already saying Peter!

& Peter said Giles! Good to see you! How are you keeping?

& Giles said Exciting times.

So it was not a good time to intrude. I mingled casually with a nearby group.

Peter said something and Giles said something and Peter said something and Giles said Good Lord No not at all in fact if anything and they talked for quite a long time. They talked for half an hour or so and suddenly they paused, and Peter said Well this is hardly and Giles said Quite, and they paused again and without another word left the room.

I had meant to leave after 10 minutes; it was high time to leave. But now there was more noise by the door and Liberace appeared smiling and kissing women on the cheek and apologising to people for being so late. Several people in my group seemed to know him and tried to catch his eye, and I hastily murmured something about a drink and slipped away. I was nervous of heading for the door, because I was afraid someone might introduce me to Liberace as a special favour, but it seemed safe enough to stand by the buffet. Phrases

from Schoenberg kept coming back. At this time I had never heard
any of his music but the book on harmony seemed a real work of genius.

I stood by the buffet eating cheese sticks, looking up from time to
time at the door—but though Liberace moved gradually into the
room he was still between me and the door. So I stood thinking
about this brilliant book, I thought, I must buy a piano, & after a
while who should come up but Liberace.

He said Are you as bored and frustrated as you look?

It was not easy to think of a reply which would not be rude or
flirtatious or both.

I said I never answer trick questions.

He said It's not a trick question. You look completely fed up.

I realised that, faced with coming up with a reply, I had thought
of the question and not the questioner. Some people would see that
until you have determined how bored and frustrated you look you
have no way of knowing whether your sentiments match your appearance—but Liberace had proved himself so innocent of logic in
all his written work—was it likely that he would marshal greater
powers of reasoning in casual conversation at a party? No.

I said I was thinking about leaving.

Liberace said So you *were* fed up. I don't blame you. These things
are horrible aren't they?

I said I had never been to one before.

He said I thought I hadn't seen you before. Are you with Pearce?

I said Yes I am.

I had a brilliant idea. I said I work for Emma Russell. Everyone
in the office was so excited when they heard you'd be here. You must
let me introduce you.

He said Would you mind if I didn't?

And he smiled and said I was just about to leave when I saw you.
You know misery loves company.

I knew nothing of the kind but I said So they say.

And I said If we leave we won't have any misery to share.

He said Where do you live? Maybe I can give you a lift.

I told him where I lived and he said it was not far out of his way.

I realised too late that I should have said I did not need a lift. I said it now and he said No I insist.

I said That's OK and he said Don't believe everything you hear.

We walked along Park Lane and then along various streets of Mayfair, while Liberace said this and that, in a way that seemed intentionally flirtatious and unintentionally rude.

I realised suddenly that if the Chinese characters were the same as the Japanese I knew the characters for White Rain Black Tree: 白雨黒木! I put these provisionally into the mind of Yu and laughed out loud and Liberace said What's funny. I said Nothing and he said No tell me.

At last in despair I said You know the Rosetta Stone.

What? said Liberace.

I said The Rosetta Stone. I think we need more.

He said One's not enough?

I said What I mean is, though I believe the Stone was originally a rather pompous thing to erect, it was a gift to posterity. Being written in hieroglyphics, demotic and Greek, it only required that one language survive for all to be accessible. Probably one day English will be a much-studied dead language; we should use this fact to preserve other languages to posterity. You could have Homer with translation and marginal notes on vocabulary and grammar, so that if that single book happened to be dug up in 2,000 years or so the people of the day would be able to read Homer, or better yet, we could disseminate the text as widely as possible to give it the best possible chance of survival.

What we should do, I said, is have legislation so that every book published was obliged to have, say, a page of Sophocles or Homer in the original with appropriate marginalia bound into the binding, so that even if you bought an airport novel if your plane crashed you would have something to reread on the desert island. The great thing is that people who were put off Greek at school would then have another chance, I think they're put off by the alphabet but if you've learned one at the age of six how hard can it be? It's not a particularly difficult language.

Liberace said When you get the bit between your teeth you really get carried away don't you? One minute you're so quiet I can hardly get a word out of you, then all of a sudden there's no stopping you. It's rather engaging.

I did not know what to say and he said after a pause What's funny about that?

Nothing, I said and he said Oh, I see.

I asked after a pause where his car was. He said that it should be here. He said that it must have been towed, and he swore The bastards! The bastards! and then he said abruptly that it would just have to be the Tube.

I walked with him to the Tube, and when we got to his stop he said I must come back to his place to take his mind off his car. He said I could not imagine the horror of going to a party such as the one we had left and then discovering that it had cost you fifty pounds or so plus the sheer horror of going to West Croydon or wherever it was they kept the cars to get it back. I said something sympathetic. I had left the train to continue the conversation and now I found myself leaving the Tube station and walking through the streets with Liberace to his place.

We walked up the steps and upstairs inside and Liberace started up a little conversational medley on the subject of cars and towing and wheel clamps. He improvised on the subject of the depot for the towed-away cars. He improvised on the officials who obstructed attempts to reclaim a car.

His way of talking was a little like his writing: it was quick and nervous and anxious to seem anxious to please, and every so often he would say Oh God I'm talking too much I'm boring you you'll walk out on me and leave me alone to brood on my you know I don't personally consider my car I mean if you could see it you'd see I couldn't possibly consider it a phallic but the meaning's out there isn't it there's something potentially horribly symbolic isn't there about having it towed away just when you've offered a lift to I mean you may think that's too obvious I couldn't agree more but fuck, and he would say Tell me if I'm boring you. No one had ever asked me if he was boring me who wasn't, and I never knew what to say, or rather it always seemed as though the only possible answer was No and so I now said No not at all. I thought it would be better to change the subject so I asked for a drink.

He brought drinks from the kitchen and talked about this and that, showing me souvenirs from his travels and making comments by turns cynical and sentimental. He had a new computer, an Amstrad 1512 with two 5.25 inch floppy disk drives and 512 kilobytes of RAM. He said he had installed Norton Utilities to organise his files, and he turned it on to show how Norton Utilities worked.

I asked if it could do Greek. He said he didn't think so, so I didn't ask whether it could do anything else.

We sat down and to my horror I saw on a nearby small table a brand new book by Lord Leighton.

By Lord Leighton, of course, I don't mean the Hellenising late-Victorian painter of A Syracusan Bride Leading Wild Beasts in Procession and Greek Girls Playing at Ball, but the painterly American writer who is the spiritual heir of the artist. Lord Leighton (the painter) specialised in scenes of antiquity in which marvellous perplexities of drapery roamed the canvas, tarrying only in their travels to protect the modesty of a recruit from the Tyrone Power school of acting. His fault was not a lack of skill: it is the faultlessness of his skill which makes the paintings embarrassing to watch, so bare do they strip the mind of their creator. Only the pen of Lord Leighton the writer could do justice to the brush of Lord Leighton the painter, for just so did Lord Leighton (the writer) bring the most agitated emotions to an airless to a hushed to an unhurried while each word took on because there was all the time in the world for each word to take on the bloom which only a great Master can give to a word using his time to allow all unseemly energy to become aware of its nakedness and snatch gratefully at the fig leaf provided until all passion in the airlessness in the hush in the absence of hurry sank decently down in the slow death of motion to perpetual stasis: a character could not look, or step, or speak, without a gorgeous train of sentences swathing his poor stupid thoughts and unfolding in beautiful languor on the still and breathless air.

Liberace saw my glance and said Are you a fan and I said No and he said But he's marvellous.

He picked up the book and began to read one lovely sentence after another—

& I said in despair How beautiful, as one might say Look at that feather! Look at the velvet! Look at the fur!

I have naturally often thought that it would be nice to get some money from Liberace for Ludo, and I have sometimes thought that even apart from the money I should tell him. Whenever I think this I think of this conversation and I just can't.

I would say But he is like a man who plays Yesterday on the piano with Brahmsian amplitude & lushness and so casually kicks aside the very thing which is the essence of the song he is like the Percy Faith Orchestra playing Satisfaction

and he would say Listen to this

and he would read out a sentence which was like Yesterday with Brahmsian harmony or the Percy Faith Orchestra playing Satisfaction by special request and I would say He is like a man who plays the first movement of the Moonlight Sonata so slowly he makes mistakes, these logical fallacies are more glaring because he has so much the air of taking his time

and Liberace would say But listen to this

and he would read out a lovely sentence full of logical mistakes

and I would say Or rather he is like a man who plays the third movement of the Moonlight Sonata with dazzling virtuosity & complete ignorance of the music, Schnabel's teacher once told him that he was a musician but he would never be a pianist & this writer is exactly the opposite

and Liberace would say Yes, but listen to this

and he would read out a sentence which was the work of a stupid virtuoso

and he never did seem to see what I meant. Lord Leighton was like this and like that and the other & he was like a man who piles mattresses on a pebble & I was like the princess & the pea, I was not going to say something about English & the American novel to be told I was engaging so I drank my drink and when Liberace had finished reading he talked for a while about Lord Leighton.

Now I am sure or rather I have no reason to doubt that if I had told Liberace about Ludo he would have done some decent thing. And yet— The fact is that 99 out of 100 adults spare themselves the trouble of rational thought 99% of the time (studies have not shown this, I have just invented the statistics so I should not say The fact is, but I would be surprised if the true figures were very different). In a less barbarous society children would not be in absolute economic subjection to the irrational beings into whose keeping fate has consigned them: they would be paid a decent hourly wage for attending school. As we don't live in that enlightened society any adult, and especially a parent, has a terrible power over a child— how could I give that power to a man who—sometimes I thought I could and once I even picked up the phone but when I thought about it I just couldn't. I would hear again his breathtaken boyish admiration for lovely stupidity his unswerving fidelity to the precept that ought implies cant and I just couldn't.

Liberace talked on and on and on. Gradually as we drank more drinks Liberace talked more and more and more and asked more and more if he was boring me, and as a result it seemed less and less possible to leave, because if he wasn't boring me why would I want to leave?

Then I thought, there must be some other way not to listen to all this, and of course there was a way. Surely Liberace had brought me back here to pick me up. It would be rude to put a hand over his mouth, but if I were to put my mouth on his mouth this would stop him talking just as well without being rude. His eyes were large, a clear glass green, rimmed with black like the eyes of a nocturnal animal; it seemed as though, if I only kissed him, not only would I not have to listen to him, but I would somehow be closer to the animal with these beautiful eyes.

He said something, and paused, and before he could say anything else I kissed him and there was a sudden, wonderful silence. It was silent except for the silly little laugh of Liberace, but once he had laughed it was over whereas there was no end to his conversation.

I was still drunk, and I was still trying to think of things I could do without being unpardonably rude. Well, I thought, I could sleep with him without being rude, and so I responded in a suitable manner as he unbuttoned the buttons of my dress.

This was a terrible mistake.

❖

The wind is howling. A cold rain is falling. The brown paper window pane is flapping in the fierce rain and wind.

We are sitting in bed watching a masterpiece of modern cinema. I sat at the computer for three hours this morning, & allowing for interruptions typed maybe an hour and a half. At last I said I was going upstairs to watch Seven Samurai & L said he would too. L has read *Odyssey* 1–10; he has read the story of the Cyclops six times. He has also read a voyage of Sindbad the Sailor, three chapters of *Algebra Made Easy*, and a few pages each of *Metamorphoses*, *Kalilah wa Dimnah* and I Samuel following some scheme which I don't understand, and every single one involves a constant stream of questions.

I know or at least tell myself that it is better than Japanese (since at least I know the answers to maybe 80% of the questions), & I know I told him to do it. It took him a year to read the *Iliad* so I do not know how I could have known he would read 10 books of the *Odyssey* in three weeks.

It occurs to me that the Book of Jonah is just four pages long. Questions on Hebrew have got to be better than questions on Japanese. Wonder if it's too late to say I really meant Jeremiah.

I should be typing *Advanced Angling* as they want it back by the end of the week, but it seems important to preserve my sanity. It would be a false economy to forge ahead with typing until maddened to frenzy by an innocent child.

Also in the interests of sanity I have written nothing more for posterity in several days. I have been finding this rather depressing to write—writing of Mozart I thought suddenly of my mother blundering through the accompaniment to Schubert lieder with my Uncle Buddy, *Jesus*, Buddy, said my mother, what's the *matter*, you sing

like a Goddamned accountant, and slamming down the lid stormed
out of my father's latest half-finished motel & off down the highway
while my Uncle Buddy softly whistled a little tune & said nothing
much. What's the use of remembering that?

I then thought of a priceless line I'd read somewhere or other: It
is my duty as a mother to be cheerful. It is my duty as a mother to
be cheerful, & so it is clearly my duty to watch a work of genius &
abandon *Advanced Angling* & composition.

Kambei is samurai 1. He starts to recruit the rest.

*He picks out a samurai in the street. He tells the farmer Rikichi to bring
him to a fight. He tells Katsushiro to stand inside the door with a stick and
bring it down. He sits inside waiting.*

*The samurai comes through the door, seizes the stick and throws Kat-
sushiro to the floor. Kambei tells him the deal; he isn't interested.*

Kambei picks another samurai.

Katsushiro stands inside with the stick. Kambei sits waiting.

*2 comes to the door. He sees through the trick; he stands laughing in the
street.*

*Gorobei knows the farmers have a hard time, but that's not why he accepts.
He accepts because of Kambei.*

I say to L: Kurosawa won a prize for a film he made before this
one, called Rashomon, about a woman raped by a bandit; in that one
he tells the story 4 times, & it's different each time someone tells it,
but in this one he did something more complicated, he only tells the
story once but you see it from about 8 points of view, you have to
pay attention the whole time to see whether something seems to be
true or is just what somebody says is true.

He says: Uh-huh. He is murmuring snatches of Japanese under his
breath, & also reading the subtitles out loud.

3 doesn't have to pass the test. Shichiroji is an old friend of Kambei's. He'd given him up for dead.

Gorobei finds 4 chopping wood to pay for a meal. Heihachi is a second-rate swordsman but he'll keep them in good spirits.

Kambei and Katsushiro come across two samurai stripping bamboo poles for a match.

The fight begins. A raises his pole and pauses. B holds his pole over his head and shouts.

A draws back his pole in a beautiful sweeping movement, and pauses. B runs forward.

A raises his pole suddenly and brings it down.

B says it was a draw.

A says he won. He'd have killed him with a real sword. He walks away.

B wants to fight with swords.

A says he'd kill him, it's stupid.

B draws his sword and insists.

A draws his sword.

He raises it and pauses.

B holds his sword above his head and shouts.

A draws back his sword in a beautiful sweeping movement. B runs forward.

A raises his sword suddenly and brings it down. B falls down dead.

I would like to watch the rest of the film, but there is *Advanced Angling* to consider. I tell L that I have to go downstairs & put the heater on to type, & that he will have to stay in bed and watch the video. Of course he instantly begs to come too. I say You don't understand, we need £150 for the rent and £60 for the council tax, that alone is £210 and as you know I make £5.50 an hour before tax, 210 divided by 5.50 is approximately 40—

38.1818
38.1818, fine,
18181818181818
the point being
18181818181818181818181818181818
that if I work 10 hours a day for the next 4 days I can get the disks
in Monday, we'll get the cheque on Friday, and we can pay two bills,
and if we stretch out the £22.62 we now have in the house we can
also buy food.

The master swordsman isn't interested in killing people. He only wants to perfect his art.

I can't work with you downstairs. I know you don't mean to dis-
tract me but you do.
I just want to work.
Yes but you always ask questions.
I promise I won't ask questions.
That's what you always say. You stay here and watch Seven Samu-
rai and I'll go downstairs and do some work
NOOOOOOOOOOOOOOOOOOOOOOOO

*Kambei doesn't want to take Katsushiro. They can't take a child. Rikichi
wants to take him. Gorobei says it's child's play. Heihachi says if they treat
him as an adult he'll grow into an adult.*

I'm sorry but it has got to be done. You don't have to watch Seven
Samurai, if you would rather just sit in bed you can. Do you want me
to turn it off?
NOOOOOOOOOOOOOOOOOOOOOOOO

Kambei gives in. 5 has never fought before.

All right then, I'll see you in a little while.
PLEASE let me come
I'm sorry
NOOOOOOOOOOOOOOOOOOOOOOOO
NOOOOOOOOOOOOOOOOOOOOOOOO

6 is standing at the door. The master swordsman has decided to come. You never know why Kyuzo changed his mind.

PLEASE let me come PLEASE PLEASE PLEASE I PROMISE I won't ask any questions I PROMISE
No.

I went downstairs and turned on the computer and I typed in a piece about angling in weed and another on bait. For the whole hour I could hear him howling upstairs, to a background of the samurai theme. At last I couldn't stand it.

I went upstairs and I said All right, you can come downstairs.

He kept crying into the pillow.

I picked up the remote control and turned off the video. I picked him up and kissed him and I said Please don't cry, and I took him downstairs to the warmer room with the gas fire. I said Would you like a hot drink, what about a cup of tea? Or hot chocolate, would you like some hot chocolate?

He said Hot chocolate.

I made him a cup of hot chocolate and I said What are you going to work on?

He said very softly Samuel.

I said Good. He got out the dictionary and the Tanach and *Gesenius' Hebrew Grammar* and he sat down near the fire to read.

I went back to the computer to type, and behind me I could hear the rustle of pages as he looked up word after word after word without asking questions.

An hour went by. I got up to have a cup of tea, and he said Is it all right if I ask a question now?

I said Sure.

He asked a question and he asked another question and he asked another question, and in connection with one of the questions I opened Gesenius to look at tithpa'el verbs, having looked at this and answered the question I began to leaf through the book. I would have liked to cry into a pillow myself, and with a sore heart I began to read these words of comfort:

§49. *The Perfect and Imperfect with Waw Consecutive.*

1. The use of the two tense-forms, as is shown more fully in the Syntax (§§106, 107, cf. above, §47, note on a), is by no means restricted to the expression of the past or future. One of the most striking peculiarities in the Hebrew *consecution* of tenses[1] is the phenomenon that, in representing a series of past events, only the first verb stands in the perfect, and the narration is continued in the imperfect. Conversely, the representation of a series of future events begins with the imperfect, and is continued in the perfect.

The author of the grammar discussed this marvellous grammatical feature with a kind of stiff scholarly charm, so that he would (for example) explain in a little footnote that 'the other Semitic languages do not exhibit this peculiarity, excepting the Phoenician, the most closely related to Hebrew, and of course the Moabitish dialect of the *Mêša'* inscription'—just the three words 'excepting the Phoenician' were better than hours of the kind of help you can get on a helpline.

This progress in the sequence of time, is regularly indicated by a pregnant *and* (called *wāw consecutive*[1]), which in itself is really only a variety of the ordinary *wāw copulative*, but which sometimes (in the imperf.) appears with a different vocalization.

I was beginning to feel almost not too bad.

[1] This name best expresses the prevailing syntactical relation, for by *wāw consecutive* an action is always represented as the direct, or at least temporal *consequence* of a preceding action. Moreover, it is clear from the above examples, that the *wāw consecutive* can only be thus used in immediate conjunction with the verb. As soon as *wāw*, owing to an insertion (e.g. a negative), is separated from the verb, the imperfect follows instead of the perfect *consecutive*, the perfect instead of the imperfect *consecutive*. The fact that whole Books (Lev., Num., Josh., Jud., Sam., 2 Kings, Ezek., Ruth, Esth., Neh., 2 Chron.) begin with the imperfect *consecutive*, and others (Exod., 1 Kings, Ezra) with *wāw copulative*, is taken as a sign of their close connexion with the historical Books now or originally preceding them. Cf., on the other hand, the independent beginning of Job and Daniel. It is a merely superficial description to call the wāw consecutive by the old-fashioned name *wāw conversive*, on the ground that it always converts the meaning of the respective tenses into its opposite, i.e. according to the old view, the future into the preterite, and vice versa.

I finished the section & then I turned to the cross-references in Syntax & then I read this and that & when I looked up two hours had gone by. L was sitting by the fire reading about David and Jonathan and singing a little song.

I gave him lunch and then another half hour had gone by. I returned to the computer & typed for three hours with only occasional questions from L. I took a short break and typed for half an hour; I took a break for dinner and typed for two hours; I put L to bed at 9:00 and went back downstairs at 9:30 and typed for three hours and then I went back upstairs.

It seemed to be rather cold.

I did not see how I could leave him upstairs in the morning and I also did not see how I could bring him downstairs.

The Alien whispered It's only fair to give the other side a chance. The Alien whispered He's not a bad man.

I did not really want to go to bed knowing I was just going to wake up the next day. I put on three sweaters and rewound the video. PLAY.

A striking peculiarity of the film is that though it is called Seven Samurai it is not really about seven samurai. Bandits are about to attack the village and only one farmer wants to fight; without him there would be no story. Rikichi glared from the screen with burning eyes; his pale face glowed in the cold dark room.

Interlude

My mother's father was a jeweler. He was a handsome, shrewd-looking man; he was an accomplished amateur musician. He spoke excellent English, but he could hear his own accent and he knew there was something comical about it.

Buddy said he did not want to be an accountant and his father told him he had no idea the amount of work it took to be a professional musician. Five years you studied the violin his father said and did you practice five minutes? Five years piano.

Something looked through my grandfather's eyes and it said Werner and du and mein Kind in tones of tenderness and authority. Buddy could more or less understand what was being said but he could not argue back, he tried to think of something from Schubert lieder or Wagner but it all seemed too melodramatic. Something looked through my grandfather's eyes. It said Being an accountant, it's not the end of the world.

Something looked at my Uncle Danny. Something looked at my aunts and it said A secretary, is that so terrible?

Linda had seen four before her do something that was not so terrible and already there was something about them, their whole lives ahead of them and the best thing cut off, as if something that might have been a Heifetz had been walled up inside an accountant and left to die.

Doom. Doom. Doom.

My father got straight to the point. He argued passionately that

Linda would never forgive herself if she did not give herself this chance.

Our lives are ruined, said my father, are you going to let the same thing happen to you? He argued passionately and used words like "hell" and "damn", strong words for the time, and there was something masculine and forceful about it.

What do you think? said Linda, and she looked at Buddy.

Buddy said: I think you should go.

—because of course if she went anywhere she would go to the Juilliard.

My father said: Of course she should go. She can be in New York by noon. Linda said she could pretend to be going downtown to look for a sweater, because she had just been saying she needed a new sweater.

My father said he would drive her to the station.

Buddy said he would come too in case anybody asked any questions.

Linda said: If anybody asks you just say I went to look for a sweater.

Buddy said: That's right, if anybody asks me I simply explain that you were threatening to kill yourself when you suddenly remembered you needed a sweater. I think I'll come along for the ride.

Linda said actually maybe he should come with her to New York, she needed him to carry the cello.

Buddy said: Why would you want to take the cello?

Linda said: For my audition.

Buddy said: If they don't take you on piano they sure as heck aren't going to take you on the cello.

Linda said: Don't you tell me what to do

& they got into a heated argument while my father stood idly by. My mother was convinced that the Juilliard would despise her if all she could play was the piano, whereas if she brought a selection of instruments they would see she was a real musician.

The Konigsbergs all despised the piano, there it was all the notes conveniently divided up into a keyboard you went away and when you came back there it was the notes all still attached to the keys just where you left them, how boring, a child of four could play it (they all had). They also hated sight reading, & it is a tiresome feature of piano music that (since 10 or more notes may be played simultaneously) it involves anything up to 10 times the amount of sight reading of any other instrument. It was an instrument no Konigsberg would play if someone smaller could be made to play it instead, & since my mother was the youngest she never got the chance to hand it over to someone else. It may seem odd that the youngest got the part with the most sight reading, but as four brothers & sisters a father and a mother pointed out if she got in trouble she could always play it by ear. It wasn't, anyway, that she *couldn't* play the violin, viola and cello (not to mention flute, guitar, mandolin and ukulele)—it was just that she never got the chance.

Buddy argued that he didn't think her technique on any of the stringed instruments was up to the Juilliard, & Linda said how would you know when was the last time you *heard* me.

At first she wanted to take everything to show what she could do, but at last she agreed to take just a violin because she could play some hard pieces, a viola because she got a better tone on it for some reason, a mandolin because it was quite an unusual instrument to be able to play and a flute because it never hurts to let people know you can play the flute.

Buddy: And you will tell them you want to audition on the piano.

Linda: Don't you tell me what to do.

My father: Do you mean to say you're not planning to play the piano? You've got this fantastic talent and you're not going to play it? What about that piece you were just playing, you're not going to play it for them?

Linda: Do you know anything about music?

My father: Not really.

Linda: Then mind your own business.

My father said: Well we'd better go if you're going to catch that train.

Buddy said again that he would come along for the ride & Linda said he could explain she had gone to look for a sweater why did he always make such a production out of everything & Buddy said yes she had gone to look for a sweater & had taken along a violin a viola a flute & a mandolin just in case he thought he would come along for the ride.

My father said as a matter of fact he needed to talk to him, so they all three drove down to the station.

Linda got on the train. She had the violin case & the viola case in one hand, the mandolin case and her purse in the other, and the flute under one arm.

The train pulled out & my father commented to Buddy: You guys are amazing. I always thought a musician would take some music or something along to an audition.

Buddy said: Oh. My. God.

It was too late to do anything about it, though, and anyway she could always buy some music in New York, so they went to a nearby bar, and my father said: Let's buy that motel.

Buddy said: What if that guy was wrong?

My father said: If he was wrong we'll have a worthless piece of real estate. On the other hand, old Mrs. Randolph will be reunited with her widowed daughter and spend her declining years under the sunny skies of Florida, so at least someone will be happy.

To the sunny skies of Florida, said Buddy.

To the sunny skies of Florida, said my father.

My father and Buddy decided to drive down immediately to clinch the deal. They left in my father's car, Buddy driving, my father asleep on the back seat.

My mother meanwhile reached the Juilliard. She found her way to the general office and demanded an audition. This was not a simple matter to arrange, and she was told many times that it was necessary to apply and fill in forms and be given an appointment; but she insisted. She said that she had come all the way from Philadelphia. She was very nervous, but she had an inner confidence that if she could only start to play for someone she would be safe at last.

At last a homely man wearing a bow tie came out of an office and introduced himself and said he would find a room. The Juilliard had its forms and applications and procedures, but people there were no different from people anywhere: they loved a story, they loved the idea of a brilliant young musician getting on the train in Philadelphia and going to New York and walking in off the street. So my mother (carrying violin viola mandolin handbag & flute) followed him to a room with a grand piano, and the homely man sat in a chair down the room, one leg crossed over the other, and waited.

It was only now that she realized that she had overlooked something.

Under my father's urging she had walked straight out the door. In her excitement at the idea of just walking out the door she had walked out the door without stopping to practice and without even her sheet music, and now she had nothing to play from and nothing prepared.

Some people might have been daunted by this setback. The Konigsbergs faced musical catastrophe on a daily basis, & their motto was: Never say die.

What are you going to play for me? asked the homely man.

Linda took the violin out of its case. She explained that she had left her music on the train, but that she was going to play a Bach partita.

She played a Bach partita, and the homely man looked without comment at his knee, and then she got through a Beethoven sonata with only a couple of hairy moments, and the man looked calmly at his knee.

And now what are you going to play? said the homely man without comment.

Linda asked: Would you like to hear me play the viola?

Man: If you would like to play it for me I will be happy to hear you play it.

Linda put the violin back in the case, and she took out the viola. She played an obscure sonata for viola solo which she had learned a couple of years ago. Even at the time it had seemed completely unmemorable, the type of composition which composers do for some reason foist off on the viola. For a moment she wondered whether she would be able to remember it, but it came back once she got going. She couldn't remember how to go on after the first repeat & so had to do it twice to stall for time, & she had to make up a new andante having temporarily forgotten the old one (but luckily the piece was so obscure he probably wouldn't notice), but apart from that she thought she scraped through pretty well.

The homely man continued to look at his knee.

She said: That's just to give you the general idea. Would you like me to play another piece?

He said: I think I've got the general idea.

She said: Would you like me to play the mandolin?

He said: If you would like to play it.

She played a few short pieces by Beethoven and Hummel just to give him the general idea, and then she played a few pieces on the flute so he would see she could play the flute.

He listened without comment, and then he looked at his watch and said: Is there anything else you'd like to play for me?

She said: I can also play the cello, the guitar and the ukulele, but I left them at home.

He said: Would you say that one of those was your best instrument?

She said: I wouldn't say best instrument. My cello teacher said I showed promise, and of course any idiot can play the guitar, and if you can play the guitar you don't have to be a genius to play the ukulele, but I don't know that I would say best instrument.

A musician can develop a kind of sixth sense for the mood of his audience. My mother sensed that the audition was not going well.

The man in the bow tie looked at his watch again, and he stood up and paced up and down and said: I'm afraid I have an appointment so—

I can play the piano, she said reluctantly, & she said vivaciously: Might as well be hung for a sheep as a lamb!

I'm a little pressed for time, said the man, but he sat down again & crossed one leg over the other & looked at his knee.

My mother went to the piano and sat down. She had not practiced, but in the last week she had played Chopin's Prelude No. 24 in D minor 217 times. She began to play Chopin's Prelude No. 24 in D minor for the 218th time that week, and for the first time the homely man looked up from his knee.

He said: I'd like to hear something else.

He said: Do you want me to find you some music? If there's something you need we can get it from the library.

She shook her head. She must play something. She began to play the Moonlight Sonata. There was something odd about this; it was odd not to be playing Chopin's Prelude No. 24 in D minor for the 219th time.

And what are you going to play for me now? asked the man.

She began to play a Brahms intermezzo. This time she did not wait for him to ask but launched into another piece and another and another, filling in more and more as she went along, her hands skittering up and down the keyboard.

In the middle of the piece the man stood up and said That's enough.

He walked quickly over the creaking boards toward her; he was saying No, no, no, no, no. She thought at first he was complaining because she was improvising where she couldn't remember the piece.

No no no no, he said stopping beside her.

You can't play the piano like that.

He said: There's no weight in your hands.

Linda took her hands off the keys. She did not understand what he meant. And he said: Can't you FEEL how tense your wrists are? You've got to play with the whole arm. Don't play from the wrist. You've got to relax or you'll never be in control.

He asked her to play a C major scale and before she had played 3 notes he said No. He told her to play with the whole weight of her arm on each note. He told her not to worry about mistakes.

Someone knocked on the door and looked in & he said Not now.

He stood by for an hour while her clever hand moved stupidly over the white keys.

At last he said that was enough. He gave her a simple exercise & he said: I want you to play this four hours a day for two months the way I showed you. After that you can go back to one of your pieces, but you must play with a relaxed wrist. If you can't play with a relaxed wrist don't play it. And you should play the exercise for two hours before you practice anything.

He said: Go back to the beginning and in a year you may have something to show me. I don't promise we'll take you, but I promise we'll hear you play.

He said: You may think that promise isn't worth a year of your life.

And he said: You may be right, but it's the best I can do.

My mother shook his hand and said thank you politely.

She said: What about the violin? Is there anything you'd like me to do on the violin?

The homely man started to laugh & said No I don't think so. He said he also had no advice to offer on the viola, the mandolin or the flute.

He said: Still, Rubinstein never played the flute and it doesn't seem to have hurt him.

He said: I don't know who's been teaching you, but— Where is it you're from, Philadelphia? Give this man a call, you can mention my name. Don't call him if you're not going to work, he'll never speak to me again, but if you're serious— Actually don't call him for a couple of months, try it and see if you really want to put in the time, and if you're serious give him a call.

He wrote a name & a phone number on a piece of paper and gave it to her and she put it in her bag. She asked if it was all right to play the exercise in B major instead, and he laughed and said she could play it 50% of the time in B major as long as she played it with a relaxed wrist. So she thanked him again, and she picked up the violin viola mandolin handbag and flute and left the room.

Another minute and she was outside in the street, staring up at the buildings. It was early afternoon.

If she had been accepted by the Juilliard she would have gone to the top of the Empire State Building and looked down on the city she had conquered; New York would have lain at her feet.

She did not want to go to the Empire State Building, so she walked to the Plaza Hotel to see the fountain where Fitzgerald and Zelda had danced in the nude. She said later that she stood by the fountain crying and shaking & yet thinking that it was the happiest day of her life, because if you were the youngest of five no one ever took you seriously, & now someone had taken her so seriously as a musician that he had told her to spend four hours a day on a single exercise. If the Juilliard said something like that even her father would have to take her seriously, & by some miracle she out of the whole family would be a real musician.

It was true that she actually wanted to be a singer but at least it was a start.

It began to drizzle, so she went to Saks Fifth Avenue to look at sweaters, and then she went back to the station and caught a train back to Philadelphia.

She got home and explained and nobody seemed to understand that somebody had taken her seriously.

What does he know? said my grandfather. Who ever heard of him? If he's such a genius how come we never heard of him, eh?

I have to practice, said my mother, and she went to the piano. The memory of her heavy arm, with the weighted hand stumbling over the keys, was still new. She put her hands on the keys and for an hour a terrible, jerking noise came from the front room. All of the children had played the piano attractively from the age of three; no Konigsberg had ever played a scale in living memory; my grandparents had never heard anything so horrible in all their lives.

My grandparents had previously thought that nothing could be worse than to hear Chopin's Prelude No. 24 in D minor 30 times a day. They now thought they should have known when they were lucky. My grandmother went so far as to say Why don't you play that lovely piece you were playing the other day, Linda?

My mother said she could not play anything but the exercise for two months.

Meanwhile everybody was wondering what had happened to Buddy, who had just driven off with his friend without a word to anybody.

My mother said maybe he went downtown to look for a sweater.

My mother practiced hours every day, hours as painful to hear as to play. At first everybody thought she would give in. Day followed day, and the terrible stumbling sounds went on for hours on end.

She did not know what else to do.

In retrospect almost every aspect of the audition was much more hideously embarrassing than it had been at the time, the viola sonata in particular with the three repeats and the new andante kept coming back to haunt her. The only good thing about it was that at least she hadn't opened her mouth to sing. But even after just three weeks of the exercise she thought that she would never again be able to walk innocently into a room to show what she could do.

Uncle Buddy and my mother had wanted to be singers because they loved opera, but they did not really know what you had to do to become one.

The way they saw it was, obviously a music school couldn't let in every Tom Dick and Harry, it would assess people on the basis of their instruments, once you got in you could start singing. But after the audition my mother thought it might work some other way. If there was this desert of technical work to be crossed before you could play the piano, maybe every other instrument and maybe the voice was also surrounded by a desert.

My mother kept playing the exercise. She did not belong to the school choir because it spent most of its time preparing for the Christian highlights of the year. Who knew what you had to do to be a singer?

My mother kept playing the exercise because the Juilliard had said the piano was her instrument.

One day my grandmother came into the room. She said You know your father only wants what's best for you. She said You're driving him crazy, what do you think it's like for a man like that to hear this day after day? She said Look. Don't decide today. You've done two hours already, enough for one day, come downtown with me and help me pick out a blouse for your sister.

They went shopping and her mother bought her a dress for $200 and another dress for $250 and a hat and another hat that looked better and a pair of shoes to go with one of the hats. They went home and her father offered her a trip to Florida which she declined. They went shopping and her mother bought her six cashmere sweaters in pastel shades.

My grandmother kept coming in whenever my mother tried to practice and my mother got angrier and angrier. What had happened was this:

My grandfather had left Vienna in 1922 and he had settled in Philadelphia and done pretty well. The quality of the music available was not really comparable to what he was used to, but otherwise it was not too bad. He married and got through the Depression all right and from a business point of view the War was a good thing because sales of wedding rings shot up. From another point of view the War changed his views.

Most of his family was still in Austria. If you are a jeweler people think you are made of money and sooner or later a letter would come, probably from someone he had never liked, he would have to come up with several thousand dollars for a surety and then he would get involved in a protracted correspondence. Say you have a man who has an advanced degree in engineering and a year of teaching at university level, say he has had to resign his position at the end of the year because students of Aryan stock should not be defiled by instruction from a person of impure blood, say he has spent some time in industry though not at the level you would expect for his qualifications, say he has an actual offer of a teaching position at an American college, you write to the State Department and the State Department explains that unfortunately a minimum of two years' teaching experience is required for the application to be approved. You get into a protracted correspondence and one day you write to the applicant to explain what is happening and get no reply.

Mr. Konigsberg did not talk about this much, and when his children said they wanted to be musicians he did not even touch on it lightly, but he said you can never tell what will happen. He said being an accountant was not the end of the world. He said being a secretary was not so terrible.

It seemed as though the things he did not say were so terrible they could not be said, and of course it's not so terrible to be a secretary or an accountant. But Linda had seen four before her do something that was not so terrible. Now it turned out that it had absolutely nothing to do with whether McCarthyism was anti-Semitism dressed up as an attack on the Communists or with their chances of resettling in Canada or Brazil should the need arise. What it really was was that their father couldn't stand to be around people who were practicing to the standard set by the finest conservatory in the country. Well, if you want to ruin people's lives, fine. You want to reenact the Goddamned Sound of Music in the home, fine. But you don't have to blame it on Hitler.

Then Buddy and the atheist came back and the atheist said they could just buy a piano for the motel and Linda could practice there. Linda said wouldn't it bother the guests and the atheist explained that the guests would arrive in the evening after a long day's driving and be on their way first thing the next morning, that was the beauty of a motel. He said grinning that what's more he would take her to Helene's and teach her to play pool so that she would always have something to fall back on.

Sometimes my mother did practice but one thing led to another and sometimes she did not. The advice of the homely man was something of a curse. She would not practice at all if she could not practice right so that gradually she played less and less and sometimes not at all.

I used to think that things might have been different. Gieseking never played a scale and Glenn Gould hardly practiced at all, they would just look at the score and think and think and think. If the homely man had said to go away and think this would have been every bit as revolutionary a concept for a Konigsberg. Perhaps he even thought that you had to think. But you can't show someone how to think in an hour; you can give someone an exercise to take away. My grandfather would not have been troubled by silent thought; he would not have kindly commanded my mother to enjoy her music & so driven her out of the house; and everything might have been different.

ii

—*A real samurai would never get so drunk. If he's as good*
as you say he'll parry the blow.

Samurai leader as an impostor
tries to join the band of six

It is not surprising that *Seven Samurai* was remade
by Hollywood because it is already close to the
Western in its use of an elite body of brave warriors.

David Thomson,
A Biographical Dictionary of Film

1

We Never Get Off at Sloane Square for Nebraska Fried Chicken

We've just pulled into the Motel Del Mar, a.k.a. Aldgate: we are taking the Circle Line in a counterclockwise direction. The pillars are covered in pale turquoise tiles, with lilac diamonds on a single band of cream—it's a colour scheme I associate with paper-wrapped soaplets & tiny towels with embroidered anchors. What kind of childhood is this for a child? He's never even been to Daytona.

I've been taking him every day to ride the Circle Line to stay out of the cold: I can type at night when he goes to bed, but we can't have the fire on 20 hours a day. He hates it because I won't let him bring Cunliffe. Too bad.

I remember once about 10 years ago, or rather 8, reading *Nicomachean Ethics* Book X in a Circle Line train that had stopped at Baker Street. That lovely soft-grained sepia light filtered down; it was about 11:00 and very quiet. I thought: Yes, to live the life of the mind is the truest form of happiness. Reading Aristotle was not even then my idea of intellectual felicity, but after all it is possible to lead the life of the mind without reading Aristotle. If I could read anything I wanted I would read *The Semantic Tradition from Kant to Carnap*.

This is absolutely not possible today, with L interrupting every minute or so to ask a word. He is in a bad mood because he hates having to ask; I think he thinks if he asks enough I will let him bring the Homeric dictionary tomorrow. James Mill wrote an entire history of India in the intervals of providing lexical assistance to little

John—but he did not have to load a twin pushchair with a small library, a small child, Repulsive, Junior Birdman & Bit—and with all
the advantages of a wife, servants & a fire in the room he was still impatient and short-tempered. Repulsive is a three-foot stuffed gorilla;
the Birdman is a two-foot fighting turtle misnamed Donatello by its
maker; & Bit is a one-inch rubber mouse designed to be lost 30 or
40 times a day.

Even when he is not interrupting people keep coming up. Sometimes they scold him playfully for colouring in a book, and sometimes they stare goggle-eyed when they realise he is reading it. They
don't seem to realise how bad this is for him. Today a man came up
and said playfully: You shouldn't colour in a book.

L: Why not?

Playful: It's not nice if somebody wants to read it.

L: But I am reading it.

Idiot, winking idiotically at me: Oh really? What's it about then?

L: I'm at the bit where they go to the land of the dead and this
is the bit where she changes them into pigs and this is the bit
where they go to the king of the winds and this is the bit where
they sharpen a stick in the fire and gouge out the eye of the
Cyclops because it only had one eye so if they gouged it out it
couldn't see.

Brain left school at six while body did time: Well that wasn't very
nice now was it?

L: If someone's about to eat you you don't have to be nice. It's
acceptable to kill in self-defence.

Slow on the uptake (goggle-eyed): Blimey.

L (for the five-hundredth time that day): What does that mean?

Slow: It means that's absolutely amazing. (To me) Aren't you
worried about what will happen when he goes to school?

I: Desperately.

Only trying to be helpful: There's no need to be sarcastic.

L: It's not a particularly difficult language. The alphabet is a precursor to the one in which English is written, and very similar to it.

Now Only is amazed and goggle-eyed not only at the Homerolexic infant; he is goggling as only a man can goggle who has applied Occam's razor to syllables all his life. He looks at me and asks if he can sit down.

The train pulls into Embankment. I shout 'No Exit!' and dart onto the platform, manhandling the pushchair.

L does the same, then dashes down the stairs marked No Exit. I follow my child, a mother following her child. We lurk behind a corner until the train pulls out, then return to the platform and buy a couple of bags of peanuts.

Of course L has not been reading the *Odyssey* the whole time. The pushchair is also loaded with *White Fang, VIKING!, Tar-Kutu: Dog of the Frozen North, Marduk: Dog of the Mongolian Steppes, Pete: Black Dog of the Dakota, THE CARNIVORES, THE PREDATORS, THE BIG CATS* and *The House at Pooh Corner.* For the past few days he has also been reading *White Fang* for the third time. Sometimes we get off the train and he runs up and down the platform. Sometimes he counts up to 100 or so in one or more languages while eyes glaze up and down the car. Still he has been reading the *Odyssey* enough for a straw poll of Circle Line opinion on the subject of small children & Greek.

Amazing: 7

Far too young: 10

Only pretending to read it: 6

Excellent idea as etymology so helpful for spelling: 19

Excellent idea as inflected languages so helpful for computer programming: 8

Excellent idea as classics indispensable for understanding of English literature: 7

Excellent idea as Greek so helpful for reading New Testament, camel through eye of needle for example mistranslation of very similar word for rope: 3

Terrible idea as study of classical languages embedded in educational system productive of divisive society: 5

Terrible idea as overemphasis on study of dead languages directly responsible for neglect of sciences and industrial decline and uncompetitiveness of Britain: 10

Stupid idea as he should be playing football: 1

Stupid idea as he should be studying Hebrew & learning about his Jewish heritage: 1

Marvellous idea as spelling and grammar not taught in schools: 24

(Respondents: 35; Abstentions: 1,000?)

Oh, & almost forgot:

Marvellous idea as Homer so marvellous in Greek: 0
Marvellous idea as Greek such a marvellous language: 0

Oh & also:

Marvellous idea but how did you teach it to a child that young: 8

I once read somewhere that Sean Connery left school at the age of 13 and later went on to read Proust and *Finnegans Wake* and I keep expecting to meet an enthusiastic school leaver on the train, the type of person who only ever reads something because it is marvellous (and so hated school). Unfortunately the enthusiastic school leavers are all minding their own business.

Faced with officious advice feel almost overwhelming temptation to say:

You know, I've been in a terrible *quandary* over this, I've been racking my brains for *weeks* trying to decide whether I was doing the right thing, finally this morning I thought—I know, I'll take the *Tube*, somebody on the Tube will be able to advise me, & sure enough you were able to tell me just what to do. Thank you *so* much, I don't know *what* I would have done if you hadn't come along—

So far have been able to resist temptation 34 times out of 35. Pas mal.

When able to resist temptation I say (which is perfectly true) that I never meant this to happen.

TEMPLE EMBANKMENT WESTMINSTER ST. JAMES'S PARK

Etymology so helpful for spelling 2
How did you teach so young a child 1

VICTORIA SLOANE SQUARE SOUTH KENSINGTON

Etymology so helpful for spelling

GLOUCESTER ROAD HIGH STREET KENSINGTON NOTTING HILL GATE

Wonderful
Wonderful
Wonderful
Etymology so helpful

PADDINGTON EDGWARE ROAD BAKER STREET and around and around and around

A man got on the train at Great Portland Street & expressed surprise & approval.

He said his youngest was about that age but of course no genius—

I said I thought small children had an aptitude for languages

He said Was it very hard to teach him

& I said No not very

& he said Well hats off to you both it's bound to be a big help to him think of all those words heavy weather for the average boy all in a day's work for this little chap. Hydrophobia! Haemophilia!

The train stopped at Euston Square but no stopping Hats Off— Microscopic! Macrobiotic! Palaeontological ornithological anthropological archaeological!

[King's Cross but no]

Hats: Photography! Telepathy! [OK] Psychopath! Polygraph! [OK OK] Democracy! Hypocrisy! Ecstasy! Epitome! [OK OK OK] Trilogy Tetralogy Pentalogy! [OH NO] Pentagon! Hexagon! [STOP] Octagon Octopus [*STOP*]

Enapus

What'll He Think Of Next [chuckling]: That's a new one on me

Dekapus

What'll [still chuckling]: This is my stop. [Gets off at Farringdon—how like a man]

Hendekapus

[NO]

Dodekapus

[NO]

Treiskaidekapus

[Oh well]

Tessareskaidekapus

[You win some you lose some]

pentekaidekapus hekkaidekapus heptakaidekapus OKTOKAIDEKAPUS enneakaidekapus eikosapus

I never meant this to happen.

I meant to follow the example of Mr. Ma (father of the famous cellist), and I still don't know where I went wrong. I did say though that if I knew for a fact that even 10 people would like to know how you teach a four-year-old Greek I would explain it. 11 riders of the Circle Line have now said they would like to know this. I rather wish now that I had said 10 people not including people who think it is a marvellous idea because grammar & spelling not taught in schools, but it was an unconditional offer & if I say I will do a thing I try to do it.

It seems to me that the last time I approached this subject I had explained how I had taken a break from typing in an interview with John Denver & had been interrupted while reading *Iliad* 6 by L. The last thing I wanted was to be teaching a four-year-old Greek, and now the Alien spoke & its voice was mild as milk.

What is the Alien asks a reader.

The Alien is whatever you want to call the thing that finds specious reasons for cruelty and how do you expect me to finish with these constant interruptions.

And now the Alien spoke & its voice was mild as milk, and it said He's just a baby.

And J. S. Mill said:

In the course of instruction which I have partially retraced, the point most superficially apparent is the great effort to give, during the years of childhood, an amount of knowledge in what are considered the higher branches of education, which is seldom acquired (if acquired at all) until the age of manhood.

And I said: NO NO NO NO NO

And Mr. Mill said:

The result of the experiment shows the ease with which this may be done,

And I said *EASE*

& he resumed implacably,

and places in a strong light the wretched waste of so many precious years as are spent in acquiring the modicum of Latin and Greek commonly taught to schoolboys; a waste which has led so many educational reformers to entertain the ill-judged proposal of discarding these languages altogether from general education. If I had been by nature extremely quick of apprehension, or had possessed a very accurate and retentive memory, or were of a remarkably active and energetic character, the trial would not be conclusive; but in all these natural gifts I am rather below than above par; what I could do, could assuredly be done by any boy or girl of average capacity and healthy physical constitution.

The Alien said it would be kinder to say no & I longed to believe it, for the ease with which a small child may be introduced to what are commonly considered the higher branches of education is nothing to the ease with which it may not. I thought: Well maybe he'll just. I thought: Well.

So I gave L a little table for the alphabet & said there's the alphabet & he looked perplexed. When I learned the language the first thing we were given was a list of words like φιλοσοφία θεολογία ἀνθρωπολογία & so on and we would see the similarity to philosophy theology anthropology and get excited, this type of word tends not to turn up in *Hop on Pop* & so is not very helpful for teaching a four-year-old. So I said a lot of the letters were the same and when he still looked perplexed I explained patiently—

There are a lot of Greek letters that are like English letters. See if you can read this, and I wrote on a piece of paper:

ατ

And he said at.

And I wrote down βατ and he said bat.

And I wrote down εατ and he said eat.

ατε. ate. ιτ. it. κιτ. kit. τοε. toe. βοατ. boat. βυτ. but. αβουτ. about.

And I said That's good.

And I said There are some other letters that are different, and I wrote down γ = g, δ = d, λ = l, μ = m, ν = n, π = p, ρ = r, & σ = s & I said see if you can read these.

I wrote down γατε and he said Gate!

And I wrote down δατε and he said Date!

And I wrote down λατε and he said Late!

ματε. Mate! ρατε. Rate! λετ Let μετ Met νετ Net πετ Pet σετ Set!!!!!!

The Alien said that that was enough for today.

Mr. Mill said his father had started him on cards with Greek vocables at the age of three and that what he had done could assuredly be done by any boy or girl of average capacity and healthy physical constitution.

Mr. Ma said that was far too much for one day & that too much material had been covered in a superficial manner without being thoroughly mastered.

I said I think that's enough for one day

& he said NO! NO NO NO NO

So I wrote down ξ = x. ζ = z.

μιξ. Mix! λιξ. Lix—oh Licks! πιξ Picks! στιξ Sticks! ζιπ Zip!

I said Now you know the sound H makes, and he said Huh.

I said Right. I said Now in Greek they don't use a letter for that sound, but a little hook over the first letter of the word, that looks like this: ʽ. It's called a rough breathing. If a word starts with a vowel & doesn't have an H sound it gets a smooth breathing, which is a hook facing the other way: ʼ. So how would you say this:

ἑλπ.

He thought about it for a while & at last he said Help?

I said Good. And this? ὁπ

And he said Hop.

ὁτ. Hot! ἱτ. Hit! ἱτ. It? ἁτ. Hat! ἁτ At! ἁτε Hate! ἁτε Ate!

And I said Brilliant!

And he said This is easy!

And the Alien made a rattling sound in its throat. Coupez la difficulté en quatre, it said, with a ghastly grin.

Mr. Ma said You know my methods.

I thought: Just five more minutes. I can stand five minutes.

I said That's good, because the next bit is a little harder. There are four letters that stand for sounds that we write with two letters. There's θ which is th, but it's not the th of the or thin, it's more like what you say if you say SPIT HARD. And there's φ which is ph as in SLAP HARD. And there's χ which is kh as in WALK HOME. And there's ψ, which is ps, as in NAPS. Do you want to try or do you want to stop for now? And he said he would try.

So I wrote παθιμ

and he looked for a very long time & at last I said Pat him.

And I wrote παθερ

and he said Pat HER.

And I wrote μεεθιμ & he said Meet him and I wrote μεεθερ & he said Meet HER & I said Terrific.

βλαχεαρτεδ Blackhearted? βλοχεαδ Blockhead. βλαχαιρεδ Blackhaired.

ἑλφερ Help her. ἑλφιμ Help him. ριψ Rips! λιψ Lips! νιψ Nips! πιψ Pips!

And I said Brilliant.

Then he picked up the book and looked at it and he said he couldn't read any of it.

I said patiently That's because it's a different language so all the words are different. If you could read the words it would be English in different letters.

I said:

Look, I'll get out some pages I've done on this book and you can work on that.

He said:

OK.

So I went to find the four pages I had managed to finish. Four years earlier I had started work on a sort of *Teach Yourself Iliad*, with text vocabulary at bottom of page translation on facing page. I had finished four pages which had been stuck in the back of the Homeric dictionary for the past four years & I had still not progressed beyond *Iliad* 1.68. This was depressing but at least it meant I had some pages for him to work on with vocabulary at the bottom of the page.

I said This is just to get you started reading the words, yes? I'll give you some words and you can use one of my Schwan Stabilo highlighters that I use for my Arabic. Which colour would you like to use?

And he said Green.

So I gave him a Schwan Stabilo 33 & I picked some words that turned up a lot, but because I remembered Roemer and the something in the something with the something I tried to make sure they were not all prepositions & articles & connectives.

Then I realised that I had forgotten to go over the long vowels & diphthongs.

I did not want to go over the long vowels & diphthongs. I don't want to go over them now. But I knew of course that if I did not L would be interrupting & pestering me to explain them within the hour, and if I do not explain them again I know what will happen: the poet Keats will haunt my dreams. Bearing in one hand Chapman's Homer in the other the Oxford Classical Text, he will gaze at me fixedly with an expression of inexpressible sorrow before opening the Chapman with a piteous sigh. A Connery lookalike pacing through the mists will look up in silent indignation and stalk off without a word. Well—long e has its own letter, η, like the e of bed stretched out; long o has its own letter ω, like the o of hot stretched out; παι rhymes with pie, παυ pow δει day βοι boy μου moo—I explained this in a manner which I leave to the imagination & returned to the words.

How would you say this? πολλὰς. Pollas? Terrific. That means many.

And this? ψυχὰς Psukhas. YES. That's something like souls or spirits.

And what about these? ἡρώων θεῶν ἀνδρῶν. Heeroooon theoon androon. Right. They mean, of heroes, of gods, of men. Now all I want you to do is go through as much as you can and colour in all the places where you see those words. We'll worry about the grammar later. OK?

And he said OK.

So I handed over the pages and said There you go.

We have come all the way around to Blackfriars. L is up to the pentekaipentekontapus under the admiring & indulgent eyes of people who get on and are able to get off again after a few stops.

He looked at the pages and he looked at me.

I said It isn't as hard as it looks. Look carefully and show me one of your words.

& he looked at the page and he found πολλὰς in line 3 & I said That's right, so colour that green & look for the rest, OK?

& he said OK.

OKTOkaipentekontapus ENNEAkaipentekontapus HEX-EKONTApus

[Well anyway]

I turned again to *Iliad* 6 and in two minutes Baby Driver was back. He said he was going to colour in the names of people because he could read them & he was not finding very many words to colour. I said that was a very good idea & he went away & I turned my attention to Hector & Andromache & he was back again. He said θεοῖς looked like θεῶν and could he count it because he was not finding many words to colour.

I was not looking forward to simplifying and explaining even the simplest points of grammar to a four-year-old & I can't say I am looking forward to going through it all again now but I said I would so I

HEKkaiHEXeKONtapus   HEPtakaiHEXeKONtapus
OKTOkaiHEXeKONtapus

will.

I am finding it rather hard to concentrate however so may salve conscience by just touching on highlights like Sound of Music cutting from Doe A Deer to seven-part harmony or heptaphony as some people (naming no names) would probably call it.

I said Yes you can and I said Do you remember what θεῶν meant and he said Of gods, I said Right, well θεοῖς means to gods or by gods & do you remember what ἡρώων and ἀνδρῶν meant & he said Of heroes and of men & I said But there's no separate word meaning 'of', is there, it's all in the word so there must be a bit of the word that means 'of' & what do you think that would be & I don't know about you but I am about ready for The hills are alive (A-a-a-ah).

heptakaihebdomekontapus
[Ah. Forget it]

Another day on the Circle Line, house too cold to stay in. An icy rain sweeps the city, underground it is warm and dry.

LIVERPOOL STREET ALDGATE TOWER HILL MONUMENT

Far too young

CANNON STREET MANSION HOUSE BLACKFRIARS

Etymology so helpful

TEMPLE EMBANKMENT WESTMINSTER and around and around

At St. James's Park a woman gets on and sees the tiny head bent over a book, pudgy fingers dragging a blue Schwan Stabilo highlighter across the page. Twinkling eyes share the joke, she longs for adult bonding. He looks up & gives her an enchanting smile, all chubby cheeks and sparkling black eyes & tiny milk teeth. He says: I've almost finished Book 15!

She says: I SEE you have! You must have been working very hard.

Another Shirley Temple special for the nice lady. L: I only started it yesterday!

Isn't He Adorable: Did you REALLY?

Adorable: Today I read this and this and this and this and yesterday I did this and this and this and this and this and this! [tiny fingers flip back through pages covered with fluorescent pink and orange and blue and green]

Isn't: Isn't that wonderful!

Wonderful: I've read the *Iliad* and *De Amicitia* and three stories in *Kalilah wa Dimnah* & one Arabian Night and Moses & the Bullrushes and Joseph and his Manycoloured Coat and now I have to read the *Odyssey* and *Metamorphoses* 1–8 and the *whole Kalilah wa Dimnah* and 30 *Arabian Nights and* I Samuel *and* the Book of Jonah *and* learn the cantellation, *and* do 10 chapters in *Algebra Made Easy.*

Slightly Taken Aback: Why do you have to do that?

All Innocence: Sibylla says I have to.

Appalled: Isn't he rather young etymology so helpful of course for spelling inflected language so helpful of course for grammar not taught in schools but classics after all part & parcel of old divisive educational system wouldn't he really be better off playing football I think you are making a terrible mistake.

Standard reply.

SLOANE SQUARE SOUTH KENSINGTON

Four hours have gone by. We have taken the Circle Line around four times. We have been to the toilet twice; L has hopped the length of the platform at Mansion House on one foot and back on the other foot; we have left the train each time at Tower Hill to make faces at the video camera & watch ourselves making faces in the banks of TVs. Or rather—you see yourself in one TV. In the others you do not appear—they show sometimes an empty platform, sometimes a platform with a few people, sometimes a platform with a train pulling around a bend. I think these are images from cameras further down the platform, but they look like glimpses into possible worlds, worlds where the sun rises and the trains run without you. There are pushchairs to be pushed but not by you, bad memories to be dodged but not by you.

2

99, 98, 97, 96

12 December, 1992

My name is Ludo. I am 5 years and 267 days old. It is 99 days to my sixth birthday. Sibylla gave me this book today to write in because she said I should practise writing because my handwriting is atrocious, and they will not let me write on a computer all the time at school. I said I didn't know what to write and Sibylla said I could write about things I liked so that in later years I would be able to see what I liked as a child. Also I could write about interesting things that happened so that in later years I would be able to remember things that had happened.

One thing that I like a lot is polynomials but I do not like the word binomial because it is wrong. I have decided never to use it. I always use the right word for a polynomial whatever anybody else does. My favourite Greek word is γαγγλίον and that is all the things I like today

13 December, 1992

It is 98 days to my birthday. One interesting thing that happened today was that I took Kalilah wa Dimnah on the Circle Line too and somebody asked if my father was an Arab. Sibylla said whatever gave you that idea. The person said isn't that Arabic. Sibylla said Yes. Then she said but my father wasn't an Arab. I was going to ask her what he was but then I decided not to.

I think that Greek and Arabic and Hebrew are my favourite languages because they have a dual. Greek has better moods and tenses but Arabic and Hebrew have better duals because they have a feminine dual and a masculine dual but Greek just has the one. I asked Sibylla if there was a language with a trial number and she said not that she was aware but she didn't know all the languages in the world. I wish there was a language with a dual trial quadral quincal sextal septal octal nonal and decal, if there was that would be my favourite language.

It is boring on the Circle Line but I am up to Odyssey 15.305. 9 books to go.

14 December, 1992

97 days to my birthday.

One interesting thing that happened today is that we took the Tube one way and then we took it the other way and a lady got into an argument with Sibylla. Sibylla said let's take the example of two men about to be burned at the stake, A dies at time t of heart failure while B burns to death at time $t + n$, I think we can all agree that B's life would be better if it were n minutes shorter. The lady said she thought it was rather different and Sibylla said she thought it was exactly the same and the lady said there was no need to shout. Sibylla said she wasn't shouting she just thought it was barbaric to force people to die at time $t + n$ and she said barbaric so loud that everyone in the train looked around!

Barbaric comes from the Greek word βάρβαρος which means a non-Greek but in English it means something completely different.

15 December, 1992

96 days to my birthday.

Today I was reading the Odyssey on the Tube and a man got on and said it was good that I was starting so young. He said he started Hebrew when he was three and I said I knew Hebrew and he said what have you read in Hebrew. I said I had read Moses in the bullrushes and he taught me this song:

Pharaoh had a daughter with a very winning smile
She found the baby Moses while swimming in the Nile
She took him home to Pharaoh, said I found him on the shore
Pharaoh winked at her and said I've heard that one before.

I sang it three times and he said splendid and he said it was never too soon to start on your religious education. He asked Sibylla if my father was teaching me or if I was studying at school or with a rabbi and Sibylla said she was teaching me herself. He said it was a shame all Jewish mothers did not take religious education so seriously. Sibylla said she was really only teaching me the language and he said of course, of course. I was hoping he would ask if my father was Jewish but he didn't. When he got off the train I asked Sibylla and she said she didn't know, it didn't come up in the conversation, but she didn't think so.

16 December, 1992

95 days to my birthday.

One thing that is funny is that even though I have been reading the Odyssey on the Tube for a long time nobody ever asked if my father was Greek. Today I read Babar but nobody asked if he was French.

Speaking of French a funny thing happened today on the Tube. A lady got into an argument with Sibylla who said let's take the example of two men who are about to be ritually disembowelled. A dies at time t of heart failure and B dies at time t + n from having someone plunge a stone knife into his chest and rip the beating heart out with his bare hands, I think we would agree that B's life was not improved by the additional n minutes in which the stone knife was plunged into his and the lady said pas devant les enfants. I said parlez-vous français? The lady looked very surprised. Sibylla said would you be more comfortable if we continued the discussion in Bengali? The lady said pardon? Sibylla said or perhaps some other language he does not know? She said her Russian, Hungarian, Finnish, Basque and Icelandic were not up to much but she thought she could manage something in Spanish, Portuguese, Italian, German, Swedish, Danish or Bengali. I was surprised because I didn't know Sibylla knew any of those languages. I don't think the lady did. I asked when I could learn those other languages and Sibylla said after I have learned Japanese. I asked if my father was French and Sibylla said no.

17 December, 1992

We took the Tube again today. It was boring. I read Odyssey 17 part of the time and the rest of the time White Fang. On the way home I asked Sibylla if my father was Russian, Hungarian, Finnish, Basque, Icelandic, Spanish, Portuguese, Italian, German, Swedish, Danish or Bengali. She said No.

94 days to my birthday.

3

We Never Get Off at Embankment to Go to McDonald's

and around and around and around and a

L is up to *Odyssey* 17. This is so bad for him. Hundreds of people saying wonderful marvellous far too young what a genius. It seems to me that it is does not take miraculous intelligence to master the simple fact that Ὀδυσσεύς is Odysseus, if you go on to master 5,000 similar simple facts you have only shown that you are a miracle of obstinacy.

Anyway I have been watching Seven Samurai once a week with L to counteract the deplorable influence of the Circle Line. But today something terrible happened.

A woman sitting across from me saw the *Reader of Handwritten Japanese* sitting unopened in my lap and said Are you studying Japanese & I said Sort of.

Nine green bottles hanging on the wall

I said I was mainly learning the language so I could understand Kurosawa's Seven Samurai and also (if it ever came out on video) Mizoguchi's Five Women Around Utamaro which I had watched five days in a row when it showed at the Phoenix, and that I was also interested in a text called Tsurezuregusa by a 14th-century Buddhist priest.

NINE GREEN BOTTLES HANGING ON THE WALL

She said Oh and she said she had seen Seven Samurai though not the other one and what a marvellous film

I said Yes

and she said It's a little on the long side but what a marvellous film, of course it's basically so simple isn't it I suppose that's the source of its appeal, sort of like the Three Musketeers, an elite band—

and I said WHAT?

and she said Sorry?

ELITE BAND! I said staring aghast

and she said there was no need to shout.

And if ONE GREEN BOTTLE should accidentally fall
There'll be EIGHT GREEN BOTTLES hanging on the wall

I began to imagine L seeing all kinds of things in the film which would not be incompatible with throwing a person from a plane on orders from a third party

EIGHT GREEN BOTTLES HANGING ON THE WALL

I said politely but firmly I think if you see the film again you will find that the samurai are not, in fact, an elite band. Lesser directors have of course succumbed to the glamour of the eliteness of a band, with predictable results; not Kurosawa.

She said there was no need to take that tone

EIGHT GREEN BOTTLES HANGING ON THE WALL

& I said politely Essentially the film is about the importance of rational thought. We should draw our conclusions from the evidence available rather than from hearsay and try not to be influenced by our preconceptions. We should strive to see what we can see for ourselves rather than what we would like to see.

She said What?

And if one green bottle should accidentally fall

I said Also, we should remember that appearances can be deceptive. We may not *have* all the relevant evidence. Just because somebody is smiling doesn't mean he wouldn't be better off dead.

She said I really don't think

SEVEN GREEN BOTTLES, HANGING ON THE WALL

I said Let's say A sees his wife, B, burned alive at time t. A survives. Later we see A singing in a local ritual. C, observing the ritual, thinks A has come out ahead. We infer that C is not in full possession of the facts & has been influenced by his own preconceptions since

She said It all seems rather clinical

I said Clinical!

THERE'LL BE SIX GREEN BOTTLES, HANGING ON THE WALL

She said & isn't this rather morbid—

I pointed out that if she were thrown into a tank of man-eating sharks she would not think it morbid to consider the possibility of exit from the tank.

After all we both when it comes down to it we both think it's a marvellous film, she said pleasantly.

I was afraid she might give some other example but luckily the train pulled into Moorgate and this was her stop.

SIX GREEN BOTTLES, HANGING ON THE WALL
SIX GREEN BOTTLES

[Could be worse. He could be singing 100 bottles of beer on the wall, instead of a song that not only counts down, but starts at 10.]

277 degrees above absolute zero.

I said All right, we'll take the Circle Line again, and we had another argument about Cunliffe.

I: Look, there's no point in bringing a dictionary when there is no place to put it. You can't use it if you are holding it in your lap with the book on top. We tried that before and it didn't work.

L: Please

I: No

L: Please

I: No

L: Please

I: No

L: Please

I: No

The ideal thing would be to go somewhere with tables, such as the Barbican or South Bank Centre—but it is impossible to go to either without being faced at every turn with bars and cafés and restaurants and ice-cream vendors, all selling expensive appealing food which L wants & we cannot afford.

Please No Please No Please

I thought about another day like the last 17, 10 hours of marvellous wonderful far too young what a genius; I thought about another day like yesterday, more marvellous wonderful far too young what a genius *plus* nonsense about elite bands not to mention 10 hours explaining every single word/visiting toilet inaccessible to pushchair/smiling pleasantly through 273 verses $(10 + 0 + -262)$ of the green bottles song. Could I be sure that he would not start up again at

—263 or rather would anyone familiar with the child offer even straight odds that he would not? No.

So I said All right, forget the Circle Line. We'll take Cunliffe and we'll go to the National Gallery, but I don't want you to say ONE WORD. And no running through doors that say No Entry or Authorised Personnel Only. We've got to be inconspicuous. We've got to look as though we've come to look at the paintings. We've been looking at the paintings and our feet are tired so we're just sitting down to rest our feet. We're just sitting down to rest our feet so we can get up and look at more paintings.

Natürlich, said the Phenomenon.

I've heard that one before, said I, but I put Cunliffe under the pushchair along with *Odyssey 13–24, Fergus: Dog of the Scottish Glens, Tar-Kutu, Marduk, Pete, WOLF!, Kingdom of the Octopus, SQUID!, The House at Pooh Corner, White Fang, Kanji ABC, Kanji from the Start, A Reader of Handwritten Japanese,* this notebook and several peanut butter and jam sandwiches. I put L in the pushchair with *Les Inséparables* and we set off.

We are now sitting in front of Bellini's Portrait of the Doge. L is reading *Odyssey* 18, consulting Cunliffe at intervals—*infrequent* intervals. I have been looking at the Portrait of the Doge—*somebody's* got to.

I have brought things to read myself but the room is so warm I keep falling asleep and then jerking awake to stare. In a half-dream I see the monstrous heiskaihekatontapus prowling the ocean bed, pentekaipentekontapods flying before it, Come back & fight like a man, it jeers, I can beat you with one hand tied behind my back (heh heh heh). Strange to think Thatcher could work on three hours sleep, five hours & I am an idiot. Should never never never have told him to read all those things—but too late to retract.

I think the guard looks suspicious.

Pretend to take notes.

❖

No sooner were Liberace and I in his bed without our clothes than I realised how stupid I had been. At this distance I can naturally not remember every little detail, but if there is one musical form that I hate more than any other, it is the medley. One minute the musician, or more likely aged band, is playing an overorchestrated version of The Impossible Dream; all of a sudden, mid-verse, for no reason, there's a stomach-turning swerve into another key and you're in the middle of Over the Rainbow, swerve, Climb Every Mountain, swerve, Ain't No Mountain High Enough, swerve, swerve, swerve. Well then, you have only to imagine Liberace, hands, mouth, penis now here, now there, no sooner here than there, no sooner there than here again, starting something only to stop and start something else instead, and you will have a pretty accurate picture of the Drunken Medley.

The Medley came at last to an end and Liberace fell into a deep sleep.

I wanted to clear my head. I wanted strangeness and coldness and precision.

I listened for a little while to Glenn Gould playing pieces from The Well-Tempered Clavier. In recording sessions Gould would often make nine or ten different versions of a piece, each note perfect, each perfectly distinct from the others in character, and each note played bears the mark of all those to which it was preferred. I am not really capable of replaying a fugue in my head so I listened to his queer performance of the C minor prelude, Book 1, which begins with each note staccato, and then two-thirds of the way down the first page the notes suddenly run very smoothly and softly, and then I listened to Prelude No. 22 in B flat minor which I could never play without the pedal. I think that though perhaps it should not be played with the pedal it should at least be played legato, and yet the harsh abruptness with which Gould plays this piece displaced with its coldness, its lack of ease, the wilful expressiveness with which Liberace wearies the heart.

Liberace was still asleep. His head lay on the pillow, face as I had seen it, skull encasing a sleeping brain; how cruel that we must wake each time to answer to the same name, revive the same memories, take up the same habits and stupidities that we shouldered the day before and lay down to sleep. I did not want to watch him wake to go on as he had begun.

I did not want to be there when he woke up but it would be rude to leave without a word. On the other hand almost any note would be impossible to write. I could not say thank you for a lovely evening because you can't. I could not say hope to see you again because what if he took this as encouragement to see me again? I could not say I had a horrible time and I hope I never see you again because you just can't. If I tried to write a short note that said something without saying any of these things I would still be there five or six hours later when he woke up.

Then I had an idea.

The thing to do, I thought, was to *imply* that we had had an interesting conversation which just happened to be interrupted by the fact that I had to leave (for some sort of appointment, for example). Instead of marking the close of the occasion the note should present itself as a further element of a conversation which was still in progress & only suspended. The note should appear to assume that Liberace was interested in things like the Rosetta Stone & should purport to answer a perceived scepticism as to the possibility of putting together such a thing in such a way as to be generally comprehensible, thus presenting itself as part of an ongoing discussion to be resumed at some unspecified later date. All I would have to do was write down a short passage of Greek, as if for this interested sceptic, with translation transliteration vocabulary and grammatical comments—taking pains, of course, to write the latter as if for the type of person who can't get enough of things like the middle voice, dual number, aorist and tmesis. I am usually not very good at dealing with social dilemmas, but this seemed a stroke of genius. It would take about an hour (comparing favourably with the five-hour unwritable note), and the final tissue of false implication would practically guarantee (while avoiding gratuitous cruelty and yet not departing for one instant from the truth) that Liberace would never want to see me again.

I got up and got dressed and I went into the next room and got a piece of paper from his desk. Then I took my Edding 0.1 pen from my bag, because I was going to try to fit it all on one page, and I sat down and got to work. It was about 3:00 a.m.

You seemed to doubt that a Rosetta Stone would be possible (I began casually). What do you think of this?

Iliad 17, Zeus pities the horses of Achilles mourning the death of Patroclus

Μυρομένω δ' ἄρα τώ γε ἰδὼν ἐλέησε Κρονίων,
muromenō   d'   ara   tō   ge idōn   eleēse   Kroniōn

Seeing them grieving the son of Kronos took pity

κινήσας δὲ κάρη προτὶ ὃν μυθήσατο θυμόν·
kinēsas   de   karē   proti   hon muthēsato   thumon

And moving his head spoke his mind

ἆ δειλώ, τί σφῶϊ δόμεν Πηλῆϊ ἄνακτι
a   deilō, ti sphōi domen   Pēlēi   anakti

'Ah wretched things, why did we give you to King Peleus,

θνητῷ, ὑμεῖς δ' ἐστὸν ἀγήρω τ' ἀθανάτω τε;
thnētōi, humeis d' eston   agērō   t' athanatō   te

A mortal, when you are ageless and deathless?

ἦ ἵνα δυστήνοισι μετ' ἀνδράσιν ἄλγε' ἔχητον;
ē hina dustēnoisi   met' andrasin   alge' ekhēton

Was it that you might have sorrows with wretched men?

οὐ μὲν γάρ τί πού ἐστιν ὀϊζυρώτερον ἀνδρὸς
ou men gar ti pou estin   oizurōteron   andros

For there is nothing more wretched than man

πάντων ὅσσα τε γαῖαν ἔπι πνείει τε καὶ ἕρπει.
pantōn   hossa te gaian epi pneiei te kai herpei

Of all things that breathe and creep upon the earth.

ἀλλ' οὐ μὰν ὑμῖν γε καὶ ἅρμασι δαιδαλέοισιν
all'   ou man humin ge kai harmasi   daidaleoisin

But not by you and the glittering chariot will

"Εκτωρ Πριαμίδης ἐποχήσεται· οὐ γὰρ ἐάσω.
Hektōr   Priamidēs   epokhēsetai   ou gar easō.

Hector son of Priam be carried; for I will not allow it.'

So far so good. It was only 3:15, and here already was more help for the decipherer than the Rosetta Stone ever gave Champollion. In fact I could not help thinking how much easier life would be if I proceeded without further ado to a noncommittal Ciao, rather than struggling hungover and sleepless with grammatical detail. And yet the text as it stood looked so thin. Apart from the transliteration, it offered nothing not readily available in the pages of the Loeb Classical Library. It was completely unconvincing as a message in a bottle and besides, it would be only too obvious that it could not have taken more than 15 minutes to write. So it would still be necessary to leave a note unless, of course, I left a more plausible sample of the gift to posterity, and I wrote

Μυρομένω grieving [masculine/feminine accusative dual middle participle] δ' ἄρα and then, and so [connective particles] τώ them [M/F accusative dual pronoun] γε emphatic particle ἰδών seeing [M. nominative singular aorist participle] ἐλέησε took pity [3rd person singular aorist indicative] Κρονίων the son of Kronos (Zeus)

and I still did not have something on the page that could be concluded with an airy Ciao.

It was also useless as a message in a bottle because full of unexplained grammatical terms which should really be explained or taken out. But I could not take them out without writing it all out again, and I could not explain them without going on for pages. But what if I had got carried away going through the passage word by word and not noticed this problem till later?

κινήσας moving [masculine nominative singular aorist participle] δὲ and [connective particle] κάρη head προτὶ . . . μυθήσατο addressed [3rd person singular aorist middle indicative] ὃν his θυμόν soul/spirit/ mind/heart [masculine accusative singular] ἆ Ah δειλώ wretched [masculine/feminine vocative dual] τί why σφῶϊ you [2nd person accusative dual] δόμεν did we give [1st person plural aorist indicative] Πηλῆϊ Peleus (father of Achilles) ἄνακτι king [masculine dative singular 3rd declension]

θνητῷ mortal [masc. dative sing. 2nd declension] ὑμεῖς you [2nd person nominative plural] δ' [connective particle] but, yet ἐστὸν you are [2nd person dual indicative] ἀγήρω ageless [M/F nominative dual] τ' . . . τε both...and ἀθανάτω immortal [M/F nom. dual]

ἦ 'forsooth' [exclamatory particle] ἵνα so that δυστήνοισι wretched [M. dative plural] μετ' with ἀνδράσιν men [M. dative plural] ἄλγε᾽ [= algea] pains, sorrows [neuter accusative plural] ἔχητον you should have [2nd person dual subjunctve]

οὐ not μὲν introductory particle γάρ for τί anything [neuter nominative singular] πού anywhere ἐστιν is [3rd person singular present indicative] ὀϊζυρώτερον more miserable/wretched [neuter nom. sing. comparative] ἀνδρὸς than man [M. genitive singular after comparative adjective]

πάντων of all things [neuter genitive plural] ὅσσα as many things [neuter nominative plural] τε particle showing generalisation γαῖαν earth [fem. accusative singular] ἔπι upon [here postpositive] πνείει breathe [3rd person singular present indicative dependent on neuter plural noun] τε καὶ both and ἕρπει creep [3rd person sing. pres. indicative]

ἀλλ' but οὐ not μὰν emphatic particle ὑμῖν by you [2nd p. dative plural] γε emphatic particle καὶ and ἅρμασι chariot [neuter dative plural] δαιδαλέοισιν glittering, cunningly made [neuter dative plural]

Ἕκτωρ Hector Πριαμίδης son of Priam ἐποχήσεται will be carried [3rd p. singular future passive indicative] οὐ not γὰρ for ἐάσω I will allow [1st p. singular future active indicative]

It seemed to be rather longer than I had expected.

It had also taken a bit longer to write than I had expected (two hours). This still compared favourably with a five-hour unwritable note. I wrote a final paragraph pointing out that for a real Rosetta Stone you would probably want to have a third column with Chinese but unfortunately I did not know any of the characters, and then I said that if he had ever come across the poem of Keats on looking into Chapman's Homer he would probably be interested and surprised to see that this was what Chapman had written:

De dumty dumty dumty dum Iove saw their heavy chear,
And (pittying them) spake to his minde; Poor wretched beasts
(said he)
Why gave we you t'a mortall king? De dumty dumty dum
De dumty dumty dumty dum de dumty dumty dum?
De dumty dumty dumty dum de dumty dumty dum?
Of all the miserable'st things that breathe and creepe on earth,
No one more wretched is then man. And for your deathless
birth,
Hector must faile to make you prise de dumty dumty dum

and then I just said you see how easy it would be I hope you like it Must dash—S and after the S I put an illegible dashing scrawl because I thought there was a good chance he had not caught my name the night before.

Then I put this on a table where he would be bound to see it. It had seemed so plausible and suave when I had had the idea in bed, and yet now I wondered whether Liberace would realise that I was politely implying etc. etc. or whether it just looked outré. Too late, and so good-bye.

I got home and I thought I should stop leading so aimless an existence. It is harder than you might think to stop leading an existence, & if you can't do that the only thing you can do is try to introduce an element of purposefulness.

Whether Liberace liked the Horses of Achilles I do not know (going by his other remarks it would not surprise me to learn that he felt like Cortez gazing on the Pacific on reading the Chapman). It had made me happy to write down the passage, anyway, & I thought that I could now do this for the whole *Iliad* and *Odyssey* with interleaved pages explaining various features of grammar and dialect and formulaic composition. I could print them up for a few thousand pounds and sell them at a market stall and people would be able to read them regardless of whether they had studied French or Latin or some other irrelevant subject at school. Then I could do something similar for other languages which are even harder to study at school than Greek, and though I might have to wait another 30 or 40 years for my body to join the non-sentient things in the world at least in the meantime it would be a less absolutely senseless sentience. OK.

One day Emma invited me into her office for a talk. She explained that she would be leaving the company. What would I do? If her job disappeared, so would mine. I hadn't been with the firm long enough to be entitled to maternity pay. Was I planning to go back to the States to have the baby?

I did not know what to say.

I didn't say anything, and Emma made practical suggestions. She said the publisher was launching a project into 20th-century language which involved typing and tagging magazine text for computer; she said she had made inquiries, and thought she could get me smuggled onto this under my work permit. She said there would be no problem about taking the computer to work from the home since the office had been downsized out of existence. She said that she knew of a house whose owner could not afford to fix it and who was afraid it would be occupied by squatters if she did not rent it; she said that the owner would let me have it for £150 a month if I did not ask her to fix it. I did not know what to say. She said she would understand if I wanted to go back to the States to be with my family. I knew what not to say: I did not say no one could understand that, for I would have to be mad to do it. I said: Thank you very much.

❖

I looked up to see how L was getting on. *Odyssey* 13–24 was lying face down on the bench; L was nowhere to be seen. I couldn't remember when I had seen him last. I thought of going to look for him, but then this would mean leaving the one place he knew to look for me.

I looked at the *Odyssey* to see how far he had got. My chances of not teaching him Japanese did not look good. I began leafing idly through *White Fang.*

After a while I heard a voice I knew.

Would you like to hear me count to a thousand in Arabic? said the voice.

I thought you said your mum was in Room 61?

She is.

Then we'll have to leave it for another time.

When?

Some other time. Is this your little boy?

A security guard was standing in front of me, as was L.

I said: Yes.

L said: I went to the toilet all by myself.

I said: Good for you.

Guard: You'll never guess where I found him.

I: Where did you find him?

Guard: You'll never guess in a million years.

I: Where?

Guard: All the way down in the basement in one of the restoring rooms. Seems he must have nipped down the stairs and gone through one of the staff doors.

I: Oh.

Guard: No harm done, but you ought to keep a closer eye on him.

I: Well, there's no harm done.

Guard: No, but you ought to keep a closer eye on him.

I: Well, I'll bear that in mind.

Guard: What's his name?

I wish people wouldn't ask that kind of question.

When I was pregnant I kept thinking of appealing names such as Hasdrubal and Isambard Kingdom and Thelonius, and Rabindranath, and Darius Xerxes (Darius X.) and Amédée and Fabius Cunctator. Hasdrubal was the brother of Hannibal, the Carthaginian general who crossed the Alps with elephants in the 3rd century BC to wage war with Rome; Isambard Kingdom Brunel was a 19th-century British engineer of genius; Thelonius Monk was a jazz pianist of genius; Rabindranath Tagore was a Bengali polymath; Darius was a Persian king, as was Xerxes; Amédée is the first name of the narrator's grandfather in *A la recherche du temps perdu*, and Fabius Cunctator was the Roman general who saved the Roman state from Hannibal by delaying. They all had names one should really not give to a child, and once he was born I had to think fast.

I thought that ideally it should be a name which could work whether he was serious and reserved or butch, a name like Stephen which could be Steve or David which could be Dave. The problem was that I liked David better than Stephen, and Steve better than Dave, and I couldn't get round it by calling him Stephen David or David Stephen because a series of two trochees with a v in the middle would sound ridiculous. I couldn't call him David and Steve for short; that would be quaint. People kept coming up to the bed saying what's his name, and I would say, Well, I was thinking of Stephen, or I was thinking about David, and on one occasion it turned out the person was a nurse with a form who wrote down whatever it was I was thinking about and took it away again and that was that.

They did give me the birth certificate when I left and it was one or the other. When I got home it was obvious that his name was actually Ludovic so I called him that having really no choice in the matter.

I now replied evasively: I call him Ludo.

Guard: Well, keep an eye on Ludo in future.

I: Well, thank you for your help. I think we'll just go to Room 34 and look at the Turners if you don't mind. Thank you again for your help.

It was much easier when he was small. I had one of those Kanga carriers; in warm weather I would type at home with him in front and in cold weather I would go to the British Museum and sit in the Egyptian gallery near the changing room, reading *Al Hayah* to keep my hand in. Then at night I would go home and type *Pig Fancier's Monthly* or *Weaseller's Companion*. And now four years have gone by.

4

19, 18, 17

19 days to my birthday.

I am reading Call of the Wild again. I don't like it as well as White Fang but I have just finished White Fang again.

I am up to Odyssey 19.322. I have stopped making cards for all the words because there would be too much to carry around but I just make cards for words that look useful. Today we went to the museum and they have a picture of the Odyssey, it is supposed to show the Cyclops but you can't actually see him. It is called Ulysses Deriding Polyphemus. Ulysses is the Latin name for Odysseus. There was a card on the wall saying you can see Polyphemus on the mountain but you can't. I told the guard they should change it and he said it was not up to him. I asked who it was up to and he said maybe the head of the gallery. I tried to get Sibylla to take me to see the head but she said he was too busy and it would be more polite to write him a letter, she said I could write him a letter and practise my handwriting. I said why don't you write a letter. She said he had probably never had a letter from a five-year-old before, if I wrote a letter and signed it Ludo Aged Five he would pay attention to it. I think this is stupid because anybody could sign a letter Aged Five. Sibylla said true, one look at your handwriting and he won't believe you're a day over two. She seemed to think this was hysterically funny.

2 March, 1993

18 days to my birthday. I have been on the planet 5 years and 348 days.

3 March, 1993

17 days to my birthday. We rode the Circle Line today because we couldn't go back to any museums. It was tedious in the extreme. One funny thing that happened is that a lady got into an argument with Sibylla about two men who were about to be flayed alive. Sibylla explained that one of the men dies of heart failure at time t and the other at time t + n after having someone peel off his skin with a knife for n seconds and the lady said pas dev and Sibylla said I should warn you that he speaks French. Then the lady said non um non avanty il ragatso and Sibylla said not forward the boy. Not forward the boy. Not. Forward. The boy. Hmmm. I'm afraid I don't quite understand, you clearly have a command of Italian idiom which I cannot match and the lady said she thought it was not a suitable subject for discussion in the presence of a small child and Sibylla said oh I see, and that's how you say it in Italian. Non avanty il ragatso. I must remember that. The lady said what kind of example do you think you are setting and Sibylla said would you mind if we continued this discussion in Italian, I feel that it is not a suitable subject for discussion in the presence of a small child or as they say in Italian non avanty il ragatso. After she got off the train Sibylla said she should not really have been so rude because we should be polite to people however provoking and I should not follow her example but learn to keep my inevitable reflections to myself. She said it was only because she was a bit tired because she had not been getting much sleep and otherwise she would never have been so rude. I am not so sure but I kept my inevitable reflections to myself.

5

We Never Go Anywhere

Early March, winter nearly over. Ludo still following scheme I do not understand: found him reading *Metamorphoses* the other day though he is only up to *Odyssey* 22. Seems to have slowed down on *Odyssey*, has only been reading 100 lines or so a day for past few weeks. Too tired to think of new places to go, where is there besides National Gallery National Portrait Gallery Tate Whitechapel British Museum Wallace Collection that is free? Financially in fairly good position as have typed *Advanced Angling* 1969–present, *Mother and Child* 1952–present, *You and Your Garden* 1932–1989, *British Home Decorator* 1961–present, *Horn & Hound* 1920–1976, and am now making good progress with *The Poodle Breeder*, 1924–1982. Have made virtually no progress with Japanese.

Another argument about Cunliffe. L: Why can't we go to the National Gallery again?

I: You promised you wouldn't go through doors marked Authorised Personnel Only.

L: It didn't say Authorised Personnel Only. It said Staff.

I: Exactly. In other words people who worked there, because the people who work there want to get on with their work without being disturbed by people who don't work there. If at some stage you decide to reject the theory of a Ludocentric universe do let me know.

We go to Tower Hill to catch a Circle Line train. The Circle Line is experiencing delays, so we sit down & I discover that Ludo has smuggled *Kalilah wa Dimnah* into the pushchair. He takes it out and starts reading, turning the pages quickly—the vocabulary is pretty easy and repetitive, should really have picked something harder but too late now.

A woman comes up & stares & admires & comments, How on earth did you teach so young a child?

She says she has a five-year-old herself & presses me for my methods which I explain, such as they are, & she says surely there must be more to it than that.

L: I know French and Greek and Arabic and Hebrew and Latin and I'm going to start Japanese when I finish this book and the *Odyssey*.

[What?]

L: I had to read 8 books of the *Metamorphoses* and 30 stories in the *Thousand & One Nights* and I Samuel and the Book of Jonah *and* learn the cantellation *and* do 10 chapters of *Algebra Made Easy* and now I just have to finish this book and one book of the *Odyssey*.

[*What!!!!?*]

My admirer says that's wonderful & that it's so important for small children to have a sense of achievement, & then drawing me slightly aside says that all the same it's important to keep a sense of proportion, one needs to strike a balance, dangerous to carry things to extremes, moderation in all things, not that she means to interfere.

By the looks of things I have about three days' grace before I start teaching Japanese to a child with no sense of proportion whatsoever.

My admirer is still hovering & hesitating, having struck a blow for moderation she says something or other about her own child who is no genius.

I say What about French, she might like to learn French

& she says I know it sounds awful but I haven't the time.

I say she is probably expecting too much, why not teach her just one word a day & let her colour it in in a book wherever she finds it, the secret of success is to complete a single simple task on a daily basis.

Is that what you did? she asks looking awestruck at *Kalilah wa Dimnah* (which is completely ridiculous as it is a very easy text, far *too* easy in my opinion).

No, I say. But it is still the best method.

Two Circle Line trains came and went and a District Line train pulled in and pulled out on its way to Upminster. She said But how did you get him to do all that work and I explained about the five words and the Schwan Stabilo highlighter & she said Yes but there must be more to it than that, there must be more to it than that—

so that I could not help thinking of things I would rather not think about, such as how hard it is to be nice and how hard it was going to be to be nice.

She seemed to be really interested because now a Barking train came and went and still she was here. She said what she meant was for example she had studied Latin herself, well if you teach a child French the simple task could be a word whereas in an inflected language the grammar was so frightfully complicated surely beyond the grasp of a four-year-old child.

I said I thought small children liked matching things up, it was not that big a deal, I just explained that the words had to match and he could see that they matched, though of course it probably made more sense when he got used to the idea.

She was smiling sympathetically. What a nice thing to explain to a four-year-old child.

I had not planned to give him a whole declension on the first day as I knew very well what Mr. Ma would think. L seemed to be having such a good time colouring in words with his highlighter, though, and it is always such a relief when a small child finds something to do that it is happy to go on doing, that I wrote out some tables for him (including the dual), with the comforting reflection that Mr. Ma was not there to see it.

I had to consult the dictionary to make sure of finding all the dialect forms and in the end he had lots and lots and lots of words that he could colour in and that was nice.

I told him he could colour in any of the words that he found & then I went back to John Denver leaving *Iliad* 1–12 on the chair.

Four or five hours went by. After a while I looked up and he was doing something on the floor. I went over to him and he smiled up at me. He had gone back to the beginning of *Iliad* 1 in my Oxford Classical Text, and he had highlighted his five words *and* all occurrences of the definite article all the way to the end of *Iliad* 12, so that every page had blocks of green scattered over it.

He said Where is Volume II? I need to finish this.

I said patiently after a short pause I don't know where it is, I was looking for it earlier, and I added patiently Perhaps you should learn some more words and go back over Volume I again instead. You could use a different colour. If you need more practice you can go on to Volume II.

He said All right. Can I have ten words this time?

I said Natürlich. You can have as many as you want. This is tremendously good. I thought it would be too hard for you.

He said Of course it's not too hard for me.

& I looked again at the coloured page and I said

And DON'T YOU DARE colour in ANY OTHER BOOK without ASKING ME FIRST.

That was all I said, & it was too much. A chittering Alien bursts from the breast to devour your child before your eyes. He looked down at the page,

& I returned to my work and he returned to his work.

I had tried to be patient and kind but this was not very nice.

A week went by. I have heard it said that small children have no powers of concentration. What in God's name is to keep a small child from concentrating on something? L anyway was a monomaniac. He would leap out of bed at 5:00 in the morning, put on four or five sweaters, go downstairs to get out his eight Schwan Stabilo highlighters and get to work. At about 6:30 or so he would rush upstairs to report on his progress waving a fluorescent page in my face and I disapproving of the type of parent who fobs a child off with Wonderful Wonderful would murmur Wonderful and then disarmed by a face like a new penny ask questions. Elephant stampede up and down stairs for a couple of hours & time to get up.

A week as I say went by. One day I snatched a few moments from typing to read Ibn Battuta & L came up and just looked. He didn't say anything. I knew what this meant: it meant for all my good intentions I had not been very nice. So I said: Would you like to learn it? And he naturally said he would so I went through the whole procedure again, and I gave him a little animal fable to read in *Kalilah wa Dimnah*. And now each night I would look up the next twenty words in each book and write them down for him so that it would not be so boring for him at 5:00 in the morning.

Four days went by. I tried to be careful but you can't always be careful and one day I went to look something up in Isaiah. I got out my Tanach and he came over and looked and that was that.

◉

I am reading *Let's Learn Kana—the EASY Way!!!!* L is reading *Jock of the Bushveld*.

	あ a	い i	う u	え e	お o
k	か ka	き ki	く ku	け ke	こ ko
g	が ga	ぎ gi	ぐ gu	げ ge	ご go
s	さ sa	し shi	す su	せ se	そ so
z	ざ za	じ ji	ず zu	ぜ ze	ぞ zo
t	た ta	ち chi	つ tsu	て te	と to
d	だ da	ぢ ji	づ zu	で de	ど do
n	な na	に ni	ぬ nu	ね ne	の no
h	は ha	ひ hi	ふ fu	へ he	ほ ho
b	ば ba	び bi	ぶ bu	べ be	ぼ bo
p	ぱ pa	ぴ pi	ぷ pu	ぺ pe	ぽ po
m	ま ma	み mi	む mu	め me	も mo
y	や ya		ゆ yu		よ yo
r	ら ra	り ri	る ru	れ re	ろ ro
	わ wa				を o
	ん -n				

I try to imagine presenting this to a small child.

て　かった　いん　て　はった
Te　Katta　In　Te　Hatta

ほっぽ　おん　ぽっぽ
Hoppo　On　Poppo

This is not going to work.

6

We Never Do Anything

A week went by and it was a bright, windy day. There were pale green buds on the bare black boughs of the trees. I thought we should get some fresh air but the wind was too bitter.

We took the Circle Line in a counterclockwise direction. I was still struggling to devise a system for explaining the kana (let alone the badly eroded remains of the 262 kanji once known to me let alone the 1,945 kanji in common use in Japan let alone the fragments of grammar gleaned from *Kanji from the Start* and the *Reader of Handwritten Japanese*). L was reading *Odyssey* 24. The problem was not so much a dictionary problem as the fact that L was completely fed up with the Circle Line.

After a couple of hours I began to look through one of the papers. There was an interview of the pianist Kenzo Yamamoto, who was currently on concert tour in Britain.

Whether Yamamoto was taught a simple task on a daily basis I do not know, but he had once been famous for being a prodigy. He was older now, and for the past two years he had just been notorious.

Yamamoto had started winning prizes and giving concerts when he was about 14; when he was 19 he had gone to Chad. He had then returned to concertising & created a sensation at the Wigmore Hall. People had of course gone to the Wigmore Hall expecting a sensation, but they had not expected him to play about 20 minutes of drum music after each of six Mazurkas of a Chopin recital. This was followed by the rest of the advertised programme (which was also expanded slightly to permit an unexpected replay of the six Mazurkas), with the result that the concert ended at 2:30 in the morning & people missed their trains & were unhappy.

After the Wigmore Hall episode his agent was quoted as saying that on a purely personal level he looked on him as a son but on a purely business level there were a lot of considerations, obviously they were both professionals & he wouldn't be doing him any favours if he continued to handle him purely as a personal favour.

Yamamoto hardly ever gave concerts now & no one knew whether this was his own choice or forced on him by prudent managements. The interviewer of the *Sunday Times* was trying to probe this and other hot topics while Yamamoto tried to explore the nature of percussion & other musical issues.

ST: I don't think anyone really understands why you went to Chad—

Yamamoto: Well, my teacher had always emphasised that one should keep the piano from sounding like a percussive instrument— you probably know that Chopin tried to produce the effect of a vocal line on the piano—and for years I kept thinking: But if it's a percussive instrument why shouldn't it sound like one?

He said that at the time he had this idea that drums were percussion in its purest form & that he would never understand the piano until he understood percussion in its purest form. He said he had come to see later that in a lot of ways this was an overreaction and that any sound that the instrument could make was obviously a sound it could make so that it was oversimplistic not to let it sound like a voice or a cello to the extent that it could, but at the time he was obsessed with drums & percussion.

ST: Interesting.

Yamamoto said the other thing his teacher had always emphasised had been what she called the backbone of the piece. It was not enough to perfect a beautiful surface which sounded like the human voice or a cello or some other non-percussive instrument because in the final analysis attention should not stop at the surface but be directed to the musical structure.

He said that when he was small he would sometimes work day and night to get some passage the way she wanted, at last he would think Yes, that sounds good & she would say Yes, that is very pretty but where is the music? And she would say of this or that international star, Oh so and so, he's just a virtuoso, with the utmost contempt, because if someone was not a musician he was a charlatan.

ST: Interesting.

He said: Now the thing is of course I could see what she meant, but later I started to think, Yes, but why are we so afraid of everything and what are we afraid of? We're afraid of the surface, we're afraid it will sound like what it is, what terrible thing will happen if we stop running away from these things?

Then when he was 16 he came across a book called *Drums over Africa*.

Drums over Africa was written by an Australian named Peter McPherson who had travelled around Africa in the early 20s. He took with him a wind-up gramophone and several recordings of Mozart, and the book was full of amusing episodes in which he astounded the natives with the machine or kept his wits about him to keep them from stealing it.

Most of the time people simply admired the machine itself without commenting on the music, but in one village he met a critic. This man said that the music seemed thin and uninteresting, and when he had said it several other people agreed but they could not explain why. At last they brought out a collection of drums and began to play on these—it is common in African music for two competing rhythms to be played simultaneously, but here the players unleashed six or seven. McPherson said it took some time to get used to, but as no one showed the slightest interest in appropriating the gramophone he stayed there for some time. For two months he saw nothing but the small-to-medium-sized drums brought out on the first day, but one day he saw an extraordinary ceremony.

The village was described by McPherson as a 20-day trek from St. Pierre, in a kind of desert scrub, on the edge of a small desert lake, with a sheer rock bluff at the other side, and though the first mountain foothills were maybe 20 miles away this seemed to be the same kind of rock. He had often noticed one hut a little distance from the rest, but when he had once approached it he had been warned away, and he had never seen anyone enter or leave it.

One day in the late afternoon he saw seven men enter the hut. They came out each carrying a drum taller than a man, and they carried the drums in silence to the edge of the lake and set them down in a row on the shore. Then a group of women came from another house. They carried a boy on a pallet; he seemed to have some fever, for he was wasted away and shivered and trembled as they carried him. They were singing a song in which one woman called out a line and then the others called softly back, and they laid the pallet on the shore. They stopped singing and stepped away.

The sun was near the horizon; at any moment it would be dark, for it sets quickly in the tropics. The sky was a deep dark blue. The men tilted the drums against wooden rests; they began to tap the drums very lightly with sticks, and the sound seemed to melt away over the lake. Then they stopped, and at a gesture from the leader they struck the drums a single louder blow. They stopped. Another beat. Another beat. Another beat. When they had struck the drums six times like this the sun vanished and they struck the drums once, very loudly, and stopped. Several seconds went by, until at last, from over the dark water, the sound of the drums came back. Again they struck the drums, and again the sound came back, and when this had happened seven times they laid down their sticks and walked away, and the women picked up the pallet and walked away, and McPherson saw that the boy was dead. In the morning the drums were gone.

Yamamoto said: There was something about this, the idea of percussion in its purest form coming through the air & at the same time over water, and at last hitting rock & coming back, you know coming through this very thin medium & also over a denser one & against a very solid one—& I thought I just have to hear this. I don't know how but I've got to.

For the next few years whenever Yamamoto met someone from Africa he would describe this episode in *Drums over Africa* but no one seemed to know about percussion in its purest form and the rock and water and air.

When he was 19 it was arranged that he would spend six months studying in Paris. One of the other students was from Chad, and Yamamoto asked again about percussion in its purest form and the student was rather annoyed, because whenever people thought of African music all they thought of was drums.

Drums drums drums, said this friend, if anything the most important element in African music (insofar as it made sense to generalise about *African* music which it did not) was the voice.

Don't talk to me about the voice, I said, I am not interested in the voice but in percussion in its purest form, & I told him about the drums & the lake, & I said it was a 20-day trek from a place that used to be called St. Pierre

& he said he did know of a place that used to be called that but it couldn't be the one because the people in that area had a totally different kind of music, they have these professional musicians, these griots who sing ballads and nothing like what I had described would happen there

& I said But is it a desert and is there a lake

& he said Yes but it can't possibly be there

& then he said Forget about Africa, you don't know what you want, I'm getting together some people to put on Boulez's Eclat/Multiples stick around & you can have the piano

ST: So you went to Chad.

Yamamoto: That's right.

Yamamoto said that when he finally found the place there was something almost magical about it—the lake was there, and the hill, and the hut a little way apart, and the people who would play a piece of music with six or seven rhythms all at once. The things they played while he was there melted away over the lake, and he never got to hear the other drums.

Yamamoto: I'd managed to set aside two months, which was practically unheard of; got to Chad; *incredible* hassle getting out to the village, isn't there some movie about a guy who tries to take Caruso up the Amazon?

ST: Yes?

Yamamoto: With Klaus Kinski?

ST: Yes?

Yamamoto: Well, that gives you some idea, and then to top it all I get maybe two weeks, maximum, in the village with the drums and then Kaboom! It's gone.

ST: This is the part a lot of people find hard to believe.

Yamamoto: I know, I know, how could I even *think* of going two months without practising? Sometimes I have trouble believing it myself.

Yamamoto had been staying in the village and one day he bicycled over to the mountains to see some rock paintings, taking a boy from the village as his guide. He had noticed a lot of soldiers around but he had never had the time to be interested in politics. When they got back to the village everyone in it was dead. The boy said they would kill him if they found him and Yamamoto had to help him get away. At first Yamamoto said there was nothing he could do but the boy said you've got to help me.

They were alone in a village full of dead bodies. Yamamoto said Don't you have to beat the drum for them? Or is that only for the dying?

The boy said I am too young, and then he said No, you are right.

He went to the hut. Yamamoto followed him. Inside were seven drums, but five were almost eaten away by termites, and one was quite badly damaged, and only one still stood upright. The boy took it from the hut and set it up on the shore of the lake. It seemed to be made from the trunk of some hardwood tree, though Yamamoto had never seen anything but low twisted bushes of scrub in the area.

The boy tilted the drum back against a stand, and when it was late afternoon he began to strike the drum very lightly with a stick. When the sun was close to the horizon he struck eight louder blows, and then, when the sun dropped below the horizon, he brought the stick down on the drumhead with all his might. Then he held the stick at his side and waited for several seconds, but no sound came back over the water. Again he struck the drum, and again the sound died away over the water and did not return. Then he struck it a third time so hard the drum quivered and trembled, but no sound came back and he dropped the stick in the sand.

No, he said, it will not come back, there is nothing to come back to—

And he said that they must cut it open and he would hide inside and Yamamoto would take the drum with him when he went.

Yamamoto said this was a stupid plan, the boy would be safer just—

But he couldn't think of some way the boy would be safer.

The boy was 16, the age Yamamoto had been when he first played Carnegie Hall. He said All right, we'll see what we can do.

The boy took off the top and got inside, and Yamamoto fastened the covering back on. Then he bicycled to another village and he said he needed transportation back to N'Djamena. He managed eventually to get a small truck that could take the drum, and they drove back to the village. The drum stood by the shore. The boy was inside it. The owner of the truck put the drum on the truck and they drove off.

Fifty miles down the road the truck was stopped by troops. They made the driver take the drum off the truck and they said what's in that. Nothing said Yamamoto it's just a drum I'm taking back to Japan. All right then play it said one soldier and Yamamoto tapped it lightly with a stick.

A soldier took off the cover but they had fitted another cover just inside so that it looked as though the drum was solid inside.

Yamamoto said: You see there's nothing there.

A soldier held up his machine gun, aimed at the drum, and fired a round. There was a scream, and then a whimper, and then all the soldiers fired at the drum while splinters flew up and blood seeped out onto the dirt and when they got tired of shooting they stopped and there was silence.

The soldier said: You're right there's nothing there.

Yamamoto thought his turn would be next. A soldier swung up his gun by the barrel and hit him once on the head with the handle. He fell to the ground. He said later that he wasn't afraid at first because he assumed he was going to die. Then he realised that his hands were lying in the dirt next to the boots of a soldier. He thought they would destroy his hands and he could not move for terror. Then three of them kicked him in the ribs, and he passed out.

When he came to the soldiers and the truck were gone. All that was left was the drum riddled with bullets, the ground beside it wet with blood. His papers and money were gone. His hands were all right.

He checked to see that the boy was dead and he was dead. He had nothing to bury him with, so he started walking. He walked for two days without food or water. Twice trucks passed him and refused to stop. At last one stopped and much much later he got back to Paris.

People were prepared to be sympathetic but he alienated everyone by saying Well obviously my trip didn't work out the way I'd hoped but the one bright spot is that I got back in time to take part in a production of Boulez's Eclat/Multiples.

Or people would say was it hard to put it behind you and Yamamoto would say Well when I got back Claude said I was stupid to go he said why are you so obsessed with drums drums are beside the point listen to Messiaen's Mode de valeurs et d'intensités—

—so the first thing I did when I got back was listen to the Messiaen which is about, well basically it's about the dying sound. That's what a piano produces, a dying sound. You know, the hammer strikes the string and then it bounces away again and you just have the string vibrating until it stops, and you can just let that happen or you can prolong it with a pedal or and this is where it gets interesting you have the fact that other strings will vibrate in sympathy with certain frequencies & you can just let *that* happen or you can come in with a pedal at one place or another as it dies—

Or people would say Do you think you'll ever go back to Africa and he would say Well I'd like to go back someday because my last visit wasn't as helpful as I had hoped from a musical point of view.

ST: How did this lead up to what people have called the Wigmore Hall debacle?

Yamamoto: Well my agent had made the booking a long time before. What I thought at this time was that music was not about sound but about perception of sound which means in a sense that to perceive what it is you need also some sense of what it could be but is not which includes other types of sounds and also silence.

ST: The Wigmore Hall?

Yamamoto: To put it another way, let's just take a little phrase on the piano, it sounds one way if you've just heard a big drum and another way if you've heard a gourd and another way if you've heard the phrase on another instrument and another way again if you've just heard nothing at all—there are all kinds of ways you can hear the same sound. And then, if you're practising, you hear a phrase differently depending on how you've just played it, you might play it twenty or thirty different ways and what it actually is at any time depends on all those things it might be—

ST: It sounds a little like Gould's decision to leave the concert stage because he could get a better piece of music in the recording studio.

Yamamoto: No, not at all, Gould would play the same piece nine or ten times and probably each one would be perfect and different and then using the technology he'd produce a single version which would amalgamate one or more of those, in other words there's the idea that multiplicity and the possibility of failure and perception of the taking of decisions are only for the performer, what you give the audience is a single thing. As far as I'm concerned it doesn't really matter whether you give them that one thing in a concert hall or in a recording that lets them play around with the settings on their sound system.

ST: The Wigmore Hall?

Yamamoto began to talk about the idea of a fragment, he said for instance when you were working on a piece you might take a section in one direction, let's say you might keep scaling it down and down until it was barely there & then that barely there section would sometimes be enchantingly beautiful but you would realise when you came to relate it to the next section that you could only get from that to the next section by means of something crass and stupid, some stupid violent crescendo that wasn't right or even an abrupt transition that wasn't right or it might be that you could get from one to the other but still you wanted the next part to be hard & bright and you didn't want something quite so bare before. Well everyone knew there were unfinished pieces Schubert's unfinished symphony the Mozart Requiem Mahler's Tenth Moses and Aaron & what made them unfinished was the stupid fact that the composer had not put an end to them, but if you worked on a section & got an enchantingly beautiful version that could not be used what you had in effect was a fragment, a thing that was not part of the finished work. Once you saw that you saw that you could potentially have dozens of fragments that could not be part of the finished work, and what you saw was that it was perceiving these fragments as fragments that made it possible to have a real conception of what wholeness might be in a work—and once you saw this you naturally wanted an audience to see it too because otherwise

ST: But people already complain that people listen to music in too fragmented a way. There's already a tendency to play single movements. Aren't you just taking this toward playing not even a movement but just part of a part of a piece? Where does that leave the composer?

Yamamoto said he thought you had to be able to hear how something did not work as part of a bigger thing to hear how it did and it was precisely because people couldn't hear that that they were willing to let movements be taken out of pieces.

He said: Getting back to Gould I think he had a, maybe horror is the wrong word but something like a contempt for what you could call the surface of a piece, for the aspect of a piece of music that is somehow tied to the instrument, the place where you would see showmanship. The funny thing is that I somehow feel I agree with him more than anyone else even though in a way I totally disagree with him, because I agree that what you can do physically is not the thing that's interesting. I mean, say you do a run of double octaves and maybe there's one person in the audience who could do it or maybe nobody else in the auditorium that day could do it, that's completely uninteresting, but of course if you've worked on a piece and thought about it you don't just (you hope) play it more intelligently you hear it more intelligently, and if you're the only person in the room really able to *hear* it that's horrible. But I think you get around that by showing people as much of the surface as possible

The *Sunday Times* said: Getting back to the Wigmore Hall

Yamamoto said: Sure, well I said to my agent that I'd really like to play the same piece twenty times or so to give people an idea of the piece and he said even with my name the Wigmore Hall would not be able to sell tickets.

His agent had reminded him of various clauses in his contract and he had reminded him of the obligations of a professional musician.

Yamamoto said: My agent always liked to say that you could count on a Japanese to act like a true professional. He kept saying that the booking had been made and people had already bought tickets in a way that was obviously meant to appeal to a true professional. I thought: What does that mean, to be a true professional? What's so Japanese about that?

Well, as you probably know the exchange of gifts is quite a big thing in Japan and part of it is that the gift has to be wrapped up the right way. People go there and they miss the point. They think the thing the Japanese are really worried about is wrapping it up to look right it doesn't matter if what's inside is a piece of shit. I thought: That's what I'm supposed to do, they've already bought the wrapping paper and now I'm expected to give them a piece of shit that will fit the paper, I'm supposed to be a *true professional* and feel good about it because I gave them something that would fit the paper. I thought: There's no point in talking about this.

Well, the big night came and people had bought their tickets to hear I think it was six Chopin Mazurkas the Barcarolle three Nocturnes and a Sonata. I thought: Well as long as I play the Mazurkas Barcarolle Nocturnes and Sonata it can't matter what *else* I play. I'm not saying the total package was what I would have chosen but I wanted to have the sound of the piano against the contrast of percussion in its purest form and the Chopin part had already been agreed. So I had I think it was about four hours of the drums and then also six Mazurkas one Barcarolle three Nocturnes one Sonata and six Mazurkas.

ST: With the result that a lot of people missed the 11:52 out of Paddington and were not very happy.

Yamamoto: With the result that people missed the 11:52 out of Paddington.

ST: And now you haven't given a concert in about two years?

Yamamoto: That's right.

ST: But you've promised the Royal Festival Hall that no one is going to miss their train this time.

Yamamoto: Nobody is going to be walking the streets of London at two in the morning.

ST: Was that hard?

Yamamoto: I feel pretty good about it.

It said at the end that Yamamoto was appearing that night at the Royal Festival Hall.

L though not complaining looked miserable. I kept thinking about the enchantingly beautiful fragments which could not be part of the finished whole. I kept thinking of the Mazurkas against a background of percussion in its purest form. Then I thought I should be attentive to the needs of my child, who looked absolutely miserable.

I said: How would you like to go to the South Bank Centre?

L looked surprised.

I said: We can get a table to work at, and afterwards we can go to a concert.

He said: I don't want to go to a concert.

I said: You can have a table all to yourself.

He said: Can I have an ice cream?

I said: Yes

He said: Can I have Häagen-Dazs?

I said: Yes. If they have it.

He said: Done.

I said: OK. Try to act like a rational human being.

We went to the Royal Festival Hall and I found a table as far as possible from any place selling something to eat. Ludo spread out *Call of the Wild, White Fang, Fergus, Pete, Tar-Kutu, Marduk, SQUID!, SHARK!, WOLF!, KILLER WHALE!,* and *True Tales of Survival* on a separate table. Every so often he ran off to run up and downstairs then came back then ran off then came back to work on *Odyssey* 24. Oh well.

I had already bought Ludo a pencil flashlight at Embankment. I now bought two tickets for the concert at the cheapest price. At 8:00 I checked the pushchair, minus *Call of the Wild*, at the cloakroom over stiff opposition from an unhelpful attendant, and I explained to Ludo that if he got bored he could read *Call of the Wild*. I took him to the toilet and he said he didn't have to go. I pointed out that he now knew where the toilets were, & I said that if he needed to go in the middle of the concert he could go because we had aisle seats.

I bought a programme because I thought it might have some more interesting remarks by Yamamoto. The programme for the evening was: Beethoven: 15 Variations in E♭ and Fugue on a Theme from Prometheus, Op. 35 (Eroica Variations); Brahms: Variations on a Theme by Robert Schumann, Op. 9; Webern: Variations for Piano,

Op. 27. Interval. Brahms Ballades, Op. 10: No. 1 in D minor, based on the old Scottish ballad Edward; No. 2 in D major; No. 3 in B minor; No. 4 in B major.

There was a certain feeling of suspense (or at least I thought there was) as the concertgoers walked through the doors, because people were half expecting to see a collection of drums. Instead there was only a grand piano. Yamamoto walked onstage and there was a round of applause. He sat down and began to play the Eroica Variations.

The Eroica Variations came to an end and there was a round of applause. Yamamoto walked offstage and returned and sat down. He began to play the Variations on a Theme by Robert Schumann.

The Variations on a Theme by Robert Schumann came to an end and there was a round of applause. Yamamoto walked offstage and returned and sat down. He began to play Webern's Variations for Piano, Op. 27.

The Variations for Piano came to an end in six minutes flat and there was a round of applause. Yamamoto walked offstage and it was time for the interval.

I bought Ludo an ice cream and I read the Scottish ballad Edward, which was reprinted in the programme.

The interval came to an end. It was about 9:00.

We walked back into the hall and there was a soft noise as of eight out of ten people laughing softly in quick succession in the audience. There were a lot of things on stage that had not been there before. There were a lot of drums, and a set of hand bells, and two glasses of water on a stand—you couldn't take in everything all at once. Yamamoto came back onstage to a round of applause and sat down and began to play.

At first I thought he had begun to play Op. 10 No. 1 based on the old Scottish ballad Edward, a piece I had never heard before. I realised after a while that this was not what he was doing. He was playing a couple of bars—maybe five or six chords—over and over. I had no idea whether these featured in Op. 10 No. 1 or not. Sometimes you see a painting where the painter has put paint on the canvas and then scraped almost all of it away; at first he seemed to be scraping the sound away until there was almost nothing there, but even the softest sound on a piano dies away & 9 or 10 times he seemed to bring in a pedal at different stages of this dying so that you heard the other chords over different forms of the first, or he used the sustaining pedal or no pedal at all. It was hard to know what was going on—I thought maybe this phrase did come from Op. 10 No. 1 and you were supposed to see that these were variations, but though in a sense they were variations they were not a piece. This went on for about 20 minutes or half an hour. Then there was a pause, and then he began to do the same thing with a different phrase. This went on for about 20 minutes or half an hour. Then there was a pause, and then he began to play a piece which seemed likely to be Op. 10 No. 1 based on the Scottish ballad Edward, and which did contain the two phrases he had been playing for the last hour. This went on for seven minutes. He stopped and there was a round of applause.

Yamamoto stood up & walked upstage to a drum and struck the drum, and in the aftermath of the soft boom he returned to the piano and sat down and began to play Op. 10 No. 1 in D minor. This went on for five minutes. He stopped and there was a round of applause and a lot of people left.

It was about 10:15. Ludo said Didn't he play that before and I said Yes and he said Why did he play it again and I said I'll explain later and somebody laughed and said he'd love to be a fly on the wall. Ludo went back to reading *Call of the Wild*.

For the next seven and a half hours Yamamoto played Op. 10 No. 1 in D minor, & sometimes he seemed to play it exactly the same five times running but next to the sound of a bell or an electric drill or once even a bagpipe and sometimes he played it one way next to one thing and another way next to another. Some of these sounds were produced at the time and others were recordings, and after six and a half hours he stopped stopping to start the other sounds: a tape began to run & he kept playing. The tape was of traffic and footsteps & people talking and he played Op. 10 No. 1 nine times while it ran, and naturally you could see that you couldn't really hear how he was playing it or even how he was dealing with the two phrases. At 5:45 the tape came to an end and the piece came to an end and there was silence for 20 seconds or so, and then he played the piece so that you heard it after and over the silence. This went on for six minutes and then he stopped and there was a moment of silence and then he raised his hands to the keys.

You expected to hear Op. 10 No. 1 in D minor for the 60th time, but instead were shocked to hear in quick succession Op. 10 No. 2 in D major, Op. 10 No. 3 in B minor and Op. 10 No. 4 in B major, and you only heard them once each. It was as if after the illusion that you could have a thing 500 ways without giving up one he said No, there is only one chance at life once gone it is gone for good you must seize the moment before it goes, tears were streaming down my face as I heard these three pieces each with just one chance of being heard if there was a mistake then the piece was played just once with a mistake if there was some other way to play the piece you heard what you heard and it was time to go home.

The three pieces were over in about 20 minutes. He took his hands from the keys and the room was absolutely silent.

At last he stood up and bowed and there was a round of applause from the 25 people left in the room. He walked to the centre of the stage and picked up a microphone, and he said:

I think the trains will be running by now. I hope you all get home safely. Thanks for staying.

He put the microphone down & walked to the box with the two

glasses of water & took a sip from one, and then he put it back and walked offstage.

I thought: How can he ever play in public again?

I started thinking about the best way to get home, should I cross the river & take the District Line or maybe it would actually be easier to walk right up to Tottenham Court Road & catch a Number 8, & then I remembered that I had moved since I last went to a concert & that I now had a son. The reason this had slipped my mind was that the seat beside me was empty.

I made my way calmly toward the nearest exit where a couple of ushers were talking in low, angry voices. I asked if they had seen a little boy. They said they had not. I asked politely whether he could be paged, and one said not at this time of the morning. I was about to demand hysterically that he be paged when my eye was caught by my programme, on which was the following reassuring message:

Dear Sibylla I am tired so I have decided to walk home.

I thought: Let's think about this rationally. There is no point in getting worried or upset when for all I know he may be safe at home. First I will get the pushchair & go home, and then if he is not there I can decide whether to get worried.

I got the pushchair from the cloakroom & I took a taxi home so that I would know as soon as possible whether to be worried. The house was still locked & he did not have a key. I opened the door and went inside. I thought: Well, of course if he got in somehow he would be upstairs in bed, so I went upstairs. He was lying asleep in his bed still wearing his clothes. His window was open. He had scraped the skin on one cheek.

I went back downstairs and I thought: Let's think about this rationally. This has been terrifying but should I tell him never to do it again just because I was terrified? What are the risks that were run?

Traffic: negligible at that time of night. Muggers: possible but surely less likely to attack a small child than (say) a man likely to be carrying cash or wearing an expensive watch. Rapists: possible but surely less likely to attack a small child than (say) me & I would not have thought I was running a big risk if I had walked home. Kidnappers: distinguish possible from likely. Satanists: distinguish possible from likely. Type of person who enjoys inflicting pain on the defenceless: distinguish possible from likely.

Then I thought: Anyway this is stupid. When am I ever going to go to a concert? So why scare him with a lot of things that might have happened? I'll just say that if it happens again he should ask me for money for a taxi because it's a long walk home. And thinking of taxis I realised that I had spent some £35 that I could not afford. I turned on the computer and I turned to page 27 of *The Poodle Breeder*, 1972 (Vol. 48, No. 3): 'Clipping the Country Poodle—Secrets of Success'.

❖

Ludo got up at 11:00. I went on typing until 2:00. That was about seven hours which was good going for the day, and paid off for the concert and taxi and ice cream. I thought: 1: If I could do this every day I would have hours left over and 2: If I could play a piece 60 times in seven hours I could probably learn to play the piece. I had a longing to hear again Brahms' Ballade Op. 10 No. 2 which I had heard only once at the concert the night before.

I took Ludo to the Barbican & I borrowed Brahms Piano Works Vol. 1 & took it home. As I had done so much typing already that day & as I had had no sleep I thought I would try to play the piece, and I began to play just one little phrase over and over. I tried to vary it this way & that but it always sounded pretty much the same except sometimes with a few mistakes and sometimes with several and once in a while with none. I played the phrase again and again until at last I could play it with a lot of mistakes every single time and when I had played it with a lot of mistakes for the tenth time in a row Ludo began to laugh.

I turned around on the chair and looked at him. He was still laughing.

I thought I would probably hit him if I stayed in the room, so I went upstairs into the bathroom and shut the door. It was bitterly cold. I put down the toilet lid and sat on it.

I once read somewhere about some research that was done on baby monkeys who were given cloth surrogate mothers which became monsters: one expelled jets of air—one had an embedded wire frame that sprang out and threw the baby to the floor—another ejected sharp brass spikes on command. The response of the baby monkeys was always the same: they clung ever more tightly to the monster, or if thrown off waited for spikes to disappear & returned to cling to their mother. Though sometimes I think I am the monster of spikes & wire & jets of air that is not so bad for the researchers were not able, through these methods, to produce psychopathology in the young monkeys, but perhaps

The researchers stopped working with mothers of cloth & went on to produce monstrous mothers of flesh, they reared female monkeys in isolation & arranged for their impregnation & when the babies were born some mothers were indifferent & others were brutal or lethal they would crush the infant's skull with their teeth or smash its face to the floor & rub it back & forth and what if

I thought: Let's think about this rationally or rather let's not think about this at all. I thought: I have not slept for a long time, I will go to bed and when I wake up everything will look different.

I thought: This research raises more questions than it answers, the thing that would be really interesting would be a psychological profile of the type of person who instead of occupying himself with Aristarchus and Zenodotus and Didymus addresses himself to producing psychopathology in the infant monkey. I tried to persuade myself that the chief researcher was probably a pre-Spock baby, I thought there was a doctor pre-Spock who for a while held the influential theory that a baby should be held to a timetable & fed according to timetable regardless of cries screams etc., but I would have liked to know for sure. What was to stop Ludo from reading of monkeys placed for 45 days in a vertical chamber with stainless-steel sides producing severe and persistent psychopathological behaviour of a depressive nature for 9 months or more & determining that much remained to be done in examining the relative importance of chamber size, chamber shape, duration of confinement, age at time of confinement & other factors & how could I be sure that on reaching adulthood he would not always be looking for a surrogate monkey for a mother

I slept for a long time and when I woke up I felt better.

I thought: He starts school in the fall.

I thought if I went downstairs I would probably not bite his head off so I went downstairs.

Ludo was sitting on the floor.

He said I've finished *Odyssey* 24!

I said cordially That's WONDERFUL

and because I always do what I say I'll do I said Well, shall I teach you the hiragana?

And he said It's all right, I already know it.

I said What?

He said I learned it myself. Out of the *Japanese Reader*.

I said Well, do you want me to teach you the katakana?

He said I know that too. It wasn't too hard.

I said When did you do this?

He said A couple of weeks ago. I thought I would spare you the hassle.

I said that was wonderful. I said Write it down for me now so I can see you got it right,

and he wrote on a piece of graph paper the little grid of hiragana and the little grid of katakana and he said See? It's easy.

I looked at it and it looked right so I said That's fantastic. I kissed him four or five thousand times & I said Aren't you smart? I said What else do you know? Do you know lots of words?

He said he knew some words. He said he knew Tadaima and Ohaiyogozaimasu and Konnichiwa and Sayonara and Tada kassen ni wa zuibun deta ga.

I said this was very good. I said Well do you want me to show you some kanji?

He said I think I can probably do it myself.

I knew what this meant, it meant for all my good intentions I had been a monster. I said I'm sure you can do it yourself. I said Well would you like me to explain the system?

He said OK.
I explained the system.

7

End of the Line

I came downstairs early to get ready for his birthday.

I put things away for three hours and I found various notes I had made for posterity. I am not sure how helpful they will be for posterity—but on reflection I think the thing to do is approach the subject in a systematic way once he is in school. He starts in a few months; the fact is that in five consecutive hours I could say everything that needs to be said. I have put the notes in a file.

Ludo is still sleeping—he stayed up till 3:00 in the morning last night because it was the night before his birthday and I said he could stay up as late as he wanted. I will watch a video until he gets up.

40 bandits stop on a hill above a village in Japan. They decide to raid it after the barley harvest. A farmer overhears.

A village meeting is held. The farmers despair.

1 leaps to his feet with burning eyes.

Let's make bamboo spears! Let's kill all the bandits!

You can't, says 2.

Impossible, says 3.

A soft rain is falling. The brown paper window pane is fluttering in the air.

The farmers consult the village patriarch.

He tells them to find hungry samurai.

4 farmers go in search of samurai: Rikichi of burning eyes, Yohei (can't), Manzo (impossible) and no name.

I think spring is here.

The farmers see a crowd of people. A samurai has gone to the river's edge to be shaved by a monk.

A man with a moustache and a sword pushes his way through the crowd and squats scratching his chin. (It's Toshiro Mifune)

This is really shocking. I fell asleep 10 minutes into a masterpiece of modern cinema, and when I woke up the whole recruitment section was over.

STOP. REWIND.

Signs of life in the next room.

STOP. PLAY.

The master swordsman has changed his mind, you don't know why. 6 samurai get ready to leave for the hills in the morning.

In comes a gambler, who says they've found a really tough samurai.

Katsushiro picks up a stick and strides to the door: one last test.

Gambler: That's unfair

Kambei: If he's as good as you say he'll parry the blow

Gambler: But he's drunk

Kambei: A good samurai would never get so drunk

A man runs through the door; Katsushiro brings down the stick hard on his head. It's Toshiro Mifune, who falls to the ground.

Mifune looks at the samurai. He recognises Kambei.

You had the nerve to ask whether I was a samurai

I'm a samurai all right
Don't go away. I'll show you something [takes out scroll]
Look at this
Handed down in my family for generations

Mifune is making strange faces and noises now replicated in miniature by my side. Kurosawa is right, he can turn on a dime & watching quicksilver Mifune stern Shimura ardent Kimura I suddenly
realise that everything is going to be all right, I am providing my fa-
therless uncleless boy not with 8 male role models (6 samurai 1 gate-
crashing farmer's son 1 fearless farmer) but 16 (8 characters 8 actors)
17 including Kurosawa who does not appear. Only one of the characters is a perfectionist in the practice of his art but all 8 actors & the
director who does not appear show this terrible perfectionism making a total of 17 male role models (not including the extras).

[Kambei, reading] You're this Kikuchiyo?
Born in the Second Year of Tensho . . . [bursts out laughing]
You look remarkably old for your age
Looking at you I can hardly believe that you are 13
[All the samurai burst out laughing]

L: Where did you steal this?
L: Who do you think you are, calling me a thief?

Now we are six.

iii

After this superb battle . . . one might expect the picture to end with some kind of statement that he has at last grown-up, that he has arrived, that he has *become* something—the great judo champion.

Donald Richie, *"Sugata Sanshiro,"*
The Films of Akira Kurosawa

1

1, 2, 3

20 March, 1993

Today is my sixth birthday.

I got an Oxford-Duden Japanese Pictorial Dictionary and a little book about a cat in Japanese that was all in kana and a book which I couldn't tell what it was because it was all in Japanese, but Sibylla said it was Sugata Sanshiro by Tomita Tsuneo. She said I would have to share her kanji dictionary and her Kodansha romanised dictionary and her grammar and she said unfortunately Sugata Sanshiro was not available in English so I might find it rather hard going, but that it seemed to be a marvellous story going by what Mr. Richie says about the film and she got out a book by Mr. Richie and said look at this, can you read this? I asked if it was in English and she said yes so of course I could read it. Apparently there is quite a dramatic scene in the book when Sugata's judo teacher tells him to kill himself. This is what Mr. Richie says about my book:

He is using all of the correct judo procedures, besting one man after the other. All of this is shown with fast cutting at its most seductive. It is an exhilarating passage. It is like something from the ordinary Japanese fight-picture, only much more skillfully done. We—not yet guessing what the picture is about—think: that Sugata is a real man, a real hero. The crowd thinks so. There are cries of how wonderful he is, how marvelous. Sugata, carried away, attacks one man after the other, always winning.

There is a cut to the judo teacher's room. Everything is still. He does not move, there is no movement on the screen, and after the furious motion of the sequence directly before it is like an admonition. He sits there, as though waiting, the seconds pass. Then Sugata, his kimono torn, comes in.

Teacher: Well, you must feel good after having thrown so many people around.

Sugata: I'm sorry.

Teacher: I rather wanted to see you in action. You're very strong, really very strong indeed. Maybe you are even stronger than I am now. But, you know, there is very little similarity between your kind of judo and my kind of judo. Do you know what I mean? You do not know how to use it, you do not know the way of life. And to teach judo to someone who does not know that is like giving a knife to a madman.

Sugata: But I know it.

Teacher: That is a lie. To act as you do, without meaning or purpose, to hate and attack—is that the way of life? No—the way is loyalty and love. This is the natural truth of heaven and earth. It is the ultimate truth and only through it can a man face death.

Sugata: I can face death. I'm not afraid to die right now, if you order it.

Teacher: Shut up, you're nothing but a common street-fighter.

Sugata: I'm not afraid to die.

Teacher: Then go and die.

Then Sugata does an extraordinary thing. He opens the shoji and without a look backward or below he leaps.

I am really looking forward to reading the book.

The Pictorial Dictionary had a picture of a samurai on the front so first I looked for that. It was quite hard to find because it is in Ethnology, and when I found it the only words it gave were the words for samurai and for armour, and it didn't even give the character for samurai it just spelled it out in hiragana.

I did not want to say anything to Sibylla because I did not want to hurt her feelings but I think she guessed something because she asked what's the matter. I said Nothing and she said Doh ka na? very sceptically. Doh ka na? means Really? in Japanese. I showed her the samurai and she said it was absolutely appalling that it did not give the kanji and that it was probably because they thought it was too hard for people, so what I should do was write a letter to the editor and sign it Ludo Age Six. I asked if I could write it on the computer and she said how will he know you are really six? She said to be sure to put the character in my letter so I am going to.

侍

Sibylla is watching Seven Samurai again. I have seen it before several times so I decided to start reading Sugata Sanshiro. We are each going to pick a character every day and master them thoroughly on a daily basis starting tomorrow. Today I just learned two words that Sibylla gave me that come up in the book.

柔術 jujitsu   柔道 judo

Ju means soft and jitsu means art or skill and do means way and apparently the characters turn up in other compounds. I already know all the hiragana and katakana.

Finally I looked at the first page of the book. Japanese is the hardest language in the world.

I did not want to colour in the characters that I knew because this is the only Japanese book that we have apart from two of Sibylla's. So I decided to try to find another character in the dictionary and it took about an hour to find it. The characters all look quite similar so it is hard to remember anything if you do not colour them in as you go along. After a while Sibylla looked up. She stopped the video and said what's the matter. I said Nothing. She came over and looked at the page of the book and said how are you ever going to learn this if you don't colour in the characters? She said these little Japanese books are so cheap, it only cost a fiver, we can always get another. She said she wanted me to enjoy my birthday, and she said if anything was bothering me I should let her know.

She said I could ask as many questions as I wanted because it was my birthday. I said who is my father? Sibylla said she was sorry, but she could not tell me. She said he was a travel writer and she had only met him once.

I think maybe he is somebody famous.

21 March, 1993

Today we each picked a character. We are going to do this every day until we know them all. There are 1945 and I already know three so if we do two a day we will know them all in 971 days. I wanted to do 20 a day because then we would be finished in three months but Sibylla said no it would be terrible to wake up thinking we had to do 20 whereas we could always do more if we felt like it.

Sibylla picked 人 JIN person/hito person. JIN is the exogenous Chinese lexeme and hito is an indigenous Japanese lexeme.

I picked

 yaku flute 17-stroke radical for musical instrument

Unfortunately Halpern does not seem to have any characters that use the radical.

After we had thoroughly mastered our characters I asked Sibylla where she met my father. Apparently Sibylla met my father at a party. Everyone at the party wanted to talk to him but he decided to talk to Sibylla and when she decided to leave the party he decided to leave too.

22 March, 1993

Sibylla picked 大 DAI TAI (big)/ō/(big) and she wanted me to pick 太 TAI huge/futo(i) (thick) because it would be easy to remember.

I picked 璽 JI (imperial seal). I said if I could have 爾 JI (that) she could have 太 but she said we could do them tomorrow.

After breakfast I started going through Sugata Sanshiro. I coloured in Sugata Sanshiro wherever it appeared and also the characters for judo and jujitsu in the second half of the book. The ones I picked have not come up yet.

Today I asked Sibylla about my father but she said she did not want to talk about it. I said at least tell me his first name but she said No. I said she could just tell me the letter it starts with but she said No.

23 March, 1993

太 TAI huge/futo(i) (thick)

爾 JI (that)

24 March, 1993

Today Sibylla picked 水 SUI (water)/mizu (water). This time she wanted me to pick 氷 HYŌ (ice)/kōri (ice)/hi (ice)/kō(ru) (freeze)(!). I said I thought that was boring because it was almost exactly like mizu and Sibylla said that was the whole point. I said if she wanted to pick boring characters she could but I was picking

 SŌ (algae, seaweed; elegant expression, rhetorical flourish)/ mo (algae, duckweed, seaweed)

I said I would learn 氷 if we could also learn

 KEN (cocoon)/mayu (cocoon)

25 March, 1993

氷 HYŌ (ice)/kōri (ice)/hi (ice)/kō(ru) (freeze)

 KEN (cocoon)/mayu (cocoon)

26 March, 1993

木 BOKU MOKU (tree, wood)/ki (tree, wood)
大木 taiboku (gigantic tree)

 SUI (jade green, emerald green, verdure; kingfisher)

27 March, 1993

森 SHIN (thick woods)/mori (thick woods)
森森 shinshin deeply forested

亀 KI (turtle, tortoise)/kame (turtle, tortoise)

    After we had thoroughly mastered our characters we went to the library. I have been trying all week to find out my father's name but Sibylla will not even tell me the first letter. I decided to borrow Kon Tiki.

28 March, 1993

Sibylla and I had another argument today about characters. Sibylla said if she picked 火 KA (fire)/hi (fire) and I picked 炎 EN (flame, blaze)/honō (flame, blaze) and if we bore in mind the fact that 巛 was the radical magarigawa for river we would understand in an intuitive way why 災 SAI/wazawa(i) meant natural calamity/disaster and we would then see why 人災 jinsai was a manmade calamity and 火災 kasai was fire or conflagration. I said is Thor Heyerdahl my father? Sibylla said certainly not. I said well if you want to pick all those characters you can, are you picking them? Sibylla said aren't you? I said if she got four including the radical for river I wanted

翳 EI (shade, gloom)/kage(ri) (shade, gloom)

鼎 kanae (ritual cauldron, tripod vessel)/TEI (triangular)

黽 BŌ (toad, frog) and

201

虎 KO (tiger)/tora (tiger)

I said so are you picking four, and Sibylla said yes because she could not wait four days for the term jinsai which was obviously an indispensable euphemism for small child. I said in that case I wanted

虐 GYAKU (cruel, savage, tyrannical, oppressive)/shiita(geru) (oppress, persecute, tyrannise, grind down)

instead of

黽 BŌ (toad, frog).

Sibylla said Dozo, jinsai. She obviously thought this was very funny.

29 March. Today I finished Kon Tiki. I have decided to learn how to clean a fish.

30 March. Today Sibylla and I practised cleaning a fish. Sibylla was rather annoyed because I did not want to eat it.

31 March. I have started reading Into the Heart of Borneo. I wanted to practise cleaning a chicken but Sibylla said she was not in the mood. We went to Ohio Fried Chicken instead.

1 April. Sibylla still did not feel like cleaning a chicken today. I asked if my father's name was Ludo and she said no. I asked if it was David and she said no. I asked if it was Steven and she said no. I said well what is it then and she said Rumpelstiltskin. Then she suggested we go out to Ohio Fried Chicken. I asked if it was really Rumpelstiltskin and she said no.

2 April. Today I finished Into the Heart of Borneo. I have decided to practise sleeping on the floor. I have started Arabian Sands.

3 April. Today I was still reading Arabian Sands. It was interesting. The Bedou do not wear shoes. This is to harden their feet. I asked Sibylla if we could clean a chicken today and she said No.

25 April

I have read Kon Tiki, Into the Heart of Borneo, Arabian Sands, Journey into Danger!, Quest for Adventure!, The Snow Leopard, In Patagonia, Amazon Nights, To Caucasus, Tents on the Steppe, Igloo Winter, With Camel and Compass, Among Pygmies and After Alexander. Today I asked Sibylla if she ever read any of them. She was watching Seven Samurai and I thought she might drop a clue while her mind was otherwise occupied. It was at the part where Kyuzo fights the other samurai. She said she had read In Patagonia. After Kyuzo killed the other samurai she burst out laughing. She said she had never even met Bruce Chatwin. I asked if she had ever met any of the others. She turned and looked at me without a word and then she looked back at the TV.

I am a bit fed up with these Japanese characters as none of them turn up in Sugata Sanshiro. We have mastered 98 so far. A few of Sibylla's characters have turned up but not one of mine. Also I have looked up most of the characters in the book now and some of them are not even in the dictionary! It is extremely frustrating.

26 April

Today we went to the library. I got Tracks Across Alaska, Ticket to Latvia, Night Train to Turkestan, Idle Days in Patagonia, In the Steps of Stanley, In Search of Genghis Khan and Danziger's Travels.

12 May

I have finished Sugata Sanshiro. There were some things that I did not understand because Sibylla could not answer a lot of my questions. Sibylla said I was being very quiet these days and she had done an enormous amount of work and we would go to Books Nippon and buy me another book in Japanese. I said I would like to get a book about an octopus. We asked at the counter and the lady said she would see if they had anything. Finally she showed us some books. We think we have bought a book about an octopus but we are not quite sure.

13 May

Today I finished Tracks Across Alaska. I decided to start reading Ticket to Latvia. Sibylla did a lot of typing and then she watched Seven Samurai for a while. When it got to where they get to the village I asked if she had actually read anything by my father. She said not if she could help it. I said what do you mean? She said someone in the office gave her one of his books so she had to read some of it. She said she said to the person that it seemed to have rather a lot of logical mistakes and the person said what difference does it make. I said casually do you still have it? She turned her head and looked at me. Then she said no, I didn't keep it and looked back at the TV. I said who was the person? She kept looking at the TV. She said she couldn't remember, they had all been crazy about him.

So all I need to do is find someone who was in the office and ask who they were all crazy about. The only problem is that I think they were all fired. When I am a bit older I can do some detective work and trace them.

14 May

Today was a real false alarm. I was practising my Japanese characters when all of a sudden I noticed that Sibylla was looking at my library books! I held my breath and watched her. After a while she picked up Danziger's Travels and started turning the pages, and then she went over and sat down! She looked at it with a very sad expression and read pages here and there, sighing from time to time. At one point she said Isfahan under her breath! And then without even looking up she said ironically don't leap to conclusions.

I said Why won't you tell me who it is?

She said Because he doesn't know about you.

I said Why didn't you tell him?

She said Because I didn't want to see him again.

1 said Why didn't you want to see him again?

She said I don't want to talk about it.

Maybe he was about to set out on an expedition when they met. He had raised all the money for the expedition and if she told him about me he would have had to give her the money. But she knew his heart was set on the expedition so she didn't tell him.

15 May

Sibylla got mad at me today because I asked a question about my father. All I did was ask if he knew any languages. She looked at me and said I want you to hear something. She had been typing but now she got up and said we had to go to the library even though we had just been there yesterday.

We went all the way to the Barbican and into the music library and she asked if they had anything by Liberace. They said they didn't. Sibylla said this couldn't wait so we took the Circle Line to King's Cross and then we took the Piccadilly Line to Pic-

cadilly Circus and we went into Tower Records. They said Liberace was in Easy Listening so we went up to Easy Listening.

They had a lot of things by Liberace but the cheapest was a
cassette for £9.99.

£9.99! exclaimed Sibylla holding it in her hand. It breaks
my heart but it must be done.

She bought the tape and we went home.

When we got home Sibylla put the tape on the tape player.
It was quite old-fashioned music, and before each piece the performer would make a few jokes to the audience. The whole time
it was playing Sibylla watched me. When it was over she said,
What do you think?

I said it was rather old-fashioned but he played the piano
quite well.

Sibylla didn't say anything. She went to a drawer and took
out a postcard. It was a picture of some Greek girls painted by
Lord Leighton.

What do you think of this? she said.

I said it was a picture about ancient Greece and they were
playing ball.

Anything else? she said.

I said it was quite good the way you could see the wind
blowing because of the way he had painted their togas.

Then she got an old magazine out of a drawer. She opened
it to a page and said Read this. So I started reading. At first I
thought maybe it was something my father had written but it
wasn't about travel.

What do you think? she said.

I said it was rather boring but I supposed it was quite well
written.

Sibylla put the magazine on the floor. She said, You will not
be ready to know your father until you can see what's wrong with
these things.

I said, When will that be?

She said, I don't know, millions of people have gone to the grave admiring them.

I said, Well why don't you tell me what's wrong?

She said, I won't say it's better for you to work it out for yourself, la formule est banale. Even when you see what's wrong you won't really be ready. You should not know your father when you have learnt to despise the people who have made these things. Perhaps it would be all right when you have learnt to pity them, or if there is some state of grace beyond pity when you have reached that state.

I said, Let me see the magazine again.

Then I read the whole article, but I couldn't see anything wrong except that it was boring. I looked at the picture again but I couldn't see what was wrong. I wanted to listen to the tape again but Sibylla said she could not stand to hear it again in one day.

I said, It's not fair, nobody else has to wait until they're old enough to know who their father is.

She said, We should not elevate the fortuitous to the desirable.

I said, How do you know I'm old enough to know YOU?

She said, What makes you think I think you are?

28 May

Sibylla has stopped mastering Japanese characters because she has too much work to do. I have mastered 243 thoroughly. Today she started typing and then she watched me working on my characters and then she sighed and got out a book. Later she put it down and I saw that it was the Autobiography of J. S. Mill. Rather surprisingly when she put it down she got out Mr. Richie's book and she said, Can you read this? Mr. Richie's book is in English so obviously I can read it. She said, Well read this for me. So I read a paragraph. It was about the villain in Sugata Sanshiro.

He is a man of the world—which Sugata is certainly not. He is well dressed, wears a moustache, is even slightly foppish. Also, he obviously knows what he is about. He is so good that he need never show his strength. He would not, one feels, ever resort to throwing people around as we know Sugata has done. And yet something is missing in him. Sugata may not know the "way of life" but at least he is learning. This man will never know it. He shows it in little ways. At one point, smoking a cigarette—the mark of a dandy in Meiji Japan—he does not bother to look for an ashtray. Instead, he disposes of his ash in an open flower, part of an arrangement on a nearby table.

Sibylla asked, What do you think it means?
I said, I think it means we should respect nature.
Sibylla asked, What?
I said, The villain puts ash in a flower whereas the hero is inspired by the natural beauty of the world around us.
Sibylla said, Hmmm.
I couldn't think of what else it could mean and Sibylla didn't say. After a while she went into the kitchen to make a cup of coffee and I went to look at the book by J. S. Mill. It was blood chilling!
J. S. Mill started to learn to read when he was two, just like me, but he started Greek when he was three. I only started when I was four. By the time he was seven he had read the whole of Herodotus, Xenophon's Cyropaedia and Memorials of Socrates, some of the lives of the philosophers by Diogenes Laertius, portions of Lucian and Isocrates' ad Demonicum and ad Nicoclem, as well as the first six dialogues of Plato, from the Euthyphro to the Theaetetus!!!! He also read a lot of historians I have never even

heard of. He didn't start the Iliad and Odyssey until later whereas I have read both but they are the only thing I have read. I don't think he did any Arabic or Hebrew but the things I have read in them are rather easy and anyway I have not read a lot.

The thing that is worrying me is that Mr. Mill was rather stupid and had a bad memory and he grew up 180 years ago. I thought that it was quite unusual for a boy my age to read Greek because a lot of people on the Circle Line were surprised that I was reading it but now I think that this is probably fallacious. Most of the people on the Circle Line did not say anything at all but I thought they would be surprised because the people who said something were surprised. This is stupid because if they were not surprised why would they say something? And now I am supposed to start school in three months.

2

a, b, c

6 September, 1993

Today we went to the school to talk to my teacher. Sibylla was very nervous about it. I think she was worried because she knew I would be behind. Every time I asked her she said not to worry about it. She has an old book called Six Theories of Child Development but it is not very specific.

When we reached the school we encountered an unexpected setback.

We went into the year one classroom and Sibylla introduced herself.

'I'm Sibylla Newman, and this is Stephen,' she explained to the teacher, though actually she hadn't been able to find the birth certificate to make sure before we left.

'I think you may be his teacher this year,' she added. 'I thought I should talk to you.'

The teacher's name was Linda Thompson. 'I'll just check the print-out,' she replied.

She took out a print-out and perused it.

'I can't seem to find Stephen,' she reported at last!

'Who?' queried Sibylla.

'Stephen? You did say his name was Stephen?' enquired Ms. Thompson.

'Oh yes, yes I did,' confirmed Sibylla. 'Stephen. Or Steve. It's a bit soon to tell.'

'Pardon?'

'He's a bit young to reach a final decision.'

'Are you sure this is the right school?' asked Ms. Thompson.

'Well, we live right down the street,' replied Sibylla.

'You should have registered for a place last year,' Ms. Thompson informed her.

'Good heavens,' exclaimed Sibylla. 'I had no idea. But what do I do now?'

Ms. Thompson said she thought all the places were filled.

'So does that mean he should wait another year?' enquired Sibylla.

'Oh no. He's legally required to attend school. Besides, you wouldn't want him to fall behind. It's very important for children to be at the same level as others in their age group.'

'That's what I wanted to talk to you about,' commented Sibylla. 'He's never been to play group or anything. I just did things with him at home, and I'm a little worried . . .'

'Oh, he'll catch up in no time,' Ms. Thompson assured her. 'But he really mustn't miss a year. How old is Stephen now?'

'Six,' Sibylla informed her.

'SIX!' ejaculated Ms. Thompson. She glanced at me in dismay. 'Stephen,' she said cordially, 'why don't you go and look at the building blocks down at the end of the classroom?'

'Surely we should not discuss his education in his absence,' demurred Sibylla.

Ms. Thompson appeared agitated. She exclaimed, 'He should have started when he was five!!!'

Sibylla replied, 'Five! I'm sure I started school when I was six.'

Ms. Thompson observed that in Britain all children started school at the age of five, and that a year or two of nursery school was recommended.

Sibylla queried, 'So you mean he could have started school last year?'

Ms. Thompson asseverated, 'Not only could but should, it is extremely important for a child to be with his peers as part of the learning experience.'

This is exactly what it said in the book. 'During the crucial formative period of children's lives, the school functions as the primary setting for the cultivation and social validation of cognitive competencies,' I concurred.

'What was that?' questioned Ms. Thompson.

'I'll just go and have a word with the head,' interpolated Sibylla. 'Lu— Stephen, you wait here.'

I did not want to make Sibylla feel guilty because I had missed a year of school so I thought this would be a good time to find out what I had missed.

I remarked to Ms. Thompson, 'Could you give me some idea of the material covered in year one because I am afraid I am a long way behind the rest.'

'I'm sure you'll adjust beautifully,' assured Ms. Thompson, with a warm smile.

I persevered, 'Have they read Isocrates' Ad Demonicum?'

Ms. Thompson said they had not. I was glad because it sounds hard. I probed, 'What about the Cyropaedia?'

Ms. Thompson asked what it was. I explained that it was by Xenophon and I did not really know what it was about. Ms. Thompson said she had never heard of anyone reading it in year one.

I enquired, 'Well, what *do* people read?'

Ms. Thompson said abilities and interests differed and people read different things.

I said, 'Well, I have only read the Iliad and the Odyssey in Greek and De Amicitia and Metamorphoses 1–8 in Latin and Moses and the Bullrushes and Joseph and his Manycoloured Coat and Jonah and I Samuel in Hebrew and Kalilah wa Dimnah and 31 Arabian Nights in Arabic and just Yaortu la Tortue and Babar and Tintin in French and I have only just started Japanese.'

Ms. Thompson smiled at me. She is very pretty. She has wavy blond hair and blue eyes. She said usually people would not study Arabic or Hebrew or Japanese at school at all and they would usually not start French or Greek or Latin until the age of twelve or so!

I was absolutely amazed!!!! I said that J. S. Mill had begun Greek at the age of three.

Ms. Thompson asked who was J. S. Mill!!!!!!!!

I explained that Mr. Mill was a Utilitarian who died 120 years ago.

'Oh, a Victorian,' commented Ms. Thompson. 'Well, you know, Stephen, the Victorians placed a much greater value on facts for their own sake than we do. Now we're more interested in what someone can do with what they know. One of the most important parts of school is just learning to work as a member of a group.'

'Yes,' I replied, 'but Mr. Mill said he was never allowed merely to fill his head with unexamined facts. He was always forced to examine arguments and to justify his position.'

Ms. Thompson remarked, 'Well, obviously there's a lot to be said for that, but just the same things have moved on since Victorian times. People just don't have the time to spend years learning dead languages any more.'

'That was why Mr. Mill thought people should start when they were three,' I observed.

Ms. Thompson rejoined, 'Well, the fact is children develop at different rates, Stephen, and a lot of children would find those subjects rather off-putting. Any school system has to set priorities, so we concentrate on the things that everyone is going to be able to use. We can't take it for granted that *everyone* is a genius.'

I explained that Mr. Mill thought that he was not a genius but that he had accomplished a lot because of getting a head start. I said I had not even done as much as Mr. Mill and anybody who read the book could say what was in it so I did not think I could be a genius.

Ms. Thompson answered, 'The fact is, Stephen, that while your degree of articulateness would not be so surprising in an educated person, the reason it is not surprising is that the average educated person has developed their mind over the course of their education. It is not so common in a boy your age.'

I thought that this was probably a fallacious argument. It was quite hard to explain things to Ms. Thompson. I said, 'In my opinion this argument is completely fallacious. How can you say that you will not let a stupid person start something until the age of 12 and then say the reason you know they are stupid is they do not know something another person knows because they got to start at the age of 3? In my opinion this is completely preposterous.'

Ms. Thompson asserted, 'Be that as it may.'

At this point Sibylla returned to the room.

'It's all set!' she exclaimed. 'I talked to the head and he said they could probably squeeze one more in and that the school always treats every child as an individual.'

'Obviously we make every attempt,' began Ms. Thompson.

'But it looks as though he won't be in your class.'

'What a shame,' regretted Ms. Thompson.

'Anyway, we won't take up any more of your time. Come along, David. Everything's going to be all right.'

MY FIRST WEEK AT SCHOOL

13 September, 1993

Today was my first day at school. I thought maybe now that I was old enough to go to school Sibylla would tell me about my father but she didn't. Sibylla walked me to school and I was very nervous because if people did not study any languages until they were 12 they must study some other thing and I was a whole year behind.

I thought maybe other people studied more mathematics and science and I had not even finished Algebra Made Easy.

When we got to school Miss Lewis explained that school had started last Thursday. Sibylla said she was sure she had started school on Monday when she was a child.

We didn't do any science today so I could not tell if that was what people had been doing.

When I got home I started reading The Voyage of the Beagle. This is an excellent book. I have worked out that Charles Darwin could not be my father, because he died in 1882, but I am going to finish the book anyway.

14 September, 1993

Today was my second day at school.

We started the day off by painting pictures of animals. I did a picture of a tarantula with 88 legs. Miss Lewis asked what it was and I explained that it was an oktokaiogdoekontapodal tarantula. I don't know if there are any real ones, I think this is just something I made up. Then I did another picture. This one was of a heptakaiogdoekontapodal tarantula because the first one got in a fight and lost a leg. Then I did a picture of two monster tarantulas fighting, each one had 55 legs and it took a long time to draw all the legs. Before I had finished Miss Lewis said we should put away our drawings because it was time to do some arithmetic. We were supposed to go to the addition positions and work at our own speed. At addition position 1 you do a worksheet adding 1 to a number and at addition position 2 you add 2 to a number.

When I finished all the worksheets I was the only one at position 9 so I decided to do some multiplication. Addition takes quite a long time to get anywhere unless you are adding big numbers and all the numbers at the positions were quite small. I practised multiplying 99 × 99 and 199 × 199 and some other interesting numbers. I like numbers that are almost some other number.

I read three more chapters of The Voyage of the Beagle tonight. I was too tired to work on Japanese.

15 September

Today was my third day of school. I was still at addition position 9. I decided to practise using the distributive principle of multiplication. The distributive principle of multiplication is in chapter 1 of Algebra Made Easy but it was my own idea to use it with 9 because it is almost 10.

$$9 \times 9 = [(10 - 1) \times 9] = (10 \times 9) - (1 \times 9) = 90 - 9 = 81$$
$$99 \times 99 = [(100 - 1) \times 99]$$
$$= (100 \times 99) - (1 \times 99)$$
$$= 9900 - 99$$
$$= 9801$$

9	99	999	9999	99999
× 9	× 99	× 999	× 9999	× 99999
90	9900	999000	99990000	9999900000
− 9	− 99	− 999	− 9999	− 99999
81	9801	998001	99980001	9999800001

$999999 \times 999999 = 999998000001$

$9999999 \times 9999999 = 99999980000001$

$99999999 \times 99999999 = 9999999800000001$

$999999999 \times 999999999 = 999999998000000001$

$9999999999 \times 9999999999 = 99999999980000000001$

$99999999999 \times 99999999999 = 9999999999800000000001$

$999999999999 \times 999999999999 = 999999999998000000000001$

$9999999999999 \times 9999999999999 = 99999999999980000000000001$

16 September

Today was my fourth day of school.

17 September

Today was my fifth day of school. It was boring.

18 September

Today is Saturday. I mastered 20 characters in Halpern. 417 to go. I told Sibylla I thought I should do some more French and Greek and Latin and Hebrew and Arabic even though I was doing Japanese because apparently I will not get to do them at school until I am 12 and I was afraid I would forget them by then. I thought Sibylla would be appalled but she just said all right. I also pointed out that they probably would not teach me German either until I was 12 so it might be a good idea if she taught me instead. I thought she was going to say I would have to do a lot of Japanese first but instead she said she would show me a little poem because I had been so good all week. The poem was called Erlkönig by Goethe, about a boy who is riding on a horse behind his father and the Erlking keeps calling the boy and the father doesn't hear and then the boy dies.

19 September

Today was Sunday so I did not have to go to school. I read Amundsen and Scott. I mastered 30 Japanese characters thoroughly and Sibylla commented, 'Well, at least Mr. Ma will never know, I shudder to think what he would think.' I asked, 'Who is Mr. Ma?' Sibylla said he was the father of a famous cellist. I asked, 'Is he a travel writer?' Sibylla said, 'Not to my knowledge, jinsai.'

MY SECOND WEEK AT SCHOOL

20 September

Today when I got home from school Sibylla was in a terrible state. She said Red Devlin had been taken hostage in Azerbaijan. I asked who was Red Devlin. She said he was a journalist. She said everyone said he could persuade anyone to do anything. He was called Red because he didn't have red hair and because he was brave to the point of insanity. He had been in Lebanon and then he had gone to Azerbaijan and been kidnapped after three days.

I asked, 'Was he a good writer?'

'Oh no,' said Sibylla, 'He's a lousy writer, he goes to all these amazing places and sees tumbledown cottages and ragged urchins and girls with coltlike grace. But what a terrible thing to happen.'

Suddenly I had an idea.

Only time will tell.

21 September

$1 \times 11 = 11$

$11 \times 11 = (10 \times 11) + (1 \times 11) = 121$

$111 \times 111 = (100 \times 111) + (10 \times 111) + (1 \times 111) = 12321$

$1111 \times 1111 = (1000 \times 1111) + (100 \times 1111) + (10 \times 1111) + (1 \times 1111) = 1234321$

$11111 \times 11111 = 123454321$

$111111 \times 111111 = 12345654321$

$1111111 \times 1111111 = 1234567654321$

$11111111 \times 11111111 = 123456787654321$

$111111111 \times 111111111 = 12345678987654321$

22 September

11 × 11 = 121
11 × 111 = 1221
11 × 1111 = 12221
11 × 11111 = 122221

23 September

111 × 111 = 12321
111 × 1111 = 123321
111 × 11111 = 1233321
111 × 111111 = 12333321

1111 × 1111 = 1234321
1111 × 11111 = 12344321

11111 × 111111 = 1234554321
111111 × 1111111 = 123456654321
1111111 × 11111111 = 12345677654321

24 September

111111111 × 11 = 1222222221
111111111 × 111 = 12333333321
111111111 × 1111 = 123444444321
111111111 × 11111 = 1234555554321
111111111 × 111111 = 12345666654321
111111111 × 1111111 = 123456777654321
111111111 × 11111111 = 1234567887654321
111111111 × 111111111 = 12345678987654321

MY THIRD WEEK AT SCHOOL

27 September

Today as soon as I got into class Miss Lewis took me to one side and said, 'Stephen, I want you to make a real effort to be a cooperative member of the class.'

I said it was hardly necessary to remind me of this as Dr. Bandura had underlined the importance of cooperative behaviour. Miss Lewis said, 'Good.'

28 September

Today when I got to school Miss Lewis said it was important for people to do their own work and what was she to think when she found that five other children had 111×111 and 1111×1111 and 11111×11111 on their addition sheets. I said they would appear to have used the distributive principle of multiplication. Miss Lewis said I must understand that it was important for people to work at their own rate. I said I did understand. Miss Lewis said, 'Good.'

I worked out that I have spent 12 days in school which is 84 hours so I could have read 8400 lines of the Odyssey. I could have read Herodotus or ad Nicoclem or Cyropaedia and Memorials of Socrates. I could have finished Algebra Made Easy. I could have started Calculus Made Easy. I could have mastered all the Japanese characters thoroughly.

The thing that is worrying me is that J. S. Mill did not go to school. He was taught by his father and that was why he was 25 years ahead of everybody else.

I decided to take the Argonautica to school.

29 September

Today I took the Argonautica to school. Miss Lewis took it away and made me take it home again at the end of the day.

30 September

Today I could have read Book 2 of the Argonautica.

1 October

Today I could have read Book 3 of the Argonautica.

2 October

Today was Saturday. I read Book 1 of the Argonautica. It is longer than I thought. I read up to line 558 and I mastered 30 Japanese characters thoroughly and the rest of the time I practised tying knots.

3 October

Today was Sunday. I read Book 1 of the Argonautica up to line 1011 and I mastered another 30 Japanese characters and I practised some more knots and I read Half Mile Down.

MY FOURTH WEEK AT SCHOOL

4 October

Today I could have finished the Argonautica.

$9 \times 9 \times 9 = (10 - 1) \times (9 \times 9)$
$= (10 \times 9 \times 9) - (1 \times 9 \times 9) = 810 - 81 = 729$
$99 \times 99 \times 99 = (100 \times 9801) - 9801$
$= 980100 - 9801 = 970299$
$999 \times 999 \times 999 = 997002999$
$9999 \times 9999 \times 9999 = 999700029999$
$99999 \times 99999 \times 99999 = 999970000299999$
$999999 \times 999999 \times 999999 = 999997000002999999$
$9999999 \times 9999999 \times 9999999 = 999999700000029999999$
$99999999 \times 99999999 \times 99999999 = 999999970000000299999999$

$99 \times 99 \times 99 \times 99 = [(99 \times 99 \times 99) \times 100] - (99 \times 99 \times 99)$
$= 97029900 - 970299 = 96059601$
$999 \times 999 \times 999 \times 999 = 996005996001$
$9999 \times 9999 \times 9999 \times 9999 = 9996000599960001$
$99999 \times 99999 \times 99999 \times 99999 = 99996000059999600001$
$999999^4 = 999996000005999996000001$
$9999999^4 = 9999996000000599999960000001$

$99^5 = (99^4 \times 100) - 99^4$
$= 9605960100 - 96059601 = 9509900499$
$999^5 = 995009990004999$
$9999^5 = 99950009999000049999$
$99999^5 = 9999500009999900000499999$

$99^6 = 950990049900 - 9509900499 = 941480149401$
$999^6 = 994014980014994001$
$9999^6 = 9994001499800014999400001$
$99999^6 = 999940001499980000149999400001$

3

$999999^7 = 9999930000209999650000349999790000006999999$

11 October, 1993

Today Miss Lewis gave me a note to take to Sibylla. She said this could not go on.

I gave the note to Sibylla and I do not know what it said but I do not think Miss Lewis told her what really happened. Sibylla read the note and she said, 'What!' and then she looked at me and said, 'Well, you must feel good after throwing so many people around.'

I said, 'Well, do you want me to go and die? Do you want me to jump out a window?'

Sibylla said now that I was 6 I was old enough to act like a rational human being.

I said Miss Lewis told me to be a cooperative member of the class but when I tried to help people she said they should do their own work but when I tried to do *my* own work and take Algebra Made Easy to class she said I should try to be more involved and be a cooperative member of the class. I said, 'We are supposed to be working at our own speed but whenever I try she tells me to stop and whenever I ask a question she does not know the answer. She does not know anything I do not know already so I don't think there is any point in going to school.'

Sibylla said, 'But you've only been at school a month. How do you know Miss Lewis doesn't know anything you don't know? You can't possibly make up your mind on so little evidence.'

I said, 'Well, how much more evidence do you need?'

Sibylla said, 'What?'

I said, 'How much more evidence? Do you want me to go for another week or another two weeks or how long?'

Sibylla said, 'I think you are legally required to go until you are 16.'

Sibylla said, 'Please don't cry,' but at first I couldn't stop. No wonder Miss Lewis doesn't know anything because we have to go whether she knows anything or not.

I said, 'Let's take two people about to undergo 10 years of horrible excruciating boredom at school, A dies at the age of 6 from falling out a window and B dies at the age of 6 + n where n is a number less than 10, I think we would all agree that B's life was not *improved* by the additional n years.'

Sibylla started walking up and down.

I said, 'I could just take some books and ride the Circle Line or go to a museum by *myself* every day. Or I could take the bus over to the Royal Festival Hall and work there, and I could save up my questions and you could just explain things for an hour a day.'

Sibylla said, 'I'm sorry but you are too small to go out by yourself.'

I said I could work here and I wouldn't be in the way. I said, 'What if I promised to ask just 10 questions a day and only at one time it would hardly take any time at all.'

Sibylla said, 'No.'

I said 5 questions which was still more than Miss Lewis ever answered and Sibylla shook her head and I said, 'Well, I won't ask any questions ever again, if I ever ask a question you can make me go back to school but I promise I won't.'

Sibylla just said she was sorry.

I said, 'What kind of argument is that?'

Sibylla said, 'There is an argument but it is not one I can

discuss with you. You will have to go to school and do the best you can.'

She said she would go and talk to Miss Lewis tomorrow after school.

12 October, 1993

Today Sibylla came after school to talk to Miss Lewis. Miss Lewis said I should go to the other end of the class but Sibylla said, 'No.'

Miss Lewis said, 'All right, then.' She said I was a disruptive element in the class. She said there were other things in life besides academic achievement and that often children who had been forcefed at an early age had trouble adjusting to their peers and were often socially maladjusted all their lives.

'La formule est banale,' I said.

Miss Lewis said, 'That will do, Stephen.' She said she was prepared to adapt the programme to stimulate a gifted child but that it must be made clear to me that whatever my achievements they did not give me the right to disrupt the class and interfere with the learning process of the other children. She said that whenever I was in a group with other children she invariably found that the other children had failed to remain on task. She said she would make every effort to integrate me into the class but that she could not do this if everything she tried to achieve during the day was undermined as soon as I went home, and that it would only work if there was a genuine partnership between home and school.

I said, 'Does that mean I don't have to go to school any more?'

Sibylla said, 'Lu— Stephen. We can't, that is even if I *wanted* you to stop working with Miss Lewis which I don't we can't afford to hire people who know about quantum mechanics and we especially can't afford it on £5.50 an hour.'

I said, 'Although the capacity to think vastly expands human capabilities, if put to faulty use, it can also serve as a major source of personal distress. Many human dysfunctions and torments stem from problems of thought. This is because, in their thoughts, people often dwell on painful pasts and on perturbing futures of their own invention. They burden themselves with stressful arousal through anxiety-provoking rumination. They debilitate their own efforts by self-doubting and other self-defeating ideation. They constrain and impoverish their lives through phobic thinking.'

Sibylla said I should not just quote things uncritically, the writer seemed to assume there was no such thing as an unsolicited memory, an assumption for which there seemed to be no evidence whatsoever.

I said that was exactly why it would be better for me not to go to school, I needed to learn to argue like J. S. Mill.

Miss Lewis said that while she did not mean to belittle what Sibylla had achieved there was a real danger of being cut off from reality.

Sibylla said Miss Lewis did not know what it was like to go to school in the type of place that was excited to be getting its first motel.

Miss Lewis said, 'What?'

Sibylla said when she was growing up she only ever went to one school that even taught Greek and you had to have three years of French or Spanish and two years of Latin when she only had one year of French so she had to say she had two years of French and Latin lessons with a defrocked Jesuit priest from Quebec and forge a letter from the priest and most people couldn't learn Arabic or Hebrew or Japanese even if they invented a defrocked Jesuit *priest*.

Miss Lewis said, 'I think we are getting a little off the subject here. What do you think is the effect on a child who is progressing satisfactorily at Key Level Two and in fact is doing work if anything *ahead* of her age group, what do you think is the effect, as I say, on a child who has every reason to take pride in her achievements and have her self-confidence *bolstered* when Stephen comes up with a page covered with problems in six or seven figures and tells her there is no point in doing a problem unless the answer won't fit on the display of a calculator? To say nothing of the effect on children who are having difficulty with the material. I have one boy who has been working his way through the alphabet one letter at a time and just last week he finally reached the stage where he could recognise all the letters with confidence, well, I am not saying Stephen necessarily means to be unkind but what do you think the effect is if Stephen starts writing all the names of the dinosaurs in Greek and explaining that a lot of the letters are the same? If you want my opinion that boy has more of an accomplishment to be genuinely proud of in that single alphabet than Stephen with dozens, but he was absolutely devastated. Weeks of work undone at a stroke. It has got to stop. Stephen has got to understand that there is more to life than how much you know.'

I said, 'Does that mean I don't have to go to school any more?'

Sibylla said, 'I couldn't agree with you more, we have been watching Seven Samurai on a weekly basis for about a year.'

Miss Lewis said, 'I beg your pardon?'

Sibylla said, 'Well, as I'm sure you know the whole issue of a skill in Kurosawa is highly— Why *look*, you've got a little book about samurai in the classroom, how marvellous!'

She picked up SAMURAI WARRIORS off my desk and she began to peruse it.

Miss Lewis said, 'I think we should.'

Suddenly Sibylla exclaimed in accents of horror, 'WHAT!'

'What is it?' asked Miss Lewis.

'EXPERT IN A DIFFERENT COMBAT SKILL!' cried Sibylla.

'What?' reiterated Miss Lewis.

'How can they SLEEP AT NIGHT,' said Sibylla, 'having foisted this FABRICATION on unsuspecting SCHOOL-CHILDREN! It says each of the samurai is an expert in a different combat skill. Combat skill my foot. What's Katsushiro's, the STICK? Or Heihachi's—the AXE? What a SHAME he had to leave it behind with its owner so he couldn't actually use it on the ENEMY.'

Miss Lewis said, 'I really think.'

Sibylla said, 'It's only the merest CHANCE that we happen to know the facts of the matter, for all we know the school is crammed to the rafters with books full of mistakes on subjects where my son might have been hoping to LEARN something he didn't already KNOW, which I had SUPPOSED was the object of EDUCATION. Oh what am I to do?'

Miss Lewis said, 'I really don't think.'

Sibylla said, 'You might as well call a book the GENIUS OF SHAKESPEARE and then explain to a Japanese schoolchild that Laertes is the hero of HAMLET under the impression that he is the more INTERESTING CHARACTER. Oh what shall I do?'

Miss Lewis said, 'I think we've talked enough for one day. Stephen, I want you to think very carefully about what has been said.'

I said I would think about it very carefully.

If I ever have a son and he wants to leave school I will let him because I will remember what it is like.

We went home and Sibylla walked up and down.

'What shall I do?' she said. 'What shall I do?'

I said, 'Maybe I should just study at home.'

Sibylla said, 'Hmm.' She said, 'Let us consult Mr. Richie,' and she gave me another page about Sugata Sanshiro to read.

The hero is a man actively engaged in becoming himself— never a very reassuring sight. The villain, on the other hand, has already become something. Everything about Tsukigata suggests that he has arrived. There is not a wasted gesture, not an uncalculated movement. He has found what is to his advantage and acts accordingly. Sugata, by comparison, is all thumbs.

Kurosawa's preference is the preference we all have for the formed man. In the ordinary film this man would be the hero. But he is not and, despite his admiration, Kurosawa has told us why. One of the attributes of all of his heroes, beginning with Sugata, is that they are all unformed in just this way. For this reason, all of his pictures are about education—the education of the hero.

After this superb battle . . . one might expect the picture to end with some kind of statement that he has at last grown-up, that he has arrived, that he has become something—the great judo champion. This would be the logical Western conclusion to a film about the education of a hero.

Kurosawa, however, has seen that this cannot be true. A hero who actually becomes is tantamount to a villain—for this was the only tangible aspect of the villain's villainy. To suggest that peace, contentment, happiness, follows a single battle, no matter how important, is literally untrue—and it would limit Sugata precisely because of the limitations suggested in the words "happiness" or "judo champion."

I asked, 'Is that enough?'
Sibylla said, 'That's enough. What do you think it all means?'
I thought if I get this right I don't have to go to school. I've got to get this right. I looked at the page to stall for time.

I said, 'It means that it is literally untrue to suggest that peace, contentment, happiness, follows a single battle, no matter how important, and that a hero who actually becomes is tantamount to a villain.'

Sibylla said, 'A hero who actually becomes what?'

I said, 'Becomes a villain?'

Sibylla said, 'Oh what shall I do?'

I said, 'Becomes himself?'

Sibylla said, 'What shall I DO?'

I said, 'Becomes a great judo champion?'

Sibylla said, 'What shall I DO?'

I said, 'Becomes happy! Becomes content! Becomes a hero! Becomes something!!!!'

Sibylla said, 'WHAT shall I DO?'

I thought about 10 years in school and I said, 'I think what it's really saying is that you can't understand something until you go through it. You think you know what something is about and that's why you do it but then when you do it you realise it's about something else. What it's saying is that that's why it's important to study judo.'

Sibylla said, 'JUDO! Why there's a judo club just up the road! So you COULD study judo COULDN'T you.'

To tell the truth I think I would rather study tae kwon do, but I said, 'Yes.'

Sibylla said, 'It does not solve everything but at least it solves one thing. You will meet other children your age in a structured and moral environment and strive to achieve satori. It would not be actually wrong for me to teach you at home.'

She walked up and down. I could see something was bothering her.

I said, 'I promise not to ask any questions.'

Sibylla kept walking up and down.

I said, 'I think it solves everything.'

iv

If we fought with real swords I would kill you

1

Trying to feel sorry for Lord Leighton

The man was almost dead.

He should not have been moved after the accident, but they were short of supplies. They had been travelling now for ten days, stopping only to rest the dogs and to snatch a quick mouthful of pemmican.

Now they were down to their last dog. They had eaten Wolf two days before. Soon it would be Dixie's turn. But without a dog . . .

The boy put the thought out of his mind. Cross that bridge when we come to it. At least the wind had died down. The only sounds were the squeak of the runners on the snow, the loud panting of Dixie as she struggled with the unaccustomed load, his own quick breath and the groans of the injured man.

The air was clear as crystal. Was that an igloo in the distance? It must be an Inuit encampment. Only the Inuit stayed so far north so late in the season.

Two hours later they staggered into the settlement.

'Where are we?' muttered the man.

'It's an Inuit camp,' the boy replied.

'Will they speak English?'

'I speak Inuit,' said the boy.

'Good thing I brought you,' said the man with a ghastly grin.

Two fur-clad figures approached. The boy struggled to remember a few phrases picked up from The Eskimo Book of Knowledge months before.

Taimaimat ᴋanimajut âniasiortauningine maligaksat sivorlerpângat imaipoᴋ:
ANIASIORTIB PERKOJANGIT NALETSIARLUGIT.

The two men turned without a word and returned to their igloos. The only sound was the fine snow drifting through the encampment.

The boy tried again:

Ilapse ilangat killerpat aggangminik âniasiortib mangipserpâ ajoкertorpâselo killeк mangipsertautsainartuksaungmat. Ilanganele killertub mangiptaк pêjarpâ, kingornganelo tataminiarpoк killeк âкivalialugane piungilivaliatuinarmat. Nerriukkisê âniasiortib mangiptaк najumitsainarniarmago uvlut magguk pingasullônêt nâvlugit killeк mamitsiarкârtinagô?

Silence was the only reply.

Desperately he summoned up a few words of greeting from that half-remembered book:

Sorlo inôкatigêksoaкarjmat unuktunik adsigêngitunik taimaкtauк ataneкarpoк unuktunik adsigêngitunik, anginerpaujorle tamainit, idluartomik ataniortoк inungnik кaкortanik кernângajuniglo кernertaniglo, tagva ataneк George, ataniojoк Britishit atanioviksoanganut. Tâmna atanerivase.

Suddenly a shot rang out, and the boy fell lifeless to the snow.

As far as I can see, *The Eskimo Book of Knowledge* is completely useless. 'The first rule in curing sickness or injury is TO OBEY THE INSTRUCTIONS OF THE WHITE MAN.' When am I ever going to use that? They should have called it *A Hundred and One Things Not to Say Where the Inuit Can Hear You.*

When one of your people cuts his hand, the Trader covers the wound with a bandage and instructs the man to keep the wound covered. Often the man throws away the bandage and wonders why the wound grows worse instead of better. Do you expect the Trader to hold the bandage round the man's hand for two or three days until the wound is healed?

That's going to make us popular.

As there are many different races, so there are many different rulers, but the greatest ruler of all, who governs with justice White Men, Brown Men and Black Men in very many countries, is KING GEORGE the ruler of the British Empire. He is your King.

Another winner. Unfortunately it was the only thing on Inuit I could find. Of course, he may not be going where they speak Inuit. I could work out some of the words and grammar if I knew I was going to need it, but Sibylla still won't say. It would help if she would just tell me *something* about him. I can't believe I'm almost 11 and the only thing I know is that he's not Thor Heyerdahl.

Not only is King George a man of great prudence and a hard worker; he is also a great hunter. Whether it be in the hunting of fierce animals like the bear, or in the crafty stalking of the deer or in the shooting of partridges while they fly, no man in the British Empire takes surer aim than our King.

AtaneκGeorge silatudlartuinalungilaκ angijomiglo suliaκarpak-lune, ômajoκsiorteogivorletauκ—

OK, that's an exaggeration. That's not the only thing I know. I also know he's not Egon Larsen. He's not Chatwin. She likes Thubron, so he's out. I think I've narrowed it down to 8 or 9. For a while I thought it was Red Devlin: she always laughs at the gap-toothed urchins, and since he was captured five years ago his wife's been campaigning for his release, so Sibylla might have thought it was safer not to tell me. But then last week James Hatton got back from the Arctic Circle and wrote an article for the *Independent Magazine* that used the phrase 'veritable cathedral of ice'. VERITABLE CATHEDRAL OF ICE shouted Sibylla and she walked up and down saying veritable cathedral of ice and reading out other priceless phrases and suddenly I had a hunch that it was Hatton. So I got *The Eskimo Book of Knowledge* and started to work on Inuit.

Before returning to London to take pen in hand Hatton walked solo to the North Pole and back without telling anyone where he was going. At one point he was attacked by a walrus. It was so cold the action on his gun wouldn't work, so he had to throw a knife at it. He got it in one eye (Hatton: 'Bull's-eye!'), and then was able to harpoon it. He had to eat some of the meat raw and then trek on another 15 miles, even though he'd been going for 20 hours, because he knew the smell of the blood would attract other predators. At one point the frostbite in one toe was so bad he had to cut it off.

If it *is* Hatton I've wasted years learning Xhosa, Swahili, Zulu, Hausa, Quechua, Faroese and Mongolian. If it isn't I'm wasting my time on *The Eskimo Book of Knowledge*. I think I may be wasting my time anyway.

> If you hunters used half the CARE of the White Men in setting your traps skilfully and in keeping your furs free from dirt, every Innuit family would gain greater possessions from the Company's Trader.

If I get us both lynched my long lost father will probably tell his long lost son to get lost and stay lost.

Sibylla is supposed to be typing and is reading the paper. I've got the Kanji dictionary on one arm of my chair, and the little Kodansha Romaji on the other. If she asks what I'm reading I'll tell her, but she probably won't ask when she sees the Japanese dictionaries; she knows I've got a new book on judo. I don't want to hear about how pay for schoolchildren, the right to death, homosexual marriage and all the other basic requirements of a culture not irredeemably sunk in barbarism will be commonplace by the year 2065.

No wonder your beautiful damsels prefer to marry a good hunter, a man who is an honour to his camp and can provide for his family comforts and new possessions! In all parts of the world such men are favoured by fair damsels—

OH MY GOD! shouted Sibylla. He's OUT! He ESCAPED! This is WONDERFUL!

And striding up and down she said that Red Devlin had escaped three months ago and had just walked into the British Embassy in Tbilisi. She said: I've actually kind of MISSED those gap-toothed urchins toting Kalashnikovs. She was bounding around as though the gravitational force of the planet had suddenly dropped by a third.

I thought: It's got to be Devlin.

I read one of his books a long time ago. It was called *Get Out Before I Throw You Out.* He wasn't much of a writer; his talent was for making outrageous demands which people found impossible to refuse. For instance he once asked to go up with some paratroopers over a war zone and was told this was against all regulations.

Oh go on, said Red Devlin.

X: Oh all right then but no one must know this is strictly on the Q.T.

Red Devlin was equipped with a parachute purely as a safety precaution and then when the paratroopers jumped he jumped out too before anyone could stop him and got some story that no one could have got who had not gone in with the paratroopers. A newspaper hired him on the strength of this story and then fired him for refusing to file some other story, and then another newspaper hired him because he had penetrated a guerrilla hideout by going into a local bar and saying 'I'd like to visit that guerrilla hideout.'

Barman: Nobody knows where it is. It's a secret.

Red Devlin: Oh go on, you can tell *me.*

Barman: Oh all right then, you take the first right— Tell you what, we'll go in my car.

Sceptics had pointed out that there was only Red Devlin's word for this, but since most of the people he talked to refused to talk to anyone else you could either argue that he must have been telling the truth or that there was no way to prove that he wasn't.

Red Devlin had once helped a couple to adopt an orphan from Romania. The couple had visited Romania and seen an orphanage and on their return to Britain they had decided to adopt a little girl. They had immersed themselves in Romanian and they had talked to people who had adopted Romanian children and they had tried to initiate adoption procedures and had been told it was out of the question. Both were women so that they were a man short and one woman too many. The couple argued passionately and described in graphic detail the conditions of the orphanage but rules were rules and there was nothing to be done.

The couple went outside and sat shivering in the sun. And now by a piece of luck Red Devlin came down the street. He had lost a job again so his time was his own.

What's the matter? said Red Devlin.

They explained and he said he would help them.

The couple were so convinced that rules were rules that they thought he was offering to marry one of them. Red Devlin laughed. He said he was a married man. He said he would go to Romania and get the child. The couple explained patiently that you could not get the child out of Romania or into Britain without the adoption papers.

Is that a fact? said Red Devlin.

Red Devlin knew maybe three words of Romanian. They may have meant 'Oh go on' to start with; if they didn't, they did by the time Red Devlin was through with them. He went to the orphanage and asked for the girl, and each time someone objected he brought out his three words of Romanian and the long and the short of it was that in three days he drove out of Bucharest with the girl beside him.

Some people smuggle children over borders in the boots of cars. Some people dress them as giant dolls, or stuff them in suitcases. Some people stick them under a blanket and hope for the best. Red Devlin would drive up to the border with the girl in the front seat.

Official: Where are her papers?

Red Devlin: She doesn't have any papers.

Red Devlin would explain the situation.

I'm sorry, but she will have to go back.

Red Devlin would explain the situation again.

Believe me, I sympathise, but there's nothing I can do.

Sure you can, said Red Devlin. Anyone can say it, but Red Devlin really believed it, and every time he said it people who had only been doing their job stopped doing their job. Back he came to Britain with the girl to discuss the matter with a member of the Social Services.

This was not a pushover. The woman said she was only doing her job and Red Devlin said Oh go on, and instead of saying Oh all right then the woman came back with Rules are rules. Red Devlin said Oh go on again and this time the woman said there was nothing she could do. Red Devlin said Sure you can and the woman said My hands are tied. They talked for a whole hour, and the whole time they talked Red Devlin never once argued passionately or said but SURELY or but can't you SEE or How would you feel if it were YOUR child. They talked and talked and talked and talked and talked and even after an hour of Red Devlin the woman didn't say Oh all right then, but she said she would see what she could do. The long and the short of it was that the girl got to stay. There were hundreds of episodes like this but then he had been taken captive and held hostage.

Sibylla said what had probably happened was that they had kept him gagged for five years and then one day someone accidentally took off the gag and Red Devlin said I'd like to go home and they said Oh all right then.

I waited for her to say something else but she just walked up and down and suddenly as she walked by she saw *The Eskimo Book of Knowledge.*

What's this? she asked, and picking it up began to look at it and to read out *as soon as it pleased White damsels to adorn their necks and shoulders with the soft white fur of the fox, then there were many young men eager to make glad the hearts (and the vanity) of their damsels with gifts of white fox skins; and when their wives were sad, husbands learned to make them happy with gifts of white fox-skins* and to say This is amazing and When was it published?

1931 I said.

1931 said Sibylla and this is, let's see

1998

1998 so that's 67 years, so in 67 years it will be

2065

2065. Exactly. Just think Ludo in 2065 people will probably consider it absolutely BARBARIC that a child should be condemned to work 12 years without pay in absolute economic subjection to the adults into whose keeping fate has consigned it and BARBARIC that people should be brought into the world into circumstances they did not choose and then COMPELLED to remain REGARDLESS and they will not know which is more surprising, the absolute SILENCE on these subjects at the present time or the absolute RUBBISH routinely published on the subject of marriage between members of the same sex in papers which PURPORT to

Is Red Devlin my father? I asked.

She said:

I don't want to talk about it.

She did not come to earth. My mother was now on a planet with a deadly atmosphere and gravitational force of 17. Leaning heavily on the chair and looking down at *The Eskimo Book of Knowledge* she said after a pause with a gallant effort:

But what a marvellous language let's see *kakortarsu* is obviously the white fox so we've got *kakortarsu kakortarsuk kakortarsungnik kakortarsuit* and there's *puije* and *puijit* for seal further up the page it looks like *puije* is the accusative *puijit* is the nominative which would make *kakortarsuit* nominative *piojorniningillo* is vanity on the previous page we seem to have *puijevinit* seal meat *puijevinekarnersaularposelo* you will also gain a greater supply of seal meat I've always wanted to learn a agglutinative language

I said: Three's not enough?

She said: I feel like learning another it's wonderful to think of a language like this in DAILY USE. She said: I wonder what the Inuit would be for veritable cathedral of ice!

I didn't say anything.

She said:

Oh LOOK it's got the Inuit for God Save the King!

The planet Saturn has a gravitational force of only 1.07 and she began to sing

> Gûdib saimarliuk
> Adanterijavut
> Nâlengnartoκ.
> Piloridlarlune
> Nertornadlarlune
> Ataniotile
> Uvaptingnut.

I said:

Is it James Hatton?

JAMES HATTON! said Sibylla. Why the man's a veritable colossus!

She said:

I've got to work.

I got the impression I was wasting my time on *The Eskimo Book of Knowledge*. I thought: Well, maybe this year I'll pass the test, and I went to look at the postcard of Greek Girls Playing at Ball, by Lord Leighton, which Sibylla had shown me years before. Abstract expressionism this is not, but I still couldn't see what I was supposed to see. Then I read the magazine article for the 500th time, but I couldn't see what I was supposed to see. Then I listened to the tape of Liberace, which is obviously complete and utter crap.

Sibylla said: Would you mind not playing that? I'm trying to work.

I said: I can see the tape is crap. Isn't that enough?

She looked at me.

I said: How do you know you're not wrong about the other two?

She looked at me.

I said: Why don't you tell me what you think is wrong so I can decide for myself?

She looked at me with burning eyes.

I said: Why won't you tell me who he is? Do you want me to promise not to tell him? I have a right to know.

She said: Well I have a right to remain silent.

She said: If you don't need me for anything I'm going to watch Seven Samurai for a while.

She turned off the computer. It was about 11:30. So far she had spent about 8 minutes typing which at £6.25 an hour meant she had earned about 83p.

She picked up the remote and pressed ON and PLAY.

*40 bandits stop on a hill above a village in Japan. They decide to raid it
after the barley harvest. A farmer overhears.*

A village meeting is held. The farmers despair.

Rikichi leaps to his feet with burning eyes.

Let's make bamboo spears! Let's run 'em all through!

Not me, says Yohei.

Impossible, says Manzo.

I used to take her word for it. But what if she's wrong? A new
book by the author of the magazine article came out last month. According to the reviews he is one of the greatest writers of our time.

The farmers consult old Giseku.

I said: According to the reviews the author of the magazine article is one of the greatest writers of our time.

Sibylla said yes and Alma-Tadema fetched more than Michelangelo for a while.

He tells them to find hungry samurai.

I said: According to one reviewer this writer I am supposed to re-
gard from a state of grace beyond pity is the greatest writer in English in the world today. Another described him as America's answer
to Flaubert. A third referred to him as the great chronicler of the
American experience. Nine out of ten reviewers gave him a rating
of 'great' or better. Five used the word 'genius'.

She said: Anything follows from a false premise. If you accept that
American novels should be written in English then it also follows
that the Pope is a Jew.

I said: Well in that case Seven Samurai can't be any good because it's in black and white and Japanese. You're being completely inconsistent. I thought: This is insane. Why don't we just talk about the decline of traditional Zulu raindances or mutations in inland water algae in the Urals or some other randomly chosen completely irrelevant subject? I have a right to know who he is whoever he is.

She said: I wish you wouldn't say the first thing that comes into your head, Ludo. There is an obvious difference between someone who works within the technical limitations of his time which are beyond his control and someone who accepts without thinking limitations which are entirely within his own power to set aside.

She said: It may have escaped your notice but I am *trying* to watch one of the masterpieces of modern cinema.

The farmers see a crowd of people. A samurai has gone to the river's edge to be shaved by a monk.
Mifune pushes his way through the crowd and squats scratching his chin.
Katsushiro asks his neighbour what's happening.

I said So you think Proust would have been better with some English and German added in & she looked at me with burning eyes & I said Why don't we talk about the impact of tourism on the traditional Zulu raindance why don't you test me on 50 capitals of the world this is completely irrelevant I have a right to know.

She looked at me with burning eyes.

I said: Well just tell me this. He didn't rape you did he? (Everything I know about delicacy I learned at my mother's knee.) For one horrible moment I thought he really had: increase Rikichi factor by power of 10.

She said: No.

I said: So there must have been something you liked about him. He must have had SOME redeeming quality.

She said: That's one way of looking at it.

I said: What other way is there of looking at it?

She said: In our society one of the most highly prized virtues if not *the* most highly prized virtue is that of sleeping with someone you don't desire for free, if it is prized in people who have to do it surely it would be a supererogatory virtue in someone who wasn't even married.

I said: Is that what you did?

She said: Well, I was trying to be polite.

I was not going to be struck speechless now. I said: What word has escaped the barrier of your teeth?

She said: There is a strange taboo in our society against ending something merely because it is not pleasant—life, love, a conversation, you name it, the etiquette is that you must begin in ignorance & persevere in the face of knowledge, & though I naturally believe that this is profoundly wrong it's not nice to go around constantly offending people.

I had heard this a million times. I said: Does that mean there WASN'T anything you liked about him?

She said: How can you be so sure something you don't know is something you want to know? Look at Oedipus.

I said: What are you afraid of, that I'll kill him or sleep with him?

She said, or rather riposted: Well, I wouldn't sleep with him if I were you, and she said: Tiresias has spoken.

There is a strange taboo in our society against matricide.

She rewound the video ostentatiously to the place where I had interrupted.

The thief runs from the barn and falls down dead.

The parents of the child rush forward to take it.

Mifune rushes forward brandishing his sword. He jumps up and down on the body.

The samurai walks off without a backward look.

I've been telling her for years about Dervla Murphy who rode through the Andes on a mule with her eight-year-old daughter. My father probably does that kind of thing the whole time for a living. The most we've ever done is hitchhike through France. My father might like the chance to spend some time with the son he never knew he had. We could go to the source of the Amazon by canoe, or trek overland to the Arctic Circle, or live six months with the Masai (my Masai is pretty good). I know 54 edible plants, 23 edible mushrooms and 8 insects that you can keep down if you don't think about what you're eating; I think I could live off the land in any continent. For the last two years I've been sleeping on the ground outside even in the winter, and I walk for an hour without shoes every day to toughen my feet, and I've practised climbing trees and buildings and telephone poles. If she would just tell me who he is I could stop wasting my time on things that might just happen to come in handy and concentrate on the things I actually need to know. I've had to learn five major trade languages and eight nomadic languages just in case. It's insane.

My name is Katsushiro Okamoto. Please, please let me become one of your followers.

Followers? I am Kambei Shimada. I am only a ronin. I have no followers

I thought about Liberace and Lord Leighton and the author of the magazine article. Even if she's right, what's bad about these people is that they are bad artists. Maybe my father was a bad writer— but it could be because he had more important things to think about. If you're travelling across Siberia with a team of huskies you may not have time to polish every word. Sibylla does tend to take art too seriously.

I went up to my room after a while. She has been watching Seven Samurai for the last 10 years and she still has trouble with the Japanese. I could hear it downstairs. I knew she'd be there for at least another hour.

I had once seen an envelope in her room marked To Be Opened In Case of Death. I thought—well surely if she thought she'd be dead she'd say who my father was. I thought—I've tried to play by the rules, but this is ridiculous. I could just see myself in 10 years looking at the picture by Lord Leighton and not seeing anything wrong, or trying to find something wrong with one of the greatest writers of our time.

I had practised walking silently. I walked silently across the landing to her room. There's a drawer where she keeps her passport. I thought the envelope might be there. I crossed the room and opened the drawer.

There was a folder with a thick stack of papers in it.

2

I know all the words

I read through the papers quickly.

There was quite a lot about my father, but she'd thought of a nickname and stuck to it. I kept thinking she'd say who Liberace was, or at least mention the title of one of his books, but she didn't. Before I could start looking again for the envelope Sibylla called from downstairs

LUDO! ARE YOU UPSTAIRS?

I said

YES

and she said

WOULD YOU MIND BRINGING ME THE DUVET?

I put the folder of papers back in the drawer and took the duvet downstairs. I don't know what I thought. I think I thought It's not too late not to know and But I have to know.

The first part of the recruitment was over, the part where Katsushiro stands behind a door with a stick. When I was very little I would practise reading fast from the subtitles and Sibylla would say why do you think he did this and why do you think he did that and why doesn't Shichiroji have to take the test and why does Gorobei take Heihachi if he says he always runs away? I would say something and she would laugh and say she never thought of that.

Kambei and Katsushiro find two samurai stripping bamboo poles for a match.

259

The fight begins. Kyuzo raises his pole. X holds his pole over his head and shouts.

Kyuzo draws back his pole. X runs forward.

Kyuzo raises his pole suddenly and brings it down.

X: Sorry, that was a draw

No. I won

Nonsense

If it had been with real swords you'd be dead.

Sibylla put the duvet around her shoulders. She said she would start typing soon.

I wanted to say: Was he really as bad as Liberace?

Liberace was the one thing she'd shown me that I could see was bad. Could my father really be that bad? Could he be worse? I wanted to say: How bad is bad? Is it worse than gap-toothed urchins and coltish grace? Worse than scrap of humanity? Worse than veritable cathedral of ice? I wanted to say: But at least he's seen the world.

I thought of saying to Sibylla, If I'm such a genius why won't you let me decide for myself? I thought of saying, I thought you disapproved people who purely because they happened to arrive on the planet a few years earlier make other people who happened to arrive on the planet a few years later obey them without persuading them of the justice of their position. I thought you thought disenfranchisement on grounds of age the hallmark of a BARBARIC SOCIETY. I thought of saying, How do you know something I don't know is something I *don't* want to know?

In runs the gambler, who says they've found a really tough samurai.

Katsushiro runs to stand behind the door with a stick.

Gambler: You dirty cheat!

Kambei: If he's a real samurai he won't be hit.

Gambler: But he's drunk.

Kambei: A samurai doesn't get so drunk that he loses his senses.

A man runs through the door; Katsushiro brings the stick down hard. This samurai doesn't parry the blow. He falls moaning to the ground.

This was the first scene I understood. It was because the scroll made me realise I could see the words. Obviously hearing something is just reading backwards, what I mean is, when you read you hear the word in your mind, and when you talk or hear someone say something you see an image of the word in your mind: if someone says *someone* you see a word in Roman letters, and if they say *philosophia* you see φιλοσοφία, and if they say *kataba* you see كتب, you actually see an image of something you read from right to left. But for a long time I didn't realise this worked with Japanese. I'd hear *Nihon* in my head if I saw 日本 on the page, say, but I didn't realise I could see something in my head if I heard something. Anyway Kambei picks up the end and reads from it—what he actually says is 'Tenshō second year second month seventeenth day born', he says the sounds *Tenshō ninen nigatsu jūshichinichi umare* and suddenly I realised I could see some of the words, he was seeing them on the scroll and saying and when he said *ninen nigatsu jūshichinichi* in my mind I could see 二年二月十七日. Second year second month seventeenth day. Probably because I was obsessed with Japanese numbers at the time.

For the rest of the film sounds would sort of crystallise here and there around an image and then I went back and tried to work the others out and by the time I was eight the images came into my head for most of the film and I could understand almost all of it.

Mifune recognises Kambei.

Hey you! Asking me 'Are you a samurai?' like that—don't laugh at me.

Even though I look like this, I'm a genuine samurai.

Hey—I've been looking for you the whole time ever since then. . . . thinking I'd like to show you this [pulls out a scroll]

Look at this

This genealogy

This genealogy of my ancestors handed down for generations

(You bastard, you're making a fool of me)

Look at this (you're making a fool of me)

This is me.

[Kambei, reading] This Kikuchiyo it talks about is you?

[Mifune] That's right

[Kambei] Born on the seventeenth day of the second month of the second year of Tensho . . . [bursts out laughing]

[Mifune] What's funny?

[Kambei] You don't look thirteen

Listen, if you're definitely this Kikuchiyo you must be thirteen this year.

[All the samurai burst out laughing]

Where did you steal this?

[Mifune] What! It's a lie! Shit! What are you saying?

Sibylla said: Can you really understand it?

I said: Of course I can understand it.

Sibylla said: Well what's he saying then?

and she rewound the video to the place where Mifune staggers to his feet.

I said, Well he says *Yai! Kisama! yoku mo ore no koto o samurai ka nante nukashiyagatte . . . fuzakeruna!*

and Sib said for all she knew she might actually know these words, she never recognised a word when she heard it

so I wrote on a piece of paper explaining as I went, he says やい *yai* hey 貴様 ! *kisama* you (the Kodansha Romaji says it's CRUDE and very insulting) よく *yoku* well も *mo* intensifying particle 俺の

ore no me possessive particle 事を *koto o*, thing object particle, i.e. periphrasis for me 侍 *samurai* か *ka* interrogative particle なんて *nante* COLLOQ. for *nan-to* what, how, as in how cold it is ぬかしやがって *nukashiyagatte* gerund of *nukasu*, to say, i.e. Asking me 'Are you a samurai?' like that, ふざけるな！ *fuzakeruna* negative imperative of fuzakeru, to joke, i.e. don't laugh at me.

I explained that according to *Japanese Street Slang shiyagatte* was the gerund of *shiyagaru*, the common contraction of *shite agaru*, which was the offensive form of the verb *suru*, to do. So if *nukasu* was to say *nukashiyagatte* would be the offensive gerund.

What a wonderful language, said Sib, they seem to have toned it down quite a bit for the subtitles. I knew *Japanese Street Slang* was a bargain at £6.88.

In other words Asking me 'Are you a samurai?' like that—how dare you!

All right, said Sib, & then what?

俺はなこう見えてもちゃんとした侍だ

俺はな *ore wa na* I topic particle emphatic particle こう *kō*, in this way 見えて *miete*, present participle of *mieru*, appearing も *mo* even, i.e. even appearing like this.

Sib said she might not know much Japanese but she did not believe for one nanosecond that Mifune said Even appearing like this.

I said I did not think consciousness was capable of operating in units of nanoseconds.

Sib said she did not believe it for the smallest unit at which consciousness was capable of operating and then what?

ちゃんとした *chanto shita*, precise, proper, up-to-standard

Up-to-standard! said Sib

侍 *samurai* だ *da*, I am, i.e. Even though I look like this I'm a genuine samurai.

Which subtitle is that, said Sib, I don't recognise any of this.

I said it came up roughly where he said I'm a samurai all right. Hmm, said Sib.

やい俺はなあれからお前の事をずっと捜してたんだぞ

やい *yai* hey 俺はな *ore wa na*

I topic particle emphatic particle said Sib

あれから *arekara* since that time お前の *omae no* of you 事を *koto o* thing object particle, i.e. periphrasis for you ずっと *zutto* the whole (time), I said talking fast

捜してたんだ *sagashitetanda* contraction of *sagashite ita*, I was searching, contraction of *no da* it is a fact that, *no* nominalising particle *da* verb to be ぞ *zo* sentence-final particle expressing strong exclamation generally used only by male speakers, I said even faster

これを *kore o* this object particle 見せよう *miseyō* plain volitional I'd like to show と *to*, quotative particle applying to previous phrase, 思ってな *omotte na* present participle of *omou* to think plus *na* emphatic particle, i.e. thinking that I'd like to show you this—

I know all those words, said Sib.

Well, do you want me to just write it down for you? I said. I wrote down a few lines and Sib said I might not be aware of it but writing was generally considered a means of communication & my handwriting in Japanese was even more enigmatic than the scripts I had introduced to English, Greek, Arabic, Hebrew, Bengali, Russian, Armenian and other languages too numerous to enumerate.

これを見ろ, I said, *kore o miro*

I know that, said Sib, Look at this

この系図はな *kono keizu*, this genealogy, *wa na*

topic particle particle said Sib

俺様の *ore sama no*

my said Sib

先祖 *senzo*, ancestors 代々 *daidai* counter for generations の *no* possessive particle said Sib

系図よ *keizu yo*

genealogy exclamatory particle said Sib

このやろうばかにしやがってなんでい *kono yarō baka ni shiyagatte nandei*

この *kono*, this, やろう *yarō* boor, bumpkin, *kono yarō* you swine according to Sanseido, ばか *baka* idiot most popular Japanese swear word according to *Japanese Street Slang, baka ni suru* is literally you're making a fool of me but ruder in Japanese, don't fuckin' fuck with me according to *Japanese Street Slang,* so if しやがって *shiyagatte* is the offensive form of *suru* it's probably even ruder, なんでい *nandei* whatever.

The subtitles don't really seem to capture the flavour, said Sib.

Anyway you get the picture, I said, and Sib said But you've only done a couple of lines, how can you stop after two lines of one of the CENTRAL SCENES of the FILM?

oK,oK,oK I said. The great thing about having two parents is that each protects you from the other. If I had a father he would notice that I was getting fed up and say Leave the boy alone, Sibylla. Or he would say tactfully I'm going over to the park to kick a ball around before it gets dark and he would offer to explain the scene to Sib himself later on.

Where are we up to? said Sib.

We're up to where Kambei looks at the scroll, I said.

Sib went back to the beginning of the scene again and replayed it and she said she still couldn't understand a word. I think you're making all this up said Sib

I said it's probably Mifune's delivery that's giving you trouble

& Sib said she would not hear a word against Mifune

I said Kurosawa said himself

& Sib said yes but it is part of the character and do go on.

I said would you mind if I just wrote it down neatly for you

Sib said she wouldn't mind so I wrote it down starting at 'You're this Kikuchiyo born in the second year of Tensho,' and I transliterated everything because Sib has a tendency to forget the kana from time to time. It seemed to be getting rather complicated to explain so I said I thought I would do the rest later and Sib said OK. She rewound the film to the very beginning of the scene, where Katsushiro begs to go, we can't take a child says Kambei, at the end of it all I've no parents, no family—I'm alone in the world, & Heihachi looks up to see Kyuzo standing silently at the door.

Did you know that E. V. Rieu has Odysseus address his companions as lads? said Sib.

You may have mentioned it, I said.

These subtitles said Sib seem to stand at a similarly respectful distance from what the characters actually say. I am going to try not to think about it. One good thing though is that it hardly affects some of the best things about the film, look at Miyoguchi standing silently in the door, he is like a great actor of silent film I have no idea how many LINES they gave Kyuzo but the lines are completely beside the point. How long did it take you to work out what everybody was saying?

I said I didn't know. I spent a whole day on one scene one day and after that it got easier.

Well how many times did you watch this scene said Sib

& I said I didn't know, not that many, maybe 50

The film reached Manzo's return to the village to cut off Shino's hair. This is supposed to make her look like a boy and so of no interest to the samurai. It's not much of a disguise. Sibylla is bored by Shino; she stopped the video and said she had to work.

She turned on the computer and began typing in text from *Practical Caravanning* 1982. Rikichi factor 5. She looked about the way you'd expect someone to look who'd once made a terrible mistake.

She might be waiting for my birthday, which was only a day away. Or maybe I could pretend to sudden insight into the defects of Lord

Leighton and Lord Leighton—the writer was obviously the author of the magazine article she once showed me.

If I said anything about the Moonlight Sonata or Yesterday or drapery it would be a dead giveaway, but suppose I said: the problem is that they are classicistic rather than classic, pursuing both truth and beauty not for themselves but because manifested in these forms in the great works of the past. It would be harder, of course, to seem as though I saw these faults from a state of grace, but maybe she would overlook that.

I picked up the postcard and gave it a piercing look, as though suddenly struck by something. As a matter of fact there did seem to be rather a lot of cloth in the air. Now all I had to do was casually comment on this superfluity of airborne material in a way that would show not only pity for the perpetrator but a grace beyond pity.

PRACTICAL CARAVANNING said Sibylla. What in God's name is practical about caravanning and why in God's name should the word 'Practical' be thought to add appeal to the activity am I yet again a market of one? *Impractical Caravanning. Impractical Boating. Impractical Knitting.* I would buy any of the above and I have not the slightest interest in knitting, boating or, God help me, caravanning.

I unfolded the magazine article yet again. This was a lot harder. Moonlight Sonata, I said to myself. Yesterday. I read through it trying to see what she had seen.

The horror! The horror! said Sibylla.

She had been typing for about 5 minutes. Earnings for the day so far: about £1.35.

If I interrupted the most likely thing was not that she would change her mind but that she would go back to watching Seven Samurai.

I went back upstairs. She didn't look up.

I looked everywhere in her room, but I couldn't find the envelope.

❖

Today is my birthday. Sibylla hasn't said anything. I thought she
might when I opened my presents, but she didn't.

I said: I think what's wrong with Lord Leighton is that he is classicistic rather than classic, pursuing both truth and beauty not for
themselves but because manifested in these forms in the great works
of the past. Something similar seems to be wrong with the author of
the magazine article.

Hmm said Sibylla.

I was afraid she was going to say in what way similar so I said
quickly:

I'm sorry I said the tape was crap. He deserves our pity.

Sibylla looked as though she was trying not to laugh.

I said: What do I have to say?

She said: You're looking for something in the wrong place.

I said: I just want to know who he is.

She said: Are you telling me you don't care what he's like? You've
read hundreds of travel books. Who's the worst writer you can think
of?

I didn't even have to think.

Val Peters, I said.

He had had an affair with a Cambodian girl with one leg and he
had written a book about Cambodia and the girl and the stump with
poetic evocations of what remained of the countryside and the leg.
This was the worst book I had ever read. It wasn't really that he was
a bad writer, though—even though I was only eight I could see he
was quite a good writer.

She said: If that was who it was would you still want to know?

I said: Is that who it is?

She said: VAL PETERS! Why the man's a veritable Don Swan.

I said: Well then who is it?

She said: You don't want to know. Why won't you take my word for it?

I said: Because you're a market of one.

Sibylla said: Well, you may be right. Would you mind if I had a look at that book on aerodynamics I got you for your birthday?

and without waiting for a reply she took the book from the table and opened it and reading began to smile.

The present was not much of a surprise. Sib came across it at Dillon's Gower Street and about three pages into the book began to laugh and to pace up and down repeating the words THICK MANTLE OF FEATHERS while the three other people in the room got out of the way. WE APPROXIMATE THE BIRD'S BODY BY A SPHERE OF RADIUS 5CM, said Sib, I had no idea aerodynamics was so entertaining, and under the impression that everyone in Dillons would like to share the joke she said Just listen to this example:

Grebes (an example is the common 'hell-diver') are among the birds that hunt their prey underwater. Unlike ducks and other surface water birds, whose feathers are completely water repellent, the outer two-thirds of the grebes' body feathers are wettable. However, like the duck, they require the buoyancy as well as the thermal insulation of the air trapped by a thick mantle of feathers when they are on the surface. In order to facilitate the underwater maneuverability required to catch its prey, the grebe increases its specific gravity to near that of the water by drawing its feathers close to its body (each feather has eight muscles); their partial wettability assists in expelling most of the air, leaving only a thin layer at the skin surface for thermal insulation.

We approximate the bird's body by a sphere of radius $r = 5cm$ and assume it has a specific gravity of 1.1, and find the thickness Δr of the layer of air under sea level conditions required to bring the specific gravity of the combination to unity.

Did you know that each grebe's feather has eight muscles? asked Sib.

No, I said.

Did you know that the outer two-thirds of their body feathers were wettable?

No, I said.

I did not point out that everyone within a radius of 10 metres knew it now. I said I didn't think I was ready for aerodynamics, not because I didn't think I was ready for aerodynamics but because the cheap books in the room were £20.

Of course you're ready for it, said Sib flipping through the book. You can tell just from the names of the mathematicians. Bernoulli's equation—Euler's equation—Gauss's divergence theorem—I have no idea what these actually ARE, but essentially the mathematics at the heart of the subject seems to be post-Newtonian developments in calculus, 18th 19th century stuff. How hard can it be? And look, it's got an appendix on natural prototypes with a discussion of the hummingbird and aerodynamics of insect flight.

I said: When was it published?

1986, said Sibylla.

I said in that case maybe we could get it secondhand at Skoob.

Good point, said Sib. Would you like something on Laplace transforms?

No.

What about Fourier analysis? Not for your birthday, obviously you can't have Schaum's Outline Series for your birthday, but just to have? It says it's a crucial mathematical tool for modern engineering.

No.

We'll see if they've got it at Skoob, said Sibylla, and of course when I opened my presents not only were there the books on aerodynamics, Fourier analysis and Laplace transforms, but also Gordon's

Introduction to Old Norse, Njal's Saga in Icelandic & in the Penguin, various other bargains and a new skateboard.

I wanted to throw everything on the table to the floor and shout. All I wanted was something that everyone else in the world takes for granted and instead I got Laplace transforms and the aerodynamics of insect flight. I was about to say this when I saw that Sib had stopped smiling and was now holding her head in her hand, even thick mantle of feathers had not kept away whatever it was she didn't want to think about. I thought I might say something anyway if I stayed, so I went out to ride my skateboard.

3

Funeral Games

Well, now I know.

When I got back to the house Sib said she was going out. I had seen that look on her face before. While at Skoob we had seen a secondhand copy of *The History of the Jewish People in the Age of Jesus Christ*, the brilliant four-volume updated version which had come out in the early 80s, an amazing bargain at just £100. We had had a long argument in which Sibylla had said I ought to have it and I had said we could not afford it and Sibylla had said it was a superb work of scholarship which no home should be without and I had said we could not afford it.

I said: You know we can't afford *The History of the Jewish People in the Age of Jesus Christ*. Sibylla said she was going to Grant & Cutler. I said we couldn't afford to go to Grant & Cutler and Sibylla said I didn't have to come. The last time Sibylla went to Grant & Cutler alone—actually I don't want to think about the last time Sibylla went to Grant & Cutler alone. I said I thought I'd come too.

You're right, she said. We can't afford it

and she turned on the computer and then sat curled up in a chair not doing anything at all.

I thought: This is insane. I thought: Who cares what's wrong with Lord Leighton? We've got to get out of here. But I still didn't know where she kept the envelope.

I had to do something, so I went out on my bike to Blockbuster Video to see what I could find. At last I found something.

I went back to the house. Sibylla was still sitting in the chair. I said: I got you a video, and I put the cassette in the TV and turned it on.

A copyright warning came and went.

Sib sat up.

OHHHH, said Sib, Tall Men in Tight Jeans!

What? I said.

I haven't seen this in YEARS, said Sib.

It says on the cover that it's a western based on the story of Seven Samurai, so I thought you'd like it.

LIKE it! said Sib. I ADORE it. You KNOW how much I like the Tyrone Power school of acting.

Do you want me to take it back? I said.

But it was too late. Sib was sitting alertly on the arm of her chair like a terrier with its eye on the ball. Ball flies through air, terrier flies over ground; terrier gets ball, terrier barks insanely, terrier spends hour growling if anyone tries to get ball & whining if no one shows interest. No sooner had the film begun than gleeful Sib pounced on some point in which it was inferior to Seven Samurai and for the next hour there was an almost constant stream of comment, interrupted only by howls of laughter at each appearance of the recruit from the Tyrone Power school of acting & by occasional silences in which I was meant to disagree so she could argue some more. There may have been some dialogue—if there was, I couldn't hear it.

Brynner began to recruit men for the job.

It's a difficult assignment, said Sibylla. It will be hard to find so many tall men in tight jeans.

Will you shut up? I said.

I'm sorry, said Sib shutting up.

Isn't there ANYTHING you like about it? I said.

How can you ask? said Sib. Not ONE but SEVEN tall men in tight jeans—it's simply MAGNIFICENT.

Never mind, I said.

And it's so easy to follow, you can tell which one is the mercenary because he has a stomach.

Never mind, I said.

The villain is the short one, said Sib. The starving peasants are fat. If they were tall and lean it would be too confusing.

I looked at the screen without saying anything.

James Coburn, said Sib. I always like watching James Coburn. And Eli Wallach is brilliant. And then, one of the problems with Seven Samurai is that none of the actors has the faintest idea of how to do Oriental inscrutability. Mifune is HOPELESS, and are the rest any better? Shimura, Kimura, Miyaguchi, Chiaki, Inaba, Kato, Tsuchiya—pathetic. It's only when you see Tall Men in Tight Jeans that you realise what a *handicap* it was to Kurosawa in not being able to draw on the genius of Charles Bronson. If he had had an actor with a face like a Japanese woodcut who knows what he might have achieved—

I'm trying to watch the film, I said.

I won't say another word, said Sib. I'll be as silent as the grave.

And suddenly I knew where she kept the envelope.

For as long as I can remember Sib has been pining for Fraser's *Ptolemaic Alexandria* (a superb work of scholarship which no home should be without). It is not available in public libraries (or at least in none known to us) but sometimes we would come across a secondhand copy in a bookshop and visit it on a daily basis. Sib would draw attention to marvellous footnotes on Eratosthenes (who worked out the circumference of the world) or the *Alexandra* of Lycophron which was a whole poem narrated by Cassandra in a prophetic frenzy and which made so little sense that scholars could never tell whether textual corruption or the madness of Cassandra was to blame for their difficulties, or the *Theriaca* of Nicander which was a long poem in hexameters about snakes. It was always too expensive, and sooner or later somebody richer would buy it.

Four months ago Sib found another copy and this time she bought it. I don't know where or what she paid for it—she wouldn't tell me. She said she would ask to be buried with it but it would be cruel to rob posterity of one of the few copies in existence, she would be willing to bet that if she died 50 *years* from now Oxford University Press would still be pretending to be about to reprint it, and she said if she had a funeral perhaps I could pass the book around and people could read out interesting passages from it. I promised that if I had any say in the matter it would be read at her funeral.

The last time I had seen the envelope in the drawer had been six months ago; the reason it was no longer there was that in the meantime she had got the book.

I had to watch the rest of the film but I couldn't concentrate. I don't know whether it was any good; all I could think about was the envelope and the book.

At last it was over. Sib said Thank you. She said she'd better do some work.

Ptolemaic Alexandria was in a bookcase behind her back. I got out Volume II and opened it to the description of a tragedy portraying the events of Exodus (Fraser quotes an exchange between God and Moses in iambic trimeters), and there it was. To Be Opened In Case of Death.

I thought: If 'twere done, 'twere well 'twere done quickly. I thought: What's a sealed envelope? A door marked No Entry or Authorized Personnel Only. Something to ignore if the circumstances warrant it.

I put it inside my shirt and went upstairs. When I got to my room I opened the envelope.

It wasn't Red Devlin. It wasn't anyone like that.

I remembered one of his books that I hadn't bothered to finish. He'd gone to Bali. The men there walk barefoot across the lava field of a live volcano. He didn't. He stood watching them walk across the lava and then he went back to the hotel and wrote about how he'd watched them. He didn't know any Balinese. He fucked a woman back at the hotel on the basis of three words of Balinese. Maybe she liked nocturnal animals.

4

Steven, age 11

Three days after I learned his name I realised I'd jumped to conclusions. Quite often in travel books the writer goes from being naive or ignorant or cowardly to doing something quite brave later on. It was stupid to judge him with so little to go on. So I went to the library to look for the rest of his books. Sibylla is right, he's very popular—they have everything he's written, but only two books were there.

Right beside them on the shelf was my old favourite, *Journey into Danger!* I must have read that about 20 times. Well, too bad.

I took down *The Lotus-Eaters*. There was a picture of my father on the back, taking up the whole back cover. He stared frowning into the distance. He was less handsome than I'd imagined, but it might be a bad picture.

An Antique Land had a different picture on the back. Another audition for the Tyrone Power school of acting.

If the books had been fiction the librarian probably wouldn't have let an 11-year-old borrow them, but because they were travel writing it did not occur to her to object. She was used to my borrowing from the grown-up section, especially travel books; she probably didn't realise these were X-rated.

I read the two books I'd found, and then I got three more at the Barbican, and I read the latest one at the Marylebone Library because I didn't have a ticket. By the end of the week I had read all my father's books.

Well. I have to admit I'd hoped to find some spark of genius or heroism unnoticed by Sibylla. I wanted to open a page and think But this is brilliant! This didn't happen. I kept reading anyway. I don't know what I was hoping to find.

❖

When I didn't find anything in the books I thought he might be different in person.

He had been married to his first wife when he met my mother, it had ended, and he had married again and moved to another house. So even if I could have discovered the location of the Medley, it would now be occupied only by his ex-wife.

Then I thought he might give a talk somewhere, and I could follow him home. But I thought it would end in drinks, and be hard for me to follow. I could try the hunchbacked midget costume I had to wear when we went to see The Crying Game—but I thought I might have trouble getting into a bar even as a midget sensitive about his height.

Then I had an idea. My father wrote a lot of journalism, and he always got a lot of things wrong. Science held a fatal fascination for him. He had never really mastered the difference between the special and general theories of relativity, but for some reason could not keep from bringing both into his articles whenever he could. Sometimes he would take a word which had both a technical meaning and an ordinary meaning (chaos, string, relativity, positive/negative, half-life, you get the idea) and then take statements applicable to the word in its technical sense to support generalisations about the word in its common sense. Sometimes the technical meaning would be something that could only be expressed in mathematics, so that it didn't really have a correlate in ordinary language—that never stopped him. It was really just a matter of waiting for his next piece to come out & then writing to correct the mistakes in an engaging, innocent, boyish way, signing the letter Steven aged 11—this would be bound to get a response, and with luck he would put his address on the letter.

The next day was Monday. I went back to the library and went through all the Sunday papers, but there was nothing by my father. I went through all the Saturday papers, but there was nothing there either. Then I went through the papers for Monday, 30 March. Nothing there. I had known who he was for 10 days.

I went back to the library every day to go through the papers. There was nothing by my father. I would stand at the table, leafing through the pages, and sometimes I'd see an interesting story and get excited and suddenly remember. I knew who he was.

On Saturday I went back to the library again, and this time there was a piece in the *Independent Magazine* on the Galapagos. It talked about extinction and selection. There were lots of logical fallacies, and also some factual mistakes about dinosaurs, and he seemed to have misunderstood the selfish gene theory. Here was my chance!

I wasn't going to point out the logical errors, which might put his back up, and I decided not to say anything about the part where he mixed up DNA and RNA because I thought that would be too embarrassing, but I thought I could safely point out more abstruse errors of fact, and this would be the type of thing I could sign Steven aged 11. It was hard to know how simply I should put the selfish gene theory: since he hadn't understood it I didn't want to make the explanation complicated, but I thought it would sound obnoxious if I stuck to words of one syllable.

I wrote the letter ten times trying to sound clever and not obnoxious. I could have printed it out on the word processor, but I thought my atrocious handwriting might be more appealing, so I wrote the final version out by hand.

It took two days to write. I could have written it in 15 minutes if I hadn't had to worry about sounding obnoxious. Still, as Sibylla would say, it's not nice to go around constantly offending people.

❖

A week went by and I thought the *Independent* might not have passed it on straight away.

A week went by.

A week went by and I thought he must have it by now.

Three days went by and April was over. I thought he might actually be travelling. A day went by and I thought he might have a secretary to deal with correspondence. Four days went by. The secretary might have instructions not to answer letters unaccompanied by SAE.

His letter came the next day.

I took it to my room to read.

The address was handwritten; I thought this looked promising. The envelope was one of those self-stick envelopes; he'd written in black ballpoint. I opened it slowly; there was a sheet of A5, folded once, inside. I unfolded it. It said:

6 May, 1998

Dear Steven,

Thank you for your letter. As you probably know, there are a lot of different theories about why the dinosaurs became extinct. I admit I used the one most convenient for my argument. The point about the selfish gene theory would be fair enough if that was what I was relying on, but in fact Dawkins' theory does have some rivals.

I hope you won't be discouraged if I stand my ground. I think it's wonderful that you show such a grasp of the importance of the theory, and I'm thrilled that you like my writing.

Yours,
Val Peters

I had told myself not to expect anything, but I must have been expecting something. In spite of the article, in spite of all the books, I'd kept hoping for something so brilliant I couldn't have thought of it myself. I looked down at the piece of paper in my hand with its bold careless signature, and I wished more than anything in the world that it had not been written by my father.

If anyone else had written it, I would have written back to point out that the whole article talked as if selection at the level of genes, individuals and species were the same thing and that he needed to clear up this confusion even if he was arguing against Dawkins as the article claimed to, and I would have pointed out that he hadn't answered any of my arguments. I still didn't want to annoy, however, so I let it pass. The crucial thing was that he had put his address at the top of the page. I looked the street up in the A–Z, and it was not far from the Circle Line.

5

For David, with best wishes

I took the Circle Line and I went to my father's house and stood outside.

I knew I had two half-brothers and a half-sister, but I was pretty sure they lived with their mother. At about 10:30 a woman came out of the house. She got in a car and drove off.

I wasn't sure whether to go up to the door. I didn't know what I'd say—I thought I'd blurt out something stupid. I crossed the street and looked at the windows. I couldn't see any movement. At about 11:00 I saw a face.

At 11:30 the door opened again and a man came out and down the steps. He looked older than I'd imagined him; the pictures I'd seen must have been taken years ago. He was less handsome than I'd imagined, even after the pictures; I'd forgotten that she had been rather drunk by the time she kissed him.

He reached the street and turned right. At the corner he turned right again.

I went back again the next day. I had in my backpack the introduction to aerodynamics, a book on calculus for engineers, the Penguin translation of *Njal's Saga, Brennu-njalssaga,* Gordon's *Introduction to Old Norse* and *The Count of Monte Cristo* in case I got bored, plus four peanut butter and jam sandwiches and a tangerine. There was a bus stop with a low wall beside it across the street from his house. I sat watching the house, reading *Njal's*

Saga and flipping back and forth between the Icelandic and the Penguin.

Njal and his sons were at a court called the Althing. Skarp-Hedin, one of Njal's sons, had killed a priest. I did not really understand how the court worked. Njal's son-in-law Asgrim and the Njalssons went from booth to booth looking for support. First they went to Gizurr's booth and then they went to the Olfus booth to see Skapti Thoroddson.

'Lát heyra þat,' segir Skapti.
> *'Let us hear your errand,' said Skapti.*

'Ek vil biðja þik liðsinnis,' segir Ásgrímr, 'at þú veitir mér lið ok mágum mínum.'
> *'I need your help,' said Asgrim, 'for myself and my kinsmen.'*

I had been working on Icelandic for three weeks so it wasn't too bad. There were some things I couldn't do without a dictionary. Nothing happened in the house.

'Hitt hafða ek ætlat,' segir Skapti, 'at ekki skyldi koma vandræði yður í híbýli mín.'
> *'I have no intention,' said Skapti, 'of letting your troubles into my house.'*

Ásgrímr segir: 'Illa er slíkt mælt, at verða mǫnnum þá sízt at liði, er mest liggr við.'
> *Asgrim said, 'These are mean words; you are of least use when the need is greatest.'*

The postman came to the house with the second post. The woman came to the door to take it; there seemed to be a lot of letters. I ate a peanut butter sandwich.

'Hverr er sá maðr,' segir Skapti, 'er fjórir menn
ganga fyrir, mikill maðr ok fǫlleitr, ógæfusamligr,
harðligr ok trǫllsligr?'

> *'Who is that man,' said Skapti, 'the fifth in the line,*
> *that tall, fierce-looking, troll-like man with the pale, ill-*
> *starred look?'*

Nothing happened in the house.

Hann segir: 'Skarpheðinn heiti ek, ok hefir þú sét
mik jafnan á þingi, en vera mun ek því vitrari en
þú, at ek þarf eigi at spyrja, hvat þú heitir. Þú heitir
Skapti Þóroddsson, en fyrr kallaðir þú þik
Burstakoll, þá er þú hafðir drepit Ketil ór Eldu;
gerðir þú þér þá koll ok bart tjǫru í hǫfuð þér.
Síðan keyptir þú at prælum, at rísta upp jarðarmen,
ok skreitt þú þar undir um nóttina. Síðan fórt þú
til Þórólfs Loptssonar á Eyrum, ok tók hann við
þér ok bar þik út í mjǫlsekkum sínum.'

> *'Skarp-Hedin is my name,' he replied, 'and you have*
> *often seen me here at the Althing. But I must be*
> *sharper than you, for I have no need to ask you your*
> *name. You are called Skapti Thoroddsson, but once you*
> *called yourself Bristle-Head, when you had just killed*
> *Ketil of Elda; that was the time you shaved your head*
> *and smeared it with tar, and bribed some slaves to cut*
> *you a strip of turf to cower under for the night. Later*
> *you fled to Thorolf Loptsson of Eyrar, who took you in*
> *and then smuggled you abroad in his flour sacks.'*

Eptir þat gengu þeir Ásgrímr út.

> *With that they all left the booth.*

Nothing happened in the house.

Skarpheðinn mælti: 'Hvert skulu vér nú ganga?'

> *'Where shall we go now?' asked Skarp-Hedin.*

'Til búðar Snorra goða,' segir Ásgrímr.

> *'To Snorri the Priest's booth,' said Asgrim.*

Njal's Saga was a bit hard in places but not too hard. The aerodynamics was a real killer. I read a couple of pages but I wasn't in the mood. Nothing happened in the house.

I went back to *Njal's Saga*. Snorri said that their own lawsuits were going badly, but he promised not to take sides against the Njalssons or support their enemies. He said:

'Hverr er sá maðr, er fjórir ganga fyrir, fǫlleitr ok
skarpleitr ok glottir við tǫnn ok hefir øxi reidda um
ǫxl?'

> *'Who is that man, fifth in the line, the pale, sharp-featured man with a grin on his face and an axe on his shoulder?'*

'Heðinn heiti ek,' segir hann, 'en sumir kalla mik
Skarpheðinn ǫllu nafni, eða hvat vilt þú fleira til
mín tala?'

> *'My name is Hedin,' he replied, 'but some call me Skarp-Hedin in full. Have you anything else to say to me?'*

Snorri maelti: 'Þat at mér, þykki maðr harðligr ok
mikilfengligr, en þó get ek, at þrotin sé nú þín en
mesta gæfa, ok skamt get ek eptir þinnar æfi.'

> *'I think you look very ruthless and formidable,' said Snorri, 'but my guess is that you have exhausted your store of good luck, and that you have not long to live.'*

The Asgrimssons went from booth to booth with mixed success and each time someone said there is just one thing I'd like to know, who is that ill-starred looking man the fifth in line and each time Skarp-Hedin said something insulting with predictable results. It was quite different from Homer or from Malory because it was very plain but I still rather liked it. There was a glossary in Gordon and some grammatical tips so it was not too bad on the whole.

I read a few more pages and then I read *The Count of Monte Cristo* for a couple of hours and went home.

I went back the next day and I read three pages of aerodynamics but I wasn't in the mood. Then I read some more of *Njal's Saga*.

At about 12:30 he passed by a window on the ground floor eating a sandwich. I had four peanut butter and jam sandwiches and two banana and Marmite sandwiches and a bag of crisps in my backpack. I ate one of the sandwiches and then read *The Count of Monte Cristo*. Nothing else happened in the house.

I let two days go by. It was raining hard and cold. Then the weather cleared. I went back to sit on the wall. I had three peanut butter and jam sandwiches, one peanut butter and honey sandwich and a bottle of Ribena.

It started to rain again, so I walked back to the Circle Line and spent the rest of the day reading *The Count of Monte Cristo*. I could have worked on aerodynamics but I wasn't in the mood.

Third week of May, typical English cold snap. 283 degrees above absolute zero. I went to the house just to look at it. I saw him talking to the woman in an upstairs room but I couldn't hear what they were saying. I made myself sit reading on the wall just in case I ever had to go to the North Pole.

My teeth started chattering. Magnusson seemed to have used a different text from the one Sibylla had given me; I thought I could work out the extra bits. Then I remembered I wasn't going to be going to the North Pole. There was nothing going on in the house. I went back to the Circle Line and ate my sandwiches.

I let four days go by and then I had to go back. I sat on the wall and made myself read a whole chapter on aerodynamics just to prove I could still do it. I ate a peanut butter sandwich. I was still reading

Njal's Saga. I hadn't worked on it very much. It was stupid to stand here. I couldn't really work, either I should do something or I should go somewhere else where I could work. It would be stupid to go away after standing outside at a bus stop for a week.

Then I knew what I would do.

I would ask my father for an autograph.

❖

I came back the next day, and I took with me a paperback copy of
Stout Cortez (the book with the Balinese woman), which I had
bought at an Oxfam shop for 50p. I also had *Brennu-njalssaga*, Magnusson, Gordon, the book on Laplace transforms and a book on edible insects which the library was selling off for 10p. I could spend
the rest of the day on the Circle Line. I wasn't expecting this to take
long; it was just something I had to do.

I reached the house at 10:00. A window was open on the ground
floor; people were talking quietly. I stood by the wall listening.

Are you sure you don't want to come? You hardly ever get to see
them.

It's not really my kind of thing. It won't help if I'm bored out of
my skull, and if we do something else they'll hate me. The only question is, are you sure you don't mind?

It's not that I mind, I just thought you'd like to spend some time
with them.

I would, obviously, but they've got school all week. They've got
their own ideas about how they spend the weekend. It's not the end
of the world.

A car drew up outside the house and three children got out.

The car drove off.

The children looked up at the house.

Well, come on, said one.

They headed up the walk. The door opened. There was some sort
of discussion just inside it. The children came back down the steps
with the woman I'd seen before. The man stood in the doorway.

We'll go to Planet Hollywood when you get back, he said.

They got into a car and drove off. He closed the door.

I was tired of walking up and down the street and watching that
door. I didn't want to walk away again. I was tired of wondering

whether it was a bad time. I was tired of wondering whether it would be better to interrupt him before he'd had a chance to start work.

I went to the door and rang the bell. I waited a minute. Then I counted a minute, and then I counted two minutes. I knocked on the door and counted another minute. If he didn't come I would go away. I thought I'd annoy him if I kept knocking and ringing the bell. Two minutes went by. I turned and went down the steps.

A window shot up on the second floor.

Hang on, I'll be down in a minute, he shouted.

I went back to the door.

A couple of minutes went by, and the door opened.

What can I do for you? he asked.

His hair was medium brown, with some grey; his forehead was quite deeply lined; there were grey hairs in the eyebrows, and the eyes under them were large and light, a little like a night animal's. His voice was rather light and soft.

Can I help you? he asked.

I've come for the Christian Aid envelope, I found myself saying.

I don't see it anywhere, he said, not looking. Anyway, we're not Christians.

That's OK, I said. I'm a Jewish atheist myself.

All right, I'll ask, he said smiling now. If you're a Jewish atheist what are you doing collecting for Christian Aid?

My mother makes me, I said.

But if you're Jewish, doesn't your mother have to be Jewish too? he asked.

She is, I said. That's why she won't let me steal from Jewish charities.

It worked like a charm. He laughed helplessly. He said: Shouldn't you save this for Comic Relief?

I said: A red nose is funny? I know, I know, they only laugh when it hurts.

He said: Why do I get the feeling you're not here for Christian Aid?

I said: I wanted an autograph, but you have to break these things gradually.

He said: You want an autograph? Really? How old are you?

I said: Why, is your signature 15-certificate?

He said: Well, there may be a few people who think my name is a dirty word, but no. You seem a little young, though. Or is this another scam? Are you going to flog it?

I said: Could I get a lot of money for it?

And he said quite confidently: I think you'll have to wait a while.

I said: Well, I don't mind. I've got a book with me.

I took off my backpack.

He said: Is it a first edition?

I said: I don't think so. It's a paperback.

He said: Then it won't be worth a lot of money.

I said: Well, I guess I'll just have to keep it.

He said: I guess you will. Come inside and I'll sign it for you.

I followed him down a corridor to a kitchen at the back of the house. He asked whether I would like anything. I said an orange juice.

He poured two and handed me one. I handed him the book.

He said:

It's always strange when they come back to you. It's like sending children out into the world with no idea where they'll end up. Look at this. Third printing, 1986. 1986! It could have been around the world. Some clapped-out hippy in Kathmandu could have carried it on a trek; passed it to a mate on his way to Australia; a tourist might have picked it up in an airport before meeting one of those cruise ships that go to the Antarctic. What shall I put?

I felt cold. I could say To Ludo, with love from Dad. In ten seconds there would not be an object in the room that was not there now, and yet everything would be different.

He had a pen in his hand and had been through this all before.

The hand that had been now here now there held the pen. His mouth was slightly pursed. He was wearing a blue shirt and brown corduroys.

He said: What's your name?

David.

Is To David with best wishes all right? he asked.

I nodded.

He scrawled something in the book and handed it back.

I wondered whether I would throw up.

He asked me something about school.

I said I didn't go to school.

He asked me about that.

I said something about that.

He said something else. He was being pleasant. There seemed to be a lot of grey in his hair; that wouldn't have been there at the time of the Medley.

I said: Can I see where you work?

He said: Sure. He sounded surprised and pleased.

I followed him up to the top of the house. This was not the same house, but they had gone to his study for the Medley, so some of the books and things would probably be here. I don't know why I had to see this but I had to see it.

He had the whole top of the house for a study. He showed me his computer. He said he used to have a lot of games on it but he had to take them off because he wasted too much time playing games. He gave me an engaging boyish grin. He showed me his database on different countries. He showed me boxes of record cards for different books.

On a bookshelf I saw 10 books by the author of the magazine article Sibylla had shown me. I walked over and took one off the shelf. It was signed. I said:

Are they all signed?

He said:

I'm a big fan.

He said:

I think he is one of the greatest writers in English this century.

I did not laugh hysterically. I said:

My mother says I will be able to appreciate him when I am older.

He said:

What other books do you like?

I was about to say Other?

I said:

Do you mean in English?

He said:

In anything.

I said:

I like *Kon Tiki*.

He said:

Fair enough.

I said I liked *Amundsen and Scott* and I liked *King Solomon's Mines* and I liked everything by Dumas and I liked *The Bad Seed* and *The Hound of the Baskervilles* and I liked *The Name of the Rose* but the Italian was rather difficult.

I said:

I like Malory a lot. I like the *Odyssey*. I read the *Iliad* a long time ago but I was too young to appreciate it. I'm reading *Njal's Saga* right now. My favourite part is where they go around the booths asking for help and Skarp-Hedin insults everybody.

He had been making a thing of being wide-eyed and open mouthed. He said humorously: I don't think I've come across it.

I said: Do you want to see my Penguin translation? I've got it with me.

He said: Sure.

I opened my backpack and took out the Penguin translation by Magnus Magnusson. The Icelandic dictionary is about £140 & I had told Sibylla we could not afford it.

I opened it to the page. I said: It's only a couple of pages, and I handed it to him.

He turned the pages, chuckling as he read. At last he handed it back to me.

You're right, it's a scream, he said. I'll have to get a copy. Thanks.

I said: The translation isn't very much like the Icelandic though. You can't really imagine a Viking warrior saying don't interfere in the conversation. The Icelandic is *vil ek nú biðja þik, Skarpheðinn! at þú létir ekki til þín taka um mál várt.* Though of course the Icelandic words don't really have the same register as English words of Anglo-Saxon derivation because they're not in opposition to a register of Latinate vocabulary.

He said: You know Icelandic?

I said: No, I've only just started. That's why I need the Penguin.

He said: Isn't that cheating?

I said: It's harder than using a dictionary.

He said: Then why don't you use a dictionary?

I said: It costs £140.

He said: £140!

I said: Well it stands to reason there's not much of a market for it. People only study it at university if at *all*; the only way you can get anything in Icelandic is to order it specially from Iceland; who's going to buy the dictionary? If there was a groundswell of interest in the population at large maybe the price would come down, or at least maybe libraries would get a copy, but obviously people aren't going to develop an interest in something they've never heard of.

He said: Well how did you develop an interest in it?

I said: I read some of the Penguin translations when I was younger. I said: The interesting thing is that according to Hainsworth's classic article on Homer & the epic cycle the mark of Homer's superiority to the cycle is supposed to be richness and expansiveness, & yet it seems as though bareness is the thing that is good in the Icelandic saga. You could say Well, Schoenberg is obviously wrong to dismiss the Japanese print as primitive and superficial, why is he wrong?

He was giving me another humorous wide-eyed look. He said: Now I believe you read my book.

I did not know what to say.

I said:

I've read all your books.

And he said: Thanks.

He said: I mean that. That's the nicest thing I've heard in a long time.

I thought: I can't stand this.

I thought of the three Prisoners of Fate. I could walk out any time. I wanted to walk out and I wanted to drop hints. I wanted to mention the Rosetta Stone and watch realisation dawn. I don't know what I was going to say.

I was just about to say something when I saw Fraser's *Ptolemaic Alexandria* on a shelf. I exclaimed artlessly:

Oh, you've got *Ptolemaic Alexandria*!

He said:

I shouldn't really have bought it but I couldn't resist.

I didn't ask where he'd heard of it. Somebody had obviously told him it was a superb work of scholarship which no home should be without.

I said:

Well, it's a brilliant book.

He said:

Not that it's much use to me. Did you know there was a Greek tragedy about God and Moses? It's got it at the back but it's all in Greek.

I said:

Would you like me to read some for you?

He said:

Oh—

and he said

Well, why not?

I got Volume II off the shelf and I started reading where God is saying Stretch out thy rod in iambic trimeters and I translated as I went along and after about three lines I could see he was looking bored and amazed.

I said:

Well, you get the drift.

He said:

How old are you?

I said I was 11. I said there was nothing very difficult about the passage and anyone who had studied the language for a few months would be able to read it and I had known it for years.

He said: Christ.

I said it was not such a big deal and that J. S. Mill had started Greek at the age of 3.

He said: How old were you when you started?

I said: 4.

He said: *Christ.*

Then he said:

Sorry, I don't mean to make you self-conscious, it's just that I've got kids of my own.

I was looking down at *Ptolemaic Alexandria* thinking I've got to say something. I said What did he try to teach them and he said nothing in a formal way but the point was they had watched Sesame Street and it was about the right level. There was a piece of paper at the front of the book. I said: What's this?

He said: Don't you recognise it?

and I thought: So he knows

and I thought: How did he know?

I said: Recognise it?

He said: It's from the *Iliad*. I thought you'd recognise it. Somebody gave it to me.

I said: Oh, of course.

I said: Have you read it then?

He said: I keep meaning to get around to it.

He said: I think subconsciously it reminds me of Latin.

I said: Of Latin?

He said: I took a year at school and I spent most of it smoking behind the bike shed.

I said I had heard the things worth reading in Latin were things you couldn't appreciate until you were 15 so maybe it was just the texts.

He said: I don't think we made it as far as texts, I just remember on the first day the teacher writing some noun on the board with nominative genitive bla bla bla. It all seemed so fucking pointless. I mean, look at the Romance languages. As far as I know every single one got rid of the case endings because the people actually speaking the language thought they were a complete waste of time. I kept thinking why do I have to sit here learning this evolutionary failure of a language?

He was grinning broadly as he said it and he said he thought whatever it was that had made him get out of the class and smoke behind the bike shed instead of sitting in the class learning case endings was probably the thing that had helped most to make him successful if you could call it success.

I was looking at a piece of paper that ended hope you like it Must dash S[illegible scrawl].

 I thought: My father is Val Peters.

He said: But I really should read it one of these days, she obviously went to a lot of trouble.

He said: I'm kind of glad mine weren't put under any pressure to start early, they grow up so fast and they spend so much time in school anyway, but I think it's amazing what you've done I really do and it really does mean a lot that you like my books, I wasn't just saying that, because at the end of the day it's not just how many people buy them.

I thought I should say something.

He said: Look, let me give you something else, something that'll be worth something some day. I mean I don't know what you think, but maybe you'd like one of these, it's not as if I'm ever going to read them, they get translated into about 17 languages and you don't necessarily do signings every time so if I signed one it would be unique,

and he went to another bookcase that was full of books and he said why didn't I take one of his books in Czech or Finnish or something and he would sign it and it would be unique.

I said You don't have to do that and he said No I insist, and he asked me which language I would like and I said Well how about Finnish?

He said Don't tell me you know Finnish and I said Do you want me to lie about something like that and he said Gordon Bennett.

He said Just out of curiosity is there any language here you don't know? I looked at the books and I said No but there are a lot I don't know very well and he said Sorry I asked and gave me another humorous look.

He said:

Why don't I make this one more personal, is there something you'd like me to say?

I thought: I've got to say something. I thought: Am I just going to go away without saying anything? I said: What did you have in mind?

He said: How about, for David, I promise never to decrease the market value of this book by signing another Finnish edition, your friend in Mammon Val Peters? He was grinning at me and holding a pen.

I said: Say whatever you want.

He said: I'd like to say something more personal but everything you think of saying always sounds so wet.

I said I probably wouldn't sell it anyway so it didn't have to be unique.

He said: Well in that case why don't I just put For David with best wishes Val but you'll know it came from the heart. He did not really say this with another humorous smile because he was smiling humorously throughout. I said Fine, thanks, and he scrawled something in the book and handed it over.

It was not hard to imagine a world where my body stood in this room with something else inside it. If I said something he would see that other world. I thought: Well am I going to go away?

I said:

Do you ever bury your books?

He said: What?

I said: You could bury your books in a plastic bag a few metres down, one on each continent. Then if there was a cataclysm they'd be preserved for posterity. They could dig them up again.

He said he hadn't tried it.

I said: What they should really do is bury a book in the foundation of each house. Sealed in plastic. It would help archaeologists in a millennium or so.

He smiled. He said: I hate to throw you out, but I'm gonna have to throw you out. I've got work to do.

I thought again that I could say something and everything would be different, and seeing his casual slightly complimented look I wanted to say it.

Then I thought:

If we fought with real swords I would kill him.

I thought:

I can't say I'm his son, because it's true.

V

He obviously thinks he's a samurai

1

A good samurai will parry the blow

The night I met him I went outside to sleep on the ground. It was stupid, I wasn't going anywhere. I rolled up my sleeping bag and brought it inside. I went upstairs and slept on the mattress, covered in blankets.

I could sleep outside if I had to.

I finished *Njal's Saga*. I had planned to go back to Inuit when I had finished but now there did not seem to be any immediate point so I decided to go on with aerodynamics.

I put the book on aerodynamics in my backpack as well as the two Schaum Outlines in case I needed Laplace transforms or Fourier analysis. I went to the National Gallery and sat on a bench in front of The Virgin & Child Enthroned between a Soldier Saint and St. John the Baptist.

4.9 Bound Vortex

It was shown in the last section that the force on a body is determined entirely by the circulation around it and by the free stream velocity.

Now I believe you read my book, said my father.

In an identical manner, it can be shown that the force on a vortex that is stationary relative to a uniform flow is given by the Kutta-Joukowski law.

Thanks, said my father. I mean that. That's the nicest thing I've heard in a long time.

The vortex that represents the circulation around the body

Thanks, said my father. I mean that.

departs in its characteristics from that of a vortex in the external flow

Thanks, said my father.

in that it does not remain attached to the same fluid particles

I mean that, said my father. That's the nicest thing

I got up and went to the main wing and sat in front of *A Young Man Holding a Skull* by Frans Hals. My father didn't say anything. I opened Kuethe & Chow on *Foundations of Aerodynamics* to page 85.

4.10 Kutta Condition

The Kutta-Joukowski theorem states that the force experienced by a body in a uniform stream is equal to the product of the fluid density, stream velocity, and circulation and has a direction perpendicular to the stream velocity.

I think you're going to have to wait a while, said my father.

The Kutta-Joukowski theorem states that the force experienced by a body in a uniform stream is equal to the product of the fluid density, stream velocity, and circulation and has a direction perpendicular to the stream velocity.

I think he's one of the greatest writers this century, said my father.

The *Kutta-Joukowski* theorem states that the *force* experienced by a *body* in a *uniform stream*

Thanks, said my father.

I stood up and left the room. I went this time to Room 34, and I took the corner seat by Ulysses Deriding Polyphemus. Still no sign of Polyphemus. I couldn't really remember the Kutta-Joukowski theorem but I wasn't going back to it again. I opened the book to page 86 and I started reading down the page very fast

The above discussion applies to an inviscid flow, but in a viscous fluid (however small the viscosity), the circulation is fixed by the imposition of an empirical observation. Experiments show that when a body with a sharp trailing edge is set in motion, the action of the fluid viscosity causes the flow over the upper and lower surfaces to merge smoothly at the trailing edge; this circumstance, which fixes the magnitude of the circulation around the body, is termed the *Kutta condition*, which may be stated as follows: *A body with a sharp trailing edge in motion through a fluid creates about itself a circulation of sufficient strength to hold the rear stagnation point at the trailing edge.*

The flow around an airfoil at an angle of attack in an inviscid flow develops no circulation and the rear stagnation point occurs Thanks Sure Now I believe you read my book. Isn't that cheating? Why don't you use a dictionary?

It wasn't all that easy to understand the book anyway, and with my father interrupting all the time it was practically impossible; what if he never stopped? What was it going to be like hearing it for 80 years? I thought of giving up and going home. Then I thought of Sibylla, jumping up and sitting down, jumping up to walk here and there, jumping up to read this book and that book a paragraph a sentence a word at a time.

I got up again, and I started walking quickly through the gallery, past the Fragonards, past the Caravaggios, past a room of Rembrandts and a room of followers of Rembrandt, looking for one of the boring little rooms people never visit to hide from him there. What about this? Still Life with Drinking Horn of the Saint Sebastian Archer's Guild, Lobster and Glasses, not to mention a half-peeled lemon—but beside it was a Vanitas by Jan Jansz Tech, a picture of a skull, an hourglass, a silk scarf, a drawing & other precious things, meant according to the caption to remind the viewer of the absurdity of human ambition. This was exactly the type of thing my father liked to comment on in philosophical moments, generally in the presence of a crumbling temple or tomb, what about the next room? Here was Cuyp's large painting, A Distant View of Dordrecht with a Milkmaid and Four Cows, and his small painting, A Distant View of Dordrecht with a Sleeping Herdsman and Five Cows—*no one* would look for me here.

I made myself read to the end of the chapter. I had to read every paragraph about eight times but at last I had finished it. I reread the Kutta-Joukowski Theorem five or six times. I thought of reading another chapter, but he kept saying Thanks, & instead I started flipping through the book, stopping at one page or another, looking for something so fascinating I wouldn't hear him any more. Mach Waves —incompressible flows—Tollmien-Schlichting instability—Flight of small insects—Control and Maneuvering in Bird Flight—

'My observation of the flight of buzzards leads me to believe that they regain their lateral balance, when partly overturned by a gust of wind, by a torsion of the tips of the wings . . .' This passage is from Wilbur Wright's first letter to Octave Chanute, dated 13 May 1900. It describes the crucial observation that led the Wright brothers to the invention of the aileron and thus to the achievement of lateral control and in turn to man's first powered flight.

Now I believe you read my book, said my father. I really mean that I'm not just saying that said my father. It means a lot said my father. At the end of the day it's not just how many buy them said my father. I've got kids of my own said my father Sesame Street was about the right level said my father Now I believe you read my book said my father Now I believe you read my book.

There was no point in staying so I left. There is a painting over the main stairs by Lord Leighton of Cimabue's Celebrated Image of the Virgin Borne in Procession; for years I had looked at this painting every time I left, wondering what was wrong with it.

When I got home Sibylla was watching Seven Samurai. She couldn't have been watching long; the farmers had only just left the village. Tough-looking samurai were striding through the streets of a large town; you'd have to have a lot of nerve to ask one to fight for three meals a day.

I sat on the sofa beside her. Fair enough, said my father.

Kambei was handing a razor to the priest with a bow. He sat by the river and splashed water on his head; the priest began to shave off his hair.

Fair enough, said my father.

Kambei put on the clothes which the priest had brought. He met the eyes of the shiftless Mifune with a face of stone. I think you're going to have to wait a while, said my father.

Kambei took the two rice cakes and walked to the barn. The thief shrieked inside. I am only a priest, said Kambei. I won't arrest you. I won't come in. I've brought food for the child. Thanks, said my father. I mean that. That's the nicest thing I've heard in a long time.

I stood up and began walking around the room, looking for something I could do for an hour or even ten minutes without hearing his voice. I picked up my book on judo but after two lines I saw his face, and I started reading Ibn Khaldun and he said Now I believe you read my books.

Have you seen him yet? asked Sibylla. This was her idea of delicacy, to bring the thing out in the open rather than leave me to wonder what she knew & whether I should say anything.

I saw him, I said. I don't know what you saw in him.

You know as much as I know, said Sib, delicately indicating that she knew for a fact that I'd also read through her papers.

I didn't tell him, I said.

Selbstverständlich, said Sib. I never could. I kept thinking I should, but I just couldn't. I'd read something he'd written, thinking he might have changed, and he did change, but only in the way that someone from the Tyrone Power school of acting would show maturity: mouth set, furrowed brow, this is someone thinking tough thoughts. He woke up a boy and went to bed—a man. I'm sorry to speak ill of your sperm donor, though. I'd better stop.

It's all right, I said.

No, it's not all right, said Sib. She turned off the video. It is shocking to stop in the middle, she said, still at least Kurosawa will never know.

It doesn't matter, I said.

All right, said Sib. Just remember that you are perfect, whatever your father may be. It may be that other people need a sensible father more.

We're not talking about an exhaustible resource, I said.

We're talking about luck, said Sib. Why should you have all of it?

Was I complaining? I said.

Look at it from his point of view, said Sib. It's hard for a man to be upstaged by his son.

I wasn't complaining, I said.

Of course you weren't, said Sib.

He said he had kids of his own, I said. He said they watched Sesame Street and it was about the right level.

At what age? said Sib.

He didn't say.

Hmmm, said Sib.

She stood up and turned on the computer and picked up the *Independent* and sat down to read it.

Did I tell you I was reading *Die Zeit*? said Sib. I was reading *Die Zeit* and I came across this lovely line, Es regnete ununterbrochen. It rained uninterruptedly. It sounded so lovely in the German. Es regnete ununterbrochen. Es regnete ununterbrochen. I shall think of it whenever it rains.

Did you ever think of having an abortion? I said.

I did, said Sib, but it was very late and I had to have counselling, they counselled adoption & I said Yes but how could I be sure your adoptive parents would teach you how to leave life if you did not care for it & they said What and I said—well you know I said what any rational person would say and we had an unprofitable discussion & she said

Oh look! Hugh Carey is back in England.

I said: Who?

Sibylla said: He was the best friend of Raymond Decker.

I said: Who?

Sibylla: You've never heard of Raymond Decker!

And then: But then who has?

She said that Carey was an explorer and Decker, she did not know what Decker was doing these days but in the early 60s they had been legendary classicists at Oxford. A pirate copy of Carey's translation of Wee sleekit cow'rin' tim'rous beastie into Greek for the verse paper in the Ireland was passed from hand to hand, & Decker had won the Chancellor's Latin with an amazing translation of Johnson on Pope, not said Sibylla the bit where he says It is a very pretty poem Mr. Pope but it is not Homer which was actually Bentley anyway now I think of it but the bit that goes

. . . the distance is commonly very great between actual perfor-
mances and speculative possibility. It is natural to suppose, that as
much as has been done to-day may be done to-morrow; but on
the morrow some difficulty emerges, or some external impedi-
ment obstructs. Indolence, interruption, business, and pleasure; all
take their turns of retardation; and every long work is lengthened
by a thousand causes that can, and ten thousand that cannot, be re-
counted. Perhaps no extensive and multifarious performance was
ever effected within the term originally fixed in the undertaker's
mind. He that runs against Time, has an antagonist not subject to
casualities.

Sib explained that this though Latinate was a diabolical piece to put
into Latin because all the abstract nouns would have to be turned
into clauses, she digressed to explain that Lytton Strachey on Johnson on the Poets, on the other hand, was the type of thing that was
very easy to turn into Latin, Strachey she said for example said

Johnson's aesthetic judgements are almost invariably subtle, or
solid, or bold; they have always some good quality to recommend
them—except one: they are never right. That is an unfortunate
deficiency; but no one can doubt that Johnson has made up for it,
and that his wit has saved all

the Latin she said practically wrote itself she seemed on the point of
digressing to some other point of similar interest so before she could
discuss somebody else on Strachey on Johnson and how they might
easily be translated into Phoenician or Linear B or Hittite I said
quickly
    But who ARE these people?

❖

Hugh Carey and Raymond Decker met when HC was 15 and RD was 19. HC was from Edinburgh. He had told his teacher he wanted to apply to Oxford and the teacher had told him to wait, & HC thought—but that's stupid, if I get in at 15 people will always say He got into Oxford when he was 15. So he wrote independently to Merton to apply to take the exam, & he went down to take the exam.

RD was largely self-taught.

RD had read Plato's *Gorgias* even before he came up, and being the type to take things to heart he had taken it to heart. In the *Phaedrus* the rhetorician Gorgias is said to boast that he can give a long or a short answer to any question, and in the *Gorgias* he says that when it comes to giving short answers he is unsurpassed. Socrates, on the other hand, knows only one way to answer a question, some questions can be answered with one word and others may take five thousand, and the philosopher, unlike the rhetorician or the politician, will take as long as he needs. This placed RD in a terrible dilemma. He had bought copies of past papers from the University Press & now he paced up and down declaiming to HC: All the interesting questions require a *minimum* of three hours apiece to answer and the rest are so stupid it is impossible to say anything intelligent about them, how can you make an intelligent reply to a stupid question? And he would tear his hair and say What am I to *do*?

HC was surprised. He had done 13 O-levels because he had heard the most anyone had ever done before was 12, and he had done them at the age of 12 because he had heard when he was 9 that the youngest anyone had ever done more than 5 was 13 & he had instantly decided to beat the record.

He said: Well what did you do for A-level?

RD: I don't want to talk about it.

HC: Well what about O-level?

RD: I don't want to talk about it.

HC: Well surely you must have taken some exam.

RD: Of course I've taken an exam. It was horrible. Full of questions about long division. I don't want to talk about it.

Long division? said HC.

RD: I don't want to TALK about it. And he paced up and down the common room making further anguished references to the *Gorgias* crying What am I to *do*?

HC said: Do you play chess?

What? said RD.

And HC said: Do you play chess?

And RD said: Of course.

And HC said Let's play a game. He took out from one pocket a pocket chess set, and from his other pocket he took out a chess clock which he took with him wherever he went. It was the night before the first exam, and he had been planning to go over the chorus to Zeus of Aeschylus' *Agamemnon*. He set out the board. RD was white.

HC set the timer & he said: 20 minute game.

And RD said: I don't play that way.

HC: 10 minutes each.

And RD said: But that's stupid.

HC: I don't have time to play longer. I need to look at the chorus to Zeus.

RD: P-K4.

HC: P-QB4.

RD knew many responses to the Sicilian Defence but the question was what could be developed in the time available, still pondering this question he had not even moved his knight to KB3 when the timer went off, he moved his knight now to KB3 and HC said:

Sorry. Game's over.

RD was furious & he started to argue but in the meantime HC had moved all the pieces back and turned the clock back & this time HC was white.

HC: P-K4.

RD liked the Sicilian Defence himself but debating inwardly the merits in the time allowed of the Najdorf Variation, the Scheveningen (which he generally preferred), the Nimzowitsch & others too numerous to mention he nearly made the same mistake, suddenly pulling himself together (P-QB4) he managed to make 10 moves before falling again into deep thought interrupted only by the timer.

He reached his 10th move & the timer went off before he had moved a piece & HC said game's over and moved the pieces back again and started the clock.

By now RD was really furious. HC was only 15 and looked young for his age. RD made his first move and HC made his and this time RD made a move the instant it was his turn and HC won in 25 moves.

RD put the pieces back. HC said he had to read the *Agamemnon*. RD said This won't take long. He was black. This time he played the defence he knew the best, and he played a version of a middle game he had read in Keres & Kotov, and the end played itself.

He said: Checkmate. And he said: I know what you think you're doing, but it's stupid. It's not the same.

And HC said: It's a game. It's a stupid game. Opening, middle game, endgame, opening, middle game, endgame, opening middle game endgame. Let's set the clock to 5 minutes.

RD said: It's not the same.

HC said: 10 minute game.

HC set out the pieces and he started the clock. They played 5 games and RD won 4.

RD said: It's not the same.

They played until 2:00 in the morning. RD kept saying It's not the same, but he was laughing now because he was winning most of the time. You are probably thinking that HC was letting him win but he wasn't. HC had none of the Socratic scruples that plagued RD, but he carried sportsmanship to so fanatical an extreme that it had a very similar effect; he knew he would have no real competition if RD was not there, & left to his own devices & composing Socratic answers to Gorgianic questions RD was certainly not going to be there. So even though he could hardly keep his eyes open he said to RD: Don't think of arguments. Look at a question and say: Queen's Indian. Sicilian Defence.

RD thought this was ridiculous but no sooner had he dismissed it as ridiculous than it suddenly seemed to him, as a matter of fact, that you actually could start a discussion of the influence of Homer on Virgil using the Sicilian Defence.

Ruy Lopez, said HC, pursuing his advantage.

RD: Ruy LOPEZ! How can I POSSIBLY use the Ruy LOPEZ?

HC hesitated—

RD: If they set the question they are OBVIOUSLY, ALWAYS white.

& he was again briefly plunged into despair.

HC: Black to win in 4 moves. Two knights & a rook, checkmate in 6.

No, said RD, and he stood up and wrapped his arms around his head in a pretzel formation. He paced up and down & at last he said: Yes. NOW I see. He said: You don't actually ARGUE all the way THROUGH you decide the endgame you want to play you incorporate an opening which might lead to it by REFERENCE as it might be Black played an unusual version of the Queen's Indian you incorporate the middle game largely by REFERENCE—

Whether this really is what you do or not RD did get in under the impression that you did and get a scholarship on the strength of [opening] [middle game] endgame, and he and HC were friends & rivals. HC made him go in for prizes because if he won a prize RD had not gone in for it would not really count, & every time he had to play chess with RD to counterbalance the hold Socrates had regained on his mind in the meantime. He had to play chess to counteract the influence of Fraenkel.

Fraenkel was a Jewish refugee from the Nazis, and on coming to England he had been made Professor of Latin at Corpus Christi College and gave seminars on Greek. Very few undergraduates went to these, and the few that went went with the approval of their tutor because Fraenkel was very formidable. Somehow or other HC heard of these seminars and instantly decided to go. He asked his tutor and his tutor said he thought it would be better to wait, and HC thought: But that's stupid, if I go now people will always say He went to Fraenkel's seminar in his first term when he was only 15. His birthday was in mid-October, and if he waited even a term it would be too late.

Now if HC went RD had to go too, because otherwise HC would have felt he was getting an unfair advantage. RD was naturally diffident and said he thought he should wait till his second or even third year; a chessboard was no use in a situation like this, but HC with the genius of desperation said That's ridiculous, and stealing shamelessly from Socrates he said there was no shame in ignorance but in the refusal to learn. He said he had heard that Fraenkel had deplored the lack of rigour in English scholarship; he said surely it was of the ESSENCE that they should not pick up slipshod methods at the very OUTSET of their scholarly careers. RD said Yes but he probably won't let us in the class and HC said Leave everything to me.

HC was 15 and looked 12. He went over to Corpus before breakfast and waited outside Fraenkel's room, and when the great man appeared he brought out the phrases 'slipshod methods' and 'outset of scholarly career'. He was taken into the room and shown some Greek he had never seen before and made to comment on it, and when he did not absolutely disgrace himself he was told that he and his friend could come to the class on probation.

Now Fraenkel once said in a class that a scholar should be able to look at any word in a passage and instantly think of another passage where it occurred; HC was unperturbed by this remark, but RD took it to heart, and the longer he worked the more any text was like a pack of icebergs each word a snowy peak with a huge frozen mass of cross-references beneath the surface. So that now in addition to Socratic reservations on answering any question was added a conviction that in any linguistic analysis a real scholar would haul up the whole iceberg. Meanwhile HC was horribly bored by the class, he found the business of loading a line with comment excruciatingly boring; he was only able to cheer himself up by remembering that he had only just turned 16.

Five terms passed and it was time for Mods.

The night before the first exam other candidates went over the arguments for and against a single author of the *Iliad* and *Odyssey* while HC and RD sat over a chessboard with HC saying Opening middle game end game and RD saying it's not the same and HC saying 5 minutes.

HC and RD had now come to the part of the course which concentrated on history and philosophy. HC wanted to change courses & study Arabic & dazzle the Oriental Institute, but not only had RD taken to heart the words of Fraenkel and Socrates, he had also taken to heart the words of Wilamowitz, and he said in anguish that Wilamowitz had said that the study of history and philosophy was an essential part of Altertumswissenschaft and what was he to do? HC said they should study Arabic and dazzle the Oriental Institute, but RD said the core of the subject was the exploration of valid modes of reasoning about the subject. Whether this carried weight with HC is not known. He was not one to take things to heart, but he was a sportsman, and he could not bring himself to go into a course where he would have no competition.

Seven terms went by and it was time for Greats, the last exams of the course. RD came to HC's room. RD felt that having spent two and a half years learning valid methods of argument it was contemptible to cast them aside just as though he were a 19-year-old entrance candidate with no real training in philosophy, and on the other hand he thought he must be missing something since philosophers and historians did after all set the exams and appeared to expect the candidates to take them. He walked up and down talking about Socrates & Wilamowitz & Mommsen waiting for HC to get out the chessboard, & sure enough HC brought out his chessboard.

They began to play without a word. The timer went before RD had made his fifth move. HC set the clock back & began putting the pieces back. RD put his head on his hand.

He said: It's not the same.

He said: Is there no END to this?

HC said: You'll never have to take an exam again.

HC said: Well maybe just one.

What? said RD.

All Souls! said HC, who hoped to be the youngest fellow in a hundred years.

RD said: I can't do this any more. I can't do this to PHILOSO-PHY. I can't write some piece of rubbish in half an hour and say they MADE me do it.

HC said: Opening middle game endgame.

RD said: I can't do this anymore. He said in anguish: What am I to *do*?

HC set out the game. He set the clock. RD raised his head. He stopped saying what am I to do. He played rapidly and confidently. He won in 23 moves and he said

But it's not the same.

They played, and RD won 10 games out of 10.

He said: But it's not the same.

5 minutes, said HC.

RD won 10 games out of 10. He did not say But it's not the same. He did not say What am I to do?

The first exam was the Plato and Aristotle paper.

RD put on a black suit and white tie. He put on his scholar's gown. The icebergs bore down on him. Socrates stood silent at his shoulder. He looked silently down at the paper.

Looking up he saw that the invigilator was JH, a man who had been working for the last 20 years on a book on *Republic* X. In those days it was possible for a man to be the finest Platonist of his generation and not publish for 20 years. There was a question on *Republic* X. Now RD saw what he must do.

He wrote: I am not so presumptuous as to attempt in 40 minutes what Mr. JH has not achieved in 20 years. That took a minute. The implication of the sentence, however, was that Mr. JH had been wrong to set the paper, & it took him 2 hours and 57 minutes to decide that it would be more insulting to spare a philosopher what he believed to be the truth than to hand in the notebook with this sentence on the page.

He spent the rest of the week punting on the Cherwell.

HC got the top first that year, and RD got no degree of any kind.

Now as soon as HC saw the list of vivas he knew that he had got a very good first and RD had not, because RD's name was not on the list. There were three days of vivas after HC's: he had three days in which to enjoy his victory.

Then the class list went up and he discovered that RD's name was not on it. He had TRICKED HC into going on with the course with all his talk of Wilamowitz, and then he had cheated. Now the congratulations of the examiners seemed empty and stupid. HC stalked up and down shouting, he said no one would give RD a job, no one would give him teaching, he would end up working on a dictionary or an Oxford Companion, he'd get kicked off for missed deadlines, he'd end up marking A-levels and getting kicked off the board, he'd end up teaching *English* as a foreign *language*. RD was rather tired. Everyone can imagine a life's regret for a moment of cowardice, but you could just as easily regret a moment's courage; RD thought that everything HC said might well be true (as in fact it was), and the years after this moment of courage might make him capable of regretting it. Still, it was done.

HC stalked out of the room. He got a Fellowship at All Souls at the age of 19 but all the fun had gone out of it.

RD got a job at a crammer's.

I said I thought a crammer was a place that helped people to pass exams.

Sibylla said Yes.

I: Wasn't that a problem?

Sib: Well, it wasn't a problem in one sense in that RD thought it was perfectly acceptable to take an exam to get INTO a place where you might improve your logical faculties, he just thought once your faculties were improved you shouldn't trample underfoot what you had learned and accept an accolade for doing so, but it was kind of a problem in that the students found the chess rather hard to follow. RD would start talking about Lucretian elements in the *Aeneid* & go to the board & talk about developing the argument on the queenside under the impression that he was helping the students with their exam technique, or he would say Now let's look at some basic mating positions & have trouble with discipline. So he lost the job and got another job.

HC & RD still went to Fraenkel's classes. Afterwards they would come out into the front quadrangle at Corpus, there is a statue of a pelican on a pillar in the centre of the quad and RD would pace in anguish around the pelican. HC was getting more and more depressed. Each day he went into the Bodleian at 9:00. At 1:00 he went back to college for lunch, and at 2:15 he was back in the Bodleian. At 6:15 he went back to his college unless of course it was the day of the seminar. Sometimes he worked in the Lower Reading Room, and sometimes he called up a manuscript and worked in Duke Humfrey. There would never be anyone to compete with ever again.

He was weary of philology, weary of tracing the corruption of sounds in their written relics. He wanted to go where a language was not written. He wanted to go where all utterances died with breath.

Then he heard that there was a strange silent tribe in the desert of Kyzylkum. They refused to let anyone who was not of the tribe know its language and any member of the tribe who repeated a word in the presence of a foreigner was punished by death.

HC did some research and he eventually came to the exciting conclusion that the references to a lost silent tribe in four or five separate historical traditions might be to the same tribe which being nomadic had ranged over thousands of miles for thousands of years. He decided to find it.

He spent seven years learning Chinese and Uralic and Altaic and Slavic and Semitic languages, and at the end of his Fellowship he set off for the desert.

It was not easy to get to Kyzylkum. He tried to fly to Moscow but he could not get a visa. He tried to get over the border into Turkmenistan from Iran & was turned back. He went to Afghanistan & tried to cross the border into Uzbekistan & was turned back. Then he thought perhaps he could go to Pakistan and cross the Pamirs to Tajikistan and so trek on to Kyzylkum but he was turned back again.

Then he decided to start his quest at the other end. His theory was that the tribe ranged all the way from the Mongolian plateau to the desert of Kyzylkum and he now decided to make for Mongolia instead.

He travelled to China, pretending to be a simple tourist.

HC joined a package tour to avoid suspicion. The tour included a visit to Xinjiang, a province in the far northwest of the country; his plan was to leave the group at Ürümqi and make his way to the Mongolian border. On the second day of the tour it was announced that the Xinjiang leg of the tour had been cancelled to allow more time for celebrated landscapes of art and poetry.

The group took a train to a town in the south. The buildings had posters of Chairman Mao on their sides. No one in the town had a copy of the *Dream of the Red Chamber*. There were no books in the town or if there were no one would tell HC. There was no jade, there were no pictures. It was an odd place he said for the children all seemed to be boys. The people there seemed to work very hard, but on a field outside the town the parents and the little boys would gather to fly kites, and these were the most beautiful kites he had ever seen. They were a brilliant red, and each had a picture of Chairman Mao on the body of the kite, or two or three characters representing one of the sayings of the Chairman. A steady wind always seemed to flow across the field, and the fiery dragons shot up into the air as soon as they were released.

He did not think he would find the silent tribe, but if he did not go forward where else was there to go? As long as he felt that he had turned his back on England he was all right, but if he turned his face to it he thought that he would turn to stone.

He pretended to be sick, and when the group went on he stayed behind.

One day he stood watching as the kites flew far overhead, the Chinese characters tossing this way and that in the air. The written language was constructed of ideograms compatible with many spoken realisations of the words & he felt that people spoke here any way they liked, while the written language flew on kites overhead. He felt at last free of philology. He thought Why should I inspect the lost silent tribe are they not just as silent if I am not there? But what was he to do if he had no quest?

He watched the kiteflyers and he saw that there was a child with no kite. The child would run now to this group now to another and be pushed away. Once the child ran by HC. It was snivelling and covered with sores and it looked different from the other children in the village. He said something and the child said something he could not understand, he thought that it must be the dialect. He said something else and the child said something else and suddenly he thought that he understood a word here and there, but if he understood them they were Turkic words made strange by the Chinese intonation. He said something in Turkish and he tried it in Karakalpak and Kyrgyz and Uighur and the child looked at him as though it understood. He asked someone if he could meet its parents and he was told it had no family. He thought that the child might come from some Turkic tribe in Xinjiang or perhaps it came from the lost silent tribe itself, but what difference did it make.

At last one day in despair he walked out of town, and he came to a cliff overlooking a valley. The floor of the valley was absolutely flat, a deep bright green. Through it curved a river, flat as a ribbon, a dull silver twisting back and forth. And from that plain thrust the sheer bare rock cliffs of mountains, each a boulder thousands of feet high breaking through the flat green.

The sky when he came there was grey, and shreds of mist snagged on the rock and floated motionless above the ground. It was the strangest and most beautiful place he had ever seen. England seemed far away, it contracted until dead Fraenkel and the pelican in the quad were tiny, the Bodleian and the lives buried there were no bigger than a postage stamp. Although there was no wind he saw that the rags of mist had moved, they hung now a yard or two from where they had been. He wanted to say something—he felt so far away. The opening of the *Odyssey* came to his mind. Odysseus could not rescue his companions.

αὐτῶν γὰρ σφετέρῃσιν ἀτασθαλίῃσιν ὄλοντο,
νήπιοι, οἳ κατὰ βοῦς Ὑπερίονος Ἠελίοιο
ἤσθιον· αὐτὰρ ὁ τοῖσιν ἀφείλετο νόστιμον ἦμαρ.

They perished by their own recklessness, the fools. They ate the cattle of the Sun God who took from them their day of return. νόστιμον ἦμαρ he thought, nostimon emar—What must I do so that I need never return? Shall I eat the cattle of the Sun?

He felt it would destroy him if he were to put himself back in the matchbox.

What must I do? he said.

The valley floor could not be seen. It was covered with a mist as thick and white as cloud. Out of the cloud rose the barren rocks. The sky had cleared above, as if a solution of air and fine rain had separated until the heavier of the two had silted the valley in thick white mist leaving the clear pure air above. The backs of the rocks were in black shadow, and at the edge of the black ran a glittering line of gold, as though each was a moon just past the new. On the summit of each was a little cluster of trees, black against the setting sun, and liquid flame welled through.

I can't go back, he said. What shall I do?

As he sat there a great wind suddenly blew up, so that high above he could see the branches of the trees streaming in the ferocious air. From behind him in the distance he heard a great noise, as of many people shouting—and when he looked back & then up he saw a huge dragon shooting up into the darkening sky: the best kitemakers in the village had been working on it for weeks, & now it had escaped. The field where they launched the kites was far away, but in the slanting afternoon light all the figures stood out clearly: five or six were staring up at the kite which had escaped, and further back another group was struggling to haul a kite in. One person had caught the body of the kite, and another was reeling in the line.

Suddenly the wind snatched at the kite; the lineman tripped, tearing the kite from the other man's hands; and as the kite began to lift a child ran forward and flung itself onto the frame. The kite dragged along the ground for a few feet, the tiny figure still clinging—and then the wind snatched it high into the air while the line went flying far out of reach.

Now the kiteflyers looked up in silence, while the brilliant red kite bore the child away. It sailed above HC, and when it reached the cliff a current of air tossed it high above.

The villagers stopped at the edge of the cliff. The kite began to descend. The wind snatched it this way and that, and at last hurled it at the top of one of the mountains HC had been looking at just before. The wind was blowing away from them, but in a sudden sharp twist it tossed at them a snatch of sound, the howling of a child, before wheeling away again.

The villagers looked at the mountain & HC, feeling they might now be more communicative, asked sympathetically: What is to be done?

But though he found the dialect very difficult what they seemed to be saying was that nothing could be done.

HC was sure he had not understood, but later someone explained that though of course they could request assistance it would not come and the request would count against them.

HC said: But couldn't someone climb up and get it?

And everyone said at once that this was impossible because no one had ever climbed the mountain and anyone who tried it would die.

That settled it.

HC said at once:

I will rescue the child.

He looked up at the flaming trees and laughed, and he said:

I will eat the cattle of the Sun.

Night had fallen. The moon was the colour of a pumpkin, low on the horizon, sullen brother of the Sun. Under its baleful light the white mist glimmered, and the black of the mountains was more solid than rock.

He went back to town and he said that he needed a lot of silk. He was told that this could not be had but he kept insisting. He explained what he wanted to do and now the local people took an interest. In all the terrible times they had been through they had kept their interest in kites, and almost everyone in the town took an interest in aerodynamics and in what could be done with the silk. He gave hard currency to the right people and he was given 100 or so square metres of brilliant yellow silk, and a woman sat up all night sewing it for him on an old black Singer with a foot pedal.

In the morning the mist had cleared. The green fields ran straight to the base of each rock, unbroken by any path, and so he walked straight across a field to the wall of rock. The air was still & the occasional cries of the child could be heard.

HC had done some climbing as a boy. The fact that he had climbed before meant that he had some idea of what he was taking on; sometimes he thought he could do it, and sometimes he knew that he knew the form his death would take.

He found a handhold and a foothold, and he began to climb.

After an hour his hands were scraped and there was a shooting pain in his shoulder. His face was scraped on one side where it was against the rock, and a trickle of blood and sweat ran by the corner of one eye and could not be wiped away.

Perhaps no one would back down who'd started such a thing. HC would never back down. He was a linguist, and therefore he had

pushed the bounds of obstinacy well beyond anything that is con-
ceivable to other men. He had been through the *Iliad* and *Odyssey*
and each time he had come to a word he did not know he had
looked it up in Liddell & Scott and written it down, and if there
were five words in a line he had looked up five words and written
them down before going on to a line in which there were four
words he did not know, and at the age of 14 he had worked through
Tacitus in this way and at the age of 20 he had read the *Muqaddimah*
of Ibn Khaldun and at 22 the *Dream of the Red Chamber*. Now he
moved one finger a centimetre and then another, and then he moved
the toe of his boot a centimetre and the toe of his other boot a centimetre.

For ten hours he moved up the face of the rock centimetre by
centimetre. He looked neither up nor down. But in the tenth hour
he put a boot up a centimetre and as his head rose a centimetre the
green leaf of a vine dangled by his nose. He looked up and the fringe
of the top was a few feet above him. Still obstinately, though his
hands were bloody and his face was bloody he climbed centimetre
by centimetre.

When he got to the top he could hardly get over the edge. His
arms had been stretched up for ten hours and the muscles had set.
When he bent one wrist over the edge a terrible cramp seized the
whole arm, so that for a second he hung by one hand and the tips of
two boots; blackness covered his eyes and he might have fallen back
through thousands of feet of empty air. Something saved him. He
saw a root by his left hand and grasped it, and though he groaned
with pain he pulled himself up over the edge, and he lay on the grass
and looked at the sky.

After a while he heard a little sound & still looking up he found
he was looking into the face of the child. It was the child he had spoken to the day before. Previously he had thought that the child had
been carried away by accident. Now he thought: But perhaps he

meant to do it. He saw the dragon shooting up into the air; perhaps the child had imagined being carried into the air away from its tormentors. Now its face was scratched and there was a cut on one arm. HC said something in Uzbek and then in Chinese, but the child did not seem to understand.

After a while he sat up, & the child flinched away. HC was in excruciating pain, but he said to himself Well it's not for long, and he looked out over the edge.

The valley floor was now concealed again by the thick white mist which must have gathered while he climbed. Above the cloud the mountains rose like islands, and on the nearer ones he could see the different things that grew there. On one there was only bamboo—there is nothing like bamboo for spreading—and the grove was bent almost parallel to the ground from the strong steady wind. The fronds of it were ruffled like feathers, they streamed out in the wind. On another were tortured trees, their hard trunks must have fought harder against the wind before they bent, they consisted of the bare tormented trunks and a few leaves. The light was clear and golden—everything had the clarity and beauty of things seen underwater, so that he could see the individual leaves of the bamboo, the tiny birds, the diaphanous wings of an insect. On the far horizon was a big golden cloud, and a series of smaller clouds were being carried even as he watched steadily out of sight.

I said: So what had happened? Was he rescued? Did he climb back down again?

Of course he didn't climb back down again, Sibylla said impatiently. It was bad enough going up alone; how could he possibly go back down with the child? It would have been ridiculous to go to all that trouble and go back WITHOUT the child.

Well he must have got down somehow, I said.

Of course he GOT down, said Sibylla.

Well he can't have flown himself away on a kite, I said.

Of course he didn't fly himself on a kite, said Sibylla. I wish you would think about this logically, Ludo.

He looked out to the west. The setting sun gleamed on yellow sand. The snowy peaks of a distant mountain range were as pale as the moon by day. The whole of Tibet lay between him and Xinjiang.

Now among the many O-levels HC had taken at 12 was one in physics. The result was that he knew something about aerodynamics. His first idea had been to make a parachute—but he had heard terrible stories from his father, who had been in the RAF, about parachutes failing to deploy. Then he had thought of taking dismantled kites to reassemble as a glider—but if he'd brought anything with him that could be used for stiff wings the wind would have blown him off the rock.

Then he had had an idea. Anything will have lift if its front edge is higher than its back, and it will have more if the top surface area is greater than the bottom. His idea was that if you made a pair of silk wings open at the front and cut the bottom shorter than the top the air rushing in would inflate them and the resultant taut surface would produce lift. He had had the woman sew in ribs like those on the wings of a plane, and attach ropes for a sort of harness, and this was what he had brought in his backpack.

He had thought only that he could bring the child down. Now he thought: If no one saw us leave no one would know we had not come down.

He thought: If they would not rescue the child why should they come for me?

He thought that if they flew over the mist it would be a long time before anyone knew they had gone.

Now he unpacked the wings and assembled the harness. The child stood watching him warily; it was backing toward a thicket of bamboo on top of the rock. He stepped into the harness and beckoned but the child refused to come. He was not entirely sure himself that the contraption would work, but he could not test it first—he knew he would not be able to climb up again.

Meanwhile the wind was pulling at the wings, and one gust almost pulled him off his feet; he had to grab a tree to keep from being blown away. Another gust of wind tore at him and nearly swept him off the rock. When it died down he made a sudden rush for the child; it turned and ran, and tripped, and he seized it by the foot. And now a third gust of wind snatched at him, sharper than the first two, and he had only one hand free. He was pulled loose from the tree; he could feel himself being pulled toward the cliff. Quickly he seized the child's other foot; ignoring its howls he pulled it toward him and gripped it tightly in his arms—and no sooner had he done so than the wind filled the wings and they were carried off into the air.

At once they were carried high, high above even those pinnacles of rocks which he had seen flaming the day before. A fierce wind bore them along so impetuously he was afraid it would tear the wings; up it swooped and down it dropped, and it swept them at last out of that valley and miles and miles to the west until at last it did drop him in a bare rocky plain. There was no sand, but this was what had gleamed yellow on the horizon.

There was light in the upper air, but as soon as he reached the ground the light was gone. The sun was a bloody ball on the horizon. While he was still unfastening the harness it dropped out of sight.

HC was now in a much worse position than he had been at the top of the cliff. There was no water here; before the light had gone he had seen only the endless rocky plain stretching in all directions, with no sign of human habitation. It was bitterly cold, and there was nothing to burn. But now he had no way to a quick death—both might well die slowly of cold or thirst.

But even though he might now die a painful death he could not stop laughing. The silk wings lay crumpled at his feet, and the child

was whimpering on his back, and he kept laughing and exclaiming:
It worked! It bloody worked! Christ Almighty, it bloody worked!

He realised that he could not lie down to sleep or he would freeze
to death. So he put the child on his back and he set out to walk
through the night.

HC was 6′4″ and when he walked fast he covered ground. By
morning he reckoned he must have walked a good 60 miles. And
when the sun came up he saw a railroad track. Even though he was
cold and hungry he was still laughing. When he turned to look back
the way he had come he could not even see the valley, and he said
again It bloody worked!

He walked by the track all day, and in late afternoon a train came.
It did not stop when he waved, but it was going so slowly that he was
able to jump on the last car, and it did not stop to throw him off.

The train did not stop at the next village, but he jumped off again
to buy food. They ate, and then he put the child on his back again
and followed the track. The next train was going too fast, but he
jumped on the one after that. He kept expecting to be stopped but
he thought that he would just keep going until he was stopped.

He rode trains for five days, and on the morning of the sixth day
he saw the Flaming Mountains of Gaochang.

HC was now in the heart of Xinjiang, Mongolia to the east Kazakhstan & Kyrgyzstan to the west, but he did not know which way to
go.

He left the train close to the end of the line and set off on foot.
He walked north, keeping his options open, and now he had another
piece of luck. He came to a village, and it seemed to him that the
people there looked a little like the child he had rescued.

At first he thought he might find a home for the child, but people looked at the child and shook their heads, & though he could
barely understand the local dialect he thought he was being told that
it came from the west.

There were no maps to be had. He did not have enough to buy a pack animal. So they set out on foot.

They crossed the border without being stopped, and together they went through increasingly harsh terrain.

They went very slowly for the child could not travel fast.

After many months they came out onto a plain where horses were grazing. In the distance some kind of encampment could be seen. On they went, both half-dead.

They came to the encampment but the men were gone. The women were preparing meals or repairing clothes. The man and the boy came to a halt in the centre of the tents and gradually all fell silent.

Then at the far end a woman looked up. Her black hair was as rough as a pony's; she had the broad features of a true Mongolian. She gazed intently at the boy and at last came forward. The boy walked into her arms and began to cry and she too cried. Then she stood back and hit the boy on the side of the head and shouted and cried again. The boy lay in the dirt. HC made some gesture. The woman looked at him dumbly.

HC gestured at the boy's torn feet and the woman looked at him dumbly. He gestured from himself to a pot of food and she spat at his feet.

At last one of the other women offered HC some food. None spoke while he ate and through the long afternoon there was complete silence in the encampment.

The men returned from hunting and still no one spoke, and HC at last slept in some straw by the horses and no one spoke either to protest or to offer him hospitality, and the boy slept with him.

He stayed for eight years. For five years no one spoke to him, and if they spoke to each other and he approached they fell silent, but in his fifth year he had a terrible disappointment.

HC had been thinking for some reason of RD, who had based his method of Greek pronunciation on the authoritative work on the subject, W. S. Allen's *Vox Graeca*. RD, being largely self-taught, had always made a point of pronouncing Greek with the pitch accents, with the result that no one could ever understand a word he said. Thinking of RD, HC realised suddenly after five years with the tribe that their language was in fact Indo-European, but Indo-European filtered through a Chinese system of pitch accents to the point where it sounded like nothing he knew. He was now able to recognise a few words. It was a terrible anticlimax after all the languages he had learned, but he stayed another three years and was befriended at last and mastered it.

But then he was forced to leave.

The tribe moved around as nomads do, and it had moved to an area which was disputed between the Soviet Union and China. They were close to a village which had been punished severely by both sides for not implementing government policy and thus showing where its allegiance lay. One day a plane crashed in the desert near the encampment; the survivors were arrested as spies to forestall reprisals from above. The spies were thrown into jail and beaten to give a good impression.

HC knew he had to do something. He suspected the prisoners knew no Chinese, so he went to the jail to reason with the authorities. When he got into town he was told to come back the next day. When he got back to the encampment he found that the tribe had disappeared.

The jail was badly built and badly guarded. HC broke into it and freed the prisoners. He decided that the best plan was to march south and make their way into India. It had been ten years since he had heard a European language spoken, and he found it almost unbearable to articulate the old words with his tongue, but it had to be done.

Sibylla put her head on her hand. She seemed tired of the words in her own mouth. At last she went on.

The march south was very arduous, and three of the captives died en route. The survivors walked at last into the British consulate in Peshawar and demanded repatriation. HC was almost turned away: he had no passport, of course, and no proof of identification, and as he had been missing for more than seven years he was officially dead. Luckily for HC, however, it turned out that a man he had beaten in various prize examinations was now the British consul in Bombay. A trunk call was put through, and HC was able to recite from memory his translation into Greek verse of Wee sleekit cow'rin' tim'rous beastie, and the man at the other end said there was only one man in the world who could do that. This was not strictly true, since RD could probably have done it, but HC was not about to argue.

He returned to a civilisation which in the interim had known John Travolta and the Bee Gees and he published a book in which he spoke of the silence of the lost tribe. Then people demonstrated that he could not have been where he said he had been and people who had travelled in China said that it was not like that at all and people who had climbed those strange mountains said they were in some completely different part of the country and anyway he could not have climbed one in ten hours the way he had said. Others argued that a tiny peasant village would not have had the quantities of silk he claimed to have requisitioned, and would not have had the battered old Singer sewing machine he had claimed was used, & would have had no use for hard currency even if it had. Others said kiteflying had been banned as a bourgeois practice by the Red Guard. Then HC laughed scornfully and said he certainly did not propose the lost tribe to be a subject of a documentary but if he should ever decide this was a suitable fate for it he would at once publish an accurate itinerary of his travels to facilitate location of that wandering people. Then of course there was a great hue and cry and people tried to investigate where he had really been for the public had a right to know, but no one was able to discover anything apart from the fact that he had walked into the consulate in Peshawar.

That book said Sibylla had come out in 1982 and HC had done this and that for a while. She said that she had met him at an Oxford party in the Fraenkel Room in Corpus Christi College. Skarp-Hedin had been talking to Robin Nisbet and so Sibylla had talked for a time to HC. I said Skarp-Hedin? and Sib said One of my boyfriends his real name did not do justice to his pale ill-starred look. She said that HC had spent years with the tribe though they had offered no encouragement to stay and even after his first break-through he could understand little or nothing.

Then one day everything had changed. They had he said a bar-barous initiation ceremony which he would not describe. Afterwards many of the boys required prolonged nursing. One day as he lurked behind a tent he heard one of the initiates say something to his nurse, and then when she laughed correct himself. He had under-stood everything in a flash. It was the most wonderful thing he'd ever come across. There was an elaborate system of case-endings he said which was used only by women—the thing was quite extraordinary, as if you had at once for example a group of people speaking Arabic as it is written and another group speaking it as it is spoken. Amaz-ing! And it was the same for moods and tenses. There was an indica-tive, past present and future, and an imperative, and these were used only by men—and then there were what he would call by analogy the subjunctive and the optative, and these were used only by women. It was very confusing, he said, for when presently they be-gan to speak to him at last he would find that if he asked a question of a man, no matter how slim or even non-existent the knowledge might be on which an answer might be given, it would always be given as a statement of fact—whereas you might ask a woman whether it was raining outside and she would commit herself only to saying that it might be so. He said that when he worked it out he lay flat on his back in the grass and laughed till he cried.

Now the Fraenkel Room at this time said Sib had a long table covered with a mauve corded cloth like a cheap Sears bedspread, and a black and white photo of Fraenkel on the wall.

HC took one look at the picture and another at the people there and he said Oh my God and walked out.

That is, said Sib, he said Oh my God let's get out of here, and though she knew Skarp-Hedin would complain that she did not love him she had said Yes let's get out and they had both walked out.

HC had gone off again she said and now he was back. Sibylla said of HC that he could go for months without human contact, and if he made contact the first thing he wanted to know was how his interlocutor handled sequence of tenses, and the second was whether he used a subjunctive.

I said: What happened to RD?

Sibylla said: Oh he got a job on one of the dictionaries. You can see him around the Bodleian.

I said: Was he at the seminar?

She said: Oh he goes to all the seminars.

I said: Did they say anything?

She said: Well, RD asked the speaker a question about Phrynichus.

I said: Did they say anything to each OTHER?

She said: Of course they didn't say anything to each other. As soon as HC saw who was there he said Oh my God let's get out of here.

I said: Did you play chess?

She said: No, we didn't play chess.

I thought about this for a while and I said: What's the youngest anyone has ever gone to Oxford? Sibylla said she didn't know, in the Middle Ages it was more like a boarding school & she thought a lot of boys would be sent there at 12 or so. She thought a girl had gone to read mathematics at the age of 10 a few years ago.

I said: 10!

She said: I think she'd been taught by her father, who was a mathematician.

If *I* had had a mathematician for a father I could probably have beaten the record.

I said: Well what's the youngest anyone ever did classics?

Sib said she didn't know.

I said: Younger than 11?

It seems unlikely, said Sib, but we can only surmise.

I said: Do you think I could go?

Sib said: Well you probably *could* but how would you ever learn quantum mechanics?

I said: But if I got in at 11 people would say all my life that I got in at 11!

Sib said: They certainly would. She said: Or I could give you a piece of paper certifying that you read *Sugata Sanshiro* in the original Japanese at the age of 6 and all your life people would say you read *Sugata Sanshiro* in Japanese at the age of 6.

I said: What do I have to do to get in? Do I have to read a lot about chess endings?

Sib said: Well, it worked for RD.

Sib seemed to have no interest at all in helping me set a record. I argued with her for a long time until at last she said: Why are you saying all this to me? Do whatever you want. If you pay £35 you can go to as many lectures as you want; the RATIONAL thing to do would be to pay £35 or whatever it is, get the lecture lists, go to whatever looks interesting, collect reading lists, go through the reading lists, decide on the basis of evidence which lecturers are moderately competent teachers, decide on the basis of evidence which fields you are interested in & who is doing interesting work in those fields; collect further evidence at OTHER universities (assuming THEY let in paying guests) by going to lectures given by the interesting people to see whether they are reasonably competent teachers

& then decide where to go when you are about 16.

SIXTEEN! I said.

Sib began to talk about boring people she knew who had got jobs at Oxford & someone brilliant who had just gone to Warwick.

I did not say WARWICK! but Sib said drily that I would have of course to weigh very carefully the benefit of studying with someone brilliant against the undoubted drawback that people would merely say all my life (if they bothered to mention so uninteresting a fact) that I had gone to Warwick at the age of 16.

I could see that at any moment she was going to start talking about *Sugata Sanshiro* so I said quickly that we could talk about it some other time.

I said: Aren't you supposed to be typing *The Modern Knitter*?

Indolence, interruption, business, and pleasure; all take their turns of retardation, said Sib. I'm up to 1965.

I said: I thought you were going to finish it by the end of the week.

Perhaps no extensive and multifarious performance, said Sib, was ever effected within the term originally fixed in the undertaker's mind. He that runs against Time, has an antagonist not subject to casualities.

Sib went to the computer and typed for five minutes or so and then she stood up and sat on the sofa and turned on the video.

Kambei raised the bowl of rice. I understand, he said. No more shouting. I'm not going to waste this rice. Fair enough, said my father.

Tough-looking samurai strode up and down the street. In a doorway stood the farmers, impressed, Katsushiro, impressed, Kambei, arms crossed, unimpressed. Thanks, said my father. I mean that.

Kambei sat inside facing the door. He handed Katsushiro a heavy stick. Hide behind the door, he said. Get in position. Take the overhead-sword stance. Hit the samurai when he comes in, hard. No holding back! As hard as you can. Fair e

I stared at the screen. Katsushiro stood behind the door. I stood up and began walking up and down while a samurai came through the door and parried the blow.

Now I did not hear my father's voice or see his face; though the film had moved on I saw in my mind a street full of tough-looking samurai, and Kambei in a doorway watching the street.

In my mind I saw Katsushiro standing behind the door with a stick. I saw Kyuzo slicing through a blustering second-rater. But a *good* samurai will parry the blow.

I thought: I could have James Hatton after all! *Or* Red Devlin. Or both!

I thought: I could have anyone I wanted!

I thought: Opening middle game endgame.

I thought: A good samurai will parry the blow.

I thought: A good samurai will parry the blow.

❖

I looked at Sib's paper & it said that HC was about to walk across the former Soviet Union, and that he was planning to go alone.

I thought, HE could fight with swords. Here I thought was a man to challenge, a man who knew 50 languages, a man who had faced death a hundred times, a man impervious to praise and ridicule alike. Here was a man who on meeting his son for the first time would SURELY encourage him to go to Oxford at the age of 11, or at least take him on an expedition instead.

The paper did not say where he was staying.

I called his publisher and asked whether there would be any book signings. I counted on the charm of my childish voice to elicit the information I required, and in fact after a short time I was given a list of places where books would be signed.

He was signing books the next day at the Waterstone's in Notting Hill Gate.

❖

I took the Circle Line and ascended to the street.

I went to the book signing, and as I expected HC left on foot. He was as tall as she had said and covered ground fast, but I had expected that too and had brought my skateboard.

The house was large and white, with white pillars. In front was a little square of grass and roses around a paved stone circle, with a birdbath in the middle of the flagstones. There was nowhere to leave my skateboard. I walked ten houses down to a For Sale sign and hid my skateboard in the long grass and then walked back.

I rang the doorbell, and a woman with shining hair and jewellery and makeup and a pink dress came to the door.

I stared at her in surprise. I hadn't known he was married. Or it could be his sister.

I said I had come to see Hugh Carey.

She said: I'm awfully sorry, he isn't seeing anybody.

I said I was sorry and I went away and retreated up the street. Later the woman in pink came out and went to a car and got in it and drove away. I went back to the house and rang the bell.

He came to the door and said What do you want.

His face was creased and brown and there was a badly healed scar down one cheek. His eyes blazed blue. His eyebrows were shaggy, he had a straggling moustache. His hair was bleached very light, and there were white hairs in it.

What do you want? he said again.

I have to talk to you, I said. I knew that if I walked away I would despise myself for the rest of my life.

He said he could spare a few minutes and I followed him inside. I don't know what I expected but I was surprised by the shining wooden floors and thick rugs and stuffed sofas. An interesting form of the subjunctive is not something you can bring back as a trophy but still this was not what I had expected.

We went into a room with a black and white marble floor and a pale yellow sofa and he gestured to the sofa and said again What do you want.

I looked into that face of stone and knew I was about to die. He would see instantly through the lie and be filled with contempt. I thought of him walking across China with the boy, and walking across Kazakhstan with a tiny band of men; it was cheap and contemptible to play a trick on someone like that. I should make some excuse and leave.

Kambei tells Rikichi to call a samurai to a fight. He sits inside waiting. He tells Katsushiro to stand just inside the door with a stick. A good samurai will parry the blow.

I thought that if I were a coward I really would be my father's son.

I said: I wanted to see you because I'm your son.

You're my—

I was dead.

Eyes like the burnished blade of a sword blazed in his hard face. I was dead.

His mouth tightened. I was dead.

At last he spoke.

How the hell did that happen? he said irritably. She told me she had everything taken care of.

She forgot that she'd taken the pill a day late the day before, I said truthfully. I couldn't believe this was happening.

Women! he said contemptuously. You must be older than you look, it can't have been later than 83 which would make you—

13 and 10 months, I said. I look young for my age.

Well, and so tell me about yourself, he said heartily. Where do you go to school? What are your interests?

I don't go to school, I said. I study at home.

I was about to explain that I already knew Greek, French, Hebrew, Arabic, Japanese, Spanish, Russian and some Latin (in no particular order), plus a smattering of 17 or 18 others, when he exploded.

Oh my GOD! he exclaimed in horror. What is the stupid woman thinking of? Do you know ANYTHING? What's 6 × 7?

What do you mean? I asked cautiously. I hadn't done much on philosophy of number yet.

Oh—my—God.

He began pacing up and down the room, with a heavy-footed, slightly lame step—I remembered that he had covered thousands of miles on foot. He said: We've got to get you into a school pronto, my young friend. He said: Don't get any ideas. I couldn't possibly stump up school fees. He said: I hear some of the state schools aren't bad. He said: My God, I knew the whole times table up to 12 by the time I was 6.

I'd known the times table up to 20 by the time I was 4, but I was too disgusted to say so. I said: Oh, you mean you wanted to know the *product* of 6 and 7.

What did you think I meant? he asked.

I don't know, that's why I asked what you meant, I said.

You'll soon get that sort of nonsense knocked out of you at school, he said.

I said I had always heard that logical thought was discouraged in schools. I could not believe someone so stupid had been to find the lost silent tribe; no wonder they hadn't wanted to talk to him.

He kept shooting me fierce glances out of narrowed eyes as he stumped up and down. What's the capital of Peru? he said abruptly.

Oh, does it have a capital? I said.

Oh—my—God.

Madrid? I said. Barcelona? Kiev?

What is the country *coming* to?

Buenos Aires! I said. Santiago! Cartagena—no that's Brazil isn't it don't tell me I'll have it in a minute it isn't, it wouldn't be Acapulco would it no forget I said that it's on the tip of my tongue don't tell me it's coming ancient holy city of the Zincas *Casablanca*.

He said: Lima.

I said: I thought Casablanca didn't sound quite right, ask me another one.

He said I must give him my mother's phone number and he would have a word with her.

I said I would rather not.

He said: What you want is neither here nor there.

I wanted to get this over. I hadn't come for money but I had to say something so I said: Look, I really didn't come here to discuss my education. I know the product of 7 and 6 is 42, and 13 × 17 is 221 and 18 × 19 is 342 and I know the binomial theorem and I know

$$E + \frac{p}{\rho} + \frac{q^2}{2} + \frac{\delta \Phi}{\delta t} = C(t)$$

is the Bernoulli equation for inviscid incompressible irrotational flow. I plan to learn to work as a member of a team when the other members of the team are out of their teens. My mother doesn't know I came here, she didn't want you to be bothered. But she's going insane at her work. I want to buy a mule and go down the Andes. I thought you might help.

The last thing I wanted was to be alone in the Transural with this lunatic. I also couldn't see myself confiding my ambition to go to Oxford at the age of 11. But I had to say something.

Go down the Andes on a mule? That doesn't sound very in character, he said. Are you sure this isn't something you want?

Yes it's something I want, I said.

Well, the best piece of advice I can give you is never rely on anyone but yourself for anything you want out of life, he said. Everything I've got I've got by my own efforts. You don't grow up by having people hand you things on a platter.

By the time I grow up it may be too late, I said.

You've got your whole life ahead of you, he said, and he stopped pacing to stand beside me. One hand gripped the back of the sofa; I saw that a finger was missing. He'd probably offered a piece of advice to a member of the Lost Silent Tribe.

That's what worries me, I said.

Well there's nothing I can do, he said. Nobody ever did anything for me and it never did me any harm. It made me what I am today.

I was glad we weren't fighting with real swords. If we had been this might have killed me. I said I would bear that in mind.

He said: I've got a son already. He'd be older than you are if he's still alive. Not by much, but he's already a man—they grow up fast.

He said: When a boy reaches 12 he goes through an initiation ceremony. He's stripped to the waist and flogged—not a lot, just five or six welts to make the back bleed. Then he's tied up. There's a beastly stinging fly that's attracted by blood—of course they gather. If the boy cries out he gets another lash. It's over when he's been silent for a day. You'll see them stretched out, backs solid with the feeding flies—sometimes they're unconscious for the last 12 hours or so, sometimes the father will slap a boy awake to make sure they don't get off lightly. It's hard to be a man there.

I said: Yeah, I hear they don't even use case endings.

He said: Who told you that?

It's in the book, I said.

No it's not in the book, he said.

I heard it somewhere, I said.

She must have told you. I don't suppose she told you how I found out.

He grinned at me; his teeth were yellow and brown beneath the moustache.

She said you hid behind a tent, I said.

I tried that, he said. I got nowhere. Then one day the mother of the boy came to me. She'd sold him again to some traders—they don't like impure blood in the tribe. But she was curious all the same—that's what had got her in trouble the first time. She couldn't stay away. I got her to teach me a few words and one thing led to another. The women spat at her and pulled her hair when they found out. Anyway we'd lie about in the grass and I'd copy something she'd said and she'd slap me or laugh at me for copying her. Then I overheard a couple of men talking to each other and realised what was going on. I laughed till I cried. Then she got pregnant. She made me leave. Probably sold the little bastard to the Chinese. If so he won't have been initiated, he said, and he grinned, and he said, If these things happen to anyone why shouldn't they happen to my son?

I said: In that case why should you care whether I know the multiplication table and why should you care whether I go to school?

He said: There was nothing I could do. I couldn't take her with me, and they'd have killed me if I'd stayed. This is different. Your mother has been completely irresponsible.

I began to laugh.

Steps approached the front door, which opened. The door to the room opened while I was still laughing, and the woman in pink came in.

What's going on? she asked.

This is my son, he said.

No I'm not, I said.

What do you mean? he said.

Have you seen Seven Samurai?

No.

I have, said the woman.

It was a test, I said. I couldn't tell my real father because it was true.

I don't begin to understand, said the woman, and the man said
In some parts of the world you'd be flogged for this.

I said it was not necessary to leave England to find people who
did stupid things.

Who are you? he said angrily. What's your name?

David, I said without thinking.

I don't understand, he said angrily. Did you want money? You
made it up to get money?

Of course I want money, I said, though there were other things I
wanted more. How am I supposed to buy a mule without money?

But why in God's name—

I did not know what to say. Because you were a linguist, I said. I
heard the story about the case endings and I thought you'd understand. Of course you don't understand. I've got to go.

But it's got to be true, he said. How could you know about the
case endings? She must have told you. It must be true. Where is she?

I've got to go, I said.

He said: No, don't go.

I said: Do you still play chess?

He said: She told you about the *chess*?

I said: What?

The woman said: Hugh—

He said: What does it take to get a cup of tea in this house?

She said: I was just going, but she looked at me as she went.

He said: What did she tell you about the chess?

I said: Do you mean you let him win?

He said: Didn't she tell you?

I said: She said you didn't let him win.

He said: Of course I didn't let him win, and he stumped up and
down the rug.

He said: He won 10 games out of 10. He stopped saying What am
I going to do; he sat smiling at the board. He said I do what you do

better than you can yourself, and you can't do what I do at all. I thought Where would you be if it weren't for me, you stupid bastard?

I said You talk a good game.

He said Meaning?

I said Is it a game because I say it's a game? And I said that if I treated it as a game because I thought it was a game and he treated it as a game not because he thought it was a game but because I said it was —

And he said Yes

— which of us was doing the thing he thought he did

And he said Yes

and that was the last thing I said to him

Before the exam, I said.

Yes, he said.

What was the last thing he said to you? I asked.

None of your business.

What did my mother say? I said.

I can't remember. Some daft thing.

What? I said hoping it would be something Sibylla couldn't possibly have said.

I can't remember. Something sympathetic.

I wanted to ask whether the woman had looked bored, but I thought he probably wouldn't have noticed.

He said: Tell me where she is. I've got to see her again

I said: I've got to go

He said: You've got to tell me

I opened the door and went down the front hall. I could hear him behind me. I broke into a run and slipped on a silky rug that slid on the polished wood and got my balance and caught at the first Chubb lock and I could hear him behind me coming fast. I snapped open the first lock and I opened the second Chubb lock and the third Chubb lock with both hands and I got the door open just as his hand gripped my shoulder.

I twisted away and pulled myself free. I crossed the walk in three strides and vaulted over the gate and when I looked back he was just standing at the door. He looked at me across the birdbath and the rosebushes and then he turned.

The door shut. It was just a boring house on a boring street of houses with their closed white doors.

I stumbled down the street. He had not killed to learn those moodless verbs and uninflected nouns, but he had brought a slave into existence for their sake.

I walked back to Notting Hill Gate and I took the Circle Line.

2

A good samurai will parry the blow

I decided not to apply to Oxford to read classics at the age of 11.

Sibylla asked what had happened to my skateboard. I thought of the long line of closed doors, the house for sale, the long grass. I knew I couldn't go back. I said it had got stolen. I said it didn't matter. I kept thinking of the boy who wasn't my brother.

I thought of the prisoners of fate who couldn't hope for better luck.

I thought: Why would I even WANT a father. At least I was free to come and go. Sometimes I'd pass a council bus with a message on the back: SOUTHWARK: WHERE TRUANCY IS TAKEN SERIOUSLY, and I'd walk north across Tower Bridge to the City, where truancy was not taken seriously. What kind of father would put up with that? I should quit while I was ahead.

I had stopped sleeping on the floor. I had stopped eating grasshoppers au gratin with a sauce of sautéed woodlice. Sibylla kept asking if something was wrong. I said nothing was wrong. The thing that was wrong was that nothing was ever going to change.

I decided to do something Hugh Carey would not have done at age 11. I thought if I worked through the Schaum Outline series on Fourier analysis that would be safe enough because according to Sib it is not taught in schools. HC had probably never studied it at all. I thought maybe I would do Lagrangians just to be on the safe side. Maybe I would do some Laplace transforms too.

Sibylla was typing *Tropical Fish Hobbyist*. No one was going to take me galloping across the Mongolian steppe. No one was going to take me to the North Pole any time soon.

One day I went with Sibylla to Tesco's.

A brilliant white light beat pitilessly down, like the fierce desert sun at midday on the French Foreign Legion; the glittering floor dazzled the eye with the cruel desert glare.

We walked slowly through the cereals.

Vast boxes of cornflakes and bran flakes rose on either side; as we reached the muesli a cart turned the corner and turned into the aisle, propelled by a fat woman and followed by three fat children. One was crying into a fat fist, and two were arguing about Frosties and Breakfast Boulders, and the woman was smiling.

She came down the aisle and Sibylla stopped and stood by the cart, motionless as the boxes of cornflakes on their shelves. Her eyes were like black coals, and her skin like pale dirty thick clay. From her absolute silence, from her black staring eyes, I knew that this mild fat woman was someone she had hoped never to see again.

The cart, and the woman, and the children came forward, and suddenly the woman's eyes shifted from the boxes of cereal, and across the mildness spread a look of pleased surprise.

Sybil! she exclaimed. Is it really you?

This was obviously someone who knew Sib about as well as she knew her name. No one who knew Sibylla well would have opened a conversation with a remark of such unparalleled fatuity.

Sib stared at her dumbly.

It's me! said the woman. I suppose I've changed a lot, she added grimacing comically. Kids! she added.

The little wet fist fell, and small eyes gazed at a box on which brightly coloured cartoon characters consumed representations of the product.

I want the Honey Monster, howled the child.

You picked last time, said one of the others, with unmistakable

Schadenfreude, and an argument broke out concerning the respective claims of the remaining two to choose this week.

Now two of the children wept into pudgy fingers, one screaming.

The woman tried, with small success, to restore order.

And is this your little boy? she asked brightly.

Sibylla was still silent, and now her lips were pressed tightly together.

If the woman opposite was capable of thought, something for which we had as yet no evidence, her thoughts were certainly opaque to her companions. I could see Sibylla's thoughts circling her mind like goldfish in a bowl. At last she spoke.

> To be or not to be, that is the question:
> Whether 'tis nobler in the mind to suffer
> The slings and arrows of outrageous fortune
> Or to take arms against a sea of troubles
> And by opposing, end them. To die, to sleep—
> No more and by a sleep to say we end
> The heart-ache and the thousand natural shocks
> That flesh is heir to; 'tis a consummation

The woman glanced aghast at the small fat crew and was at once relieved, for it was clear enough that they had not understood a word of this.

Well, of course we all have our cross to bear, she said cheerily.

Sibylla gazed down, eyes blazing, at a tin of baked beans.

What is your little boy's name? asked the woman.

His name is Stephen, said Sib, after a moment's hesitation.

He looks very bright, said the woman. No, Felicity, no! Micky, what did I say?

He is capable of logical thought, said Sib. It makes him appear exceptionally intelligent. The fact is that most people are illogical out of habit rather than stupidity; they could probably be rational quite easily if they were properly taught.

So it has all worked out for the best! said the woman. You know, however bad things look, something good may be just around the corner.

Or vice versa, said Sib.

We must always look on the bright side.

Again Sibylla was silent.

The children burst into quarrel again. The woman urged them mildly to stop. They paid no attention.

She looked at them mildly, her mouth crumpling a little.

Sib looked at her with terrible pity, as if wondering what death could be worse than the life which had led her to this cardboard canyon of cornflakes. She said to me in a low voice:

Ludo, take the Little Prince away.

And do what? I said.

Buy him some chocolate, said Sib, digging into her bag and giving me a pound. Buy them all some chocolate. Take them all away.

I led them away down the aisle. As we turned the corner I saw Sib put an arm around one fat shaking shoulder; now it was the fat woman who wept on a wet fist.

One of the children was about my age. He asked where I went to school. I said I didn't go to a school. He said everybody had to go to school. I said my mother thought I should identify a field of particular interest and just go straight to university, though I would probably find the students rather immature.

The conversation flagged. My companions absorbed chocolate; this gone, they turned again to combat.

Presently Sibylla and the woman came through the checkout lanes.

Sib was saying All I'm saying is if we imagine setting up a society with no knowledge of the place we are to occupy, we are highly

UNLIKELY to sentence ourselves to 16 odd years' absolute economic dependence upon persons of whose rationality there can be no guarantee, and highly LIKELY to stipulate a society in which

The woman was laughing softly.

Sibylla looked with ill-concealed horror at the bechocolated crew which now converged whining on the other trolley.

The woman smiled mildly.

No, Micky, no! Felicity, what did I say? she began—

and then she stopped. She was staring at the Schaum Outline on Fourier analysis which I had brought in case I got bored.

She said What school does he go to?

Sibylla said I was studying at home.

Now the woman stared at me, and now she stared at Sibylla like a prisoner of fate who sees hope of reprieve. She said You mean you're teaching him yourself! But that's amazing!

and she said I wonder—it would be the most enormous favour— would you consider helping Micky? I'm sure he's very bright, but he's had a few problems, and the school just doesn't want to know.

The most enormous favour did not sound good, and sure enough she went on to say Nothing formal.

Sibylla was stammering But surely you

The woman said What with the other two

Sibylla said Well

We walked home with rations for the week.

I said: Who was *that*?

Sibylla said she was someone

She said: She once saved my life.

She said: Had our positions been reversed, of course, she would have been preserved thanks to me for what we now know lay in store.

She laughed and said: This reminds me of that line in Renan!

She frowned and I thought she was not going to be able to re-member the line from Renan. She said: The Aryan language had a great superiority in the conjugation of verbs, that marvellous instru-ment, the conjugation of verbs, that marvellous instrument, that marvellous instrument of metaphysics . . . The Arab race handi-capped for fifteen hundred years by the inferiority of their moods and tenses—

and she said ce merveilleux instrument, ce merveilleux instru-ment

and suddenly she laughed and said I wonder if I can do it in Ara-bic!

I said: Do what in Arabic?

Sib said: Had our positions been reversed, of course, she would have been preserved thanks to me for what we now know lay in store.

She said: Let's do it in Hebrew and Arabic and see if he's right! You do Hebrew, I'll do Arabic—

and she said lau . . .

I said: How did she save your life?

Sib said she did not know much about it because she had been unconscious at the time but apparently the woman had called an am-bulance in the nick of time.

I said: How do you know about the case endings?

Sib said: What case endings?

I said: Of the lost silent tribe, they're not in the book

Sib said: lau . . .

I said: And the chess isn't in the book

Sib said: Isn't Robert Donat on TV tonight?

I said: Did HC tell you after the seminar?

Sib said: This thing by Renan is mysterious. It seems to me that philosophical Greek would be more troublesome to translate into Latin than Arabic. What we should do is compare a Latin translation

of, say, Plato with one in Arabic and maybe some passage of Mai-
monides on a related subject and see which is more awkward.

I said: The chess

Sib said: *Look* Ludo, an Illinois Fried Chicken!

I said: isn't in the book

Sib said: You can go to SOAS and work on it

I said: SOAS won't let me in

Sib said: You simply explain that you are working on a project for
school

She said: & if I type *Tropical Fish Hobbyist* for four hours we can
catch Robert Donat at 9:00. You can work on Plato to get ready for
this project at SOAS.

I said: Are you really going to teach the Little Prince?

She said: The Little Pauper, wits gone a-begging. It will kill me to
do it but it must be done.

The actor Robert Donat never made many films. There was The
39 Steps, in which he escaped across moors and jumped on and off
moving trains; there was The Winslow Boy, in which he played a
charismatic, controversial and highly paid barrister. In The Count
of Monte Cristo he escaped from the Chateau d'If. In The Citadel
he played a charismatic doctor who abandoned his ideals. In The
Young Mr. Pitt he played a charismatic politician. There was also
Goodbye Mr. Chips, in which he played a shy schoolmaster who
always told the same jokes. Sib thought there were some others but
she could never remember what they were. None of the films was
scheduled to be on that night. The astronomer, Nobel Prize winner and Donat lookalike George Sorabji was on TV every Thursday at 9:00. Sometimes he liked to jump onto a rope ladder
dropped from a helicopter, and sometimes he liked to stride up and
down, eyes flashing, and explain the Pauli Exclusion Principle or

the importance of the Chandrasekhar constant. He was never much like Mr. Chips.

Sorabji liked to say when asked (if not asked he would volunteer the information) that he was the descendant of a drugs baron. His great-grandfather had been a Parsi businessman in Bombay, and he had built up a fortune mainly in the opium trade. Far from being a social outcast he was a pillar of society and noted philanthropist, a man who had littered Bombay with schools and hospitals and repulsive pieces of statuary. Sorabji argued that similar benefits, only on a larger scale, would be the inevitable result of legalisation of drugs, which could be heavily taxed to pay for schools, hospitals and obscenely expensive telescopes.

The letters pages of the papers were full of heated exchanges between Sorabji and members of the public on the legalisation of drugs, astrology the pseudo-science, the absolute insignificance of our national heritage in comparison with the universe & consequent need for instant reallocation of funds to pay for obscenely expensive telescopes, and an impressive range of other subjects on which Sorabji held strong views. You could also hear Robert Donat in Winslow Boy mode on the radio or see him on TV. Last but not least he had won a Nobel Prize.

Sorabji had shared the prize with three other people; he had won it for physics because there isn't a Nobel Prize for astronomy, and people who knew said that though he was a brilliant astronomer he hadn't really won it for the thing he was brilliant at.

The thing he had been brilliant at was creating mathematical models of black holes, but the thing he had won the prize for was Colossus, a satellite for multi-wavelength astronomy which would never have got off the drawing board, let alone the ground, had it not been for Sorabji. Sorabji had extracted commitments for obscene amounts of money from the US, the EU, Australia, Japan and lots of other places that had never before thought of sponsoring a satellite, and he had helped to design ground-breaking telescopes for the satellite, which had caused the obscenely expensive project to go a heartstopping five times over budget. Then it went into orbit, and within three years information from the satellite had revolutionised understanding of quasars, pulsars and black holes.

Sorabji was interested in things that bored 90% of the country, and he had strong views with which 99% of the country strongly disagreed, but nobody held it against him. Some people said that say what you like he had the courage of his convictions, and some people said say what you like his heart is in the right place. They said he would lay down his life for his friends. Sorabji had once saved the life of a friend when, visiting the observatory at Mauna Koa, they had taken a helicopter up over a live volcano and crashed inside it, and he had rescued a member of his team, a Ugandan from the Lango tribe placed under house arrest by Idi Amin, by smuggling him out over the Kenyan border under a hail of bullets.

Sorabji had originally come to the attention of the British public through a programme called Mathematics the Universal Language. 99.99% of the British public were not interested in mathematics, but they were interested in the fact that Sorabji had succeeded in teaching mathematics to a boy from an Amazonian tribe when neither spoke a word of the other's language, and in the fact that he had nearly laid down his life for his friend.

Sorabji had been en route to a conference on pulsars in Santiago when the plane made an unscheduled stop in Belem because of mechanical difficulties. Sorabji had taken a small local plane instead; it had crashed deep in the Amazonian rainforest, the pilot dead on impact, Sorabji rescued by a local tribe but stranded for six months.

At night he would look up at the brilliant Southern sky which could be seen from the clearing, thinking about how far away everything was and how long it took the light to reach him and how little time a man did have to observe the light as it came.

He would spread soft dirt on the ground outside his hut and work on mathematical problems, because there was nothing else to do.

One day a boy from the tribe stood by him and seemed interested.

Sorabji thought: But how terrible! Suppose he is a natural mathematician, born into a society without mathematics! He had not bothered to learn the language but he had a sneaking suspicion you couldn't count in it much past four. Imagine a mathematical genius born to a language where you went one fried ant, two fried ants, three fried ants, four fried ants, lots of fried ants, lots and lots of fried ants, lots and lots and lots of— The prospect was too frightful to contemplate.

Smoothing out the dirt he gritted his teeth and addressed himself to the basics. He put a stone on the dirt, and below it he wrote: 1. He put two stones in the dirt, and he wrote: 2. He put three stones in the dirt, and he wrote: 3. Four stones: 4. Iki-go-e (or Pete, as Sorabji called him) squatted down beside him; Sorabji couldn't tell if 5 came as a surprise.

Six months later Pete and Sorabji were in jail.

A group of loggers had turned up in the jungle. A couple of members of the tribe had been killed, others had scattered in different directions, and Sorabji had set off on the tracks of the trucks for civilisation. Pete had followed. They had come to a small town deep in the jungle, and Sorabji had tried to find a telephone. There was only one in town, at a building marked Polícia; Sorabji had walked in the door and at once been arrested.

Five days later the British consul in Belem flew up the Amazon to Manaus, then headed inland in a borrowed Land Rover.

The British consul in Belem loved Brazil. He loved the language; he loved the music; he loved the wild, savage country; he loved the people. The fly in the ointment was the fact that this marvellous country had not closed its borders to all Britons not travelling on official business. The British were not, in his opinion, actually more intrepid than other nations; they merely had a boundless belief in the powers of their consul, a belief which would have been justified had the F.O. placed at his disposition, for example, a small private army and a slush fund of several millions, but which went well beyond what could be achieved on a small emergency fund and modest entertainment allowance. What do they imagine I can do? he would fume, and What on earth do they imagine *I* can do? was the refrain as the Land Rover bounced and jolted over the potholes.

He arrived at the logging town in late afternoon. He went at once to the Polícia, was shown into the jail, and nearly threw up.

It was close to 100 degrees outside; worse in the jail. Twenty men were crammed into a room in which ten could have breathed.

The jailer crunched over the cockroaches and pointed at Sorabji.

Sorabji's hair was long and matted, as was his beard. He'd spent six months in a tropical sun, and was now dark brown. His clothes had been disgusting after the first week; following local custom he had taken to wearing his shirt as a loincloth. Sorabji always liked to say that the unfortunate consul had travelled hundreds of miles into the interior to rescue a British citizen, only to find Gunga Din. It was true that the loincloth had come from Gieves & Hawkes, but this was not something you'd notice on a casual inspection.

Good of you to come, Gunga Din said suavely. So glad you could make it.

And then, because the question had been tormenting him for months, You wouldn't happen to know if they've got anywhere with binary X-ray emissions?

The consul said not to his knowledge. He introduced himself.

And you are?

The name's Sorabji, said Gunga Din. George Sorabji.

The consul explained that he would need some proof of his nationality.

Gunga Din explained that he had been on a plane that had crashed in the jungle and that his passport had gone up in flames. He suggested that the consul telephone his supervisor at Cambridge, verify his identity and determine the state of play on binary X-ray emissions. He demanded immediate release and repatriation.

And we'll have to get Pete out of here too, he added.

Who's Pete? asked his rescuer.

Gunga Din gestured to the corner.

Do you mean one of the Indians? asked the consul.

I don't think he'd get much joy at the Indian Embassy, Din replied haughtily. He is an Amazonian.

I'm sorry, but there's nothing I can do for a Brazilian national. I can tell you the procedure if you'd like to lodge a complaint—

Sorabji looked at Pete. His head had fallen back, and the whites of his eyes were showing. He would die soon but that was not good enough. He could probably get a decent mark at O-level; it was a miracle of sorts but not good enough.

Sorabji said: He is a mathematical genius. I shall take him back to Cambridge.

The consul looked at Pete. If you are a consul people are constantly spinning you ridiculous stories and expecting you to believe them, but this was the most ridiculous he had ever heard. He said correctly: If he is a Brazilian national I'm afraid there is nothing—

Sorabji said: You. Stupid. *Ignorant.* Bureaucrat.

And he said: *Newton* is sitting in this cell. If I leave they will kill him. I shall not leave this place unless he goes with me.

But what exactly do you think I can—

Sorabji said: Do you have a piece of paper?

He was handed a piece of paper and a pen, and he wrote on it

1+2+3+4+5+6+7+8+9+10+11+12+13+14+15+16+17+18+19+20

and he said: How long do you think it would take you to add it up?

The consul hesitated—

That boy, said Sorabji very gravely, can add all the numbers between 1 and 500 in 20 seconds.

The consul said: Hm.

Sorabji was a Zoroastrian but he was not much of a believer, and he had been to chapel a lot at school but he believed even less in that, and yet he found himself saying Please Please Please Please. Please let him not know about Gauss please please please please please.

Because Sorabji had taught Pete a trick that the great mathematician Gauss had discovered at the age of 8:

Suppose you want to add	$1+2+3+4+5$
Add the sequence to itself backwards:	$5+4+3+2+1$
The sum of each pair is the same:	$6+6+6+6+6$

But that's easy to work out! It's just 5×6, or 30.

So the sum of the first sequence is just 30 divided by 2, or 15!

If the sequence went up to 6, each pair would add up to 7, so the sum would be $6 \times 7 \div 2$, or 21; if the sequence went to 7, the sum would be $7 \times 8 \div 2 = 28$. If the sequence went up to 500 the sum would be half of 500×501: $250,500 \div 2 = 125,250$. Easy.

The consul was still staring at the piece of paper.

He said: But how's that *possible*?

Sorabji said: Look, don't take my word for it. Take him up to the office. Write down a sum, all the numbers between 1 and 257, 1 and 366, whatever you choose. He doesn't know how to use a pen, you'll have to spread some dirt on the floor for him to write on. Give him the problem and time him and then work it out on a calculator.

The consul said: Well . . .

He went off to speak to the head of police. It is not standard practice in the Brazilian system of justice to release convicts who can add all the numbers between 1 and 500 in 20 seconds, but all the same there was something very strange about it and the head of police said he would like to see it. So Pete was brought up from the cell.

After a little conferring they decided to try him on 30. The consul wrote out the sum on a piece of paper, and a little dirt was brought in and spread on the floor, and the piece of paper was handed to Pete. 30 times 31 is 930 divided by 2 is 465 and he squatted down and wrote 465 in the dirt while the chief of police was punching 17 into his calculator. The chief of police got up to 30. 465 appeared on the display.

The chief of police and the consul stared at the boy, and their eyes got wider, and wider, and wider.

They tried 57, and 92, and 149, and each time the same thing happened. The boy wrote a number in the dirt, and a very long time later the same number would appear on the display of the calculator.

The consul looked at the boy, and he remembered the great Indian mathematician Ramanujan. He called Sorabji's supervisor in Cambridge and received confirmation that the brilliant young astronomer had disappeared en route to a conference in Chile six months before. He hung up the phone, and he explained to the chief of police that Sorabji was a brilliant eccentric scientist. That was why he had turned up in the jungle wearing a loincloth. The boy was his pupil. The chief of police looked at him steadily. The consul made polite but firm enquiries as to the precise nature of the charges. The chief of police looked at him steadily.

Accounts differ as to what happened next.

The numbers were the only thing that Pete could understand in the proceedings, and he later said that he remembered doing the sum of numbers between 1 and 30, and the numbers between 1 and 57, and 1 and 92, and 1 and 149, and he remembered five bundles of notes with the number 10,000 changing hands.

The consul maintained that there had been absolutely no irregularity of any kind, the F.O. had extremely clear guidelines on bribery, he had made a call to Britain to speak with Sorabji's supervisor and had naturally reimbursed the chief of police for the cost of the call, and he had also authorised the purchase of clothes for which he had reimbursed the chief of police and for which he had a receipt.

The chief of police confirmed this story.

Whatever the truth of the matter, Sorabji returned to Britain and sold the story to the papers and got a TV deal and Pete went to Caltech and learned English and eventually developed an interest in physics, and he was reunited with Sorabji for the production of Mathematics the Universal Language.

Most members of the British public are not interested in mathematics, but they were intrigued enough by Pete to tune in anyway, and so got their first taste of Sorabji in action. Most had been sceptical of Sorabji's claim to have taught an Amazonian the subject from scratch. Sorabji demonstrated his methods using numbers, stones, leaves, flashing eyes, eloquent gestures and not a single word of English, and they changed their minds. Most viewers had never heard of Gauss, nor felt the lack. Seeing Sorabji they felt that things might have been different. Had they had a teacher who looked like Robert Donat, who knew what heights they might have scaled? At the end of the programme Sorabji descended into English to explain that the best-dressed Indians bought their loincloths at Gieves & Hawkes, a tip which most teachers of mathematics are not in a position to offer. Sorabji was even able to persuade people to sit still for a circle of radius 1 described in the Gaussian plane.

People said say what you like he has a sense of humour, and they watched Mathematics the Universal Language and A Funny Thing Happened on the Way to the Sun because he had a sense of humour and because he was like Robert Donat in The Winslow Boy and The 39 Steps but not Goodbye Mr. Chips.

Today the programme began at Wembley Stadium. Sorabji stood in the middle of the field.

He said how big an atom do we need to see the nucleus? He took from his pocket a tiny steel ball. He said that if this were the nucleus of a potassium atom the atom would be the size of the stadium, and 99.97% of its mass would be in the tiny steel ball, which would weigh about 105,000 kilos. For those of you who have trouble visualising 105,000 kilos, said Sorabji, that's roughly 110 Vauxhall Astras.

Wembley wouldn't let us stack 110 Vauxhall Astras on the field, he said regretfully. But here's one we made earlier.

The camera cut to a car park. The stadium was now in the background. In the foreground were 110 red Vauxhall Astras in an irregular polyhedral formation, stacked in scaffolding that looked as though it had gone a heartstopping five times over budget.

There was a helicopter standing to one side.

Sorabji looked up at the structure which was about four times his height. He said the good thing about this example is that we get a real sense of the weight of a nucleus the size of a tiny steel ball. The bad thing is that we tend to lose sight of the electrons. Literally. The electrons of this 105,000-kilo nucleus weigh about 1.5 kilos apiece, and to see what *that* means we'll have to go to Luton because the first two are in a shell 30 kilometres away.

The helicopter's propellers began to turn, and the helicopter to rise. Below it dangled a rope ladder. Sorabji leapt onto the ladder and began to climb. We were in the 39 Steps segment of the programme.

Below the helicopter you could see the red structure shrinking first to the size of a football, then a tennis ball, then a golfball, then a tiny dot and then it was gone.

A camera in the helicopter showed mile after mile of houses and

Sorabji on the rope ladder. We had seen the programme before but Sib said she wanted to see it again.

The helicopter came down 30 kilometres away at a field near Luton. Sorabji stepped onto the ground. He said: One of the things that makes electrons so hard to think about is that they don't have size in the normal sense of the word, and another is the fact that you can never know exactly where an electron is at any given time. This makes an electron highly unlike this 1.5-kilo free weight from a local gym. But a 110-Astra nucleus at Wembley weighs about 72,000 times as much as this 1.5-kilo electron at Luton, and in that it's highly *like* the relation of the nucleus of a potassium atom to an electron. He showed on a map that the second shell would be at Birmingham and the third shell would be at Sheffield and the fourth at Newcastle and he said that instead of going on to Birmingham he was going to introduce Mr. James Davis of Dunstable Tae Kwon Do. Mr. Davis was a black belt, fourth dan; he was going to break a brick with his bare hand.

The brick was on a stand. Davis stood in front of it. He raised his arm; he brought down his arm; the brick broke into two pieces and fell to the floor.

Sorabji asked how long he had had to train to learn to do it and Davis said he had been studying martial arts all his life but he would say he had started to take it seriously about ten years ago.

He said: I don't want any youngsters out there watching to get the wrong idea, obviously there is an element of hardening the body involved but I'd say the essential thing is it's about training the mind. There are a lot of misconceptions about the sport, people think it's all blokes acting out some Bruce Lee fantasy and I won't deny there are some dojangs naming no names where that's about all there is to it.

He said: Well, you've got your programme to get on with but there's just one point I'd like to make, which is that the more you study any martial art the less likely you are to actually get in a fight and the less likely you are to put yourself in the type of situation where you have to fight. A beginner might do that type of thing but the more you progress the more you realise the skill is something not to be used lightly.

He said: Also the more you progress the more you realise that there is more to it than trying to progress. As a beginner you just want to improve as fast as you can, you tend to obsess about getting to the next colour of belt, there comes a time, or there *should* come a time, when you rise above that. Obviously you improve your skill by fighting someone as good as you are or better, well, if you think about it, if the only point is to improve your skill there's nothing in it for the better fighter. There was a time when for that very reason the last thing I wanted was to open a school. But there comes a time when you realise you have to help young people coming along, and in the final analysis that was why I agreed to come on this show. If you, as a Nobel Prize winner, can take time away from the lab to help train young minds who am I to say no.

Sorabji said: Thank you for joining us.

He said: Let's see this one more time in slow motion, and they re-played the arm rising and falling and the brick splitting in two.

Sib said: Do they teach you all that in judo?

I said we didn't learn to break bricks because judo was mainly about throws and falls.

Sib said: Oh well.

He said: If the space between a nucleus and the first electron shell is like the space between 110 Vauxhall Astras at Wembley and a 1.5-kilo weight at Luton, and if the space between the first shell and the second is like the distance between Luton and Birmingham, why does it take ten years of serious mental and physical training to get a hand through a brick? At the atomic level both hand and brick are almost entirely empty space. The fact is it is not the matter in the hand which repels the matter in the brick. The repulsion is the result of electrical charge. If it were not for electrical charge we could walk through walls.

The first time I saw the programme I was very impressed by this. Now I suddenly thought Wait a minute.

I said to Sib that I did not think you could have an atom without electrical charge and if you couldn't have an atom how could you have walls and I said maybe I should write him a letter and sign it Ludo aged 11.

Sib said: If you think he is unaware of the fact you should certainly bring it to his attention. She said you should only sign a letter aged 11 if you were saying something cleverer than the average 11-year-old would say and it was not a good idea if you had completely missed the point.

She said he was obviously trying to communicate a fact to the public at large.

I said: Fine.

She said: I wonder if it's too late to move to Dunstable.

I said: What?

Sorabji explained that the electrons orbited the nucleus billions of times in a millionth of a second, the effect was similar to that of the propellers of a helicopter and it was the speed of the electrons that made the atom solid.

Sibylla commented that Sorabji was largely self-taught.

❖

Sorabji's father was a Parsi from Bombay; his mother was English. She first met his father on a visit to Cambridge: her brother was reading mathematics at Trinity College and introduced her to another man on the same staircase. At first they did not hit it off, because she made a comment about India and he had the bad manners to say that as she had never set foot in the country he would be interested to know on what she based her opinion; she said later he was the rudest man she had ever met. He went back to India and she was presented and did the usual things and it was all rather a bore. She had always been unconventional and she got the idea of going out to India just to see the place. At first her father refused his permission, but she turned down three or four offers of marriage and began taking a horse out and setting it at six-foot fences, and when she had broken an arm and a collarbone her father said he supposed he'd better let her go then, before one of the horses got hurt.

She sailed to Bombay and it was not at all what she had expected. The Club defied description. So did the people. Also, it was rather hot. That is, she had expected it to be hot, but she had expected it to be cooler. But she looked up the rudest man she had ever met and this time they got on like a house on fire. She said that now that she had set foot in the country she could say whatever she liked and he said he was delighted to hear that she had overcome the diffidence which had afflicted her on a previous occasion. She said something rather cutting and he said something quite rude. She knew he was brilliant because her brother had said he was one of the most brilliant mathematicians he knew, but though he was brilliant and rude he was not condescending. Her brother's other friends were unfailingly charming, so that she could not talk to one without instantly afterwards taking out a horse and setting it at a six-foot fence. She had never met a man who could open his mouth without imperilling the life of a horse.

They married in the teeth of opposition from his family, and now she wondered if she had made a mistake. Her husband was much richer than anyone she had ever met, but he also worked much harder than anyone she knew, and his business took up most of his time. His family took seriously things she could not take seriously at all. His mother once told her gravely about a recent gathering of the Kaisar-i-Hind, only Indian Chapter of the Canadian Daughters of Empire.

'How utterly ghastly' (the only sane response to the story) would obviously bring on palpitations. Vivian murmured some noncommittal reply and downed a gin and tonic in a single swallow. Her mother-in-law added, impressively, an illustration of the loyalty of the Guides, who had concluded an assembly by rising and shouting fervently 'One Flag, One Throne, One Empire!' It looked bad to be having another drink so soon, but what could one do?

It was terribly, terribly hot. She lost three babies and they decided not to try for a while. Then she got pregnant again, and this time she was sent immediately to the hills. Various female members of the family offered to go with her, but her husband (fearing that the cooler climate might tempt her into the saddle) put his foot down. She was allowed to go on her own, and this time the child was born alive, but she was not well for a long time afterwards so she did not see much of it.

One of her brothers was growing coffee in Kenya. She had heard the climate was better there, and she asked one day if they could go to Kenya. She did not really think they could, because the family was all in Bombay and the business there took up so much time. Her husband walked up and down for a minute or so, and he said he thought it might be quite a good idea. He said he thought there would be opportunities in Kenya. He said it would mean starting over again, but all this fanaticism was not really his cup of tea.

They left Bombay when Sorabji was five, and his first memories were of the journey by ship to Mombasa.

He would wake late at night and his mother would be by the bed. In the gloom he would see only the glint of diamonds at her neck and ears, the white of her gloves; she would take him in her arms and carry him up to the deck where his father was waiting. She would hold him on the rail; below the pale foam melted into the dark water, above the stars were brilliant and close.

Sometimes some other passenger would come and protest that the child should be in bed. His mother would laugh and say that they might see a comet.

She would point out constellations while his father stood silently smoking. She explained that she had seen different stars as a child; she explained that the earth was like a ball in the air, and that if you were at one end of it you always looked out the same way.

His mother died of malaria when he was 12. His father sent him to a school in Britain.

The head of the school interviewed Sorabji, and he agreed to admit him to the school as a special favour, but he said he would have a lot of catching up to do. He said he was the most ignorant boy he had ever seen in his life.

The fact was that Sorabji knew a lot about mathematics and science and nothing else. He had been taught by correspondence course in Kenya, and as soon as the packet came in the post he would do all the mathematics and science and send it back, so that he made rapid progress in the subjects that interested him. He kept the arts papers in a pile on the floor to be done as time allowed. One day he thought he should do something about it because the pile was five feet high, but the early papers at the base of the pile had been eaten by ants, so he had given it up as a bad job.

He told the head that he knew quite a lot about science and mathematics, and the head said what this showed was that he was completely undisciplined. As he had covered most of the mathematics, biology, chemistry and physics of the O-level syllabus, however, those periods could be used to catch up on what he had missed.

Sorabji ran away from the school 27 times and was sent back each time.

The first time he ran away was at night. He looked up at the Northern sky; it was like going from a Bond Street jeweller to a street trader hawking chips of glass on cheap velvet. The moon was 240,000 miles away and that was far enough. The second time he ran away was just after dawn. He made his way along a canal to the next town and he saw an orange ball of flame shimmering through the trees and it was 93 million miles away. He made it all the way to his father's house in London, but then he was sent back to the school. He kept running away and being sent back to the school and soon everything in the solar system was too close.

He was obsessed with distance. He had read of stars whose light had left them millions of years ago, and he had read that the light we see may come from stars now dead. He would look up and think that all the stars might now be dead; he thought that they were so far away there would be no way to know.

It was as if everything might really already be over.

One day he found a book on astronomy in the school library. Because he was interested in distance and the deaths of stars he turned first to a chapter on stellar evolution, and the book fell open on something called the Hertzsprung-Russell diagram, which used brightness and temperature to plot the evolution of stars. Sorabji had never seen anything so wonderful in his life. He had never imagined that a piece of knowledge so wonderful could exist in the universe.

He kept looking at the page thinking: Why have I never heard of this before? Why doesn't everyone know about this? He sometimes said later how strange it was being at the school, knowing that no one had ever tried to give this glorious piece of information to the boys but instead forced them to spend hours turning perfectly good English poems into atrocious Latin ones. He said the frightening thing was thinking of how many other wonderful things there might be which were kept from them at the school. He had run away one last time and put himself in for A-levels independently and got the As and got into Cambridge, and he had never forgotten the things that were kept from people at school.

I thought suddenly Look. If Kambei had stopped recruiting when the first samurai didn't work out a 205-minute masterpiece of modern cinema would have been over at minute 32. Five billion people on the planet, I'd tried one. And at least someone who'd run away from school 27 times would not leap to conclusions because I had left school at the age of six.

I was about to get excited and think This is it when I suddenly thought Wait just a minute.

I said to Sib: You know that story about the Ugandan from the Lango tribe

Sib said: Yes

I said: Is it actually true?

Sib said as far as she was aware

I said: But how do you know?

Sib said: Well there was an interview when Dr. Akii-Bua got an honorary degree from Oxford and he said he would not be there to tell the tale without the extraordinary heroism of Dr. Sorabji.

I said: And what about the volcano?

Sib said she had once read an interview of the man with the broken arm describing what it was like falling back into the volcano and then seeing Sorabji climb down inside the rim. She said: Why do you ask. I said I just wondered. I didn't ask about Pete because I had seen Mathematics the Universal Language myself. Pete called Sorabji that maniac and that lunatic, but he never said Sorabji hadn't saved his life.

❖

All the evidence suggested that Sorabji was not only brilliant but a genuine hero. The question was whether I really had the nerve to go up to someone who was not only a hero but a scientific genius.

At first I thought I was not going to be able to do it. But then I thought if you're a coward you deserve what you get. You deserve what you've got.

When I decided I was going to have to do it I realised I would have to be prepared. There was no point in going up to a Nobel Prize winner and saying the kind of thing that would make him think Sesame Street was about the right level.

The problem was that it was hard to know what would be enough. Finally I decided to do Fourier analysis *and* Laplace transforms *and* Lagrangians and I would also learn the periodic table because I had been meaning to do it for a long time and I would also learn the Lyman, Balmer, Paschen and Brackett hydrogen series because of Sorabji's early interest in spectroscopy and maybe that would be enough.

It took about a month to get ready. It was not all that easy to work in the house because Sib kept interrupting to read out amusing extracts from the *Magazine of the Parrot Society* such as Factors Affecting Parrots, A. Human Interference. Or she would jump up and look at the book on Fourier analysis and say How fascinating. Finally I went over to the Barbican and worked there. At the end of the month I wondered whether I shouldn't spend another month on it, or even a year. Wouldn't it be worth an extra year to be in with a chance? A chance of having a Nobel Prize winner for a father, and not just any Nobel Prize winner either, but a Robert Donat lookalike who jumped off trains? If I got this right—I thought if I got this right it would be like jumping *onto* a moving train, suddenly everything would be fast and easy and I would never look back.

I would have spent a year if I had known what to do, but I was not sure what to do, and I thought the more I did the older I would get and the less surprising it would be that I could do it.

I recited the periodic table one last time for good luck and I went out to look for Sorabji.

Sorabji had started out at the University of London and he still had some kind of affiliation even though he was now at Cambridge. He had kept his house in London when he got the appointment because the children were doing very well in their schools and it made sense for them to stay there. He had rooms in his college in Cambridge. He might be in Cambridge doing research or he might be in London because it was summer.

I took the Circle Line to South Kensington. I went to Imperial College and the woman in reception said there had been an unconfirmed sighting three weeks ago. I explained that I was doing an astronomy project over the summer for school and part of the project was supposed to be an interview with a famous astronomer and was there any chance I could interview Professor Sorabji? I said Please? I said couldn't she let me have his home address so I could write to him there? I said Please?

She said Professor Sorabji was a very busy man.

I said: Please?

She said she couldn't just give out his address to every Tom Dick and Harry.

I said I had been studying Fourier analysis every day for a month to surprise Professor Sorabji and Please?

She said: Fourier analysis! What's that when it's at home?

I said: Would you like to see me find the gravitational potential at any point outside a solid uniform sphere of radius a of mass m?

She said: Well—

I said: How about a problem with vibrating strings or membranes? Say a square drumhead or membrane has edges which are fixed and of unit length. If the drumhead is given an initial transverse displacement and then released, what is the subsequent motion?

She seemed to be wavering, so I snatched up a leaflet describing Imperial College and on the back hastily used the Legendre function to calculate the gravitational potential at any point outside a solid uniform sphere of radius a of mass m, and on a separate leaflet I began to calculate the subsequent motion of the drumhead but she said Oh all right. She wrote his address on a card. It was within walking distance.

I started walking to his house. I was getting more and more nervous. What if I had the chance of having a perfect father and blew it because I forgot the mass numbers of the three most abundant isotopes of hafnium?

I said: Hafnium. Symbol Hf. Atomic number 72. Relative atomic mass 178.49. Number of natural isotopes 6. Mass numbers of most abundant isotopes with percentage abundance 177, 18.6%, 178, 27.3%, 180, 35.1%. Most stable radioisotope (predominant type of decay) half-life, 181 ($\beta-,\gamma$) 42 d. First ionization energy 7.0 eV. Density in g/cm^3 at 20°C 13.31. Melting point 2227°C. Electron configuration [Xe]$4f^{14}5d^26s^2$. Oxidation state in compounds, IV. Atomic radius 156.4α pm. Covalent radius for single bonds 144 pm. Reduction potential w/ number electrons etc. etc. –1.505(4). Electronegativity 1.2. Terrestrial abundance: $4 \cdot 10^{-4}$.

I knew what some of them meant. I thought I might as well learn them all at the same time. Now I realised I should have found out what reduction potential $E°$ in V with number (n) of electrons was for, and I wished I had gone ahead and learned ionic radius in pm with oxidation number and coordination number. What if it turned out the one thing that had kept me from having Sorabji was not knowing the ionic radius with oxidation and coordination numbers? I was about to turn around and go home again but I thought that was stupid. It was just chemistry anyway so he probably wouldn't care, and anyway there would always be some other thing.

I found the house and went to the door and knocked. A woman came to the door. She had brilliant black eyes and jet black hair. She was wearing a purple sari. She seemed forceful and decisive just opening the door and listening to my explanation about the school project and the interview.

She said: We're having a guest for dinner, so I'm afraid my husband won't be able to talk to you tonight. He *may* not be able to fit you in at all, you know, he's terribly busy these days, still you may as well come in, no use letting the grass grow, if he can find a time you can fix it all up straight away. What is your name?

I said: Steve.

She said: Well come in Steve and we'll see what we can do for you.

I followed her into the house. A television was on in a room to the left off the hall. She led me into a large room to the right.

A tall, thin, grey-haired man stood by the window looking into the street. He was holding a glass of sherry. He said he thought we were a long way from understanding that.

Sorabji said he thought the next few years would be critical. He was standing by the fireplace holding a glass of sherry. He began to talk about stellar winds, gesturing with his free hand and then putting down the glass of sherry to gesture with his other hand. The only thing I could understand was that he was talking about stellar winds. I'd never thought of reading about stellar winds. The other man said something which I also could not understand and Sorabji began to talk about Wolf-Rayet stars. A Wolf-Rayet star is a highly luminous star with broad emission bands in carbon or nitrogen. I could not understand what Sorabji was saying. I would have liked to say something brilliant but the only thing I could have said was that a Wolf-Rayet star is a highly luminous star with broad emission bands in carbon or nitrogen.

Sorabji was still talking impetuously though we were standing by the door. His skin was paler than a dark tan; his eyes were piercing and black; his hair was black and wavy. It did not seem impossible that I could get away with it. He would not decide I could not be his son on the basis of abysmal ignorance of stellar winds and the single scattering maximum and Wolf-Rayet stars, but I did not want to tell him and watch him think that Sesame Street was about the right level.

He was still talking impetuously when his wife interrupted without waiting for a good moment.

She said: GEORGE. This boy wants to talk to you. It's for a school project. Can we find him a time?

He laughed. He said: Does it have to be in the next 18 months?

She said: GEORGE.

He said: I can't think about it now, I've *almost* convinced this heretic of the error of his ways, isn't that right Ken?

The man by the window gave a dry smile.

I don't know that I'd go so far as to say that.

Sorabji began to talk impetuously again and she said: GEORGE.

He said: I'd have to check my diary. I daresay I can manage something. I'll have a look later. Why don't you stay for dinner?

I said: Thank you.

He said: Splendid, my wife will find you some problems to do—

His wife said GEORGE again but he said No, a rule's a rule, and he explained that the rule was that if you finished a page of problems you got to eat with the grown-ups. He explained that his children had a page of problems to do every night. He said grinning: Don't take it too seriously, will you? God knows the girls don't, they'd far rather eat in front of the TV than sit listening to Ken and me talking nineteen to the dozen, if you find you can't hack it you can stay and watch EastEnders and we'll go through my diary later on.

His wife took me into the other room.

She said: George has this bee in his bonnet about mathematics, Steve.

I said it was all right.

The TV was on. Three girls were watching it and working on pages of problems. She introduced me and they looked up and then back at the TV. She said I could work on anything I thought I could do, and she said now she really must see about dinner.

The youngest girl was working on a page of problems in long division. I thought that they would take a long time to do, and what was the point? He was not going to think much of it if I brought in a page of long division. It wouldn't matter whether it was right or not, it would be the type of thing anyone could do.

The middle girl was working on a lot of equations in three variables. He was not going to think much of it if I just came in with solutions to three-variable equations, and they would take a long time to do.

The oldest girl was working on a page of determinants. It would be hard enough to be worth doing, but there were so many problems that it was going to take a long time.

I said to her: Are there any other problems I could do?

She said with a shrug: You can see if you can find anything in there.

She was pointing to a folder on the table. They all laughed. I said: What is it? And they said: Nothing.

I opened the folder and in it was a big pile of printed pages with problems on them. There were a lot of things I couldn't do, but I could see there were some about Fourier analysis so I thought that would probably be all right.

At the top of each paper it said 3 hours. I said: When is dinner? They said: He starts at 8:00.

It was 7:15. I thought I would just divide by three the number of problems you were supposed to do and then it would probably be all right if I went in at 8:15.

The problems on the pages were rather miscellaneous, whereas the girls were each doing all one kind of problem. So I got four problems about Fourier analysis off different pages. They were a bit more complicated than the ones in my book. It was about 8:30 by the time I finished.

I went into the dining room. He was sitting at the head of the table pouring out a glass of wine for the other man. He was saying

There's absolutely no *question*, Ken, about the importance of this proposal—Yes, what is it?

I said I had finished my problems.

He said: *Have* you now?

I said: Do you want to check them?

He said: I'm afraid it'll have to wait—

I said: Then you'll have to take my word for it.

He laughed. He said: Firoza, would you mind setting another place?

His wife set a place for me, and she gave me a big serving of curry. She told me Dr. Miller had something quite important to discuss but her husband would go through his diary with me later. Sorabji kept talking impetuously and filling Dr. Miller's glass with wine, and Dr. Miller kept saying To get back to what I was saying earlier. This went on for about two hours but the girls never came in with their problems.

After dinner Sorabji said: We'll have coffee in my study.

I was going to have to do it soon.

I followed them out of the room with my pieces of paper. We passed the room I had left; the three girls were still sitting at the table watching TV and working on their problems. They had plates of curry beside them.

Dr. Miller followed him into the study and when I followed too he looked at me and said with a smile: I'm afraid we've some business to discuss.

But Sorabji said: Oh that's all right, it's really only the finer details that need thrashing out— the main thing is that we understand each other

Miller said: I'd like to think so

Sorabji said: You can be sure of it

and he said Coffee or something stronger

Miller looked at his watch and said I really should be going, it's a bit of a trek

Sorabji said: Sure I can't tempt you

Miller said: No, better not— now where did I leave my coat?—Ah!

He picked up an old raincoat that was hanging over a chair and put it on, and he picked up an old briefcase that was standing by the chair. He said: Anyway I think we've cleared up the main issues.

Sorabji said: Absolutely. I think we've really covered a lot of ground

Miller said: Well I hope you've got a clearer picture of what we're hoping to accomplish

Sorabji said: It's been tremendously helpful, thank you for coming

Miller said: Not at all, and he said I'll try to get you something in writing by the end of the week.

Sorabji said: I'll see you to the door.

I heard the door close and he came back down the corridor whistling softly.

He came into the room and saw me. He said: You're not exactly the soul of tact, are you?

I said: What do you mean?

He said: Never mind. I owe you one. Let's have a look at these problems.

I gave him the pages. I said: I did some different problems instead because the others would take too long.

He looked down smiling. Then he looked up at me quickly and looked back; he said: Where did you get these?

I said I got them out of the folder.

He said: The folder? You mean the past papers?

He flipped through the pages quickly to see if they were all the same kind of problem and then he looked through them slowly to see if there were mistakes. At one point he picked up a pencil and crossed something out and wrote something underneath it. Finally he put the pages down on the desk. He was laughing.

He said: Good for you!

He said: I've seen first-year undergraduates who couldn't—I've seen finalists that this puts to shame.

He said: It almost restores one's faith in the educational system of this—but then I suppose you've had private tuition.

I said my mother helped me.

He said: Well I take my hat off to her!

He was grinning. He said: Make my day. Tell me you want to be an astronomer.

I said I wasn't sure what I wanted to do.

He said: But you wouldn't be here if you weren't interested in the subject. I suppose you'd be open to persuasion!

He said: I'm afraid I was rather preoccupied when you turned up, I can't quite remember exactly what it was you came for. Did you want a signed book?

I thought: I can't stop now.

He raises his bamboo sword. He draws it back with a slow sweeping motion.

I said—

I said it so quietly he couldn't hear.

He said: Sorry, what was that?

I said: I wanted to see you because I'm your son.

He drew in his breath sharply. Then he looked at me quickly, and then he picked up the pages again and looked down at them without speaking. He looked at one page, and then at another, and then he turned his head away.

He said: She told me she—

He said: She never told me—

He looked down at the pages of Fourier analysis again.

He said softly: The son I never had.

He looked up at me. His eyes were wet.

He put a hand on my shoulder and laughed, shaking his head. I don't know how I could have *missed* it, he said shaking his head and laughing, you're *exactly* what I was at that age—

I did not know what to say.

He said: Did she tell you—

I said: She never told me anything. I looked in an envelope that said To Be Opened In Case Of Death. She doesn't know—

He said: What did it say?

I said it did not say very much.

He said: And you live here? I don't quite understand—she's still in Australia, isn't she, there was an article just the other day—

I said: I'm staying with my grandmother.

I thought he would be bound to see through this.

He said: Of course. Stupid of me, she'd have had to do something like that.

He said: So you go to school here? You see her in the summers?

I said I didn't go to school, I was just working independently.

He said: I see. He looked again at the pages of problems and smiled, and he said: All the same I wonder if that's wise?

And he said suddenly: Tell me what you know about the atom.

I said: Which atom?

He said: Any atom.

I said: An atom of ytterbium has 70 electrons, a relative atomic mass of 173.04, a first ionization energy of 6.254 electrovolts—

He said: That's not quite what I meant. I was thinking more about the structure—

I thought: What happens if I explain the structure?

I said: The structure?

He said: Tell me what you know.

I explained what I knew and I explained why I did not think it made sense to say that if it were not for electric charge we could walk through walls.

He laughed and he began asking more questions. When I got a question right he would laugh; when I did not know the answer he would explain, waving his hands. It was a bit like the show except that his explanations were more complicated and sometimes he would write a mathematical formula on a piece of paper and ask if I understood it.

At last he said: We've got to get you into a school. Put you into the right school and there'll be no stopping you. What do you say to Winchester?

I said: Couldn't I just go straight to Cambridge?

He stared at me and then laughed again, slapping his knee. He said: Well you don't want for effrontery!

I said: You said you knew university students who couldn't do this.

He said: Yes, but they're not very good university students.

Then he said: Well, it depends what you want to do. Do you want to be a mathematician?

I said: I don't know.

He said: If you want to—if you're sure that's what you want to do —you might as well get on with it, the sooner the better. If you want to do any kind of science there are other considerations. Look at poor old Ken.

I said: What about him?

He said: Well just look at him! They cut our contribution to ESA last year, so he can't get on HERSCHEL. He can't get on it, his graduate students can't get on it, now they're stuck trying to scramble aboard elsewhere, you can imagine the kind of research record the department is going to have now the government has made it impossible for them to do any research, well what kind of funding do you think they'll get if they don't produce any research?

He was looking at me very seriously, the way he had looked when he had written formulae on a piece of paper that he would not have expected most people to understand. He said: Any science is expensive and astronomy is more expensive than most.

He said: More expensive than most and less likely to get any money from industry.

He said: If you need hundreds of millions of pounds sooner or later you are going to have to talk to people who don't understand what you're doing and don't want to understand because they hated science at school. You simply can't afford to cut yourself off.

I could think of two things to say. One was that I was not actually cut off because I was taking classes at Bermondsey Boys Junior Judo. The other was OK.

I said: OK.

He said: You say that but you don't understand. You think because you're clever you can understand anything. I don't suppose anything like this is going to give you problems— and he glanced at my paper. You need to be able to understand things you're going to find almost impossible to believe. If you don't learn to believe them now it will be too late.

The thing that was almost impossible to believe was that he was really saying this. A Nobel Prize winner was saying he thought I could do anything. A Nobel Prize winner was glad I was his son. The whole time he was saying it, even though he was saying it seriously, he would suddenly break into a smile as if he had been saving the

smile for the son he had always wanted and never had. He was brilliant and he thought I was brilliant. He looked like a movie star and
he thought I looked exactly like him. Instead of testing me on capitals of the world he was talking about what it would take to do the
most expensive science in the universe. Sometimes I thought, well if
he wants to be my father why shouldn't he be my father? Or I'd
think that any moment now he would suddenly decide to test me on
Lagrangians and realise I wasn't his son after all.

He said: You've got to be able to believe— It's not just that the
people who write the cheques don't like science. They are elected by
people who don't like science. They are reported by papers edited by
innumerate middlebrows who are prepared to read the odd snippet
about dinosaurs. You have got to be able to believe that the papers
which report their decisions are prepared to publish an astrology column each day which neither the publishers of the paper nor its readers believe to be entirely without foundation.

He said: What you've got to understand is that you simply can't
afford to act as if you were dealing with adults. You're not dealing
with people who want to understand how something actually happens to work. You're dealing with people who would like you to
rekindle a childlike sense of wonder. You're dealing with people who
would like you to eliminate anything tiresome and mathematical because it will impede the rekindling of a—

The phone rang. He said: Excuse me just a moment.

He went round and picked it up. He said: Yes? Oh no, not at all, I
think it went pretty well, I don't think we've anything to worry
about from that quarter. He said he'd get me something in writing
by the end of the week so you've a few days' grace.

There was a short pause and then he laughed. He said: You can't
possibly expect me to comment on that—no, no, just get it in as soon
as you can. Right. Cheerio.

He came back. He was frowning and smiling slightly.

He said: There's a cheap jibe people make sometimes at Christian fundamentalists, they say if you think the Bible is literally the word of God and that the word of God is more important than any other thing how can you possibly not learn the languages God chose for the original text, well if you think there's a Creator and if you think that matters you've only to look around you to see the language it thinks in. It's been thinking in mathematics for billions of years. Of course when you get right down to it you can't beat the religious for sheer wanton contempt for Creator and Creation alike—

He broke off and hesitated, and he said: I think you said she didn't tell you—that is, what did she say exactly?

I said: Well

He said: It doesn't matter. You've a right to know. I owe you that much.

I thought: I've got to stop this

I said: No—

He said: No let me finish. This isn't easy for me, but you've a right to know

I thought: I've got to stop this

but Sorabji had had so much practice on the programme stopping people who were trying to stop him that I did not know what to do.

I said: No. I said: You don't have to tell me anything.

I said: I'm not really your son.

He said: God knows I deserve that. You've every right to be bitter.

I said: I'm not bitter, I'm just stating a *fact*.

He said: All right, a fact, but what about this— and he smacked the pages of Fourier analysis with his hand and said That's a fact too, you can't just walk away from it. The relationship's there whether you like it or not. You know that as well as I do or you wouldn't be here. Well you may as well know *all* the facts,

and he began striding up and down the room and talking very fast to keep me from trying to interrupt—

He said: My wife is a wonderful woman. A wonderful woman. She's always done her part and God knows I entered the marriage with my eyes open. It was an arranged marriage—my father wanted to help out an old business associate, and also though he'd married out himself—perhaps because he'd married out himself—he wanted me to marry a Zoroastrian and for one reason or another he hadn't seen anyone suitable here. I don't mean there was any pressure, don't get the wrong idea about this, my father realised I'd been brought up to be thoroughly Westernised. He just asked me to meet her, he said she was a beautiful girl, well educated, delightful personality, of course if I didn't like her there was no more to be said but it wouldn't hurt to meet the girl, he'd pay all my expenses to fly out to Bombay and we could just take it from there.

Well, of course we didn't fall in love at first sight but we got on pretty well, all things considered; and I realised if I went ahead with it I could count on my family 100% in my career which frankly was the only thing I really cared about, and all in all I think it worked out pretty well. There's something to be said for it, you go into it with your eyes open.

He put up a hand to keep me from interrupting and he said—but then in the early 80s I went to a conference in Hawaii on infrared. That's where I met her. She gave a paper; one thing led to another; before we knew it we were head over heels in love. She was—I don't know what she's like now, but when I first saw her I thought she was the most beautiful girl I'd ever seen in my life. She took my breath away. It sounds trite but it's just a description of fact, it was like being kicked in the stomach. One of those things you don't believe until it's happened to you. And she was brilliant too, had some amazing insights for someone her age; I'd never imagined what it would be like to be with someone you could talk to without thinking about how to explain it.

He was silent for a moment. Before I could think of a way to take advantage of this he was talking again.

He said: It was hell to go back to London but I did it somehow. She went back to Australia. We kept meeting at conferences for the next few years. Finally I said things can't go on like this. I didn't want to hurt my wife but things couldn't go on. Colossus was about three years behind schedule but it really did look as thought it would go up in another four maybe five years, I said as soon as Colossus was in orbit I'd ask Firoza for a divorce, she could come to England if she liked, it wouldn't be hard to find her something, or I'd start looking for something in Australia, she said she was pregnant and I said What do you want to do.

He said: She just kept looking at me. I said What do you want me to do? She started to cry—it was dreadful to see her like that. I said What do you think I can do? You must be aware of the implications. I said—these things torment you later but at the time I had a terror of being swept along, of not thinking clearly—I said What is your estimate of our fossil fuel reserves? What kind of science do you think people will be able to do without petroleum by-products? How much longer do you think people will be able to do the kind of science we do? Can we be sure they will be so brilliant they will be able to do what we do without petroleum by-products?

I must have been in a state of shock myself, I realised that later, but at the time it seemed desperately important to get her to make some kind of statement about fossil fuel reserves, it used to come back to me later. It would have come to the same thing in the end, but why wasn't I kinder? I could have comforted her and instead I kept going on and on at the poor girl about petroleum by-products—it seemed desperately important that one of us should keep a clear head. She just kept crying. But what could I do? Colossus was at a stage where I couldn't possibly go through the disruption of a divorce—and anyway the financial parameters were impossible. Academic salaries in this country being what they are I couldn't possibly support two families—well, I'd had some offers from the States over the years, I might have swung it financially but the disruption of switching institutions, not to mention countries, there was simply nothing I could do.

She kept crying and looking at me. She said George—I said Why are you looking at me like that? Did I make the world? Am I a magician? Do you think I like this?

I said What do you think I can do?

She stopped crying and she said maybe she could manage something but I couldn't let her do that. She was so brilliant and she'd worked so hard—grown up in the Outback and saved up money herding sheep or knitting or some such thing to send off for her first telescope—I couldn't let her throw it all away. She'd only just got her lectureship, so she'd no entitlement to maternity leave—I said You've got to be practical, what are you going to do, go back to the sheep? Spend your life spotting comets?

She said all right, she would deal with it. She asked me for some money. There was nothing I could do. Anyway I didn't hear from her after that but of course I could see that she continued to be productive in the field and her career was going ahead full tilt, so I naturally assumed . . . I thought maybe one day she'd put in a proposal for some of the unscheduled time on Colossus and I could help push that through the unscheduled time being at such a premium, but in the event she did all her work through other observational facilities so nothing came of it.

He said: You've got to understand. If it didn't go up the chances were nothing like that ever would go up ever. I don't just mean in 10 or 20 years but in the whole lifetime of the species. The resources would be gone and there would never be another chance to find these things out for the next 10,000 or 20,000 or however many hundreds of thousands of years there are people around to want to know.

He walked up and down. He said: It's not something I did lightly but I could see she thought I should—Anyway I'm glad she found some way around it.

He put a hand on my shoulder and smiled.

He said: If she doesn't know you're here that makes things easier. I'm sure she had her reasons but you can't go on this way, you really must mix with people your own age. I'll get you an application form for Winchester; send it in and give me as a reference; you don't have to tell her you've seen me, just wait till you've got the scholarship and present it as a fait accompli.

I said: How do you know I'll get a scholarship?

He said: Why on earth shouldn't you get a scholarship? Well if there's a problem I expect I can drum up some sort of sponsorship but why should there be a problem?

I said: But isn't there a waiting list or something?

He said: I daresay there may be but it's completely beside the point. The fact that you think it could apply to you is, if I may say so, the best proof you could give that you don't understand the first thing about the system. Look at it from the point of view of the school. A boy comes to them with a reference from a Nobel Laureate who says this could be the next Newton, and that of all the schools in the country theirs is the one he thinks could best foster these extraordinary talents. Not only do they have before them the long-term prospect of a guaranteed genius as a future alumnus of the school; in the short term they can count on someone who has not only won the Nobel Prize but has also appeared on TV to add lustre to really big school events. I could get you into any school in the country; if there's one you think you'd like better by all means let me know, I don't want to ride over you roughshod—I've simply picked one I think it wouldn't drive you insane.

I tried to get excited about going to a school at the age of 12, but compared to going to Cambridge it did not seem a very in-

teresting thing to do. I said: But what if I've already done everything?

He said: You'll probably find you haven't and anyway it won't
hurt to consolidate. Besides, it won't hurt you to branch out. People
expect scientists to be well-rounded; it won't hurt you to put in
some time on the humanities. You can pick up a language or two—
that should stand you in good stead.

I tried to imagine explaining to Sibylla that I had won a scholarship to Winchester. I tried to imagine Sib not asking who had provided a reference. I tried to imagine Sib believing that Winchester
had been impressed by a reference from my teacher at Bermondsey
Boys Junior Judo.

He must have thought I didn't like the idea of studying languages,
because he said: I know how you feel, when you start out there's just
so much to know you can't stand wasting time. But it can't hurt to
keep your options open at this stage. You can get some experience
on the practical side—have you ever even been in a lab? No, I
thought not.

I tried to imagine explaining to Sorabji that I was not his son in
the genetic sense of the word.

Sorabji kept pacing up and down talking about the school. His
eyes were flashing; he waved his hands; gradually he made it sound
more and more attractive. It was not as exciting as going to the
North Pole or galloping across the Mongolian steppe, but it seemed
to be something that could definitely happen. He talked about the
teachers at the school; he talked about boys at the school who would
be friends for life. He seemed so happy and excited now that there
was something he could do. I was beginning to think if we fought
with real swords I would kill him; I couldn't tell him I wasn't his son
because it was true.

Besides, why shouldn't I go to the school?

I thought: What if there was some way to do it?

If he was right then I really could do it. I could get a scholarship and go to the school and if he ever found out about the trick it would be too late. They would not take the scholarship away just because he said to; they wouldn't take it away if he said he only gave me the reference because he thought I was his son, and anyway how could he say that was why he gave me the reference? Sibylla would have more disposable income if I went; she could buy Schürer's *History of the Jewish People in the Age of Jesus Christ*, the brilliant four-volume update by Vermes and Millar which no home should be without. If I could persuade a Nobel Laureate that I was his longlost son surely I could persuade my own mother that I had got a scholarship to Winchester.

I thought: Why can't I do that?

If it didn't work out I could always go to Cambridge at 13 instead. It might work out. At least it would be better than another winter on the Circle Line.

He was looking at me sympathetically.

I said: I don't know.

I thought: Why wouldn't it be right not to tell him? Sibylla would be happy. He'd be happy. He's obviously been going around for years feeling guilty because there was nothing he could do, and now there's something he can do. What's wrong with letting him think there's something he can do?

The phone rang.

He gave me a sort of rueful is-there-no-end-to-it smile. He said: I won't be a moment.

He went to the desk and picked up the phone. He said: Sorabji!

He said: Yes, what seems to be the problem?

There was a long pause.

He said: I couldn't agree with you more, Roy, but what do you imagine I can do about it? I'm not even on the committee—

There was another pause.

He said: I'd be only too delighted to help if there were anything I could usefully do, but I really don't see any way round it—

There was another pause.

He said: That's a very interesting suggestion.

He said: It would certainly be unorthodox, but that's not to say—

He said: Look, Roy, could I call you tomorrow? I'm in the middle of something right now. I don't want to raise false hopes, but let's not rule out any possibilities.

He said: Good. Yes. Thanks for calling.

I kept looking at him. I couldn't work out what was going on. I couldn't work out what had been going on with Dr. Miller, and I couldn't work out what had been going on with the Australian astronomer; I couldn't even really work out what was going on with his three children and the pages of problems. All the relevant evidence did not seem to be available; I could not see any way of getting all the relevant evidence. Based on the evidence available, the last person I would ask for further relevant evidence was Sorabji.

I thought that if I let him do something I would have to be his son. I wouldn't have guessed, from the TV show, that if you went to him in a crisis he'd start interrogating you on petroleum by-products —but was that the end of the world? I could avoid him in a crisis. The rest of the time he would probably take me up in a helicopter and teach me to climb a rope ladder, or take me flying across the Channel, or explain things that were so hard it helped to have them explained. There was obviously more to him than met the eye, but how much more? How much did it matter?

It seemed to me that things were easier in the days when I just had Val Peters to worry about. He had his faults. Mixing up DNA and RNA. Dabbling in sexual tourism. One could go on. But no one would ever blame *me* for having a father like that—he just came that way. Whereas—

I said: What was that about?

Sorabji looked astonished. He said: Curiosity killed the cat.

Then he smiled and shrugged. He said: Just some administrative kerfuffle. Somebody's nose out of joint.

I knew I couldn't do it. I thought: But why do I have to tell him?

I wanted to say I would send the application and then just not send it. It would be easy because once I left he would never find me. If he talked to the woman he would find out that she had not had a child. If he didn't talk to her then he would never know.

I knew I was going to have to tell him. I thought I'd better do it before I lost my nerve.

I said: You might not want to write me a reference

He said: What, because someone might suspect something? They won't think anything of it. A brilliant, self-taught boy comes to my attention; I do what I can to put him in contact with the right sort of people—what could be more natural? There's the resemblance, of course, but a lot of boys have their hair shorter than that—if you get yours cut before you go I don't think anyone will notice.

I said: You might not want to write me a reference because I'm not really your son.

He said: What?

I said: I'm really not your son.

He frowned as if to say What?

I said: I made it up.

He said: You— He said: Don't be absurd. I can understand your resentment but you can't go around with a chip on your shoulder. You look exactly like me.

I said: My mother says you look like Robert Donat. Are you related?

He stared at me. He said: So you— He said: Might I ask why?

I explained about Seven Samurai.

I don't know what he was expecting. He said: That's ridiculous. It doesn't make any sense.

I said I thought it made sense.

He looked down at the pages of Fourier analysis and spread them slightly on the table with his hand. Then he crumpled them up suddenly and dropped them in the bin. He said: So I have no son.

He said: Of course it would have been quite impossible for her, I should have seen that at once.

He looked at me.

I said: I'm sorry.

He said: Come here.

I stayed where I was. I said: I tried to tell you.

He said: It's stupid, if you were going to make it up what was the point of telling me?

I said: Is it still natural to put me in contact with the right sort of people?

He looked at me. He didn't say anything. His face was quite cold and expressionless, as if something was calculating behind it.

He said at last in an expressionless voice: You have a piece of information which you shouldn't have. You may think that piece of information is dangerous to me.

He said: I would advise you to be careful what you say. I think you will find if you try to use it that it will prove extremely dangerous to you.

I said I wasn't planning to use it and that I had tried to stop him. I thought that there had to be something I could say. He had been so excited about the Fourier analysis before; I couldn't see why it made such a difference if the person who had done it did not happen to share 50% of his genes. I sensed that this was not the moment to make this point. I said I just wanted— I said my own father tended to get the special and general theories of relativity confused.

Sorabji just looked at me.

I said I didn't really know him, it was more of a genetic relationship, and I just thought—

He just looked at me. I thought he was probably not really listening to me; he was probably just thinking that there was nothing he could do.

I said: You don't know what would have happened. Maybe it was the right thing to do. She could have gone insane. Maybe you saved her life. Just because you said the wrong thing doesn't mean you were wrong about—

I didn't even see his arm move. He got me on the side of the head with his open hand, knocking me across the room to the floor. I rolled out of the fall back onto my feet but he was already there. He hit me on the other side of my head and knocked me to the floor again. He was there before I could get up this time, but I tripped him and he fell heavily. Mainly on me.

I couldn't move because he was lying on top of me. A clock which I hadn't noticed was ticking in the room. It kept ticking. Nothing happened. He was panting as if he'd been in a worse fight; his eyes were glittering in his head. I didn't know what he would do.

There was a knock at the door, and his wife said: George?

He said: I'll just be two seconds, darling.

I could hear her footsteps retreating down the hall. I realised I could have shouted something. His eyes were still glittering—

The clock was still ticking.

Suddenly he let go of me and leapt lightly to his feet. I scrambled away across the room but he didn't come after me. He was standing by the desk with his hands in his pockets. He smiled at me and said pleasantly and conversationally:

I'm sorry, that was completely out of line. I'm sorry I got carried away. My temper flares up and then it's over, I never hold a grudge.

My head was still ringing.

His hair had fallen into his face; his eyes were sparkling. He looked like Robert Donat in The 39 Steps; he looked the way he'd looked earlier, when he'd talked about the atom and Fourier analysis.

He said: Of course you should be put in touch with the right people.

I said: So I could still go into astronomy?

He laughed. He said: I'd hate to think I'd put you off!

He raised an eyebrow in a sort of quizzical, self-mocking way. His eyes were sparkling with amusement, as if there was nothing calculating behind them.

I just hoped I wasn't going to have a black eye.

I said: Should I still apply to Winchester? Do you still want to give me a reference?

He was still smiling. He said: Yes, you should certainly apply.

He smiled and said: Be sure to mention my name.

3

A good samurai will parry the blow

Robert Donat was on again Thursday at 9:00. Sib watched enthralled. I was reading *Scientific American*.

There was an article about a man who had done research in Antarctica and was about to go back. There was an article by a man who had done pioneering work on the solar neutrino problem. I would read a paragraph or two and then turn to another page.

Sometimes I thought about the girls who were not my sisters, and sometimes I thought about Dr. Miller, but most of the time I thought of the Nobel Prize-winning Robert Donat lookalike turning through the pages of Fourier analysis, looking at me with flashing eyes, telling me I was brilliant and I was exactly the way he was at that age. I couldn't tell from the articles in *Scientific American* whether their authors thought Sesame Street was not the right level; I couldn't tell whether they had an ill-timed obsession with petroleum by-products; but I didn't have to read even a paragraph to know I'd never find another one like Sorabji.

I put down *Scientific American* and picked up my book on aerodynamics. Sometimes I thought I understood it and sometimes it was hard to follow, and when it was hard to follow it wasn't easy to tell what would help; the thing that would really help would be to be able to ask someone who didn't sum up the mathematics required as 18th 19th century stuff. Any idiot can learn a language, all you have to do is keep going and sooner or later it all makes sense, but with mathematics you have to understand one thing to understand another, and you can't always tell what the first thing is that you have to understand. And even then either you see it or you don't. You can waste a lot of time trying to work out what you need to know, and a lot more time just trying to see it.

If I hadn't said anything to Sorabji I wouldn't ever have had to waste time that way ever again. In the first place I would have gone to Winchester at the age of 12, and in the second place whenever I had a question I could have asked someone who not only knew the answer but couldn't do enough for his longlost son. And if I'd just seen Sorabji on another night—if I'd just spent one more day on the periodic table—I wouldn't have seen Dr. Miller, and I wouldn't have heard any phone calls, and I wouldn't have known there was anything to see or hear. I could have stopped wasting time and been the youngest person ever to win a Nobel Prize. Instead I was going to have to do everything myself.

I had another look at the Kutta-Joukowski theorem. It wasn't so much that I knew for a fact that I wanted to win a Nobel Prize. It's just that if you're *not* going to win a Nobel Prize you might as well do something else worth doing with the time, such as going up the Amazon or down the Andes. If you can't go down the Andes you might as well do something else worth doing, such as having a shot at a Nobel Prize. Whereas this was just stupid.

I put down my book on aerodynamics.

Sorabji looked out from the screen with flashing eyes.

I thought suddenly that it was stupid to be so sentimental.

What we needed was not a hero to worship but money.

If we had money we could go anywhere. Give us the money and we would be the heroes.

In the morning I decided to go the library. A day one way or the other was not going to have a significant effect on my chances of either winning a Nobel Prize or going down the Amazon. My chances of earning a lot of money soon were slim to non-existent. I thought I would read one of my old favourites just for fun.

Journey into Danger! was out so I got *Half Mile Down* instead.

I took the book to read on the Circle Line, and I turned to the first descent in the bathysphere before starting the whole book again.

It was of an indefinable translucent blue quite unlike anything I have ever seen in the upper world, and it excited our optic nerves in a most confusing manner. We kept thinking and calling it brilliant, and again and again I picked up a book to read the type, only to find that I could not tell the difference between a blank page and a coloured plate. I brought all my logic to bear, I put out of mind the excitement of our position in watery space and tried to think sanely of comparative colour, and I failed utterly. I flashed on the search-light, which seemed the yellowest thing I have ever seen, and let it soak into my eyes, yet the moment it was switched off, it was like the long vanished sunlight—it was as though it had never been—and the blueness of the blue, both outside and inside our sphere, seemed to pass materially through the eye into our very beings. This is all very unscientific; quite worthy of being jeered at by optician or physicist; but there it was . . . I think we both experienced a wholly new kind of mental reception of colour impression.

And I suddenly thought of someone who had made a lot of money out of reading this paragraph in *Half Mile Down*.

I thought of someone who had never pretended to be a hero.

He was a painter. He had read the passage from Dr. Beebe which I had read. He had read this passage and he had said:

How can I paint when I don't know what I paint?

He said:

I paint not things in the world but colour. How can I paint colour if I don't know what it should look like? Is blue paint merely to represent blue?

And he had said that he must find a bathysphere, or something, that would take him down to see blue.

He had found a centre for oceanography and they had refused to let him go down. And he had gone to the yard and talked to the boatman, and the boatman liked Picasso's Blue Period. The boatman would have taken him out at night, but then there would have been no blue. One weekend the oceanographers went to a conference and the boatman took him out and sent him down. And when he came up he said to the boatman Have you seen the blue, and the boatman said No. And he said You must see this. I can't paint this so you must see it. You must show me how to send this capsule up and down and you must go down. The boatman was nervous but excited. He showed him how to send the capsule up and down and he stood by while the painter practised and sent the capsule up and down. Then the boatman got into the capsule and the painter winched it over the side.

The painter never painted what he saw, for he said it could not be done.

The boatman said:

I had often sent down Dr. Cooper and the research students over the years. Sometimes a student would say This is amazing. They might say it the first time or two. But there was a lot of work to be done recording observations. Sometimes they worked with the light out, dictating observations into a machine, and other times they had a light on. I had seen a lot of photographs, and once or twice I had watched TV programmes about oceanography—I took an interest because of my connection with the field, but to tell the truth it had never had an overwhelming appeal. I went scuba diving once on a holiday in the Bahamas.

When I was growing up we had a picture from Picasso's Blue Period, and that has always been my favourite period in which he worked. Later I bought lots of books about Picasso, and the Blue Period was always my favourite. I never wanted to paint; I wanted to follow the sea. As a lad I went out on a yacht working for Dickie Lomax, as he then was, and later I was offered the job by the Oceanography Department. Sometimes it seemed to me that Dr. Cooper and his students were just making an excuse to go out to sea and go down in the capsule; they had to make up research projects to get money to do it. Sometimes I felt like saying Look, why make everything so complicated, why not just learn to sail a boat?

So when Mr. Watkins came to me I responded to him, because I thought he wasn't making excuses—he just wanted to go down there. I don't know if Picasso would have gone down, but I respected Mr. Watkins for wanting to do it.

I was very surprised when he suggested I go down, and quite nervous at the prospect. I didn't like the idea of leaving the helm to someone with so little experience. I told him I'd seen the photographs, but he kept saying No, No, that's not good enough, you must see for yourself.

At last I thought Well, it's now or never, isn't it? Because there was no way the professor was going to send me down just to have a look. It was a calm day, and I thought Well, if it's got to be, so be it. So I got into the capsule, and Mr. Watkins winched me down.

As I said before, I'd been scuba diving in the Bahamas on a holiday. This was different. You might think you would get the full effect better actually being in the water, and that might be true up to a point. But in the capsule you were inside a pocket of air. What it felt like was being in a pocket of blue light—light that was blue the way water is wet.

When I came up I got out of the capsule and he made a questioning gesture at it. I nodded and he got in and I winched him down for the last time. It was only now that I realised how low the fuel supply was. The winch runs off a generator, and we'd sent the capsule down more often than the researchers usually did—they usually went down and stayed down making observations. I sat watching the needle on the dial get closer to empty, and when I started bringing the capsule up he said not yet. So I waited and started to bring it up and he said Not yet, but I had to. Just as I brought it up to the surface the motor conked out. So he climbed back on board, and I pointed to the gauge, and he nodded and sat down. I had to take us back to land under sail. The whole time we were going neither of us said a word.

The boatman said later that though later you wanted to find words for it, at the time it was so beautiful that, or rather beautiful would be a word that you would use later but at the time it was so much bigger than that that it would have hurt to talk. He said that one thing he respected in Mr. Watkins was that he had seen just in the look in his eyes that he had seen how big it was and that it would hurt to talk. A lot of people would have had to make a joke or something, but we both knew it was too big for that and we both knew we knew it.

There were other stories about this painter, because after this he decided he could not paint blue. He decided that he must see white, and this time he persuaded the pilot of a plane to fly him to a station in the far North of Canada.

He said I must be alone in the white and the silence. He walked out into the snow and he walked for miles and he was seen by a polar bear, which is one of the swiftest and fiercest killers on earth. He saw it coming toward him with its fur dirty yellowish white against the pure white snow, and then a shot rang out and it fell down dead. The stationmaster had followed him and had shot the bear as it attacked. It lay on the snow with red spots of blood on its fur, and there were drops of red blood on the snow.

★ ★ ★

Then the painter had gone back to England. He had seen white and he had seen red and he went back to England to see more red.

He went to a slaughterhouse and he said to the manager that he wanted some blood. The manager asked how much blood he wanted, and he said he wanted enough to fill a bathtub, and the manager said he was sorry but this was too small a quantity to make it worth his while. The slaughterhouse sold its blood to the makers of sausages and haggises and pet food, and it sold it in hundreds and thousands of gallons, and it was not worth his while to sell 40 or 50 gallons of blood to fill a bathtub.

The painter thought that if it was not worth his while to sell 40 or 50 gallons he would not notice if they went missing. He waited at a pub near the slaughterhouse, and at about 7:00 a man came in with traces of blood on his hands. The painter bought him a drink, and gradually he raised the question of blood, and the man said he would see what he could do. The painter had a small white van that he sometimes used to transport paintings. He drove it to the street by the slaughterhouse, and the next day the man stayed late under some pretext, and then he came to a back door. The painter had brought five plastic bins for garden rubbish, and the man filled them with blood; it took the two of them to get them in the van. The man went with the painter to his house, and helped him to get the bins upstairs. They poured the blood into the bath and the man left.

The painter laid out sheets of paper on the floor of his studio, and he put sheets of paper on the floor from the bathroom to the studio, and on the floor of the bathroom. Then he went to the bathroom and put a video camera on a stand. He started it, and he got into the bath. He sat down in the blood, hands on the rim of the bath, and then he lay down, and he took his hands off the rim, and he turned his legs sideways until he was entirely beneath the surface. He said later that he opened his eyes, but it was not as red as he had hoped. It was not as red as he had expected.

Then he sat up, and blood streamed from his hair and down his face, and he opened his eyes facing the camera.

He stood up, and he stepped out of the bath, and he walked over the paper to his studio, and he lay down now on one piece of paper and now on another. The marks on the last sheets of paper were few and light, because most of the blood had come off and the rest had begun to dry.

When the sheets of paper had dried he put them away and put more down. He returned to the bathroom and took off the bloody clothes and dropped them to the floor, and he got into the bath again. He went through the same procedure.

He did this again and again until there was only a little puddle of blood in the bath. He scooped what he could into a cup and put it on the edge of the tub, and then he ran water and filled the bath to the brim and got into the water, and now the camera recorded his bloody body lying at the bottom of the clear water.

Then he got out and walked over the paper and lay on the paper.

He went back to the bath and let out the water and filled it again and got in it again.

When all the blood had been washed away he filled the bath one more time with clear water, and into it he poured the cup of blood.

Then he let out the bloody water, and he sold the first set of bloody canvas for £150,000. It was called Let Brown = Red.

He had been pretty well known before, which was why the new departure sold for £150,000, and when Let Brown = Red sold for £150,000 people became very interested in the other pieces, which had other interesting titles, and all of them sold for even more. The general consensus at the end of the day was that the most interesting pieces were the later ones, when the blood was drying, or when it was diluted with water, but there were two camps, and some liked the bold crude earlier pieces better. Everyone liked the photocollage of the bath which went for £250,000 and the video installation. The paintings all had interesting names, and nothing was called Blood-bath or This is Not Red because he was too clever to be obvious. And later when he was interviewed he said that all the colours around us were dead, but with blood it was easier to see, and that sometimes you had to risk banality to be clear. Then he said every-one remembered the colour of blood when they saw brown, but that no one remembered any other colour when they saw any other colour. And then he filled a bathtub with blue paint and he did the same thing and he called it Let Blue = Blue.

Let Blue = Blue was felt to be more subtle and poignant than Let Brown = Red, and it was also the kind of thing some people felt more comfortable installing in a domestic setting. Individual pieces sold for about £100,000, and an anonymous American buyer bought a complete set for £750,000, and the painter was now very rich.

What people expected, obviously, was that he would now do something similar with white, maybe a white canvas with nothing on it which was not painted but just entitled, the title would obvi-ously be Let White = White. He now had the stature where he could do something like this. That is, it was something anybody could do, but he could do it and get upwards of £100,000 for it. He was not someone who liked the obvious, however, and for many years re-fused to produce this inevitable work. Instead he tried to look for other colours: he was now rich enough so that he could afford drugs however expensive, and he did LSD mainly and some others that brought colours to life again. It would not exactly be true to say they stopped him working, since work was not exactly what was needed to produce Let White = White, or even the sly Untitled which a few people had predicted. He went to the States and people made jokes, they said he would be politically engaged now, he would paint Let Black = White and it would be very exciting. Instead he did a lot of cocaine because he said he needed to see the world the way the people who could afford to buy his paintings saw his paintings, and he was arrested and charged with attempted bribery, as well as possession, because he had told the policewoman on duty she could make a lot of money if she quietly made off with his fingerprints and mugshot.

The fact was that after Let Blue = Blue did so well he had sent a little piece to the Boatman. He had dipped his thumb in blue paint and put the thumb print on a piece of rough paper. Then he had drawn 50cc of blood from his arm with one of those needles they use for blood samples, and he had dipped a pen in it and written at the bottom, Let Blue = Blue. With it he sent a postcard saying You brought me up too soon. Now the piece was small, but it was absolutely unique. The Boatman did not like it as well as Picasso in his Blue Period, so he sold it for £100,000, and with that he bought a small yacht of his own and eventually a bathysphere, so that he was able to go into the pocket of blue whenever he liked.

The painter never saw blue again.

Sibylla took me with her when she went to see Let Brown = Red at the South Bank Gallery, but I was too young to appreciate it. Then when I was about eight we saw Let Blue = Blue at the Serpentine in 1995. Sibylla thought Let Brown = Red and Let Blue = Blue should be the Nativity and Crucifixion of the next half century and that it would receive better treatment by later artists. I was able to appreciate it now but he was still not my favourite painter.

But now I remembered that he had sent something to the Boatman, and I remembered especially the way he had insisted the Boatman should see for himself, and I remembered the way he had walked for miles into the white. I thought that if I asked for money to go through the Andes by mule I might get it.

The painter had had a studio in an old warehouse on Butler's Wharf across from Tower Bridge. Then the site was redeveloped— this was before he had started making millions of pounds out of the death of colour. So he had moved to an old factory off the Commercial Road, and he had found the bathtub in a skip and had taken it there and plumbed it in himself. Then the property market fell through just as Let Brown = Red came out, and by the time of Let Blue = Blue repossessions were falling thick and fast. So now the painter was able to buy a whole warehouse off Brick Lane which a developer had been planning to develop. This was where the painter went when he came to London, although most of the time he lived in New York. Sometimes he flew to South Africa or Polynesia, but it never seemed to help.

I had read that he was back in London for a retrospective of his work at the Whitechapel Art Gallery.

I took the Circle Line to Liverpool Street and ascended to the street.

First I went to the exhibition to be on the safe side. It was one with an entry fee—that was how big he was, and that was how fast things were in the art world. He had been exciting and promising at St. Martin's and in his early twenties, but if he had not done let Brown = Red when he was 27 he would now have been disappointing and forgotten, and because he had they were already doing a retrospective and comparing him to Yves Klein.

After I had seen the exhibition I went up to the desk and I said: Where's Mr. Watkins?

The girl behind the desk smiled at me.

She said: I don't think he's here. He came for the opening of course but he doesn't come every day.

I said: But I've got a message for him from Mr. Kramer. I thought he'd be here, I've been looking for him everywhere. Do you know where I can find him?

She said: If you want to leave it with me I can see that he gets it.

I said: But it's urgent. Mr. Kramer told me to put it in his hands. Isn't his studio just up the street?

She said: I'm not sure I can give you that information.

I said: Well, call Mr. Kramer's office and I'll get it from them.

She dialled the number, and it was busy. She tried a few more times, and it was busy. Some people came up to ask her for help. She helped them and dialled the number and it was busy.

I said: Look, I know you're just doing your job. But what's the worst that can happen? On the one hand, Mr. Kramer sent me, and Mr. Watkins loses a million-dollar deal. Or he didn't send me, and Mr. Watkins gets a strange kid asking him for an autograph. I mean, is that so terrible? Is it a million dollars terrible?

She laughed.

You're terrible, she said.

She wrote something on a piece of paper and handed it to me.

All right, she said. You can tell me the truth now. Did Mr. Kramer send you?

I said: Of course he sent me.

I pulled an envelope out of my pocket.

See? So I'd better get going.

She said: No, wait, and she handed me another piece of paper.

I ran out the door.

The factory had a big rusting double gate, big enough for lorries to get through, and a little door cut into one gate. It was locked. I rang the bell a couple of times and I banged on the gate, but no one came.

I went up to the side street and turned right, and then I turned right again on the street behind. This had also been bought by a developer and now a wooden fence closed off a row of terrace houses. The name of a security firm was on the fence, but there were gaps in the wood where boards had been torn away; and bushes growing through the gaps. I slipped through. There was a hole where a house had been, and the houses to either side were propped with metal scaffolding. I climbed through to the back. There was the back wall of the factory with glass at the top.

There was an old apple tree at the back of what had been a garden. I climbed up until I could look over the wall.

I was looking down on a concrete-paved yard, with dandelions and grass growing in the cracks. At the back of the warehouse was a metal fire escape, and a lot of broken windows.

The ground on the other side of the wall was at a lower level than on this side—there was probably a 20-foot drop from the top of the wall. But the wall was of very old bricks, and a lot of the mortar had come out.

I worked my way out the branch until it was dipping down on the other side of the wall, and I swung down to hang by my arms and tried to find a toehold in the wall. I found something for one foot, then the other, and then I found holds for my fingers. I worked my way down, going from brick to brick. Then I went over to the building.

Getting in wasn't so hard. I went up a drain pipe to the fire escape, then went up a flight of stairs and in a broken window.

I was beginning to wonder if I was in the right place. Maybe the girl at the Whitechapel had tricked me after all. I was in a room with a concrete floor, and piles of rubble in the corner. I went from room to room, and all were the same.

I went downstairs. I came into a dark room in the middle of the building. The only light was from the door, so I felt my way toward it. Now I was in another room with broken windows, cold grey light showing more crumbling concrete and rubble. There was a stack of boards along one wall piled almost to the ceiling, all cracked and warped, and on the floor beside them were little mounds of what looked like dust. I went to have a closer look, and they seemed to be heaps of tiny flakes of paint.

Now I heard a noise. It was a regular, metallic noise—the sound of a tool on stone. I followed it through another door into the next room, and the next, and the next, but there were only more piles of board, more silted paint. Then I went through another door and by the far wall a man in a black knitted hat and a faded black boiler suit sat on a milk crate. He seemed to have a chisel, or possibly just a screwdriver, in one hand, and he was chipping paint off the wall. I saw that the walls were painted a kind of shiny black up to a height of about five feet, except that for about five feet behind him, and the whole of the wall before that, which showed bare concrete, and a mound of chipped flakes of paint ran along the floor like the trail of a mole.

I said

Excuse me, can you tell me where I can find Mr. Watkins?

He said

What you see is what you get.

I did not know what to say. I said

Was it lamb's blood?

He laughed.

Yes, as a matter of fact. What made you think of that?

I said

Have you been to Jesus for the cleansing power?
    Are you washed in the blood of the Lamb?
Are you fully trusting in his grace this hour?
    Are you washed in the blood of the Lamb?

    Are you washed in the blood,
In the soul-cleansing blood of the Lamb?
Are your garments spotless? Are they white as snow?
    Are you washed in the blood of the Lamb?

He said

I didn't know those were the words, but yes.

I said

Those aren't all the words. There are two other verses. It goes:

Are you walking daily by the Saviour's side?
    Are you washed in the blood of the Lamb?
Do you rest each moment in the crucified?
    Are you washed in the blood of the Lamb?

Lay aside the garments that are stained with sin
    And be washed in the blood of the Lamb
There's a fountain flowing for the soul unclean
    O be washed in the blood of the Lamb!

Are you washed in the blood, In the soul-cleansing blood is the chorus.

He said

Funnily enough no one ever thought to ask. Funny, don't you think? You should've seen the look on his face when I asked for it.

He said

It was quite a job setting it up. They've not got much—couple pints, maybe—must've taken 50 of the little buggers.

He said

I wanted to see what difference a fact about the medium would make to what the thing was about. In the event that seemed banal. I thought well sod it, Rembrandt could start off doing Lot's wife and turn it into Bathsheba and the Elders, I've changed my mind that's all.

I said

Susanna.

He said

What?

I said

Susanna and the Elders. Bathsheba was the wife of Uriah the Hittite, who was sent into battle by King David so that he could have an affair with his wife.

He said

Whatever. The point being, when I thought about it, it was too fucking much. I mean, I really couldn't give a toss about religion. I cared about colour. I cared about that bear, I did. I could have killed the wanker who shot him. To be fair, I probably wouldn't have liked being mauled, but if he'd wanted to do me a favour he'd have shot me and left me for the bear. It would have been more use. Nice meal for the bear, and I could've stayed. It was so white there. White drifting about and frozen solid and getting inside your skin.

He put down the screwdriver and took out a packet of cigarettes.

He said

Do you smoke?

I said

No.

He lit a cigarette and said

My manners may be rough but there are limits. Here was someone who'd followed me for two days and saved my life, and anyway I was I admit a little shaken as I'd been planning on freezing to death, I didn't think I could insist on staying. So I left that white place and when I got back to England I wasn't thinking too straight. I knew I'd have to go on to red, but I wasn't thinking straight and I let my thinking get tangled up in a cliché, and while I was still confused I went to the slaughterhouse and set the thing up and got the slaughterhouse to get me the blood of 50 lambs.

He said

Well I realised as soon as I got on with it that it was a mistake. Banal, irrelevant, but I wasn't going through all that again. I thought of going back and asking for cow's blood or sheep's blood or horse's blood and going through it all again and I couldn't be bothered.

He said

So I thought I'd just leave that out and see what happened, but if anyone asked I'd tell the truth. I don't lie about my work. I was sort of surprised no one did twig it, but people aren't very interested in belief so maybe it's not so surprising.

He stuck the cigarette in his mouth, picked up the screwdriver and began chipping away at the wall.

He took out the cigarette and ground it out underfoot.

He said

Is that why you're here? To satisfy your curiosity?

I wanted to say yes.

I could imagine him lowering himself into the bathful of blood, and I couldn't imagine him sending the boatman down to a pocket of blue. I was glad to have no part of him. But I had come and I couldn't go away without doing what I'd come to do.

I drew my bamboo sword and raised it.

I said

I came to satisfy my curiosity.

I drew it back in a slow sweeping motion.

I said

I wanted to see you because I'm your son.

And he said

Out of?

And I said weak with relief

Sorry?

And he said

Who's the alleged mother?

I said

You probably wouldn't remember. She said you were both drunk at the time.

He said

How convenient.

I said

Never mind.

He said

You came here for money didn't you? You thought you could stick me. You'd better pick better next time.

I said

It's not so easy. If you pick a person to whom you could be obliged you may be disappointed.

I said

Have you seen Seven Samurai?

He said

No.

So I explained about the film and he said

I don't understand.

I said

You sent the boatman down to see the pocket of blue. He said he'd seen pictures and you said it wasn't enough. I thought you'd see why I want to go by mule through the Andes. I thought it would be worth fighting with bamboo swords.

He said

So I won.

I said

If we'd fought with real swords I'd have killed you.

He said

But we weren't.

It was true that I was not his son and that it was a trick.

I thought that he probably did not know the film very well.

Kambei tests the samurai who interest him: Katsushiro stands behind the door with a stick.

His first choice is a good fighter and no coward—he comes

through the door and parries the blow. He is offended by the trick and insulted by the idea of fighting for three meals a day. But the second spots the trick without coming through the door and he laughs, and he accepts out of interest in the samurai.

I said

You have certainly seen through the trick. I'm sorry to have bothered you. I hope you find what you're looking for

though I thought that a man with his money who had bought this grey building and its grey light would look a long time for colour here. I thought that he could probably get more money for his chippings.

I turned and walked back through the three dark rooms to the stairs, and went down to the ground floor. I had reached the gate when I heard footsteps coming down the stairs behind me.

I fumbled for the lock and turned it at last and pushed the door open, and it caught on a chain and recoiled. I closed it and undid the chain and ran into the street. I began to run down the street.

I heard footsteps behind me and sprinted ahead. His legs were longer. A hand gripped my arm and we stopped.

The sky was now completely grey. The sky was grey, and the street was grey, and a big glass office building reflected grey sky, grey street, grey man, grey boy. His face was leaden and ugly, dead and dry in the nasty light.

He said

Come on then. I'll take you to Atlantis.

He began running again, pulling me along. He ran through a lot of little streets and then we came out in Brick Lane. He began to run up the street, past the sari shops and Indian sweets shops and Islamic book shops and at last he ran up the steps of a brick building and dragged me through the door.

It was bright white, perhaps not polar white. To our right a flight of stairs ran up. To our left a door through which we went; a small entrance, walls covered with cards, another door.

We went through this door, and now we were in a very high, very long room, and along its walls and on racks across the floor were pots and tubes and sticks and papers in hundreds and hundreds of colours. We were standing by the cash register. Two people in a queue turned and stared, and one salesman said

Mr. Watkins!

And the other said

Can I help you?

And he said

No.

Then he said

Yes. I need a knife. A Stanley knife.

And while an assistant hurried to get this he was walking through the room.

His hand still gripped my arm, though not so tightly. He stopped by a display and read out 'chrome yellow' and he said

I wonder what the real thing looks like, eh my old son?

And he walked on to the back of the room where there were racks of paper.

He was walking fiercely between the racks of colours, not looking after that remark. There were large sheets of handmade paper with rose hips and other dried flowers pressed into them. There were pieces of paper of smaller sizes on a side table. He took one and looked at it and took it and he bought this and the knife. Then he resumed walking around and the sales assistant hovered at our heels until he told him to stop. He would pause behind a case and then someone would come around the case.

At last he said

All right. All right. All right.

His hand now circled my wrist loosely. He walked through the air as if it were water, by jars of colours for painting silk, and white fringed silk scarves in cellophane for painting, and white silk ties for handpainting, and white silk hearts in cellophane.

He stopped and he began to laugh a breathy scratchy laugh like the stubble on his face.

No cheap jokes, he said.

He said

This will do. This is just what I was looking for.

He picked up a silk heart and he took £10 out of his pocket and handed it to a salesperson. He had to use his other hand to get the money, so he dropped his hold on me. Now he went up a short flight of steps, then up another step to a platform overlooking the store, and I followed him up to the top. On the platform were three round black tables and three chairs with cane seats. There was a table against the wall with two coffee machines and a sign that said Help yourself to coffee and Milk in the Fridge; next to the table was a fridge. A couple of small speakers sent Virgin FM scratchily out.

He pulled a second chair to one of the tables and sat down. I sat down.

He tore open the cellophane with his teeth and unwrapped the white silk heart. He pulled the Stanley knife free of its cardboard.

He said

You know my agent? He can tell you who'd give money for this; he'll find someone who'd like to buy it.

He held his thumb up. He breathed on it, and then he ground it onto the white silk.

He said

You know the old joke. I suffered for my art and now it's your turn.

He gripped my thumb tightly. I thought he would do the same with my thumb: it was dirty enough from my climbing. He held it so tightly it hurt, and before I understood what he meant he had seized the knife and slashed my thumb with the blade.

A big gout of blood welled out of the cut. He let it gather on the blade and then he took this away and did something on the silk, and then he scooped up more blood with the knife and transferred it to the silk, and he did this nine or ten times. Then he put the knife aside and he brought my bloody thumb down on the silk beside the black mark he had made.

He lifted my hand and dropped it on the table. He retracted the blade of the knife and put the knife in his pocket.

On the white silk were the two thumbprints, one black one red with a cut across it. Underneath was written in wet letters

Washed white in the Blood of the Lamb

4

A good samurai will parry the blow

Looking for a father had turned out to be an unexpectedly high-risk activity. Stand behind the door, Kambei tells Katsushiro. Bring down the stick as hard as you can, it will be good training for you. Any more training and I might not live to see 12.

A week went by and we got three red bills on the same day. Sibylla called the project and asked when she could expect her cheque for £300 and the person she talked to was rather snide and said if they took as long to pay as she did to do the work she would probably get the cheque around Christmas. So Sibylla said she would send in 10 issues of *Carpworld* by the end of the week and the rest the week after that. They sent the cheque for £300 and Sibylla paid off the bills and we had £23.66 to keep going until she got paid for *Carpworld*.

I was reading a book on solid state physics. Sibylla gave it to me for my birthday because it said inside the front cover that the extension of our understanding of the properties of solids at the microscopic level is one of the important achievements of physics this century and because she had found a damaged copy on sale for £2.99. Unfortunately it wasn't quite the bargain it looked, because the blurb went on to say: Dr. Rosenberg's book requires only a fairly basic background in mechanics, electricity, and magnetism, and atomic physics along with relatively intuitive ideas in quantum physics. Sibylla thinks no one is put off by difficulty only by boredom and if something is interesting no one will care how hard it is;

it is certainly an absorbing subject but to follow it you really need at least some kind of introductory materials on the above-mentioned subjects. I was getting rather frustrated but I thought I would rather die than sell the heart, not because I wanted to keep it but because it would be horrible to take money for it.

I came in one night after a useless day at the Museum of Science and Technology. Considering they charge an entrance fee you'd think they'd hire people who knew about science and technology, I thought the attendants would be able to help me when I ran into trouble but the one I asked couldn't.

I was thinking about the Umklapp process, or thinking about it as much as you can think about it if you don't have a fairly basic background in mechanics, electricity, and magnetism, and atomic physics along with relatively intuitive ideas in quantum physics. The Umklapp process relates to groups of waves that cross each other's paths: there is little or no interference when the waves are in a linear medium, i.e. one in which the displacement at any point is proportional to the applied force. The waves are said to be harmonic, and the energy of the wave is proportional to the square of its amplitude; the displacement of the medium at any point can be obtained by adding the sums of the amplitudes of the individual waves at that point. If the medium is not exactly linear, on the other hand, the principle of superpositon no longer applies, and the waves are said to be anharmonic. The Umklapp process is a special case of this: if the sum of two oncoming phonons is large enough, their resultant will be a phonon with the same total energy, but travelling in the opposite direction!

The staff at the museum had not been very helpful when I had asked questions, and I knew that Sibylla would not be able to help. I was wondering whether I should try to get into a school. I came into the house and Sibylla sat at the computer with the 12 issues of *Carpworld* 1991 to her left and the 36 issues of *Carpworld* 1992 1993 and

1994 to the right. The screen was dark. I opened the door and she said:

He is a monstrous peacock, and He waveth all the night
His languid tail above us, lit with myriad spots of light.

She said:

The sun's rim dips, the stars rush out
At one stride comes the dark.

She asked if I had had a good day. I said I was reading *The Solid State* by H. M. Rosenberg. She asked if she could see it, and when I handed it over she looked inside. She said: What is a phonon?

I said: They are quanta of lattice vibrational energy.

They died as men before their bodies died, said Sibylla.

I said: What?

Never mind, said Sibylla. I believe that the body can survive 30 hours of typing *Carpworld* into a computer, for mine seems to be still of a piece.

She was flipping through the book and now she said: Oh, listen to this!

However carefully we prepare a specimen, using extremely high purity materials and very specially controlled methods of crystal growth, one form of defect will always be present—that due to the thermal vibration of the atoms. At any instant in time the atoms are never exactly at their correct lattice sites. At room temperature they are vibrating with approximately simple harmonic motion at around 10^{13}Hz about an origin which is at the geometrical lattice position. Even at very low temperatures the zero-point motion of the atoms is still present.

This is delightful, said Sibylla. If you were at school they would not let you read a book like this, they would keep you from reading it by involving you in sport. And look! It was written in 1976, so that Liberace might have read it in his intellectually malformative years and profited thereby, instead of allowing his mind to solidify, we may say, to the state where the cerebratory atoms spent their time perpetually away from their correct lattice sites. I wish I understood this, said Sibylla, and she flashed a bitter look at *Carpworld* 1991, but I'm glad that you have come upon it so young. Approximately simple harmonic motion—it sounds so Platonic, doesn't it? Plato says— oh what does Plato say? Or it may be the Stoics. But I think Plato says something about it in the *Timaeus*. And she looked even more bitterly at *Carpworld* 1992-94, and she said at last: Well anyway I know what Spinoza says, he says—and she stopped. And she said: Well I can't remember the precise words but what he says is that the mind when it becomes conscious of its own weakness is saddened. Mens blankety blankety blank tristatur.

Her face was pinched and grey. Her eyes were burning. The next day I took the heart out and put it in my backpack and left the house.

I took the Circle Line and when it stopped at Farringdon I stayed on. I didn't want to go to the agent but I was going to have to do it. Sometimes I thought the problem wasn't really money but then I remembered that someone had saved Sib's life because it wasn't worth killing yourself over money.

Someone left an *Independent* behind at Baker Street so I went around another time doing the crossword.

The train reached Farringdon. I started reading the paper. Red Devlin had come out of hiding and was publishing a book about his experiences as a hostage. There was an article about nationalism and intervention. There was a short column about Mustafa Szegeti, who had been reprimanded by the authorities in West Papua for claiming to be Belgian consul and issuing a number of Belgian visas in that capacity. Suspicions had been aroused; the Belgian embassy in Jakarta had denied any connection with Szegeti, who was in fact of Egyptian and Hungarian descent and bridge correspondent for the *Independent*. When asked why he had impersonated a member of the Belgian diplomatic corps he had replied: Well, someone had to.

This was exactly like Szegeti. He had been arrested in Burma when I was six for claiming to be a delegate from the United Nations, and in Brazil when I was seven he had passed himself off as an American commercial attaché, and he had been self-appointed deputy director of the World Bank in Uganda and Bhutanese ambassador extraordinary to Mozambique. He had helped large numbers of people to escape death and torture and flee to reluctant asylums with imaginative documentation.

That was obviously not the way he made his living.

Szegeti had learned bridge as a boy from his parents, both avid players. His mother was Egyptian, his father Hungarian. They were wealthy, but compulsive gamblers, and had lived in constant uncertainty and excitement.

They had lived in magnificent hotels when they could afford it and often when they could not. On arriving they always insisted on having a grand piano installed in the suite so that his mother could play Brahms when she was not playing roulette. They ordered lavishly from room service. Sometimes Szegeti had not seen his parents for days at a time; sometimes they had not gone outside for a week, getting up to gamble and leaving the gambling to go to bed.

His mother wore only designer clothes. Once when she had pawned all her jewellery she pawned the clothes too. Men had to wear evening dress to the casino; women were not allowed to wear trousers. She put on her husband's black tie. She did not even have the money to buy a false beard. She cut off her hair, and she glued a few wisps to her upper lip, and she went to the casino with the money raised from the clothes. She was gone for two days.

She came at last to the room. Instead of a two days' growth of beard she had only wisps of black hair coming loose from the glue. Her black hair stood in spikes. She came to the room—they had not dared to call room service for two weeks, they had been living on half-finished boxes of chocolates and leftover breadsticks—and she threw one chip on the bed.

Then you lost? said Szegeti, and the boy, too, thought that she had lost.

I lost, she said. She went to the mirror and began to pull off the moustache.

I lost, and I lost, and I lost. And then I won.

From the pockets of the suit she took sheaf after sheaf of notes, and stacked them on the dressing table. Numéro vingt-huit, she said, il ne m'a pas tout à fait oubliée. They were sheafs of 500 franc notes.

I must go to bed, she said. I have nothing to wear.

I thought: It's *not* just the money.

I thought: I can always sell the heart another time.

I thought: I can't wait to see the look on his face!

Being deported sounds rather traumatic but Szegeti had been through it so many times before I thought he would probably not let it interfere with his normal pursuits. I knew he played bridge a lot at the Portland Club, so I got off the Circle Line at Baker Street and went to the Marylebone Library to look up the Portland Club in the phone book. One should never despise the obvious, so I tried the residential directory first, but of course a man who wanted to avoid nuisance calls from the type of head of state who typically gets 99.9% of the vote from an adoring populace, not to mention the Bhutanese, American, French, German, Danish and now Belgian embassies, and not mentioning last but not least the World Bank, UN and WHO, was not listed. The Portland Club was at 42 Half Moon Street.

I took the Jubilee Line to Green Park and walked to Half Moon
Street. It was about 1:30. I sat on the curb across the street from the
Portland Club and began to peruse *The Solid State* by H. M. Rosen-
berg.

I thought: Who knows WHAT will happen?

Szegeti was not only a chronic diplomat and cardplayer, he had
had dozens, hundreds or thousands of affairs depending on your
source (Szegeti/*The Sun*/Saddam Hussein). He couldn't keep track
of them all; for all he knew one of his exes *might* have had a child. He
might accept me as his son! Perhaps I would be able to tell the story
of the moustache as a story about my grandmother.

People went in and out of the Portland Club, but none looked
like Szegeti. At about 4:00 a taxi drew up in front of the club and a
man in a white suit stepped out. It was Szegeti.

Six hours went by. I was starving. I forced myself to read H. M.
Rosenberg, *The Solid State*. I tried not to think about food.

At about 11:00 Szegeti came out. He was with another man. The
other man was saying: I just thought if I led the king it would open
up the diamonds.

Diamonds?

It was the only suit they hadn't bid.

Neither they had, said Szegeti with a sigh. One would not like to
think the spirit of adventure had wholly died out in the modern
game, but when one considers the unaccountable, indeed the apparently insuperable reluctance of the average player to bid a suit on a
void or singleton! Not to mention the pusillanimity of the partnership de nos jours which meanly settles for a suit where it has found
a fit rather than moving on to explore uncharted waters. We live in
a degenerate age.

Last time you said I should obviously have led the king.

Did I? Then I take it all back. You must certainly lead the king
every chance you get. No need to mull over your lead if you've a

king in your hand. If anyone looks surprised you may say that you have it on my authority that to lead the king is the quintessence of sound play. But here is my taxi.

He got into the taxi, and it drove off.

I had no idea where it was going.

The man left behind was staring after it. I ran up behind him and said breathlessly:

Excuse me! I was told to deliver something urgently to Mr. Szegeti at his club and now I've just missed him—do you know where he's going?

Haven't a clue. He's gone off Caprice; you could try Quaglino's. Do you play bridge?

No. Where's Quaglino's?

Oh good Lord, you can't—that is, he's in a filthy mood about something or other and if he's meeting someone he won't want you barging in. Why don't you leave it at the club?

Where's Quaglino's?

Isn't it rather late for you to be out?

Where's Quaglino's?

He probably isn't there anyway.

Then it doesn't matter if you tell me where it is, does it?

No, well, Bury Street, if you must know.

Where's that?

Miles away.

I went back to Green Park. The Tube would close in an hour. He would probably go off in a taxi again and I would not be able to follow because I only had my Travelcard and a pound. Still, maybe something would turn up.

I asked at the assistance window where Bury Street was and the man said it was just around the corner. I looked at the local area map and sure enough it was just around the corner, about a ten-minute walk from Half Moon Street. Would anyone take a taxi for that kind of distance? But it was my only lead so I walked up Piccadilly and down St. James's Street and over to Bury Street, and I looked at Quaglino's but you couldn't see much from the outside. I couldn't tell whether anyone in a white suit was inside or not.

I sat on a doorstep across the street from Quaglino's and tried to read *The Solid State*, but the light was too bad. So I started reciting *Iliad* 1. I am planning to learn the whole thing in case I am thrown in jail some day.

People went in and out of Quaglino's. I finished *Iliad* 1; it was still only 12:30. A couple of people stopped and asked if I was all right. I said I was. I started going through weak Arabic verbs. My favourites are the double and triple weak verbs because they practically shut down in the imperative, but I made myself start with initial hamza and work through.

It was a good thing I did. An hour went by; I thought he must have gone somewhere else. I might as well go home. But I'd reached my favourite verb in the whole language & I thought I would go through that first and give it just a little longer. The strange thing about يَيَّ is this: here is a triliteral verb in which all three letters are ya; a verb which only occurs in Form II, with the middle ya *reduplicated* (unfortunately this means the final ya is then written alif, but you can't have everything); a verb which means 'to write the letter ya' (Wright) or 'to write a beautiful ya' (Haywood and Nahmad)! This has got to be the best verb in the language—and Wehr doesn't even bother to put it in the dictionary! Wright, believe it or not, only mentions it to say he isn't going to discuss it because it's rare! Blachère doesn't even mention it! Haywood/Nahmad is the only one to give it decent coverage, and even they don't give the imperative. They do give the jussive, which apparently is yuyayyi; I think this means the imperative would be yayyi. So I sat across from Quaglino's saying yayya yayyat yayyayta yayyayti yayyaytu quietly to myself, and I thought that if he didn't come out by the end I'd go through Form IX (which Blachère calls nettement absurde) just for the fun of it & maybe Form XI which is the intensified form of IX & presumably so absurd it's off the charts. IX is for colours & deformities & XI is to be blackest black or whitest white. The painter would have liked that. He could do a piece called Let IX = XI. Let Deformity = Colour. Forget it.

Anyway I'd reached yuyayyi, and had just started thinking about going on to ihmarra to be red ihmaarra to be blood red, when Szegeti came out of Quaglino's with a woman.

She said:

Of course I'll drop you off.

He said:

You're an angel.

She said:

Don't be silly. But you'll have to tell me how to go, I always get lost in those little streets.

I held my breath and he said:

Well, you know Sloane Street?

She said:

Of course.

They were walking down the street away from Piccadilly. I followed on the other side of the street, and he said:

Well, you turn right onto Pont Street and then it's your fourth left —couldn't be easier.

I said: EUREKA!

I said: Sloane Street, Pont Street, fourth left. Sloane Street, Pont Street, fourth left. Sloane Street, Pont Street, fourth left.

She said:

I'm sure we'll get there somehow.

I followed them to a National Car Park. I waited by the exit so that I saw her dark blue Saab come out. Then I started walking to Knightsbridge. It was a long shot but I thought maybe she would not just drop him off but go in and if she did and I waited long enough I would see where she came out.

I got to Pont Street at about 2:15. The fourth left was Lennox Gardens. There was no sign of the Saab.

I decided to wait until the next day anyway and hope that I would see him leave. I walked back to Sloane Street where I had seen a pay phone but it only took coins. I went back to Knightsbridge and found a phone that took phonecards and called Sibylla. I said I was in Knightsbridge and needed to be there early in the morning so I thought I would just stay there but I did not want her to think I was being held hostage or sold into sexual bondage to a ring of paedophiles.

Sibylla did not say anything for a very long time. I knew what she was thinking anyway. The silence stretched out, for my mother was debating inwardly the right of one rational being to exercise arbitrary authority over another rational being on the ground of seniority. Or rather she was not debating this, for she did not believe in such a right, but she was resisting the temptation to exercise such power sanctioned only by the custom of the day. At last she said: Well then I'll see you tomorrow.

There was a locked garden in Lennox Gardens. I went over the fence and lay down on the grass behind a bench. The years of sleeping on the ground paid off: I fell asleep instantly.

At about 11:00 the next morning Szegeti came out of a block of flats at the end of the street and turned the corner.

❖

When I got home Sibylla had finished *Carpworld*. She sat in the soft chair in the front room huddled over *Teach Yourself Pali*. Her face was as dark and empty as the screen.

I thought I should be sympathetic but I was too impatient. What's the use of being so miserable? What's the point? Why can't she be like Layla Szegeti? Anything would be better than this. Is this supposed to be for my sake? How can it be for my sake if I hate it? It would be better to be wild and daring and gamble everything we had. I wish she would sell everything we had and take it to a casino and bet it all on a single turn of the wheel.

❖

The next day I went back to Knightsbridge. He had left at 11:00 the day before so I thought I'd better get there before 11:00.

I got there at 9:00, but I couldn't get in. There was a speaker phone and a buzzer: Szegeti was on the third floor. I sat on the steps to wait. Half an hour went by. I stood by the speaker phone as if looking for a name. Twenty minutes went by.

At 9:56 a woman with a bag of shopping let herself in and I followed her through. I headed for the stairs to avoid awkward questions: I ran up the stairs three at a time.

At 10:00 I went up to the door and rang the bell.

A man in a white uniform came to the door. He said:

What do you want?

I said I had come to see Mr. Szegeti.

He said: Mr. Szegeti is not receiving callers.

I said: When would be a good time to come?

He said: It is not for me to speculate. Would you like to leave your card?

But now a voice from another room called out something in Arabic. I could tell it was Arabic but I couldn't understand it; this was annoying as I thought my Arabic was pretty good. I had read 1001 of the *Thousand and One Nights* and the *Muqaddimah* and a lot of Ibn Battuta and I read *Al Hayah* whenever Sib bought a copy to keep her hand in. The voice must have said something like It's all right, I'll take care of it, because the man in white bowed and walked away, and Szegeti came into the hall. He was wearing a red and gold brocade robe; his hair was wet; he was wearing a lot of perfume. My opponent was a dandy of the Meiji period. This was it.

I wanted to meet you, I said.

He said: How very flattering. It's rather early, though, don't you think? In the days when people paid morning calls they paid them in the afternoon, you know. The custom has died out, but this civilised conception of the day is preserved in the description of a performance beginning at four o' clock as a matinee. You wouldn't expect a matinee to begin at ten in the morning.

No, I said.

As it happens, however, you would have been doomed to disappointment had you come at a more suitable time. I have an appointment at two—hence my unseasonably matutinal appearance. Why did you want to meet me?

I took a breath. He raises the bamboo sword. He draws it back with beautiful economy.

I'm your son, I said. I could not breathe.

He paused. He was perfectly still.

I see, he said. Do you mind if I smoke? This is rather sudden.

Sure.

He took a gold case—a gold case, not a pack—from a pocket. He opened it: the cigarettes had dark paper, and a gold band near one tip.

He took out a cigarette; closed the case; tapped the cigarette on the case; put the case back in his pocket. He took out a gold lighter. He put the cigarette in his mouth; cracked the lighter; held the flame to the tip. All this time he did not look at me. He put the lighter back in his pocket. He inhaled on the cigarette. He still hadn't looked at me. At last he looked at me. He said:

Would it be indelicate to ask your mother's name?

She didn't want you to know, I said. I'd rather not say, if you don't mind. I must have hurt her very badly.

No, she—she just realised it was over and thought there was no point. She had enough money and didn't want to trouble you.

How extraordinary. If we'd parted on bad terms I could understand if she'd felt miffed, but you say there was nothing of that kind.

And yet she chose not to tell me something rather momentous. She must have a very low opinion of me—I am glad it has not prejudiced you against me.

No, no, I said. She said she didn't know you very well.

Then she must have assumed the worst, surely?

He was taking slow drags on the cigarette, then speaking, then smoking again.

I'm sorry to question you so closely, but you must see that this is rather wounding to say the least. I freely admit that I have none of the uxorious virtues, but that's scarcely synonymous with an abdication of obvious responsibilities—I'd always thought the women I'd known had understood the sort of man I was. I'm not a very deep character, you know—it's pretty easy to get my measure on short acquaintance, and if women don't like it they don't stick around for very long—certainly not long enough to get to a bedroom. Or is that just shorthand for a one-night stand?

Yes, I said.

I see, yes, that makes a little more sense.

He smoked again.

If you'll forgive the question, though, am I the only candidate?

She was working in an office with mainly women, I said. Then she met you at a party.

And was swept off her feet. And this was when? How old are you?

Twelve years ago. 11.

And where? In London?

I think so.

There's just one thing I can't quite understand. What harm could there be in telling me the name of a woman I knew so briefly? Why should your mother care?

I'm not sure.

I see.

He stubbed out the cigarette.

It's all nonsense, isn't it?

I was silent.

What put you up to it, a newspaper?

No—

You want money?

No.

I felt slightly shocked. It had happened so quickly.

Have you ever seen Seven Samurai?

A long time ago. What about it?

Do you remember the scene where Kyuzo has the duel?

I'm afraid I can't remember their names.

Kyuzo is the one who isn't interested in killing people.

I forced myself to speak slowly.

He fights a match with another samurai with a bamboo sword. He wins, but the other man claims it was a draw. So Kyuzo says, If we'd been fighting with real swords I'd have killed you. So the other samurai says, All right, let's fight with real swords. So Kyuzo says, It's silly, I'll kill you. So the other samurai draws his sword, and they fight with real swords, and he's killed.

Yes?

So I went to see my real father three months ago, just to see him. I didn't say who I was. I was standing in his study, and I thought, I can't say I'm his son, because it's true.

He had been watching me with very bright, alert eyes and an impassive face. His eyes brightened further.

You could say it to me because it wasn't true? he said. I see!

He saw it in a single second. He laughed suddenly.

But this is marvellous!

He glanced at his watch (gold of course).

Come in and tell me more about it, he said. I must hear more. Was I your first victim?

The fourth, I said.

I caught myself about to apologise and stopped myself from saying something idiotic.

The first three were terrible, I said which was a little like an apology. Two believed me and one didn't. They were all terrible. Then I said it wasn't true and they didn't understand.

You astonish me.

Then I thought of you. I hadn't before because I don't play bridge.

Don't you? Pity.

I thought you'd understand. I mean, I thought if you didn't believe it you'd still understand.

He laughed again.

Have you any idea how many paternity claims I've faced?

No.

Neither have I. I lost count after the third. Usually it's the alleged mother who presents herself, with the utmost reluctance you understand, for the sake of the child.

The first time it happened was dreadful. I'd never seen the woman before in my life, or at least I'd no recollection. Instead of at once being suspicious I was horribly embarrassed—how shocking to have so little recall of a tender moment! She said it had been a few years—how wounding, you know, if she had changed so much for the worse!

At any rate I came to my senses sufficiently to ask a few questions. The thing looked more and more fishy. Then I had what I thought was a stroke of genius. I fancied myself a perfect Solomon!

I said: Very well, if the child is mine, leave it with me. I undertake to bring him up on condition that you make no further contact with either of us.

My thought was, that no mother would surrender her child on such terms to a perfect stranger. I'd scarcely uttered the words when I saw my mistake—saw the terrible temptation in the girl's eyes. It was then that I knew for a fact that the child wasn't mine: it was like playing an ace first trick and watching a rank beginner agonise over whether to trump. My heart was in my mouth, I can tell you!

What would you have done if she'd accepted? I asked.

I'd have had to take it, of course. Play or pay—not a very noble principle, perhaps, but only consider the sacrifice required to abandon it, for the mere paltry momentary advantage of ridding myself of this unexpected encumbrance. Life is such a chancy business, you may lose everything you have at any moment—if a stroke of luck can rob you of whatever it is you live by, where does that leave you? Easy enough to say now, but by God I was sweating bullets as I looked at the homely little brat—it's an absolutely infallible rule, by the way, that the infants brought forward in these circumstances are ugly as sin. Its mother holds out a little red-faced, squalling thing and assures you without a blush that there is a striking resemblance. Without being unduly vain I like to think I am at least passable; it's a terrible blow to the self-confidence to find the imposture not rejected out of hand for sheer implausibility. It is a point in your favour that you did not offer me that insult. Is your mother pretty?

Yes, I said, though it did not seem the right word. So what happened? Did she go away?

Eventually. She told me she could not let me take the child because she thought I was an immoral person. It seemed rather a case of the pot calling the kettle black, but I was too relieved to object. I assured her at once that I led a life of unparalleled viciousness, and that a child introduced to this sink of iniquity could not fail to be irredeemably corrupted. I claimed to be a regular user of a host of pharmaceutical products; I said my sexual appetite had become so jaded it could not be roused if there were fewer than four billowy beauties in the bed; I described in lurid detail sexual practices with which I will not sully your ears, to use an unhappily or, you may think, happily outmoded expression.

I was trying to keep a straight face.

And that worked?

Like a charm! Whatever the temptation to be rid of the child, she could not deliver it up to such a monster without losing face. Instead she went off and sold the story to the tabloids—how she could not reconcile it with her conscience to take money from a father of such depravity. Of course the papers adored it. I wish I'd kept a few—I remember one absolutely killing headline about Five-in-a-bed Father. I saw it unexpectedly on a newsstand and simply screamed with laughter—but like a fool I didn't buy a few hundred to send to friends. We live and learn. Of course, it's true that she hadn't retracted the claim and I suppose it may have given one or two people the wrong idea, but escape seemed cheap at the price. Have you had breakfast?

Yes.

I haven't. Have another with me.

All right.

It came as a shock to hear my own voice. Then I thought this was impolite.

Thank you.

The pleasure is mine.

I followed him through the flat. I had spent most of every winter I could remember sitting in one museum or another looking or pretending to look at the exhibits, and I was beginning to feel right at home. There were swords with Maghribi inscriptions on the blades. There was a spectacular Qur'an in Eastern Kufic on a small table. There was an equally spectacular collection of ceramics on walls, shelves and a few more strategically placed small tables, most of them again ornamented in Kufic script in its Eastern and most stylised form. Wherever a wall was not taken up with a priceless sword or piece of pottery it was taken up with a priceless Persian miniature. I thought of the heart. Maybe I could persuade Szegeti to part with some small, unmissable objet d'art and I could sell that instead.

We reached the dining room. There was a telephone on a table by the door. He lifted the receiver and spoke into it, asking someone for another place setting.

At any rate, he resumed, leading the way to the table, after that I became much more circumspect. I made it my policy to behave with perfect courtesy throughout—nothing is more infuriating to someone who is doing something quite outrageous. Goaded by frustration, they betray themselves sooner or later. There is really no need, I find, to be crude or offensive.

Practice makes perfect, I said.

Very kind of you. As you see, it's merely a by-product of a rather chequered career. I daresay your first couple of attempts were much worthier types who hadn't been involved with more than a few women. Naturally they took the whole thing much more au sérieux.

He began putting food on his plate and gestured for me to do the same. I'd never seen so much food at a single meal. About three dozen eggs had been scrambled, boiled, poached, fried, Benedicted, omeletted and whatever else you can do with an egg & then placed on silver chafing dishes to keep warm. Twenty or thirty pastries had been arranged in a tasteful mountain in a basket. Three pale green melons had been hollowed out, the edges scalloped, and the halves filled with fruit carved into crescent moons and stars. There was another big basket of fruit au naturel, most of it the kinds we never bought at Tesco's because they were 99p a shot. There was a revolving silver stand with two kinds of mustard, three kinds of chutney, five kinds of honey and twelve kinds of jam. There were crêpes with seven different fillings. There was smoked salmon, and something that I thought might be a kipper. There were glass pitchers with freshly squeezed orange, pineapple, tomato, guava and mango juice. There was silver pots of coffee, tea and hot chocolate, and a silver bowl of whipped cream for the hot chocolate.

I decided to start with a melon, a cheese omelette, three pastries, guava juice and hot chocolate.

I said: You thought she wouldn't believe twenty at a time?

He said: Why should one be less comfortable in one's home than in a decent hotel?

I said: Why should five in a bed be thought particularly immoral? Is it because a non-adulterous act is possible for at most one of the women? Or because the women might engage in homosexual practices and this is thought to be contrary to the will of a divine being?

He said: 9 times out of 10 a woman would prefer not to be told something she would rather not know.

He said: 99 times out of 100 it's more useful to know what people think is wrong. You've got to be able to read your opponent's mind in a tight spot; it's no use thinking how he ought to play his hand.

I poured out some more hot chocolate and took another pastry.

How did you take up a diplomatic career? I asked with exquisite tact.

He laughed.

Oh, it was sheer accident. I was on a cruise with some friends. The ship developed engine problems, and we ended up stranded in a small-ish town in Guatemala. Now obviously we could have got home—the company would have paid airfare out of Guatemala City—but in fact there were some really delightful people in the town. One of the big guns there was a keen bridge player, and of course rather cut off—he really couldn't do enough for us. Parties were thrown, there was a dance—better than the ship in a lot of ways. Of course a lot of the passengers cleared off, but Jeremy and I hung around.

Our host was British, but he'd married a local woman. He grew bananas—everyone did, pretty much—and he'd also been made British consul. No one else spoke much English, and we didn't speak a word of Spanish, but it didn't matter, of course, for bridge.

Well, when we'd been there a couple of weeks I got the idea of riding out into the countryside—the roads were bad to non-existent and he did a fair bit of overseeing the estate on horseback. I borrowed a horse—a big strong thing with no breeding to speak of but plenty of stamina. The saddle was a big square leather box with an enormous silver-studded pommel—not very elegant, but comfortable. Off I rode with a boy from the plantation as guide. We headed for the mountains. The boy began to get nervous after a while and made gestures that we should go back—remember I knew scarcely a word of Spanish. I ignored him—we were just getting to higher ground, and I was determined to get above the plain.

We got up into the hills at last, and got to a small village. There was no one about. I was rather thirsty, so I dismounted and began looking for a place with water. A woman came running out of a house, tears pouring down her face—she said something I did not understand and pointed up the road.

I mounted again and headed up the road. My guide flatly refused to come. I turned a corner of the road and saw—well, I saw things that make worse hearing than my hypothetical exploits with multiple companions. There were soldiers, and a lot of graves, and peasants digging at gunpoint. They saw me, and shots were fired—of course I galloped off at once.

He put three spoons of sugar in his coffee cup and poured coffee over it. He broke open a croissant and spread butter and guava conserve on it.

He said:

I say of course, and that's the way it felt at the time—nothing I could do, the only thing was to save my skin. But it got at me the whole way back. I kept thinking, what if just riding onto the field had stopped it? What if a witness was enough to stop it? But it was such a godforsaken place. They could have shot me and thrown me in a ditch and nobody the wiser. But I kept going over it, back and forth, the whole way back. I can't tell you what it's like to see something like that—that horrible place that God had turned his back on.

I thought: I'm damned if I spend the rest of my life telling myself I'm not yellow. I thought: there's got to be something I can do.

I got back to the plantation near dusk and told my host what I'd seen. He said some of the other landowners were clearing Indians off or trying to—they'd got some new machinery in, didn't need so many people with machetes. The Indians were resisting, sticking to their villages, they'd brought soldiers in—they were being killed—nothing to be done—government frightfully corrupt.

Well, of course it was obvious there was no point going to the authorities or reporting the incident. There still didn't seem to be much point in galloping in to save the day singlehanded. But suddenly I had a stroke of genius. You've heard of Raoul Wallenberg?

No?

Of course you're very young. He was Swedish consul in Budapest in WW II. The Nazis arrived and started shipping Jews out to concentration camps. Wallenberg promptly started issuing Swedish passports! Jews would be actually standing in queues on the railway platform waiting to be packed off to the slaughterhouse—and there was Wallenberg saying to the SS: This man is a Swedish citizen, I forbid you to take him! Of course not one of them knew a word of Swedish! Priceless!

At any rate, I pointed out to my friend that nothing could be simpler—we'd only to ride up with a supply of British passports, hand the things out and Bob's your uncle!

This put my host on the spot. He said a lot of rubbish I can't remember—something about his position being a sacred trust—at least, I don't think he used the word 'sacred', but you get the picture. Now I put it to you that one could scarcely represent the Queen more honourably than by extending her protection to a pack of wretched peasants being massacred by armed thugs! I put it to him—he was most unhappy about it, but really felt he couldn't. The fact was that he'd been there too long—felt he had too much to lose, that it would make his position intolerable. I've said he'd married a local woman—she may have been related to some of the culprits.

He could see I wasn't very happy about it, and the thing is, it did have an appeal for him. Finally he struck a bargain. He said he'd stake me the contents of a certain chest on a game of piquet. He couldn't precisely recall its contents; if I could win it, they were mine. I was to stake a thousand pounds.

I agreed to this since there wasn't much else I could do, but it was a maddening proposition. Piquet is not a bad game—probably one of the best for two—but chance plays a much higher part in it than in bridge, and in any case it wasn't a game I'd ever paid much attention to, so that the scope it did allow for skill did not give me much advantage. If we'd been playing bridge I'd have been sure enough of winning, though he wasn't a bad player; as it stood I couldn't be at all confident.

The game was hell from first to last. My cards were bad, and I was not playing brilliantly—I followed the principles of best play and lost steadily. It began to look as though I would lose the thousand pounds and be no closer to helping the poor bastards I'd seen. At last, when I was down to my last fifty, I thought to myself, The hell with this, I'll play against the odds—either God wants them rescued or he doesn't, I may as well find out as quickly as possible.

Of course my luck changed at once. We'd been playing five hours—it took only three to win back the money, and three after that to win the chest. We both felt like death by the end—my head was throbbing, eyes as dry as stones—and he looked worse. He can't have thought what he was about when he suggested it, you know— that he should play for a thousand quid and the right to consign a group of innocent people to perdition. God knows what it was like defending that for 11 hours. He tossed the cards down at the end— he wouldn't look at me—said he'd see me in the morning, and went to bed. Just at the door he turned back. He said if anyone harmed a

British subject he must object to the authorities in the strongest possible terms.

I went at once to the chest—there was a whole stack of passports, and some sort of official-looking stamp.

They were the old-fashioned type of passport—God knows how long he'd had them, I shouldn't be surprised if the consulship, and the passports with them, had been passed down from father to son since the last century—with a description instead of a photo. I let myself sleep four hours. In the morning I spent a few hours filling in the descriptions, writing hair: black, eyes: black; complexion: swarthy 50 or 60 times. I left the names blank, stuffed them in a couple of saddle bags, and rode off.

Well, you should have seen the look on those soldiers' faces when the first peasant brought out his British passport! I'd had my friend teach me enough Spanish for 'This man is a British subject'—there I stood among the black-haired, black-eyed, swarthy-complexioned loyal subjects of the Queen trying not to laugh my head off. The marvellous thing about it was that they couldn't prove it wasn't so—certainly none of them had any Guatemalan papers.

It did some good. Some of the Indians actually came to Britain on those wretched passports. Some went off into the hills to join a guerrilla group.

Anyway, having pulled off a trick like that once I got a taste for it. We're such cowards in front of a piece of paper these days—my mother was an Egyptian, and my father was from Hungary, both countries with a particularly impressive tradition of bureaucracy, and it gave me an indescribable frisson to cock a snook at the official channels. Once you've tried it you realise how easy it is! Half the time no one bothers to challenge you—if you say you're the Danish consul it won't even occur to most people to doubt it. I felt ashamed, really ashamed of all the times *I hadn't* claimed to be a partipotentiary of some foreign power of other.

I said:

Did it work at all in West Papua before you were deported?

He said:

Well, the visas got some people out of the country, but getting them into Belgium was pretty sticky. Shouldn't have picked Belgium, really, they've no sense of humour worth speaking of, but I was bored with being a Dane of Inuit extraction, and there'd been a picture of me in *Hello!* with Paola which I thought might give the story credibility, and anyway my French isn't half bad. My mother went to a Swiss finishing school, you see—*her* mother was Lebanese, and frightfully cosmopolitan—and the girls were all made to study French, German and English, with Italian for bad behaviour. That was how she met my father, as a matter of fact. She got sentenced to a week of Italian for some frightful breach of school regulations, walked straight out the door and found a lift down to Monte— reasoning, you know, that if she were independently wealthy she wouldn't have to be finished. She pawned the little gold crucifix she'd worn at the school—she was Muslim, of course, but it was more in the way of a fashion accessory—and spent the money, what there was of it, on chips. 28, that was her number. She couldn't lose. My father had been losing all week, but he saw the way the wind was blowing and switched to 28—he knew better than to let his luck slip once it had changed and followed her out when she left. My father had reason to curse the school; my mother took an instant antipathy to Hungarian, a language the school, she said, would not have inflicted on a girl had she enacted the 120 Journées de Sodome, and refused to learn a word of it; having heard the Arabic language put through the wringer of my father's strong Hungarian accent she declared her native tongue off-limits, and insisted that he confine his atrocities to English and to French (German he despised, though he spoke it well), in which languages my parents conversed to the exclusion of all others for the whole of their married life.

I gathered that he did not want to talk about West Papua.

I was afraid he would throw me out any minute, so I took a couple of crêpes and a croissant and I said diplomatically:

Was your father Muslim too? I saw you had an 11th-century Qur'an so I assumed you were.

He said: He wasn't, no, but there was never any question of my being anything else. Consider the matter from my mother's point of view. One day she is an oppressed schoolgirl with disgusting food to eat, an ugly uniform, exclusively female companions all kitted out in the same depressing attire and the heady prospect of putting on Racine's *Bérénice* for entertainment; no sooner does she sell her crucifix than, shazam! she wins hundreds of thousands of francs and has delicious meals, glorious clothes and a handsome and charming Hungarian at her feet. You couldn't ask for a clearer sign from God.

I said: That doesn't follow at all. If there were a divine being it would hardly arrange to communicate through a series of events which might just as well have come about through pure coincidence, and on the other hand a series of events which could come about through pure coincidence can hardly be evidence of either the wishes or existence of such a being.

He said: Not at all. You're completely missing the point. I'm not a philosopher or a theologian, so I don't know what one would look for in an uncontrovertible message from above; the question is what would convince a 17-year-old and a gambler and God the all-seeing all-knowing naturally did not waste time beaming syllogisms into the mind of a girl who found 10 minutes of Italian a crashing bore.

I said: But if God had just voted for Islam why did she marry your father?

But they were madly in love, he said. He sounded as though he'd never heard such a stupid question in his life.

He laughed. And anyway the Hungarian was part of the sign, so it was obviously God's will.

I liked this piece of logic but I was glad Sibylla wasn't there to hear it.

He said: You laugh, but you're still missing the point. The point isn't that she saw what God wanted and did it because he wanted it, like a simpering little *dévote*. She saw which way her luck lay. She wasn't going to argue with that and neither was my father. I can see you think that's frivolous, but if you'd got out of as many tight spots as I have with no better protection than a diplomatic immunity you'd invented five minutes before you'd take luck a damn sight more seriously than any arguments.

I still didn't want him to kick me out so I put a couple of pastries on my plate and tactfully changed the subject and said:

How did you like Seven Samurai?

And he said:

It is a *terrible* film. *Terrible.*

And I said:

But it's a work of genius.

He had lit another cigarette and now he raised it to his lips with the suavity of a dandy of Meiji Japan. He said: That is precisely my objection to this terrible work.

He said: I was at university at the time, in pursuit of a very beautiful, very earnest girl. I persuaded her to go out with me, but she was very serious about her studies and could only leave them for something even more serious. Seven Samurai was showing at the Phoenix for one night, and one night only: she proposed we go to that.

Consider my dilemma! That was the night of the University Bridge Club, and I had faithfully promised my partner to be there. A first-rate player, but a very short temper, and matters were at a very delicate stage—all the world had run mad for revolving discards, and Jeremy wished to follow fashion—he had devised a system of fiendish intricacy which was to be ours if I could not somehow persuade him to abandon it. The worst time in the world, in short, to annoy him, or leave him open to the influence of the fools in the club who favoured the wretched system.

But this was a chance which might not come again, and I'd been after the girl for weeks. She wouldn't take me seriously, you see, and this was a girl who, if she could not take you seriously, would not take you at all.

Well, I knew I was a fool, and certainly in the grand scheme of things bridge was a great deal closer to my heart than this wretched girl, but I agreed anyway. We went to see Seven Samurai. I knew as soon as it began that I had made a terrible mistake.

Scenes, black and white, of peasant misery rose upon the screen, and superimposed on them dreadful visions of all the appalling results to which the discard system might lead. Hand after hand flashed into my mind—nightmarish hands in which our opponents, in easily defeatable contracts, made unmakable slams doubled redoubled and vulnerable—had unearned overtricks poured into their astonished laps—and where was I while disaster loomed? Fiddling while Rome burned.

Still, there was nothing to be done about it now—I might as well try to enjoy myself.

Cast your mind back to this film for one moment. Identify, if you can, a suitable moment at which to place your arm around the shoulders of your companion and kiss her. You cannot? No more could I. After half an hour, no suitable moment presenting itself, I chose an unsuitable moment—I was rebuked. With nothing to distract me, my mind returned with ever greater foreboding to my partner, at that very moment imbibing pernicious heresy from the lips of our fellow club members. The beautiful face of the girl stared raptly at the screen.

To my unutterable chagrin, I realised that I was completely superfluous to her enjoyment of the occasion; and that for all the good it did me I might as well have spent the evening profitably ridding my partner's mind of error. In fact I could easily have gone to bridge club, left a little early, and met the girl at the end of the film.

There I was, however, trapped, while it ground inexorably on.

It ended at last. I walked the girl back to her college. She was pensive, silent; I at a loss for words.

Reflect now upon my predicament! The film portrayed a group of down-at-heels warriors who fight, many to die gallantly, amid circumstances of hardship and squalor. I could not but see that I cut no very heroic figure by comparison—and how could I expect that this girl, of all girls, would turn from heroism to my frivolous self? Remember, too, that the only love scenes in the film are presented in a very artificial, unpleasant way—I knew only too well that the girl would now be seeing herself through the clinical camera of Kurosawa, rather than through my own dazzled eyes.

We reached her college. She said that she wanted to think about the film. We kissed and parted.

A complete fiasco—and what a price I had to pay! Jeremy would scarcely speak to me. He sulked for two weeks—I could do nothing right. I am by nature an optimistic bidder; in the face of cold disapproval optimism withered on the vine, we played with only mediocre results. At last I could bear it no longer. I was forced to agree, against my better judgement, to his mad system of discards. The result was exactly as I had foreseen. We came *third* in the national championships when we might have come first, and all because I had squandered an evening watching that abominable film.

Where did you go to university? I asked, for the obvious possibility had occurred to me.

I was at Oxford. I know what you're thinking—it's a delightful thought, but surely most unlikely. How old is your mother?

36.

Well, it's not impossible.

What was the girl's name?

I think it was Rachel. What is your mother's name?

I told him my mother's name.

Are you sure it was Rachel?

No. If your mother goes home after parties and is nice to men of whom she thoroughly disapproves, however, she has changed out of all recognition from the girl I knew, or more likely is someone quite different who would have been a much more agreeable companion, and whom I did not have the good fortune to meet. What does she look like?

She has dark hair and dark eyes.

It's not impossible. You said she was pretty?

In my mind I saw the beautiful girl glowing in the light of the film. If Sibylla had always watched Seven Samurai she would always have been beautiful, but there is more to life than art.

She's not really pretty, I said. She's beautiful. When she's excited. When she's bored she looks like someone who's got two weeks to live. Someone who's got two weeks to live & is going to spend it begging the doctor for a mercy killing.

He shrugged. You could say that of any woman. They are moody creatures, up one minute down the next—it is what makes them so exasperating and delightful.

Do they all want to die?

They have all said so at one time or another, but whether they mean it! There is not a woman in a thousand who has not said she wanted to die; perhaps one in a thousand has tried to do something about it— and for every thousand who try perhaps one succeeds. There is not much logic in it, but if they were more logical they would be rather dull.

I would have liked to hear him talk this way longer. I would have liked to hear him talk this way about anything, as if you could be impervious to sorrow just by being a man. I said:

467

It's not illogical, though, not to act on a desire one thinks immoral. It's not illogical, having failed to commit an action which may be wrong, to resist the temptation to try again. It might not even be illogical even if one did not think it immoral; one might wish to act with generosity.

I said:

She tried to kill herself once and was stopped. She thinks it might have been better if she had succeeded—she thinks it when people are very banal and boring. Now she can't because of me.

He laughed, showing his gold-capped teeth.

Are you afraid she will try again?

I wish she were happier. I can't see why things make her unhappy. But if they do would it not be rational to prefer a short miserable life to a long one?

Perhaps, I said, she would be better dead.

He took out another cigarette. I saw now that when he did not want to answer immediately he became even more collected. He lit it and inhaled and exhaled.

He said:

When you play bridge with beginners—when you try to help them out—you give them some general rules to go by. Then they follow the rule and something goes wrong. But if you'd had their hand you wouldn't have played the thing you told them to play, because you'd have seen all the reasons the rule did not apply.

He said:

People who generalise about people are dismissed as superficial. It's only when you've known large numbers of people that you can spot the unusual ones—when you look at each one as if you'd never seen one before, they all look alike.

He said:

Do you really want me to pronounce on someone you've known

for 11 years and I've never met, on the basis of a lot of other people I have met?

He said:

Do you seriously expect me to argue with you?

He said:

Look here, I'm not likely to be much good to you on this one. If you need a friend one day give me a shout. In the meantime I'll give you an arrow against misfortune—I'll teach you to play piquet.

He took me into another room where there was a little table with a chessboard inlaid into it. He took two packs of cards from a drawer and began explaining the rules of piquet.

He taught me to play piquet.

He won most of the games, but I won some. I got better as we played. He said I picked it up quickly and did not play badly.

At last he said

I must dress. I've a two o'clock appointment and it's nearly four— I mustn't be too late.

He said

I wish you well. I hope you find what you're looking for. Look me up in ten years or so. If you've learnt bridge and are halfway decent I'll take you to the Jockey Club.

I went out into the street again. I walked to Sloane Square and I took the Circle Line.

5

A good samurai will parry the blow

I asked Sibylla whether she had seen Seven Samurai at Oxford. She said she had. I asked whether she had gone with someone. She said she couldn't remember. I said I'd met a man who'd seen it at Oxford with a girl whose name wasn't definitely not Sibylla.

Maybe I did, said Sib. Yes, now I think of it, I wished I hadn't. It wasn't really his kind of thing, and he wanted to hold hands. In Seven Samurai! I ask you!

Was he good looking?

He must have been, said Sib. I made him go home afterward because I wanted to be alone. You can't do that with a plain man—they look so pathetic and uncertain. The best thing is to go to mediocre films with plain boring people, and to brilliant films with beautiful, dazzlingly witty people—in a way it's a waste when your attention is otherwise engaged, but at least you can ignore them with a clear conscience.

Was he witty?

For heaven's sake, Ludo, I was watching one of the masterpieces of modern cinema. How should I know whether the silent person sitting beside me was witty?

She seemed to have made a recovery from *Carpworld*. The project had sent her *International Cricketer* which she said was not too bad. I taught her to play piquet. I taught everyone at Bermondsey Boys Junior Judo to play piquet and soon everyone was turning up half an hour early to play piquet before class. I beat Sibylla 2 times out of 3 and everyone else 9 times out of 10. I would probably have won 10 times out of 10, but as Szegeti had said there is quite a high element of chance in the game.

I looked for chances to proclaim myself the son of the Danish ambassador, but none presented itself.

Or I could be the son of a Belgian attaché.

I am ze son of ze Belgian attaché, I murmured. Release this man! My father is the Swedish DCM.

I got a book on bridge out of the library. Szegeti said he would take me to the Jockey Club when I was 21, but I thought if I got really good at the game he might settle for a mature 12. There is a Jockey Club in England, but *the* Jockey Club is in Paris; I am hoping he meant the French one. I found out what a revolving discard is: when you can't follow suit & want to tell your partner which suit to lead if he wins the trick, you play a low card in the suit above the desired suit, or a high card in the suit below it, so a low diamond means clubs a high diamond means hearts a low heart means diamonds a high heart means spades and so on. Now that everyone at judo knows piquet I am going to teach them bridge and get some practice.

I thought that I was beginning to get the hang of this. I had started by picking the wrong kind of father, but now I knew what to look for I could build up a collection of 20 or so. I felt ashamed, really ashamed of all the years I'd spent trying to identify the father who happened to be mine, instead of simply claiming the best on offer.

Today as I was riding the Circle Line a man came running down the stairs at Embankment. He ran into the car followed by three men. He ran along the car, dodging poles, and at the last moment dashed out again. The doors closed on the three men, who swore.

Hate to do it to him, in a way, said 1.

Still, he's not being exactly cooperative, said 2.

I had recognised his face. It was Red Devlin.

Red Devlin had reported on atrocities in Lebanon, and then he had been transferred to Azerbaijan and kidnapped the first day. He had been held captive for five years and then he had taught one of his captors to play chess, and then he had escaped over mountains and desert. Then he had come back to Britain and gone into hiding and he had come out of hiding to publish a book six months later. It had only just come out in hardback, so I didn't know whether it talked about ragged urchins.

It doesn't matter really, said 3. We'll catch him at his house.

Right you are, said 1.

They got off after four or five stops and I followed them to a street with semi-detached houses. A small crowd of people were standing outside one. The three men joined them.

At the other end of the street a man hurtled around the corner and stopped dead. Then he began to walk forward, very slowly. He stopped in front of the house and said something I couldn't hear. The men crowded round. I thought of going forward and saying This man is a Norwegian citizen! or My father is the Polish vice-consul! but I could not see that it would help. Even a real Danish consul could not have helped him now.

He opened a gate in a hedge and disappeared inside.

Most of the crowd dispersed. A few stayed behind.

I threw Lee and Brian at judo today. Lee is 14, and Brian is 13 but taller and heavier.

I told Sibylla & she asked what my teacher had said. I said he had said it was very good.

Sibylla said that didn't sound very character-building. I said most authorities on child psychology said a child should be given encouragement and reinforcement. Sib said Bandura and who else? I said everybody else. I didn't say that the authorities also said a parent had to be able to set limits because I was afraid she might suddenly decide to make up for lost time and set a lot of limits.

Sibylla said: Well just remember Richie, becoming the great judo champion is not the end of the story.

I said I didn't think I was the great judo champion just because I could beat Lee and Brian at Bermondsey Boys Junior Judo.

Sibylla said: It isn't a question of beating X and Y. What if there's no one you can't beat? It's a question of perfecting your skill and achieving satori. What on earth are they teaching you in this class?

I said we mainly concentrated on learning how to throw people to the ground. Sib said: Must I do *everything* myself? She was grinning from ear to ear. *Carpworld* was a thing of the past. I decided not to tell her I was beating everyone at piquet 9 times out of 10.

I have been going by the house every day for two weeks. There are still a couple of people hanging around in the street. Sometimes people go in and out of the house—mainly a woman, a girl and a boy. Once he came out and walked to the corner and turned around and came back. Once he came out and looked up at the sky and stood looking up at the sky for about ten minutes. Then he turned around and went back into the house. Once he came out in a track-suit and ran off down the street and came back walking about fifteen minutes later. Once he came out in a suit and tie and walked briskly away.

❖

I went over to the house to watch for a while. This time all of them came out the gate: Red Devlin, his wife and the boy and girl. He had his arm around his wife's shoulder. He said: What a spectacularly beautiful day! The wife and the girl said: It's lovely! and the boy said: Yeah.

I have been spending a lot of time watching his house. There is a bus stop with a bench up the street; I sit there mainly working on solid state physics. My concentration is almost back to normal.

❖

I was outside the house today when a taxi pulled up. They all came out and put suitcases in the taxi and his family got in and he said: Have a wonderful time.

The wife said: I wish you were coming too

And he said: Well, I may join you

And the taxi drove off.

It's now or never.

❖

I went to the house and knocked on the door but there was no answer. I thought he was probably there so I went around to the back of the house. I couldn't see him through any of the ground floor windows, so I climbed a tree. He was standing in a bedroom with his back to the window. He left the bedroom to go into the bathroom. There were three or four bottles of pills on the dresser and a bottle of Evian. The bottles had been emptied onto the dresser; there were probably a couple of hundred pills.

He came back into the room with another bottle of pills. He struggled with the child-proof cap, and then he struggled to get a wad of cotton wool out, and then he poured another fifty pills onto the dresser. He poured out a glass of water and picked up a couple of pills. Then he laughed and put them down. He took out a packet of cigarettes and lit one. Then he left the room.

I couldn't see what kind of pills he was planning to take.

There was a kind of narrow ornamental stone moulding around the house underneath the windows on each floor. One of the windows was open on the next floor, and a branch hung over the roof. The moulding wasn't much over an inch wide but the mortar was crumbling between the bricks so I thought there would be good handholds. I climbed up and went out the branch and lowered myself onto the moulding. Then I inched along to the window. In one place there was a lot of ivy growing over the moulding and for a moment I thought I'd have to go back—there was nowhere to put a foot, and it was impossible to get through to the wall for a grip. But when I pulled on the ivy it was tough and thick, so I took hold of that and went hand over hand. Then back to the moulding. I slipped in the window. I went through the door and ran down the stairs, not bothering to be quiet. At first I couldn't find the right room—the first door I tried was a study and the next was a broom closet. Then I found the bedroom. He was back there now. He had a drink in his hand.

I said: What are you doing?

He said without surprise: What does it look like I'm doing?

I said: Is that paracetamol?

He said: No.

I said: I think aspirin is also a bad idea.

He said: It's not aspirin.

I said: Then it's probably all right.

He laughed. He sounded surprised to be surprised. He said: Who are you?

There was no going back.

I said

I'm your son.

He said

No you're not. My son doesn't look anything like you.

I said

I'm another one.

He said

Oh, I see.

He said

Wait a minute, that's impossible. There was definitely just the one boy when I went away. One boy and one girl. You're not going to tell me you're five years old. Besides, if she'd had another child while I was away she'd have told me.

One thing was clear: if there was one thing guaranteed to make everything a hundred times worse, it was saying Well actually I'm not your son after all. I said: Not by your wife. I said: My mother told me you were my father. Maybe she made a mistake. It would have been about 12 years ago.

He said

Oh, now I see.

He finished the drink and put the glass down.

This isn't a very good time, he said. I can't put it out of my mind, you see. But I can't let people know. They don't like to see it. I don't like to see that they don't like to see it. They can see I don't like to see that they don't like to see it.

He said

I've already got too many people to protect. I can't take on any more. I'm sorry, but you'll have to go away.

I said

I don't want you to protect me.

He said

What does that mean? That I can talk about it? What do you want.

I said

I wanted to see you.

He said

You've seen me so you can go away

I said I would go away

He said

Do you know how old I am? 37. I could live another 40 years. 50 years. People live to be 100.

He said

I see it every day. It never goes away. These eyes have seen, that is they've been in the same room with, that is you've seen Lear, maybe, people flinch when Gloucester is blinded. What do you think it's like to see the bloody socket where a thumb went? He was crying with the other eye. You're not haunted by Lear, I mean it doesn't come back to haunt you, whereas the real thing—you see it day after day after day. You think of something else again and again and again. It's not the blood, it's the fact that a human did that.

He said

You need something to set against it. When you've seen that

much badness you need something to set against it—some dazzling glorious act of goodness—not to redeem your faith in humanity, whatever that might mean, but just to make you stop feeling sick.

He said

It's not fair on my family. They're fine. I mean they're perfectly OK. They're not bad. It's been hard on them, and they've responded pretty well. But not dazzling. Well, why should they be dazzling? But I feel sick.

I said

What about Raoul Wallenberg?

He said

What?

I said

Raoul Wallenberg. The Swedish consul in Budapest who handed out Swedish passports to Jews. This man is a Swedish citizen.

He said

You mean the one the Americans and the Swedes abandoned to the Russians because on top of saving 100,000 Jews he did a little spying for the Americans on the side and neither of them wanted to admit it? He was grand but it's enough to make you sick

I said

Well what about Szegeti?

And he said

That charlatan?

Mother Theresa? I said.

That nun?

Jaime Jaramillo?

He said Jaramillo was all right. He said

But I haven't seen it. What I've seen is

He said

You go into these situations as a journalist and you keep thinking you should stop reporting and just help. You have to be professional.

You tell yourself you're helping by letting people know what's happening.

Well, they know what's happening but it doesn't do any good. You try to get some people out before it's too late and you run into a blank wall of officialdom, and nothing does any good. And then it's not just that you've seen stupid thugs with another language and a foreign uniform commit atrocities, but someone pretty much like yourself say I'm sorry there's nothing I can do. If you're lucky the person says Well, I'll write to the Minister.

He said

I don't want to go on. If I've got 50 years ahead of seeing the eye and the leg and the girl and the rest and the best I can hope for is someone promising to write to the Minister I'd be better off if I were out of it now.

I know it will cause a lot of people a lot of pain. Can I go on for 50 years so they can go comfortably on saying I've adjusted?

People tell me, you can't let them win. You made it this far. If you kill yourself they've won. But it's insane. Who the fuck is they? How the fuck does it *defeat* them if I wake up howling every night?

He said

Maybe reporting does a little good. But does it do *enough* good to justify living this way? There are plenty of others who'd be glad of my job and could do it well.

I said

Well just as long as you stay off paracetamol.

He said

What?

I said

You should never try to kill yourself with paracetamol. It's a horrible way to die. People think you just pass out, but actually you don't lose consciousness, you think nothing's happened but then a day later your organs shut down. It destroys the liver. Sometimes people change their minds, but it's too late. I'm not saying you would change your mind; but almost anything is better than dying of paracetamol poisoning.

He laughed.

Where did you pick all that up? he said. He laughed again.

I said

My mother told me.

I said

A guillotine is very quick and pretty painless, though they say the head can be conscious for a minute or so before the blood supply to the brain is drained off. I made a miniature one when I was five with my Meccano set. I think it would be pretty easy to make a big one. Of course, it would be a bit gruesome for the person who found the body. You could call the police if you didn't want to upset a family member. There's no way they could reach you in time to stop you.

He laughed. I'll bear that in mind, he said. Do you know any other good ways?

I've heard that drowning is pleasant at the end, I said. A friend of my mother's was rescued when she was going down for the third time. She said it hurt at first, when her lungs filled with water, but then it was drowsy and lovely. It hurt when they pulled her out and forced the air back into her lungs. That might not be too bad. You could jump off a Channel ferry at night, or maybe it would be nicer to jump off an outboard motor in the Aegean and drown in blue. There might be a few problems for your family if the body wasn't found, but I expect it would be all right if you left a note.

Yes, he said. He was smiling. That would probably be all right. I'm going to have a drink. What do you want? A Coke?

Thank you, I said.

I followed him downstairs to the kitchen.

You seem to know a lot about it, he said.

I'm better on mechanics than pharmaceuticals, I said. I can make a noose. You want to break the neck rather than suffocate, if possible; apparently that's quite difficult to achieve with a sheet. My mother thought I should know how in case I was ever put in prison and tortured—I'm terribly sorry.

That's all right, he said. He drank a lot of the drink. She's probably right. It's not a bad thing to know—if you've use of your hands. I was tied up the whole time, so it wouldn't have helped.

Except when you played chess, I said.

No, I was tied up then too. He made my moves for me. Sometimes he'd deliberately move a piece to the wrong square and pretend not to understand if I objected. You wouldn't have thought I'd have cared, with everything else, but it made me absolutely furious. I'd refuse to play, and he'd beat me. Or he'd beat me if he lost. He didn't beat me if he beat me.

He said

He was kind of split up. He'd be quite friendly when he brought out the board, and he'd *smile*. That would last for a few moves and then sometimes he'd start to cheat, and sometimes he'd lose his temper and hit me with the gun, and sometimes. The friendliness was the horrible part, because he'd be hurt, genuinely *hurt*, when I wasn't pleased to see him or took offence because he'd beat the shit out of me the day before. And now that I'm back that's all I see. That horrible friendliness everywhere. All these people who simply don't *realise*, it just doesn't *occur* to them that

He said

That's what I mean about the ordinariness. That's why it's not enough. It's not enough to stand up to what's there, but people go on smiling pleasantly

My wife smiles and I see that horrible friendliness on her face. My children disgust me. They're delightful, extroverted, confident. They know what they want, and that's what interests them, and it disgusts me. They allowed me two weeks to be a bit strange, and then they all came to me separately.

My wife said she knew what I'd been through but this was hard on the children. My daughter came to see me and said it was hard on Mum, I didn't know what they'd been through. My son said it was hard on his Mum and sister.

So then I think, this is bloody ridiculous. It's unfair. They're perfectly OK. It's not their *fault*. What do you *want*? Do you want them to be shell-shocked and dreaming of horrors? You *want* them to be safe from all that. You want all the rest to get away to be *ordinary*. And I think, we've got so *much*. Let's celebrate *life*. We've got each other, we're so bloody lucky. And I throw my arms around them with tears in my eyes and I say, Let's go along the canal and feed the swans. I'm thinking, we can walk straight out of the house, there's no one to stop us, and we can walk by the canal because there are no land mines and no one's shelling us, let's not *waste* this. And they all look absolutely appalled because it's such a totally wet thing to do, but they come to humour me, and of course it's awful.

He said

When you've seen things, or things have been done to you, this badness gets inside you and comes back with you, and then people who've never been near a war, people who've never struck an animal never mind tortured anyone—people who are completely innocent—get hurt too. The torture comes out as disgust, and it comes out in that gush of sentimentality that chokes them. I see that but I can't kill the badness, it just sits inside like a poison toad.

He said

Is it really doing them any good to keep the toad alive? Or even if it is can I go through a lifetime of it?

I said

It would obviously be better to die before rather than after years of suffering; no one would condemn an innocent man to a life sentence to make someone else happy; the question is whether it is really the case that nothing will blot out these memories and that nothing could be good enough to make it worth undergoing them. If that's the question you can't seriously expect me to know the answer.

He began laughing again. Could I give you a word of advice? he said. Don't ever apply for a job with the Samaritans.

He could hardly speak for laughing.

My mother, I said, called the Samaritans once and asked whether research had been done on thwarted suicides to find out whether they had spent the time after the incident happily.

What did they say?

They said they didn't know.

He grinned.

I said

Sibylla said

He said

Who?

I said My mother. She said they should recruit people like Oscar Wilde, only there isn't anyone like Oscar Wilde. If there were enough people like Oscar Wilde so that you could staff Samaritans with them, no one would want to commit suicide anyway—they would joke themselves out of a job. You could call and someone would say

Do you smoke?

And you'd say

Yes.

And they'd say Good. A man needs an occupation.

My mother called once and the person kept saying Yes and I hear what you're saying, which would have been reassuring if my mother had been worried about being inaudible.

So my mother said

Do you smoke?

And the Samaritan said

Sorry?

And my mother said

Do you smoke?

And the Samaritan said

No

And my mother said

You should. A man needs an occupation.

And the Samaritan said

Sorry?

And my mother said

That's all right. It's your life. If you want to throw it away, fine. Then she ran out of 10p coins.

I said

It's your life, but you should give things a chance. You know what Jonathan Glover says.

He said

No, what does Jonathan Glover say? And who is Jonathan Glover?

I said

Jonathan Glover is a modern Utilitarian, and the author of *Causing Death and Saving Lives*. He says before committing suicide you should change your job, leave your wife, leave the country.

I said

Would it help to leave your job, leave your wife and children, leave the country?

He said

No. It would help a little not to have to fake it all the time. But wherever I went I'd see the same things. I used to think I'd like to see the Himalayas before I died. I thought I'd like to see Tierra del Fuego. The South Pacific—I've heard that's beautiful. But wherever I went I'd see a child clubbed to death with the butt of a rifle and soldiers laughing. There's nothing I can do to get it out of my mind.

He looked at his glass.
He said

> Canst thou not minister to a mind diseas'd
> Pluck from the memory a rooted sorrow
> Raze out the written troubles of the brain
> Cleanse the stuff'd bosom of that perilous stuff
> That weighs upon the heart

He said

> Therein the patient
> Must minister to himself

He put his head on his hand.
He said
It is a pretty story.
He said
The world would be quite a pretty place if the only people tormented by atrocities were those who'd committed them. Would you like another Coke?
I asked whether I could have orange juice instead.
He went to the refrigerator with his glass. He came back with the glass and a can of Coke.
He said
I don't mean it wasn't hard on my wife. She had to shoulder responsibility. She had to write a lot of letters to people who weren't very helpful. She had to keep going for the sake of the children.
I said
Does she want to die?
He said
I don't think so.
He said after a pause
It changed her a lot. She became much less

He said

Or rather she became much more

He said

That is she turned into the kind of person who

He said

That is she developed a lot of skills. She organised a successful campaign, you know, that is she organised a campaign that was successful as a campaign, it had a lot of supporters who gave money when she wrote to ask them for money and went on demonstrations when she told them there was going to be a demonstration and wrote letters to their MP when she said everyone should write to their MP. The papers published her letters when she wrote letters and they covered the demonstrations when there were demonstrations, and she got interviewed on radio and TV on a regular basis. That kind of thing doesn't just *happen,* you know. Anyway once it happens you become quite confident that you can get that kind of thing to happen.

He said

Would you like another Coke?

I said OK.

He came back with another drink. He said he was sorry but they were out of Coke, he had brought me an orange juice instead.

He said

It sort of spoiled things for the campaign, in a way, my just escaping like that. Apparently negotiations had reached quite a promising stage or anyway my wife thinks they looked quite promising, I could have jeopardised everything by just making a run for it. It's irritating for her to have this have-a-go-Grandad type of attitude to deal with because she thinks it was just luck that it worked whereas she doesn't think that if a campaign works that's luck. It's not that it's a major irritant, more of a minor irritant, it's just that I had to keep hiding how happy I was to see the dog. He practically went insane as soon as I came into the room, it was all I could do not to or actually I think I did break down and it wasn't as if he'd developed any media skills worth mentioning or made a significant contribution to the campaign or anything. What I mean is that my wife had spent, well all of them had spent five years making progress or facing setbacks whereas I'd just spent five years

He said

So obviously when the dog died

He said

Well anyway it's past history. You're bored, I'm bored, you're bored or if you're not you would be if you'd spent as much time thinking about it

I said

Have you read that book by Graham Greene?

He said

Which book by Graham Greene?

I said

The one where he kills his wife in a mercy killing and is tormented by the memory and then he loses his memory in an explosion?

He said

Oh that one. You read Graham Greene?

I said

Only that one and *Travels with My Aunt*. I liked *Travels with My Aunt* better. My mother read the other one and she thought: that's it, I'll get amnesia. So she tried banging her head on walls but she couldn't even knock herself out, and then she remembered that she'd once been knocked out by a car and she could remember everything when she came to. So she read a lot of articles on amnesia but they weren't very helpful. Then she thought: What about a hypnotist? People are always going to hypnotists and remembering things they'd forgotten that happened to them as a child, or in a previous existence when they were Cleopatra—why shouldn't it work just as well the other way?

He said

Now there's a grand idea. You go to the doctor a nervous wreck and come home Cleopatra Queen of the Nile.

I said

So she called the Samaritans.

He said

And what did they say?

I said

They said they didn't know. So she called a lot of hypnotists and they all said this was an unhealthy attitude & hypnosis as a tool of psychotherapy was aimed at helping people to confront things & no ethical practitioner would contemplate and my mother said well what about an *un*ethical practitioner? Suppose she found a rogue hypnotist, the kind who would fornicate with the unresisting body of his subject and steal her credit cards and her cashcard and ask her cashcard PIN number and take the pearls she got for her 18th birthday, would somebody like that be *able* to make her forget everything that had happened in the last 10 years or so?

He said

And what did they say?

I said

They hung up.

He said

So then what happened?

I said

She tried to kill herself.

He said

That must have been hard for you.

I said

Oh that was before I was born. I think she regrets it when people make fatuous remarks but now that she has me she thinks it would be irresponsible—sorry.

He said

It doesn't matter. It's what anyone would think. I did write the book, you know. I wrote the book and gave a lot of interviews and signed copies—funny the things people will buy.

He stood up and walked up and down. He went to the window and said

What a glorious day!

He said

Do you think sales will go up?

I said the signed copies would be worth more anyway. He said he was a fool not to have thought of it but anyway he'd given all his author's copies to prominent supporters of the campaign.

I was still feeling bad for having said my mother thought it would be irresponsible, and I was about to say that the cases were different because I didn't really have a father when I remembered that I'd said he was. Then I thought maybe it would not be too bad to say: Well, I grew up without a father and I'm all right, I mean i don't think I'd have been better off if somebody had gone through ten years of hell to be there. Then I suddenly thought, that is I suddenly thought that at that very moment Sibylla was at home teaching the Little Prince. What if at that very moment she had taken out a bottle of pills and said if she could not be a person without a past she would be a person with no future and the Little Prince had said That's all right you go right ahead?

He was still standing by the window. There were four African violets on the sill; he was running his thumb over the fuzz on a leaf. He was whistling under his breath.

I haven't described him well or at all. He was right in a way that it began to get boring after a while, but in another way it didn't really matter what he said. You could see that he was someone who could make someone who had seen his male relatives lined up and shot at the age of four and his female relatives raped and then shot want to play chess. When you were with him you wanted to go on being with him whatever he said. When you made a joke and he laughed you wanted to do ten handsprings. I wished I had had him around for ten years or even five even though he was probably the kind of parent who set limits and even though it was hard to imagine him fitting into the kind of lifestyle where you could learn Greek at a reasonable age and even though the one boy and one girl had probably watched Sesame Street and he probably thought it was about the right level. And I started thinking: What if he changed his mind?

Then I thought: What if Sibylla told the Little Prince what she wants to forget? When I asked her she always said Never you mind or Well anyway I don't know why I complain it's not as if I was tortured. At least I hadn't said that. I thought: I want him to try to go on getting over it so I can go on seeing him. I thought it was weak and cowardly to want this and it was weak and cowardly to want the Little Prince to say give it more time and if I were weak and cowardly I really would be my father's son. But I couldn't say you go right ahead.

I said

Do you want to give Oscar Wilde a chance?

He said

What?

I said

We could watch The Importance of Being Earnest. I could go to Blockbuster Video and get it out.

He said

That's OK.

Then he said

Well, OK.

I went out the front door. We kept the video card in my pocket because Sibylla tended to lose things, and I had £1.50. I ran all the way to Blockbuster Video just in case he decided to take the pills before I got back.

The set-up in Blockbuster was different from the one we went to, so it took a while to find the video. They had Seven Samurai, but so many people in it say it's better to die than face certain misery that I thought it would be better not to risk it. They had Ace Ventura Pet Detective which I had always wanted to see but Sibylla refused to get out; I suspected, however, that this might not be as efficacious as the Wilde. At last I found it. I had to argue for a long time with the girl at the register because our card was for a different branch.

I said

Please. I have to have it. It's a matter of life and death.

She said

Don't overdo it

I said

No really it's for a man who's thinking of committing suicide he was held hostage and tortured and it haunts him and I thought maybe just maybe The Importance of Being Earnest would do the trick because when my mother feels depressed it cheers her up to walk on the Wilde side.

She said

Really.

I said

Well no not really it's for my sister she's doing A-levels and they always ask a question about comparing the play with the film only she never had a chance to see the film. Our dad's unemployed so she has to work part-time so she never had the time and now the exam is tomorrow, and if she doesn't do well on the exam she won't get her grade for university because English is her best subject and it's too late to do anything about French and Sociology. According to a

recent survey in the *Independent* more and more employers expect
employees to have a university degree.

She said

Third time lucky

I said

Well actually it's for my two little brothers. Siamese twins, they
were inseparable from birth and did everything together. If one does
something the other must too, but unfortunately their heads are in-
conveniently placed so that they cannot watch the same television
screen at the same time. We tried mirrors but then whichever one
got the mirror complained. A disability allowance from a generous
government has covered the cost of an extra television and video set,
a single copy of Aladdin, and one towel. One night The Importance
of Being Earnest in the classic Redgrave/Denison production was
shown by the BBC; both twins were able to watch, enthralled. Unfortunately my mother did not have two videotapes on which to
record the film—foreseeing trouble, she did not record it at all! To no
avail, for having seen it once they must see it again—and a pair of
Siamese twins, once enraged, makes a noise which cannot easily be
ignored. In despair did my mother venture forth to our local Blockbuster, only to find that they had but a single copy of the film. Fear
not, said I, I will go to Notting Hill and get a second copy of the
film; they have few enough pleasures as it is, God knows, and my
mother agreed, for she was certain that Blockbuster would not let us
down.

She said

Why didn't you say so before

I said

You didn't ask me before

I set off at my five-minute-mile sprint.

I went up to the front door again and knocked. He came to the
door straight away.

He said

I'm sorry, I should have given you some money.

I said that was all right. He looked brighter than he had before. He led me down a hall to a room at the back of the house where they kept the TV and VCR. He had put some crisps in a bowl and some peanuts in another bowl.

I turned on the TV and VCR and put the film in. There were some ads for the Classic Collection and then the film began.

He sat in his chair watching the screen very seriously. He laughed when Lady Bracknell said Should you become engaged I, or your father if his health permits, will inform you of the fact and he laughed at some of the other jokes. After a while I forgot about him.

After a while I looked over to see whether he was enjoying the film.

He had turned his head to one side. His cheeks were wet.

He said

This isn't going to work.

I turned off the video and pressed rewind.

He said

It's not going to work and I haven't got a lot of time. They're only going for a few days. It was worth a try though.

He said

This has helped in a way, anyway. I've some letters to write. I didn't think I'd be able to because I think the important thing is to say I love them and I find it quite hard to say that because I've really only felt anything for the dog since I got back. I've said it of course but there's something that won't let me make a lie my last word. I think I can live with a penultimate lie. Whereas it can't hurt you to hear the truth.

He said

This will probably take some time. You can go or stay as you like.

I said I would stay if that was all right.

I followed him upstairs to his desk. He sat down and got out several sheets of paper and wrote Dear Marie.

I went to sit in a chair. I took out Thucydides and began to read the stasis at Corcyra.

A couple of hours went by. I got up and went to the desk; he was looking down at a sheet of paper on which were written the words Dear Marie.

He said

It's just an accident it turned out this way. I was in Beirut for a long time, but a lot of people were there a long time. Sometimes you think you'll go berserk watching the it's frustrating but there's a lot to do. You spend so much time trying to organise transportation to some place where you hear something's going on, or trying to make contacts, or trying to anyway you're always pretty busy, even so it gets to you but then you all get drunk and talk. Once I was caught there was absolutely nothing to do but think. Lie on the floor thinking will Clinton do this will the UN do that without the distraction of if I talk to this person about that jeep. It's stupid. If I'd gone out and got drunk with some mates before I left it probably wouldn't have or at least it would always have been but at least it wouldn't have been anyway other people seem to adjust insofar as you can adjust and I would probably have adjusted.

He said

maladjusted by a simple twist of fate. It's hard to know what to write.

He said

Is it patronising to say what you think someone would like you to be able to say? Or should I say

He said

You know what I'd *really* like?

I said

Apart from the obvious

He said

Cheeky bastard aren't you—*sorry*.

I said

What?

Then I said Oh. I said It doesn't matter. What would you really like?

He said:

I'd like some fish and chips. Would you like some fish and chips? Why don't we go out and get some fish and chips and I'll finish this when we get back.

I thought this might be a good sign, maybe it was an excuse to put off doing it, maybe he would realise he was making excuses and didn't really want to do it.

We went out to the High Street. I dropped off the video and we went on to get cod and chips at a place nearby. I thought people probably thought he was my father.

The staple food at home was peanut butter and jam sandwiches. Sometimes we had peanut butter and honey for a change. I was trying to eat my fish as slowly as I could to make it last. He ate two chips and a piece of the fish and he said

This is shite. They've done something to it. I can't eat this.

He was about to throw it away when I said it tasted all right to me. I said I would eat his if he didn't want it.

He handed it over and we walked through the streets while I ate.

I tried to make it last as long as I could to put off going back. I couldn't believe I was walking beside Red Devlin, that he had gone through all the years of saying Sure you can and Oh go on and all the years in the cell and the months trekking cross-country to be walking here with me.

Of course, one of the things people had always complained about was that Red Devlin was not at all particular about his friends.

At one time Red Devlin had a friend who belonged to a club. I don't think it was the Portland but it was that kind of club. They used to go there and have a few drinks and one night they ran into a man who owned a chain of supermarkets. The man was angry and aggrieved because he wanted to open a supermarket in Wales, a supermarket on a scale never before seen west of the Severn, and though he had got planning permission and carried out feasibility studies local residents were making a nuisance of themselves. The supermarket was supposed to be built on a field that wasn't being used for anything, and the local residents claimed that children played there and that their lives would be blighted if they could play there no more.

Red Devlin's friend had heard this story or others like it too often to enjoy it and he soon excused himself. Red Devlin continued to talk to the man, who pointed out that children could play anywhere, that it was not as if he were planning to build over a park it was just a field and that he was a businessman.

Red Devlin said: Kids. The things they get up to.

The man said: I am a simple businessman.

Red Devlin said: This round is on me.

The man said: No no—

Red Devlin said: I insist

The man said: I insist

I insist

I insist

I insist

I insist

But Red Devlin insisted and the man was touched because if you are rich everybody thinks you are made of money.

This time Red Devlin didn't even say Sure you can or Oh go on. The man said: As I was saying, I am only a simple businessman

and Red Devlin said: Your hands are tied.

The man said: Precisely. My hands are tied

and Red Devlin said: With the best will in the world

and the man said: My hands are tied.

Your hands are tied, said Red Devlin.

My hands are tied, said the man.

Your hands are tied, said Red Devlin.

My hands are tied, said the man.

Where is this field again? said Red Devlin.

Wales, said the man.

Much the best place for it, said Red Devlin.

It's a fantastic location, said the man.

I wish I could see it, said Red Devlin. Shame it's in Wales.

We could go in my car, said the man, but I gave my driver tomorrow off because I'm in meetings all day.

Same again? said Red Devlin.

This is mine, said the man and Red Devlin said No I insist.

They talked and talked and talked and talked and talked and the
man said My hands are tied and Red Devlin said Your hands are tied
and This is my round and the man said No I insist and Red Devlin
said No I insist.

Then the man said: *Wait* a minute! We'll take a *taxi!*

They took a taxi to Wales and in the taxi the man explained various aspects of the movement of capital, Say a bakery goes bust, he
explained, if it goes bust it's because it does not represent the most
effective use of resources in the locality, it goes bust, the stock is sold
off, of course I'm taking a very simple example, all the ovens and
mixers don't just vanish off the face of the planet they are bought and
used for another business which utilises them in a cost-effective
manner new jobs are created somewhere else people forget to look
at the bigger picture and Red Devlin agreed that they did.

They reached the field a little before 7:00. The sun was just coming up. In the middle of the field was flattened bare dirt where people played football, and around that grass, with tall weeds and some

bushes around the edges of the field and a row of willow trees where the field followed a river. The man explained the advantages of the location for a supermarket and he explained that it was too good an opportunity to pass up and that his hands were tied, and Red Devlin said Your hands are tied.

Then they went into the town to have breakfast. They talked about this and that and from time to time the man would observe that his hands were tied and Red Devlin would agree that they were. At 9:00 the man suddenly remembered why he had given his driver the day off. He began to laugh, and he said a lot of things to Red Devlin which he left to the imagination when he later told the story in 'My Biggest Mistake'. Then he called his secretary on his mobile to tell her he had food poisoning and could not make his meetings. He hung up and (as he explained in 'My Biggest Mistake') said some more things to Red Devlin until the air literally turned blue. He pointed out that Red Devlin did not know the first thing about business and Red Devlin agreed that he did not. The man said My hands are tied and Red Devlin said Your hands are tied.

They walked around the town. There was a wall along the seafront with some rocks at the bottom, and a village green a few feet across. They went back to the field and saw mothers with small children; they went away for lunch and when they came back they saw boys playing football. The man said it was too late to go back. Red Devlin agreed that it was too late to go back. But even though it was too late to go back the field was developed in a much more modest way than originally planned, and though the businessman knew he was every kind of fool he cancelled the supermarket and improved the site only by adding a set of goalposts and some swings and slides. Later the man would occasionally have a drink with Red Devlin and reminisce about Wales and turn the air blue again for old times' sake.

I remembered this story and I remembered stories about really terrible people Red Devlin had known. There was a story no one knew much about, only a few details had come out after the man in question had been found stabbed to death in a Bangkok canal, and there was a story about a man who had owned a carpet factory in Pakistan a man who prided himself on the quality of his carpets naturally he regretted the necessity but the fact was if you did not use children you did not get the same quality he was a simple businessman his hands were tied and yet one day he set aside the business habits of a lifetime.

I was down to my last chip when I thought I knew what to say.

I said: What if a person was doing something terrible because everybody else did it or anyway some people did it, and then they stopped even though everybody else was doing it and it was dangerous to stop? Wouldn't that be a dazzling act of goodness?

He said: It could be.

I said: But in that case don't you see that all the time? Or couldn't you if you wanted? I thought

I didn't know how to go on, I was embarrassed to mention all the insane things people had done because they'd talked to Red Devlin.

Red Devlin didn't say anything. He looked at me, and then he looked at two or three people walking by, and then he looked at the ground.

After a while he said

All I have to do is open my mouth.

He said

That's what I thought when I was locked up I thought I had to get out because otherwise—

He walked on for a while and then he said

—and when I got out I saw that was what everybody thought they were waiting for me to—

He stopped suddenly on the pavement. He looked at me and he said:

Open Sesame.

I said What?

He said Open Sesame. Here I am back at last to say Open Sesame so people who were just doing what they had to do because everybody has to do what they have to do because everybody is waiting for somebody to say Open Sesame and it's not a thing that just anybody can say so here I am and I'm saying it and they can stop

I said: I just meant that there was a possibility

He said: That people will do something if they hear the magic words? Or that they will by miraculous dispensation do without the magic words?

I said: That's not fair. Suppose you were born into a society

He said: Most people are

I said: A slaveowning society

He said: A society of slaves

I said: All I meant was

He said: I liked the Bad Samaritan better. I suppose a Good Samaritan sleeps better nights.

We had turned into his street again, and now he talked to me patiently. He had been saying things that he wanted to say but now he said things he didn't especially want to say but which he thought would make me sleep better nights. He said patiently

You don't understand. It's not a question of what's fair to expect. Some people do what they do because everybody does it and it doesn't make them sick that that's what everybody does it makes them feel trapped once or twice but better most of the time. If somebody says the magic words they wake up for a little while and go to sleep again. You think I should stop feeling sick if somebody does something because they hear the magic words, but it's not a question of should, it's a question of what happens. It doesn't. That is it wouldn't. It wouldn't and that's why I can't say it any more, I just look at people. Sometimes I look at them thinking What are you waiting for and sometimes I look at them and say What are you waiting for.

We went into the house. We went back upstairs and he explained patiently that if he could go on waking people up for 50 years by saying Open Sesame you could probably say he should do it even if he felt sick but actually he couldn't say it any more to anyone who was waiting for him to say it. So it just came down to what we had talked about before.

I said: Were you waiting for me to say Open Sesame?

He said: I'm not now, anyway. I'd better write those letters.

He sat down at the desk again and started writing, and I sat down in my chair. It was about midnight. After a while I fell asleep.

I woke up a couple of hours later. There were four or five envelopes on the desk. Red Devlin was sitting on the bed with his back against the wall; I could see the whites of his eyes. I turned on the lamp beside my chair, and now I could see that the pills on the dresser were gone.

He said

Are you my son?

No, I said.

He said

I didn't think so. I'm glad.

He laughed and said

I didn't mean that the way it sounds. I just meant you could do better.

That was the last time he laughed. He sat quietly, looking down, as if it tired him to look into a face. I didn't say I didn't think I could do better.

After a while his eyes closed.

I waited two or three hours until I was pretty sure there was nothing left but a thing in corduroy trousers and a blue shirt. The clubbed child and the weeping eye and the smiling chessplayer were gone. I took his hand in mine. It was still warm, but cooling. Then I sat on the bed beside him and put his arm over my shoulder.

I sat beside him while the body grew cooler. I thought at one point that if I called a hospital the organs could still be transplanted, but I thought his wife would be upset if she came home to find that even the mortal remains did not remain. In one sense, of course, it is absurd to feel better because the corpse of one's beloved is anatomically complete; to embrace a dead body with a kidney.

I wished I'd discussed it with him. I did not think his wife would enjoy arriving at a more rational position immediately after discovering the fact of his suicide.

I tried to remember how long it took rigor mortis to set in. I put his arm by his side again and cried on its chilly shoulder. It was all right to do this now that it couldn't make him feel he had to make an effort, maybe even that he had to go on being sick.

I spent the night beside it. I felt better with the dead thing beside me, reminding me that he had killed the clubbed child and the weeping eye.

In the morning his cheek was ice cold. It was about 5:00 when I woke up; the light was still on. I lay for a little while by the hard, cold thing on the bed, thinking I should get up and do something. I thought: Well anyway he doesn't have to get up. He'd said once that he woke every morning at 5:00 and lay staring at the ceiling for two or three hours, hoping to fall asleep again and telling himself he might as well get up. After five or ten minutes he would see the smiling chessplayer for the first time that day, and tell himself he might as well get up, and lie staring at the ceiling.

I put on his denim jacket, and emptied the pockets. Then I took the letters from the table and went down the street to post them.

6

A good samurai will parry the blow

I got home one night about 9:00. Sib was typing *Sportsboat and Waterski International*.

I thought I could slip upstairs, but she looked up. She said: Is something the matter?

I said: No.

She said: So what's not the matter?

I said: Well

I said: Somebody killed himself. I told him about Jonathan Glover and leaving your wife but he said that wouldn't help.

Sib said: Well

She put her hand on my shoulder.

I thought: Why am I keeping her here?

I kept thinking that I had let Red Devlin go where he wanted to go and he'd never done anything for me. I kept thinking I should say You go right ahead.

I said: Do you ever think about Jonathan Glover? Maybe you should leave the country and get another job. Go somewhere where you don't need a work permit.

Sib said: You mean go back to the States? But I don't want to go back to the States.

I said: Why not?

Sib said: You can't get Nebraska Fried Chicken. It's too depressing for words.

I thought I should not let her get away with this. I was still wearing his jacket; Red Devlin wouldn't have let her get away with this.

I said: You could stop typing *British Ostrichkeeper* and get another job.

Sib said: There are too many people I don't want to see. Anyway why are we talking about my problems? Tell me about this person who died. Were you friends?

I said: What's the point in talking about him? He doesn't have any problems. There's no one to have his problems any more. Why don't you go back?

Sib said: I don't want to talk about it

Sib said: You know, whenever my father met somebody stupid who'd been to Harvard he took it as a personal insult.

I said: This is a reason not to go back to the States?

Sib said: You should have heard him when they gave a chair to Dr. Kissinger, a man with the blood of millions on his hands.

I said: For this you're typing *British Ostrichkeeper*?

Sib said: The thing is

Sib said: It's just

Sib paced up and down. At last she said: You know, I don't know if you know this, Ludo, but if you have a motel you can always buy another motel.

I said: What?

Once you've got one motel you can always get another, said Sib. And if you can get another you can't really pass up that kind of op-portunity.

I said: What?

Sib said: It's something you only really understand once you own a motel.

I said: As I was saying

Sib said that her Uncle Buddy had vaguely imagined that making a success of a motel might be a route out of accountancy, and that

even at 30 it might not be too late to try something different. She
said her mother had imagined that making a success of a motel
might be a way of paying for musical training, since with her background she was not likely to win a scholarship anywhere she might
actually want to go. She said her father had put up the money for the
down payment and her mother and uncle had thrown themselves
into making it a success, and one day it turned out her father had
spotted the potential in another location.

I said: But

Sib said the thing was that the whole scope for profits in motels
lies in spotting previously unspotted potential, and that her father
had turned out to have an unsuspected flair for it. She said the potential of a place consisted in its being a place people were going to
want to be in a few years' time, and for it to be unspotted it had to
be a place *nobody* wanted to be when you were buying the building
or site for a future motel.

I said: But why

Sib said few places with unspotted potential boasted even an amateur chamber music society, let alone a symphony orchestra, so that
musicians were even less likely to want to spend a lot of time in one
than all the other people who had—

I waited for Sib to go on. I thought maybe if I didn't say anything
at all she would finally explain.

My father never talked about his father, said Sib. My mother
complained constantly about her parents, who were always sending
presents of sweaters from Philadelphia.

I waited for Sib to go on, and after a pause she went on:

A brown paper parcel would arrive at a motel going up on the
outskirts of Pocatello. 'Oh, my, God,' my mother would say, splashing
neat Scotch into a glass and drinking it in a single swallow. 'Well,
might as well open the damn thing.' She would tear open the brown
paper, tear open gold paper, open the shallow box from Wanamaker's

and lift from the layers of tissue paper a cashmere sweater in pale lemon or chartreuse or frosted plum, with mother-of-pearl buttons. 'Well, might as well try the damn thing on,' she'd say at last, shrugging into it and rucking the sleeves up to her elbows in the what-this-old-thing way she and her friends always wore cashmere sweaters. She'd take out a cigarette, crack a match and light up, sucking the smoke in deep though she always said it played merry hell with the voice. 'It's the hypocrisy of it that really gets to me,' she'd say, and she'd sit down to start a note that began 'Dear Mom, Thank you so much for the scrumptious sweater' and sit smoking and staring into space.

I waited for Sib to go on but she didn't go on. She picked up the remote. ON. PLAY.

I thought: This is an explanation?

STOP.

The thing is, said Sib. She walked up and down.

Do you know what Boulez says somewhere? she said.

No, what does Boulez say somewhere? I said.

Comment vivre sans inconnu devant soi. Not everyone can.

Fine, I said.

Do you know what I said when I woke up? said Sib.

No, I said.

Rage, rage against the dying of the night. You wouldn't have wanted to hear that from your friend.

No, I said.

On the other hand what's done is done and here I am and London, with all its shortcomings, is hardly a place of previously unspotted potential. How many people on the planet?

Five billion, I said.

Five billion, and as far as I know I am the only one in all those billions who thinks children should not be in absolute economic subjection to the adults into whose keeping fate has consigned them. I think I should stick around and write a letter to the *Guardian*.

I said I could write it and sign it Ludo Aged 11.

You can write to the *Independent*, said Sib. And I'll write one to the *Telegraph* signed Robert Donat just on the off-chance.

For someone who believes in the importance of rational argument Sib avoids the issue 9 times out of 10.

She began walking up and down and walking by the piano paused and sat down and started playing a short piece she has been playing off and on for years.

7

I'm a genuine samurai

My father brought out a book about his visit to Easter Island.

Hugh Carey left to walk across Russia alone.

Sorabji got a knighthood.

The painter left to walk across a desert.

Szegeti joined his partner to win the World Bridge Championship 1998 after completing a brief fact-finding mission in Jackson, Mississippi for Nelson Mandela.

People went on with their lives and got on with their jobs.

I didn't look for another father. I should have gone around saying Open Sesame, but I just wore his jacket and rode the Circle Line around and around and around.

One day I took the Circle Line to Baker Street. It didn't matter which way I went, so I walked along the Marylebone Road and then turned north. I walked up one street and turned left and down another and turned right and up a third and turned left again. Halfway up the street I heard the sound of a piano.

A herd of octaves fled up and down the keyboard like panicked giraffe; a dwarf hopped on one foot; twelve toads hopped four-footed. I sat on the doorstep while the XXV variations of Alkan's Festin d'Aesope dazzled an indifferent street. So who's this? I thought. I had heard Hamelin's recording of the piece, and I had heard recordings by Reingessen and Laurent Martin and Ronald Smith and I had once heard a broadcast of Jack Gibbons, and when you have heard these recordings you have heard the five people in the world who play it. This wasn't one of them.

Glenda the Good glided on a gleaming sea drawn by six snowy swans. The Grande Armée crossed Poland on pogo sticks. A woman with a shopping bag walked across the street and up steps. A man with briefcase walked briskly by like an overacting extra.

Six dogs tapdanced on tabletops.

The Variations came to an end. There was a short pause.

A flight of octaves took off like startled flamingoes. No one stopped and stared.

He played variations on the Variations and variations on the variations and he would play one variation next to another next to which it had not originally been juxtaposed.

Are you ready for another fight? No prospects. It could be dangerous.

I stood up and knocked on the door.

A woman came to the door. She said: What to do you want?

I said: I've come for my piano lesson.

She said: Oh.

She said: But he doesn't give lessons.

I said: He'll see me.

She said: Oh I don't know

I said: I've come for a lesson on *Alkan,* the once celebrated contemporary of Chopin and Liszt, passed over for the directorship of the Conservatoire through sordid political machinations in favour of a mediocrity and so condemned to a life of bitter obscurity only to die (as legend has it) crushed under a bookshelf while attempting to take down a volume of the Talmud. Only six people in the world today play his music of the six perhaps three are active of the active only one lives in London I have come for a piano lesson with him.

She said: He hasn't said anything to me.

I said: Oh, go on

She said: Well all right then.

I went through the door. I was in a big room with a bare floor and peeling plaster and a grand piano. Someone sat at the piano—I could only see his legs.

He said:

What do you want?

He raises his sword. He draws it back with a slow sweeping motion.

I said: I had to see you because I'm your son.

He stood up. He was about 25. He was no Mifune lookalike, but it was not likely that I was his son.

He said: What is this shit?

I didn't know what to say. Then I thought of something to say. I said:

やい！貴様！
    Yai!   Kisama!

                                 Hey you!

よくも俺の事を「侍 か？」なんてぬかしやがって
yoku mo ore no koto o   'samurai ka?'   nante   nukashiyagatte . . .

               asking me 'Are you a samurai?' like that . . .

ふざけるな！
fuzakeruna!

                             what a nerve!

He said: What?

I said:

俺はな こう見えてもちゃんとした 侍 だ。
ore wa na   kō   miete   mo   chanto   shita samurai da

      Even though I look like this, I'm a genuine samurai.

I did not seem to be making much of an impression. I persevered:

やい俺はなあれからお前の事をずっと捜してたんだぞ

 yai, ore wa na   arekara   omae no koto o   zutto   sagashitetanda   zo

    Hey, I've been looking for you the whole time ever since then

これを見せようと思ってな

kore　o　miseyō　to　omottena

thinking I'd like to show you this.

これを見ろ

kore　o　miro.

Look at this.

この系図はな

kono　keizu wa na.

This genealogy.

俺様の先祖代々の系図よ

ore sama no　senzo　daidai no　keizu　yo.

A genealogy belonging to my family for generations.

このやろう　ばかにしやがってなんでい

kono　yarō　baka　ni　shiyagatte　nandei

You bastard (you're making a fool of me)

これを見ろ　ばかにしやがって

kore　o　miro.　baka ni　shiyagatte

Look at this. (You're making a fool of me)

これがその俺様だ

kore　ga　sono oresama da

This is me.

He said Ah.

He said:

この菊千代と言うのがお前か？

kono　Kikuchiyo to　iu　no ga　omae　ka?

This Kikuchiyo it talks about is you?

I said:

さようでござる

sayō　de　gozaru

That's right

He said:

よく聞けこの菊千代申す者がお主に間違いなければ

yoku　kike　kono　Kikuchiyo mōsu mono ga onushi　ni　machigai　nakereba

Listen, if you're definitely this Kikuchiyo it talks about

お主は当年とって十三才
onushi wa tōnen   totte   jūsansai

You must be 13 this year

この系図、どこで盗んだ？
kono keizu   doko de nusunda?

This genealogy, where did you steal it?

I said:

うん？ 嘘だ！ ちくしょう！ てめえ 何 言ってんだ
uun? Uso da!   chikushō!   temē nani ittenda?

What? It's a lie! Shit! What are you saying?

He laughed.

I said

You left out some lines

He said

I haven't seen it in years, Kikuchiyo-san.

I remembered suddenly that according to the *Kodansha Romanized Japanese-English Dictionary* kisama is [CRUDE] and very insulting, that according to Sanseido's *New Crown Japanese-English Dictionary* kono yarō meant you swine, and that according to *Japanese Street Slang* baka was Japan's most popular swear word, baka ni suru meant don't fuckin' fuck with me and shiyagatte was the offensive gerund. I thought I'd better stop while I was ahead.

I went over to look at the piano. It was a Steinway, but it was the only thing in the room apart from a rolled-up sleeping bag and a suitcase.

I said

Did you know that Glenn Gould practically rebuilt CD 318 so that it wouldn't sound like a Steinway?

He said

Everybody knows that.

He said

Do you play the piano?

I said

Not Alkan.

I said

I can play Straight No Chaser.

He said

It doesn't matter. I don't give lessons. I don't even give concerts.

I said

I wasn't asking for lessons.

Then I said

Why don't you give concerts?

He started walking up and down the bare floor. He said

I kept giving the wrong size of concert. People missed their trains and they found it detracted from their enjoyment of the evening.

Then he laughed. He said: I thought a few hours one way or the other couldn't matter but people don't like to catch just any train.

He was still walking up and down. He said: People kept giving me good advice.

I said

Why don't you make a CD?

He stopped by the window. He said

No one would buy the kind of thing I'd like to put on a CD and I can't afford to make a CD that no one will buy.

I said

Variations on variations on variations

& he said

Something like that.

He said

It's funny the things people won't buy.

He started pacing up and down the floor again. He said

When you play a piece of music there are so many different ways you could play it. You keep asking yourself what if. You try this and you say but what if and you try that. When you buy a CD you get one answer to the question. You never get the what if.

He said

It's the same only worse in Japan. People take the train every day. They get on a train and get off and get on and get off day after day.

He said if that was the thinkable you'd think the unthinkable would be—

He said even if you weren't interested in music wouldn't the idea that things could be different—

He stopped by the piano. He said

But actually people don't really like a piece of music until they're used to it.

He began picking at one of the thin steel strings of the treble. Ping ping ping ping ping. Ping ping ping

He said

I'm stuck in a rut myself. I've been doing this too long. I keep telling myself I should bite the bullet, play some of my party pieces and make a comeback. What's the use of spending my life in this room?

Ping ping ping

Then I go and look at CDs.

Ping

Hundreds of CDs with whole pieces played once for the thousands of people who want CDs with whole pieces played once.

Ping

So those thousands of people are doing OK and they'll go on doing OK even if I don't play my party pieces

Ping ping

But anyone who wants to hear what if can't hear it anywhere, not in the store not in the world not with that kind of piece

Ping ping ping ping ping

He said

I can't afford to make a CD that 5 people would buy, but there's something about playing my party pieces for the thousands of people who can always find party pieces to choose from, there's something about walking away from the 5

He said

Not that I'm doing them much good in this room.

I said

Well I could afford to make a CD that no one will buy

& he said

What?

He said

Why, do you have £10,000?

I said

I've got something that's worth a lot of money. I could get a lot of money for this,

& I took the painter's heart out of my backpack. It was in a plastic folder to protect the silk, the white silk was still white and the blood was brown.

He said

What is it?

I explained what it was and he said

I've never heard of him, thanks but I can't accept this

I said he could and he said he couldn't and I said he could and he said he couldn't.

I said: But what if

He said: What if what

I said: What if it was a matter of life or death

I said: What if it was a matter of a fate worse than death

He said: What are you talking about?

I said: What if someone called the Samaritans

He said: Who?

I said: The Samaritans. They're a group of people who think anything is worse than not breathing. You can call them if you're feeling depressed.

He said: So?

I said: What if a person called the Samaritans and they weren't very helpful? What if a person kept doing the same thing day after day? What if a person kept riding the Circle Line around and around? What if there was a person who thought the world would be a better place if everyone who would enjoy seeing a Tamil syllabary had access to a Tamil syllabary? What if there was a person who kept changing the subject? What if there was a person who never listened to anything anybody ever said?

He said: Did you have anyone special in mind?

I said I was speaking hypothetically.

He said: And what exactly did you think this hypothetical CD could do for this hypothetical person?

He was smiling. He was strumming the strings of the piano softly.

I said: What if the person got off the Circle Line at Embankment, crossed the bridge to Waterloo, took a train to Paris and went to work for a famous sculptor?

He said: What, because of some stupid CD? What planet are you living on?

I said: The premise was that there were only 5 people on the planet who would buy the CD, obviously most people would not get off at Embankment because of a CD but maybe the type of person who would buy the CD would be the type of person who would.

I said

The type of person who thinks boredom a fate worse than death. The type of person who always wants things to be different. The type of person who would rather die than read *Sportsboat and Water-ski International*.

Oh, he said. *That* type of person.

He picked out the Seven Samurai theme on the treble strings.

Better not take out an ad in *Sportsboat and Waterski International* then.

He picked the theme out in the bass.

I said

Look at it this way. You don't have to make *hundreds* of CDs. You could just make 10. 5 for you and 5 for me. Then they'd be the only 10 in the world and they'd be valuable. Say we get £10,000 for the heart, say it costs £1,000 to make the CDs, say they sell for £1,000 apiece, we could either maximise our profits or we could even give one away if we happened to know the type of person who didn't mind missing trains.

He went back to the treble. Ping ping ping PING ping ping PING ping ping ping

He did not seem to be finding the argument persuasive.

I said: I could teach you a language. Would you like to learn a language?

He said: What language?

I said: What language would you like to learn?

He said: What do you recommend?

I said: I could teach you to count to 1000 in Arabic. I said: I know about 20 languages so if there's some other language you want to learn I might know it. I said: Or I could teach you the periodic table. Or I could teach you survival techniques.

He said: Survival techniques?

I said: I could teach you edible insects.

He said: What if I don't want to eat an insect?

He went back to the bass. Dum dum dum DUM dum dum DUM dum dum dum

I said: What do you want me to do? Do you want me to come back in 10 years? For all you know it may be too late.

There was a short pause. He looked thoughtfully at the strings of the piano. I thought I was really getting somewhere.

He took his other hand out of his pocket and began picking out an arrangement of the samurai theme on two strings.

I did not know what to say. I said

You could play anything you want on the CD

He said

Or I could play something by special request. Any ideas?

I said

Well

Then I said

You could play something by Brahms.

He said

By Brahms?

I said

Do you know Brahms' Ballade Op. 10 No. 2 in D major?

He said

What?

I said

Brahms' Ballade Op. 10 No. 2 in D major? It's part of a set.

He said

Yes I know.

He turned and rested his arm on the curved wooden side of the piano. He said

Do you know the rest of the set?

I said that was the only one I had heard because I knew someone who played it a lot but of course if he wanted to put the whole set on the CD he could because it was his CD and he had complete artistic control.

He said

I don't know

I did not know what to say.

I said

I could teach you judo.

He said
I don't know
I said
I could teach you piquet.
I could teach you Lagrangians.
I did not know what to say.
I said
Make this CD and I'll teach you to play Straight No Chaser.
He said
Done.